# Man
# DROUGHT

First Published 2013
Second Australian Paperback Edition 2013
ISBN 978 174356449 3

MAN DROUGHT © 2013 by Rachael Johns
Philippine Copyright 2013
Australian Copyright 2013
New Zealand Copyright 2013

This is a work of fiction. Names, characters, places, and incidents are either the
product of the author's imagination or are used fictitiously, and any resemblance
to actual persons, living or dead, business establishments, events, or locales is
entirely coincidental.

Published by
Harlequin® Mira®
An imprint of Harlequin Enterprises (Aust) Pty Ltd.
Level 19, 201 Elizabeth Street
SYDNEY 2000
AUSTRALIA

® and TM are trademarks of Harlequin Enterprises Limited or its corporate
affiliates. Trademarks indicated with ® are registered in Australia, New Zealand,
the United States Patent & Trademark Office and in other countries.

Printed and bound in Australia by McPherson's Printing Group

MIX
Paper from
responsible sources
FSC
www.fsc.org    FSC® C001695

# *Man* DROUGHT

## RACHAEL JOHNS

## Dear Reader

Thanks so much for picking up *Man Drought*. I hope you'll enjoy reading it as much as I enjoyed writing it.

The idea of The One (there being only one perfect person in the world for everyone) has always fascinated me and I decided to explore that in this book. Imogen the heroine is a widow who believes her dead husband was the only man for her. At the beginning of *Man Drought*, she's looking for new ways to live life, believing love, marriage and happily-ever-afters are things of the past for her. She takes the massive step of buying a run-down country pub to kickstart her new life.

This is where a little bit of me slipped into the book. Having lived in the country for the past nine years, I've done a fair bit of driving between rural towns. One thing that always fascinated me about these places was the pubs. They are these amazing old buildings, often oozing history, character and charm, yet more often than not they are sadly neglected and derelict. Each time I see a country pub that could do with some serious TLC, I start imagining how I'd renovate it, breathe life back into it, so I gave this role to Imogen, my heroine.

My Australian books are very much about rural communities and the people who live in them. Even if the pubs are run-down, in many of these towns they are still where locals go to socialise and therefore I'm stoked to bring you *Man Drought* – a book in which the pub gets portrayed for all its positive aspects, rather than the negative ones sometimes focused on.

I hope you'll enjoy my vibrant cast of characters and as usual I'd love to hear your thoughts about *Man Drought*. Please visit me on the web at www.rachaeljohns.com

Happy Reading!
Rachael

## *Acknowledgments*

I have so much support from family, friends and my publisher when writing a book that it is not the lonely process that some might imagine.

This time round, I want to thank Janette Radevski, who was the first person to read *Man Drought* and loved it from the get-go. Thanks for your support and advice. So many other fabulous writer friends helped me through the writing of *Man Drought* as well – thanks to Fiona Lowe, who is always generous with her wisdom and helped especially with the birth scene in this book; to Cathryn Hein for the pep talks and for constantly making me laugh; to Bec Sampson who I email at least a hundred times a day; and to Jackie Ashenden, Fiona Palmer and Joanne Levy, all great supports.

Thanks also to Peta and Chris Sattler for having me (and the boys) at your lovely farm on a research trip. We must do that again some time. Many thanks for reading the unedited version for any farming errors. As usual, any errors that did slip through are mine!

A special mention to my best friend since childhood Holly Paine – who bought FIVE copies of my last book, *Jilted*, and is continually my biggest fan. Love you always!

I don't think I could do this job and still stay on top of all the other important things in life without my fabulous home support team. To my Mum, who is undoubtedly THE BEST mother in the world, to my hubby who doesn't mind helping with the cooking or, better still, doing the vacuuming himself, to my mother-in-law who babysits during writing conferences, and to my gorgeous boys, so innocent and enthusiastic in their support – I LOVE and thank you all.

To my editor for this book – Lachlan Jobbins – thanks for all your insight and support. It never ceases to amaze me the things an editor picks up that us mere mortals don't even notice.

And lastly, but definitely not least, I need to once again offer immense thanks to Haylee Nash and the awesome team at Harlequin Australia for loving *Man Drought* and for all the other opportunities you have given me.

*This one's for Craig – for putting up with an undomestic goddess of a wifey who sits at the computer every night and demands you make Milo to feed her muse! Thank you! xo*

## FOR SALE

*The Majestic*, Gibson's Find, Western Australia
Loads of potential in this hospitality business situated on a busy national highway and surrounded by prosperous, well-established farming areas. The hotel services passing trade and loyal locals, including farmers and mining personnel.

Ideal for a husband and wife team looking for a tree change and to be their own boss. On the edge of farming land, where crops turn to pastoral stations and mining leases in the beautiful Goldfields of Western Australia, this is a unique place to live and do business.

Licensed hotel, comprising eight guest rooms, staff and manager's quarters. Great possibilities for expansion and making the most of travellers.

BE QUICK. This attractively priced business won't be on the market long!

# Chapter One

'Are you absolutely insane?'

'Please tell me you haven't signed the contract.'

'No. And yes.' Imogen grinned at her two closest friends and then gazed across at her brand new life. They'd travelled half the day to get here and she was feeling like the fizz in a can of soft drink, desperate to explode and share her excitement.

An early nineteenth-century colonial pub stood proudly in front of them – red brick and tin, verandahs along the front and sides – with the quaint charm you see on outback television dramas. The pub had definitely seen better days, and she knew not everyone would see it how she did when she closed her eyes, but just looking at the old place made her heart feel lighter than it had in years. Two years, five months and four days to be precise. But no more counting. No more dwelling on the past.

Her new life started today. Right here in the tiny precinct of Gibson's Find, not far from where the West Australian Wheatbelt met the Goldfields. Three and a half hours inland from Perth by car, far away from her memories and everything she'd shared with Jamie. It wasn't exactly the life she'd imagined, but if she didn't want to lose herself in a dark, dark hole, then she'd just have to make a go of it.

'I think I need a drink,' Jenna said with a dramatic sigh that was not at all unusual for her. Despite the heat and the fact that Amy's air conditioner had struggled on the long journey, Jenna looked like she'd stepped off the pages of a *Marie Claire* magazine.

'Me too,' Amy echoed, placing a hand on her bulging abdomen. Imogen and Jenna swung their heads to glare at her, eyebrows raised, both ready with a lecture about drinking while pregnant.

'Relax. I'm kidding.' Amy grinned and rubbed her tummy. Her face was flushed red and sweaty from the summer heat. 'As if I'd do anything to jeopardise this little bundle. But it's hot out here and my thirst needs quenching.'

Amy and her husband Ryan had been trying for a baby for the best part of five years. Her 'little bundle' was the result of a lengthy and expensive process of IVF. After supporting Amy through several failed attempts, Imogen and Jenna already felt fiercely protective of it.

'We'll get you lemonade in a champagne flute,' Jenna said, adjusting her Marc Jacobs handbag on her shoulder. 'If Imogen's really going to do this, then we may as well kill two birds with one bottle: have a stickybeak inside and toast to her insanity. What do you say?'

'I think that's a fine plan. Come on girls.' Imogen placed her hands on her hips and her two friends linked their arms in hers. Together they strode across the road and up onto the verandah, out of the hot January sun and into the building Imogen planned to make her home.

They paused in the doorway and Imogen waited as Amy and Jenna looked their fill. That unique pub aroma of beer-soaked carpets, greasy food and cigarette smoke (even though no one had been allowed to smoke inside for years) wafted out to greet them. Although her friends faces were blank, she knew them well enough to guess their thoughts. They'd already lamented about how far away she was taking them and how flat and barren the land around the town was. She wasn't sure whether to laugh or cry as they took their time, silently swivelling their heads and glancing up at sagging roof beams, looking down to the scuffed floorboards, peering through the gloom at the few redneck faces staring back at them. Actually, *ogling* was probably a better description.

Jenna took the Lord's name in vain under her breath, and Amy's grip on Imogen's arm tightened. The few men holding up the bar didn't look like the type you'd want to meet in a deserted alley on a dark night.

'I'm not crazy,' Imogen said, loud enough for only her friends to hear. Before they could challenge her, she added, 'Let's get drinks and I'll fill you in. On everything.'

'I'll buy them.' Jenna stood up straight, held her chin high as if she were about to approach a pack of wild dingoes, and disentangled her arm. 'You two get us a table.' She peered around and screwed up her otherwise perfect nose. 'If you can find a clean one.'

So The Majestic wasn't in the best shape. Yes, it would likely fail dismally in any city hygiene test – not to mention decor contest – but Imogen couldn't wait to share her vision.

While Jenna approached the old man serving behind the bar, Imogen led Amy to the table closest to an open window, furthest away from the other customers. She didn't want the locals to overhear her plans just yet. She'd asked the current owners not to blow her cover if they happened to see her here. Although she hadn't lived in a small town in donkey's years, she hadn't forgotten how fast gossip spread, and she wanted to make sure the sale went through before the bush telegraph cranked up.

'Everyone's staring at us,' Amy whispered as they sat down on rickety wooden chairs.

'There's hardly anybody here to stare,' Imogen retorted, already feeling protective of the old place.

'True.' Amy shifted around on the seat, trying to get comfortable. 'Shouldn't you be worried about that?'

Imogen tried to rein in her frustration. Explaining all this to her city friends was never going to be a walk in the park. 'No. It's two o'clock in the afternoon. I've seen the books, remember? This place isn't doing too badly in the evenings and at weekends – and it's got a lot of potential.'

Amy didn't look convinced.

They sat in silence for a few minutes, Imogen staring dreamily around and adding notes to her already massive mental project file. It included everything from the new interior paint colour to the vintage signs she planned to complement the new decoration. She'd always had an eye for design and had renovated two houses with Jamie. She could do this. She knew she could. More importantly, she wanted to. Needed to.

Soon, Jenna returned with two slightly tarnished champagne flutes and a bottle of cheap bubbly. Extremely cheap. And old, judging by the dust on the bottle and the frayed-at-the-edges label.

'Where's my lemonade?' Amy put her hand against her sweaty brow. 'I'm going to pass out if I don't get some liquid.'

'Granddad's bringing it.' Jenna nodded her head in the direction of the bar. The old bartender shuffled towards them, his wrinkled hands clasped around a glass. He stared down at the rim as if he were a small boy desperate not to spill his milk. Jenna put the champagne glasses and bottle on the table and slumped into her seat. 'You might have it by sundown.'

The three friends watched as the old man ambled over. Imogen made to get up and help him but Jenna stopped her with a hand on her forearm. 'He doesn't want help. I offered to go back but he was very insistent.'

'He probably wants to keep his independence,' Amy mused, smiling at the man.

While they waited, Jenna leaned forward and popped the cork on the bubbly. It barely made a sound and Imogen wondered how long it had been sitting in the fridge. Jenna screwed up her nose again and wiped her dusty hands on her designer jeans, then filled the two glasses.

'I thought you said you'd get me a champagne flute too?' Amy stared longingly at the bottle. 'At least that way I could pretend I was drinking the real thing.'

Jenna snorted. 'Trust me, honey, this ain't the real thing, and I did mention three glasses to granddad but he looked so confused I told him not to bother.'

'Shh.' Imogen jabbed Jenna with her elbow. The bartender had finally arrived with Amy's drink, and she didn't want him over-hearing Jenna's snide remarks.

Jenna pasted on her sweetest smile and looked up at him in much the same manner as she looked at every man over five. She batted her ludicrously long, black eyelashes and flirted. 'Thanks *so* much. My friend here's having a baby you see, so she can't touch the good stuff.'

The old man beamed at them, focusing on Amy and her bump. 'Fabulous news. Nothing more splendid than bringing a baby into the world. Charlie's the name. If I can get anything more for you ladies, just holler.' With that, he scratched his sideburns, turned around and began his slow totter back to the bar.

Despite the wobble in his walk, Imogen imagined he'd been a strapping, good-looking man in his day. Wisps of grey hair poked out from under a floppy hat and his ancient smile stretched from sideburn to sideburn.

'He's kinda sweet,' Amy said, picking up her glass. It wasn't hard to impress Amy – she was one of those constantly smiling, glass-always-half-full kind of people. Sometimes her chirpiness aggravated Jenna – who had a much sharper, cynical edge – but Imogen liked it. Before the accident, Imogen had been that kind of person too, and while she now found it much harder to summon such enthusiasm, she was thankful to have a friend who didn't let her get too pessimistic.

She smiled at her pregnant friend and picked up her drink. 'Shall we?'

Jenna and Amy raised their glasses.

'To the best friends a gal could have. If it weren't for you two, I don't know how I'd have coped these last few years. Hell, who knows if I'd have coped at all?'

'Oh, you are too sweet,' Jenna said. 'You know we'd do anything for you. And that includes toasting this crazy, harebrained scheme of yours. To you, Imogen.'

'And to this adventure being the beginning of many joyous things,' Amy added.

At their toast, Imogen lifted her glass higher. 'Thanks girls.'

They chinked the flutes and the tumbler together and took a much-needed sip.

Imogen let the bubbles dance on her tongue and savoured the taste, pretending it was better than it was and silently vowing to change the sparkling wine selection as soon as she took over.

Jenna made another face, then shrugged and downed the rest of her glass.

Amy frowned as well, then sniffed her drink. 'Ugh! This isn't lemonade. It's soda water.'

'Yuk.' The three of them had a thing about soda water. None of them could see the appeal.

'It can't be much worse than this,' Jenna announced, starting to stand, 'but I'll get you a replacement anyway.'

'No, I'll go.'

Imogen stood, not trusting Jenna not to rip into the old barman. She wasn't sure whether Charlie knew who she was yet, but she certainly didn't want to get off on his wrong side. As she approached, she smiled at the two men who sat along the bar and didn't miss the slow assessment as they looked her up and down.

They could look all they liked, but none of them stood a chance with her. No one did. Not anymore.

'Hi.' She positively beamed at Charlie. 'Hate to be a pain, but I think my friend ordered the wrong drink for my other friend. Can we have lemonade instead of soda water?' She pushed the offending drink across the counter.

Charlie blinked a couple of times and shook his head. 'Ah, maybe she did say lemonade. Sorry love.' He grabbed another glass and turned to the soft drink taps. Imogen's heart squeezed when she saw the embarrassment on Charlie's face. His smile lines drooped and the light left his eyes.

'It's fine, really. Easy mistake to make.'

'Except Charlie's been making lots of them lately,' said one of the men.

'Leave him alone,' retorted the other. 'You can't talk. You forgot where you parked your car when we went into Kalgoorlie the other day.'

While they bickered and Charlie took his sweet time filling a glass, Imogen looked around again. The bar itself wasn't in bad condition compared to the rest of the furniture, but it could do with a good spit and polish. The stools, on the other hand, belonged at the tip. She'd have to replace the furniture and lighten up the interior if she wanted to widen the clientele. And then there was the menu…

'Here you are, love.' Charlie interrupted her thoughts as he placed the glass of (what was hopefully) lemonade on the bar between them. 'Anything else I can get you? A few packets of chips maybe?'

'No thanks. Typical women, we're always watching our weight.'

That was a lie. Jenna, with her fair skin, white-gold hair and Barbie-doll curves, had never needed to watch her weight. Amy, tanned where Jenna was light, dark where Jenna was gold, always struggled with her figure – flitting from one fad diet to the next – but had given herself permission to eat whatever she felt like (within healthy reason) while pregnant. Imogen herself fell somewhere in between. She had light skin that didn't tan but freckled easily, hair her mother called strawberry but she thought more tomato, and was smack bang in the middle of her healthy weight range. Ryan and Jamie always said the trio were like neapolitan ice-cream.

Still, Imogen didn't tell Charlie any of this. She didn't want to give him the opportunity to mess up again. Picking up the drink, she turned and took a surreptitious sip. Lemonade all right. Satisfied, she headed back to her friends, putting the worry of how she'd handle her resident barman out of her mind.

'Right. Let's try again, shall we?'

Jenna lifted her glass as Imogen put Amy's drink on the table and collapsed into the rickety chair. 'To Imogen.'

Amy echoed her and took a sip. She smiled this time and took another longer one.

'To me.' Imogen took another sip of her bubbly and sighed.

Maybe they were right. Maybe this was the craziest thing she'd ever done. But dammit, she was determined to make it a success.

★★★

Three hours later, the sparkling wine didn't taste quite as bad as when they'd first assessed it. In fact, another bottle sat empty between them, as did a few empty packets of chips they'd finally risked ordering from Charlie. Even Amy, who hadn't consumed a drop of alcohol, was jovial and relaxed. The country air and atmosphere did it, Imogen was certain.

Four weeks ago, she'd driven through Gibson's Find on her way to visit her parents in Kalgoorlie. As soon as she saw the For Sale sign out the front of The Majestic, something clicked inside her. She made a few phone calls, and on the way home to Perth she'd stopped again to look through the old hotel. Before she'd taken two steps inside, she'd made up her mind. If Jamie's insurance money covered the sale, she'd buy it. She wanted to do something productive with the money – she'd come to despise it sitting there every time she checked her back account, reminding her of just how much she'd lost.

'So,' Jenna said, leaning across the table to top up Imogen's glass and then her own, 'what are you going to do with your house?'

Imogen's heart constricted a little. Her friend hadn't mentioned Jamie but they all knew the house had belonged to him as well. In fact, the last house they'd renovated – an early settler's stone cottage in Guildford – had been more about him than her. From the moment he'd seen it advertised on the net, he'd been envisaging having kids and growing old there. And she'd quickly bought into the dream. Jamie had taken leave from his job as a firefighter to do it up, while Imogen had worked extra shifts at the wine bar to pay the bills.

'I'm putting it on the market.'

'Are you sure it's the right thing to do?' Amy's caring tone conveyed her reservations.

Imogen swallowed. She didn't want to cry here. Not today, the day that marked her fresh start. 'Yes.' She paused, garnering the courage to continue. 'Even in today's property market, it's in a good location, not far from the train line. There's nothing anyone would need to do to it and it has lots of charm and style. I think it'll sell quickly, and then I can put the extra money into doing up this place.'

'No arguments here,' Jenna said, 'but I think Amy meant your emotional wellbeing.'

Amy nodded. 'Your house is the last bit of Jamie you've got.'

Imogen chuckled and shook her head at her friends. 'You two have spent the last couple of years telling me it's time to move on, and now that I'm trying to, you're worried?'

'We're your best friends. It's our job to be worried.' Amy grabbed Imogen's hand across the table and gave it a squeeze. 'It's 'cos we love you. You know that, right?'

Jenna took another sip of champagne, then added, 'You know I'm not one for warm fuzzies, but she's right. We're just looking out for you.'

'I love you guys too. And if we weren't surrounded by blokes, I'd pull you both into a group hug.' She took a deep breath, then spoke seriously. 'I am sad to sell the house, but living there isn't good for me anymore. Everywhere I look, every room I go into, he's there. And while I never ever want to forget him—'

'You won't,' interrupted the others in unison.

'I know.' Imogen smiled and placed her hand on her chest. 'He'll always be in here, but I'm only thirty. I need to get my life back. I need to find something new to live for.'

'Well, if you're sure.' Jenna turned and took another good look around the pub. 'I think your ideas are fantastic and I'll gladly offer my services on weekends. I'm always up for a good challenge, and besides, I'll need my Imogen fix every couple of weeks.'

Imogen couldn't help snorting. 'I never thought I'd hear you offer to leave the city.'

'Me neither,' laughed Amy, rubbing her tummy.

'I have ulterior motives.' Jenna leaned in towards the table and lowered her voice. The smile on her face told Imogen those motives even before her friend spoke. 'I've been watching, and some of the men I've noticed in here aren't too bad-looking.'

In the last few hours, the pub had all but filled with men as they'd knocked off work. From their outfits, Imogen guessed that most of them worked on local farms. Loud, happy men, muscular and sweaty from hard manual labour. So different to the crew that came into the Subiaco wine bar she currently worked in. Most of them wore shirts and ties even on the weekends, and thought lifting a flat pack from Ikea constituted hard manual labour.

'Ten o'clock, at the bar,' Jenna continued. 'I've had my eyes on him since he walked in the door.'

They all turned to follow Jenna's directions.

'Oh Mary, mother of Jesus.' Amy smiled and fanned her face. 'I may be happily married but I can appreciate good eye candy. And that there is *quality* candy.'

Yep, Imogen couldn't deny she'd noticed that man too. A tiny, unwanted bubble of lust had erupted low in her belly when she'd first laid eyes on him. But that hadn't been tonight. He'd been in the pub when she'd first come to see it with the real estate agent.

The man in question leaned sideways against the bar now. He was tall with liquorice-dark hair and a two-day growth along his jawline. He wore faded jeans and a flannelette shirt rolled up at the elbows. She didn't know how he could bear it in the heat, but on him flannelette looked incredibly sexy. He wasn't in a group like most of the others; rather, he nursed a lone schooner of beer and talked to Charlie whenever he wasn't busy. The current owners of the pub also attended the bar and meals were starting to be served, but Charlie made plenty of time to chat with this guy.

'Good Lord, I think we've been sprung,' said Jenna with a slight giggle.

Imogen refocused her attentions to see Charlie and the man staring at their table. The man said something to Charlie, he responded, and the man scowled and then turned back to his drink. He downed the last half in two seconds flat, then barely flicked her a glance as he stalked out of the pub.

Imogen got the distinct impression his quick departure had

something to do with them. Unease washed over her. Although she didn't care what one particular man thought of her – the only man whose opinion ever mattered was dead – she didn't like being judged without a trial. And she had a feeling that's exactly what had just happened.

'What I want to know,' Amy asked, once again jolting Imogen from her reverie, 'is where are all the women?'

So, they'd finally noticed. And finally asked a question she could answer without having to rein in her emotions. 'There hardly are any. The town's population is ninety percent male.'

'Hmm.' Jenna took a sip of her drink, leaned back in her chair and smiled. 'I'm liking this idea of yours more and more.'

★★★

Gibson had noticed the three women sitting at the table by the window the moment he entered the pub. They stood out like a mirage on a dry road. Women were few and far between in Gibson's Find and that was the way he liked it. What had been a reasonably good day spent cleaning and servicing machinery now took a nosedive.

The hairs on the back of his neck prickled at his shirt collar as he wove through the dinner crowd, nodding at a few locals, his mates Guy and Wazza, and a couple of contractors who'd been out at Roseglen before. He was one of the lucky ones who lived close enough to town to be able to come down to the pub almost every night for a cold one, not that distance seemed to keep many away. Travellers might not think The Majestic had much to offer but aside from work and sport, there wasn't much else to keep a guy occupied around here. While he'd never be such a frequent patron if it weren't for Charlie, Gibson generally enjoyed the camaraderie he found at The Majestic. As in most country towns, the pub was an icon, perhaps more vital for morale than any other business.

Today, he headed straight for the bar, not pausing to engage in small talk with anyone.

'Gibby!' Charlie beamed when he saw him. No one else in the world called him Gibby, but he didn't mind Charlie doing so. 'Your usual?'

'Yes please.' He trained his eyes on his grandfather as Charlie grabbed a glass. He refused to give in to the temptation to turn around and take a better look at the three ladies, but his mind wouldn't stop with the questions about what they were doing here. Gibson's Find wasn't exactly a holiday destination, and it was hardly the type of place three city women – and they were definitely city women – would choose.

If his ears served him correctly, the piercing giggles told him they'd already imbibed quite a lot of alcohol, which meant they had to be staying in town. He itched to ask Charlie if they'd booked a room, but that would alert him to his interest. And he wasn't interested. Well, not in the way his granddad would think, or hope.

Charlie put a glass of Carlton Dry down on the bar between them and nodded to the specials blackboard behind him. 'We've got that pasta you like tonight. Can I tempt you?'

Gibson took a sip of his drink and then wiped some foam off his upper lip with the back of his hand. He'd been ravenous when he'd parked his ute, but seeing strange women in the pub had distracted him from his hunger. He wasn't a misogynist, not at all. He liked women and sex as much as the next bloke, but his days of wanting either in Gibson's Find were over.

'What's the deal with those three?' He didn't nod his head in their direction or turn to look. Aside from Cathy, who owned the pub with her husband Trevor, the trio by the window were the only people with XX chromosomes in the joint. There were some other women in town – a couple married to middle-aged farmers, a few who worked in the shire offices, and then the few widows who tried to keep the local CWA alive – but they rarely ventured into the pub.

'You noticed them, hey?'

Gibson glared at Charlie's upturned lips. 'Of course I noticed them. I can't remember the last time there were new women round here.'

'Interested?'

'Nope. Just curious.'

Charlie's propped his elbows against the bar. 'You can't blame an old man for trying.'

Actually, he could, but he didn't see the point. Gibson had made it more than clear on a number of occasions that he wasn't interested in finding another woman to settle down with, but it seemed that the more he protested, the more Charlie ignored his wishes. Luckily, despite Charlie's fervent intentions, the lack of single women in the area hindered his efforts. Gibson wasn't complaining.

Charlie sighed, seemingly disappointed that he couldn't rouse Gibson's interest. 'One of them, I think the redhead with the big kahoonas—'

'Granddad!'

'Sorry, breasts.' He chuckled and continued. 'She's buying the pub.'

'She's what?' Gibson racked his brain, trying to think if he'd noticed a Sold sticker on the For Sale sign that had hung outside The Majestic for the last two years. One of the things about a small town with next to no women was the lack of gossip. Usually it wasn't a problem, but in situations like this…

'Buying the pub. She signed the papers last week. Handover is in a month.'

Gibson gulped and gave in to the urge he'd been fighting since he walked in the door. He turned and unashamedly stared at the female trio, zooming in on the beauty with red hair and a rather large … bust. Not too large, but big enough to cup in his hands – *shit*, what was he thinking?

He shook his head and turned back to Charlie. 'Her and her husband?'

'No. She came a few weeks ago to have a look, and I asked Cathy and Trev about her later. Only her name on the contract.'

'That's insane.' He looked around the pub at the rowdy mob of blue-collar workers. They were generally in good spirits, but if a brawl kicked off, how was she supposed to handle it? She couldn't be much over twenty-five and she couldn't rely on Charlie. At eighty-two, he wouldn't stand a chance against an irate patron, although he'd give it his best shot. 'What about you? Will she want an old bloke hanging around still?'

'Nuff of the "old", thanks. But don't worry your pretty little head about me, Gibby. Cathy and Trev wrote me into the contract. The old girl and I,' he waved his arms around, gesturing to his surroundings, 'we're a package deal.'

Gibson tapped his fingers on the bar top, resisting the urge to ball his fingers into fists. 'She'll never last. A pub's no place for a woman on her own. This town's no place for a woman.'

'We'll see.' Gibson detected a hint of amusement in his grandfather's voice. The man was mocking him. 'So, can I interest you in the pasta?'

Gibson took one more look at the girls then shook his head. 'No thanks, I'm not hungry. See you tomorrow.'

Before Charlie could say more, Gibson downed the rest of his beer, turned and walked out of the pub.

# Chapter Two

## One Month Later

Imogen spent most of her first full day in Gibson's Find in The Majestic's tiny office, sweating in the late summer heat and discussing the handover with the previous owners. According to the contract, Cathy and Trevor had to stay on site for ten days to help Imogen learn the ropes, but the middle-aged couple were eager to leave sooner if possible. They were getting ready to head off in their shiny new caravan on a tour of Australia, and Imogen was looking forward to having the place to herself.

She knew The Majestic would be hard work, but that's what she wanted – needed – to keep her mind from dwelling on the past.

Cathy was giving her a crash course – everything from the staffing arrangements and the ordering of new liquor and food supplies to the system for taking accommodation bookings. After a day of it, Imogen's head spun from all she'd learnt but she appreciated Cathy's attention to detail. With her experience of running the wine bar in Perth, she had her own ideas for overhauling some of these ancient systems, but she didn't want to sound ungrateful by telling the older woman. As helpful as Cathy and Trevor were, with them hanging around, she felt as if a teacher were constantly watching over her shoulder.

At half past five Trevor poked his head around the door. 'You girls finished yet?'

He wore a chef's outfit that could no longer be classified as white, and his round face was red and shiny from the heat in the kitchen. As a couple, he and Cathy had always held very defined roles within the pub. Trevor handled the menu, any heavy lifting and all the cooking, while Cathy did the bookkeeping, managed their limited staff and sweet-talked the boys that treated the bar as their home night after night. From what Imogen had seen, the regulars all adored Cathy – none of them seemed to care about the derelict state of the building.

Imogen had big shoes to fill. And even though she'd hired a backpacker to work the bar and had a chef arriving soon from Perth, she was more than a little nervous about what she was taking on.

Trying not to let these thoughts overwhelm her, she looked up and smiled at Trevor. 'I don't know about Cathy, but I think I've almost reached information overload.'

'Good.' Trevor grinned and scratched the back of his neck. 'Because the pub's starting to fill up. I think you're going to be thrown in the deep end tonight.'

'Sorry love,' Cathy said. 'I feel bad running out on you, but my book club would never forgive me if I didn't go to my goodbye dinner.'

Imogen nodded. Cathy had mentioned her monthly trek to the nearest town to meet with a bunch of other ladies and talk about books. She'd also confessed that they talked more about men and their unsatisfying sex lives than about literature. Tonight the group were throwing her a farewell party and Imogen had agreed to man the bar with Charlie.

'It's fine,' Imogen said, trying not to think about a bunch of fifty-something-year-old women sitting round a table, talking sex. 'I'm looking forward to meeting the locals. I'll just go get changed.'

'See you soon, then.' Trevor retreated down the corridor.

Imogen thanked Cathy for all her patience and then headed to her new abode above the pub. Like the rest of the building, the publican's residence had seen better days. Her first priority would be restoring the public parts of the building, but in the few spare moments since she'd arrived, she'd done her best to make her private quarters comfortable. Cathy and Trevor had moved out the previous week and were 'road-testing' their caravan in the hotel's car park, but Imogen didn't think she'd truly consider the apartment her home until they'd left town.

Now she slid her key into the door – Trevor had advised her to keep it locked even when she was downstairs on the premises – and headed for her new bedroom. Eerie silence filled her apartment. A silence almost as bad as the one in her house after Jamie died. She blew a kiss at his photo on her bedside table and stripped off her denim shorts and t-shirt. While in the office, she hadn't spared much thought to her appearance, but tonight she was officially stepping out as the new publican and she wanted to look the part.

She opened the wardrobe door and smiled at the neat picture in front of her. She knew it wouldn't last – Jamie found her tendency to dump clothes on the floor or at the end of the bed infuriating – but right now it did look rather nice. Maybe she'd try a little bit harder to keep her living quarters tidy. Flicking through the outfits she'd bought to wear in the pub, she chose a knee-length black skirt and a short-sleeved checked shirt. She shook her head, ran her fingers through her hair and then finished by shovelling it all into a high ponytail. She washed her face and smiled at her reflection in the mirror as she slapped on a layer of foundation, a swipe of mascara on each eyelash and then a little gloss across her lips. Professional but not overdone. Excitement kicked her stomach over as she thought about the evening ahead.

Imogen would be the first to admit she'd been a bit of a recluse since Jamie had died. Apart from work nights, she could count the number of times she'd been out in the evening on one hand. At first she hadn't been able to summon the enthusiasm to dress up, and then, staying in and dreaming of happier times became a habit. When Jenna had finally conned her into attending her work Christmas party a year ago, she spent the whole evening sick to the stomach with guilt that she was out enjoying herself (or at least trying to) when Jamie would never spend a night out with friends again.

She hated the guilt. It took over the grief for a while there, ate at her insides so that she couldn't physically stomach food if she wasn't at work or at home. It made her angry and aggressive. She'd been dragged to more parties since that first one, cringing every time someone tried to talk to her and spending most of the evening staring at her watch. She hated that everyone looked at her with pity and sympathy when they spoke. She'd got to the stage where she'd had to actively refrain from throwing glasses of wine at genuinely nice people, people she and Jamie had once considered good friends.

But the kicker had been when people stopped talking about Jamie, stopped looking at her with pity and started looking at her as potential. Potential dates. Or worse, potential for matchmaking. Friends who had given up on trying to find Jenna a partner now transferred their attentions to her. They seemed to forget she'd already found her life partner. Just because he'd died didn't change the fact Jamie was The One.

Every time she thought about those nights, her skin crawled.

She shook her head, shaking off the memories. This was a new adventure, no one here was privy to her unfortunate past. She'd be the ballbreaker publican, too busy, too ambitious for romance and love, and she'd make damn sure everyone knew it. Holding her head high, she switched on the bedside lamp so she could see her way in the dark later and blew another kiss at Jamie's photo.

'Wish me luck, good-looking.'

As she descended the stairs she could already hear the combined noise of Aussie rock music and blokes raising their voices to be heard. Mouth-watering aromas wafted up from the kitchen. She rubbed her rumbling stomach, hoping she'd get the chance to steal a bite to eat. Trevor's burgers were apparently to-die-for, and she wouldn't have many more opportunities to try one.

At the entrance to the bar she paused and took in the scene. According to local legend most country pubs struggled to lure a crowd these days, but The Majestic had no trouble tonight. At almost six o'clock the place was crammed with men in every available nook and cranny. Some played darts (she hadn't seen a dart board in a city establishment for years) and the two pool tables were heaving. She was positively dressed up compared to all the patrons, most of whom appeared to have come straight from work. Would they put a bit of effort into their appearance if there were women here as well?

Imogen's thoughts were sidelined as her gaze snapped to the bar. Old Charlie looked knackered as he shuffled back and forth pulling schooners of beer and taking money. She rushed to his aid, brushing past a couple of guys as she did so.

'Wa-hey, what have we here?'

'Nice skirt!'

She ignored their comments and launched straight into action. 'Hey Charlie,' she said, waving briefly in greeting. 'Who's next?'

Charlie grinned at her, ancient smile lines evident at the corner of his eyes. She'd got to know him better since arriving and already knew he had a heart of gold. He'd spent much of their time together telling her exactly what the town had been like in its 'heyday', as he put it. He made it sound magical.

'Him,' he said, gesturing with one thumb towards the other end of the bar.

Imogen spun on her heels and it took less than a second for her body to recognise the guy in question: the guy Jenna had gushed over the day they'd visited. Imogen's green eyes locked with his dark scowling ones, and liquid heat almost floored her. If she didn't know better, she'd say she'd just been blasted with the lust bug, but it had to be something else. The way he looked at her, like he had a personal vendetta against her, made her mouth go dry. Did *he* have to be her first customer?

Refusing to be put off by a mere male – and deciding she'd like to be the one to make the guy who never smiled smile – she summoned her most saccharine grin and spoke. 'Hi there. What can I do for you this evening?'

Although he didn't reply, he raised his eyebrows and she wanted to kick herself for her unfortunate choice of words. Did he think she was flirting? The nerve of him.

She fought the urge to roll her eyes and instead stretched her smile until her jaw ached. 'I mean, to drink?' She hoped he detected the patronising tone beneath her sickly sweet demeanour. 'What can I get you to drink?'

'Just an OJ, thanks. I'm not staying.'

*Dammit.* First night on the job and instead of buttering up the customers she'd managed to alienate one of them. Vowing to pick up her act, she glanced down the price list in front of her. 'Three dollars sixty, thanks.'

He handed her a five-dollar bill and she took it, careful not to touch him in the process. He'd no doubt assume she'd done it on purpose. She stashed the money in the till, gave him his change and was happy for the ten-second reprieve from his intense gaze as she turned away to grab a bottle of juice from the fridge. She couldn't help studying his reflection in the glass.

Despite her annoyance, she was woman enough to admit he had handsome down to a fine art, if you liked that brand of handsome. She could certainly understand what Jenna saw in him. He was just her type: tall and tanned with muscles bulging beneath his slightly-too-tight work shirt. His dark hair was a tad too long; Jenna would say perfect to rake her fingers through, Imogen would say scruffy. Jenna would also like the fashionable two-day stubble, whereas Imogen had always thought such a look signalled a man's laziness and nonchalance towards personal hygiene.

Jamie was as masculine as they come, but he'd always taken the time to shave, and she'd never had to worry about getting stubble rash when she kissed him.

Not that she'd have to worry about that with this man either.

He cleared his throat. 'Having trouble finding it?'

*Argh*, caught. She scowled a scowl she hoped he couldn't see in the reflection of the glass and summoned the plastic smile. Refusing to bite his grumpy bait, she turned back towards him. 'Would you like it in a glass?'

'If it's not too much trouble.'

'Not at all.' Her face would crack if she held it like this much longer, but she would not give him the satisfaction of flummoxing her. This was her pub and if he didn't like it, she'd be more than happy to show him the exit. She stood right in front of him as she twisted the lid off the bottle and poured the contents into a cold schooner glass, all the while praying she wouldn't spill any. 'There you go.' She placed the drink in front of him and barely waited to hear his 'Thanks'. Hopefully his grumpiness wasn't indicative of the rest of the clientele.

Ten minutes later, she'd served at least ten more men, all of whom she'd willingly given genuine smiles and friendly service. They'd offered their names and returned her smiles with goofy grins and promises to show her round Gibson's Find any time she wanted. Although she wouldn't take any of them up on their offers, each warm welcome reassured Imogen that she'd made the right decision in moving here.

There seemed to be a lull, so she told Charlie she'd go and clear a few tables. Grabbing a tray, she began weaving through the men, collecting glasses and pausing every now and then to meet someone new and answer questions. Her feet already ached but her heart felt light and happy. Everyone was just so friendly. Well, almost everyone. As long as Mr Grouchy made good on his promise to leave after the juice, she'd have an enjoyable first evening.

At the thought, her head swivelled, as if of its own free will, to where he'd been leaning against the bar. She bit her lip; no matter how dismissive he'd been, she wondered why he was drinking in solitude when everyone else appeared to be part of a group. He turned, caught her looking and glowered.

Well fine, that'd be the last bit of human sympathy she wasted on him.

'No point wasting your time lusting after Gibbo, honey.'

Embarrassed that she'd been caught looking, Imogen followed the voice to a middle-aged man sitting on a chair nearby. 'I ... I wasn't.' She hated anyone thinking she was lusting after anyone – that was sacrilege to Jamie. About to tell him exactly this, she bit her tongue at the last moment. *New start, fresh slate.*

'Right.' The man obviously didn't believe her.

Torn between having it out with him and trying to distract his misled thoughts, she chose a combination of the two. She put the tray with the empty glasses on the table and held out her hand.

'I'm Imogen Bates, the new publican. Thanks for the advice, but it's really quite unnecessary.'

'Tom Davies.' His grip was firm and warm as he shook. 'My missus cleans the rooms for you.'

'Oh yes, Karen. I'm looking forward to meeting her. I'm hoping she might be interested in some extra shifts.' She wanted to talk to her about taking on the pub cleaning as well as the rooms. The poor old building didn't look like it'd had so much as a dusting in the last decade.

He nodded, pleased. 'Anything we can do to help you get settled in, just holler. It's nice to have a new face in town.'

'It's good to be here.'

Before they could get further into conversation, the lights went off and the music stopped dead. Was this a power cut? She'd heard the electricity could be dodgy at best out here in the sticks. And dammit, Trevor hadn't shown her how to work the generator yet. She didn't want the locals to think her incompetent.

The lights flashed back on seconds later and Imogen let out the breath she'd been holding. She blinked as she noticed everyone staring at her. Trevor and Cathy were making their way over with a massive cake laden with sparklers.

Warmth rushed to her cheeks, no doubt turning them as red as the ghastly vintage carpet upstairs. She'd never liked being the centre of attention.

The previous pub owners arrived beside her. Someone swiped her tray from the table and Cathy put the cake there instead.

'I thought you had book club,' Imogen hissed as she gazed at the cake and read the pink scrawl. GIBSON'S FIND WELCOMES IMOGEN.

Her heart swelled and tears prickled at her eyes. She'd never anticipated such a welcome. Smiling faces focused on her from every corner of the pub and, gazing back, she felt completely at a loss for words. This was so much more than she'd expected. Just when she thought she might combust from the emotion, someone up near the bar cried, 'Speech!'

***

Gibson should have downed his juice and walked out the door the moment Imogen started talking. Better still, before the lights went off and the cake came out and her eyes lit up in delighted surprise. Those deep-green eyes – the colour of grass you hardly ever saw in this part of the country – had sparkled and her lips had curled, proving the smile she'd given him earlier, had been one hundred percent fake.

He should have walked out long before she started talking and definitely before she'd taken a bite of Trevor's deadly moist chocolate cake. But Charlie had reached across the bar and placed his palm against Gibson's arm. 'Stay,' he'd pleaded. 'Just a bit.'

Gibson had never been able to say no to Charlie. So he'd listened as she gushed over her surprise cake and thanked Trevor and Cathy for making her feel so welcome. 'Look around,' he'd wanted to shout. 'You're the one doing them a favour.' But he'd held his tongue. He'd watched as the other men in the pub – his neighbours, his old primary school mates, blokes who'd worked for him at one stage or another, even bloody Charlie for goodness sakes – stared open-mouthed and goggle-eyed as she spoke about her desire for a tree change. There were plenty of dry plains, salt lakes and the odd bush out here, but a tree change? He'd felt the orange juice churning in his stomach.

And they'd all been falling all over each other to ask her questions. He supposed he could sort of understand, because she was undoubtedly pretty and did have a sweet kind of voice, but what she said only got his shackles up more.

How she'd been bored and disillusioned with life in Perth. How her job in a city wine bar had been demanding but not rewarding. How she'd come into some money and wanted to do something meaningful and worthwhile with it. Apparently she had a 'vision' for the old place. If she hadn't already won everyone's hearts, she stole the last few when she mentioned wanting to become a part of the community. 'To get involved and give back.' He'd actually rolled his eyes then and earned a disapproving look from Charlie. But he'd heard it all before.

His mum – who'd spent over twenty resentful years in Gibson's Find before leaving for the coast – loved reading rural romance novels. Women writers who had no clue about outback life made out it was all homesteads the size of castles and farmers with time enough on their hands to be Prince Charming. He'd bet Imogen had read one of these books and decided it was the perfect way to catch a man. These so-called authors had a lot to answer for.

'I could watch that all night.'

Gibson didn't need to turn to the voice beside him to know where his mate Guy was looking. Imogen had stopped talking for five seconds and was finally digging into the cake. Cathy had cut her a ridiculously huge slice and she had to hold it in two hands while she nipped off tiny bites and licked her lips every few seconds to get rid of the icing smudges. You'd think she was eating in the nude the way everyone was carrying on.

He turned to Guy. 'Not much on the box tonight then, is there?'

Guy shook his head derisively. 'You're kidding me, right? Still intent on playing Oscar the Grouch?'

'I don't know what you mean.'

Guy snorted. Gibson knew his friend thought his bitterness about happily-ever-afters was all down to Serena. Guy, head of the local State Emergency Service team and a keen footballer, also managed the farm next to Gibson's, and they often helped each other with tasks that were easier with more than one person. He'd said on more than one occasion that it was time for Gibson to move on and look to the future. But Guy didn't know the half of it. No one did.

Their friend Wazza sidled up, wearing a goofy grin identical to all the other men in the pub. Just because an apparently single woman had bought the local watering hole, they'd all gone soft in the head and hard in the pants. Half of the men he hadn't seen in the pub for years, yet they'd all flocked in tonight to check out the new publican.

'So, are we taking bets on who can bed her first?'

Gibson groaned at the predictability. He'd gotten marriage out of his system after Serena, but most of his mates were still bachelors, pining for their chance at the Aussie dream. If it were just sex he could understand it, but he'd bet every available man in this room had his sights set on Imogen for more than just a quick tumble on the back of his WB ute. If it weren't so sad, it'd be funny.

One new woman and fifty single men in their twenties and thirties – it just didn't add up. And just because that one woman was talking the talk didn't mean she'd last the distance.

Wazza dug his wallet out of his back pocket and opened it up to reveal a wad of cash. He slapped a note on the table; this was the last time Gibson would listen to him complain that the crop spraying business paid badly.

'Ten bucks says I get closer than you do, Guy,' Wazza wagered.

'I'm in.' Guy fished a note out of his pocket and laid it on the bar. 'Fifty says she's mine within a month.'

Gibson loved Guy like a brother, but he'd always been a cocky sod, not to mention a Casanova whenever they took a trip into the city. And this kind of thing felt so high school.

'A month?' Wazza guffawed and theatrically pressed his hand against his heart. 'You must be losing your touch.'

Guy glowered and leaned over the bar. 'Can I get another one of these, please, Charlie old boy?'

Charlie refilled Wazza and Guy's glasses, and as the boys turned back to their gutter-level banter, Gibson tried to get Charlie's attention. They'd barely spoken since he'd arrived and Charlie was the only reason he'd ventured in here today.

Unfortunately, his granddad had already headed to the other end to serve someone else. 'Charlie,' he called.

Either Charlie was getting deaf in his old age or he was ignoring him. Gibson glanced at his watch and couldn't believe it was almost nine o'clock. How the hell had that happened? It appeared time could fly whether you were having fun or not.

Cathy approached him with the biggest smile he'd ever seen on her face. Obviously, selling the pub and the prospect of freedom agreed with her. 'Didn't your mother ever read you the story about the wind changing, Gibson Black?'

'You mean the one where the little boy grumped and his face stayed like that?'

'That's the one.'

'My mum didn't read many picture books, but I think I saw it on *Play School*.'

She laughed. 'Would a free drink encourage a smile?'

He shrugged. 'Couldn't hurt.' Not that he'd been planning on drinking tonight – he had an early start in the morning. Hell, he hadn't intended to stay more than a few minutes, but somehow his plans had changed.

Cathy gave him a bottle of beer then went back to her celebrations. He took a long sip. About to take a second one, he froze as a shadow fell over him. Even before he looked sideways, he knew the perky, pint-sized new publican had taken the stool beside him. He glanced at her as she pushed a plate with a piece of Trevor's chocolate cake on it towards him.

She smiled, and this time he thought it a real, slightly amused one. 'I think you're the only person who hasn't tasted this yet, and it's a sin not to. Trust me on that.'

She rested one elbow on the bar and held her head against her palm as she looked intently at him. A few strands of crimson hair fell across her pale cheek and he had an almost uncontrollable desire to reach out and tuck them behind her ear.

'I have tasted it. Just not tonight.' The tantalising aroma of freshly cooked cocoa wafted up to him but he resisted the urge to taste it.

'Okay, that's it.' Instead of the pout he'd expected, she folded her arms under her breasts and straightened on the stool. 'Have I done something to offend you?'

Where to start? But he knew how stupid he'd sound if he started listing the reasons. In his head, the fact he didn't want new women in Gibson's Find made sense. The fewer women around, the less likely one of his good friends would hook up with someone, get married and live the life he never would. Not that he didn't want his mates to be happy, but it was easy living here, where new relationships were even less frequent than heavy downpours, and where happily married couples weren't dancing smugly under his nose.

But if he couldn't admit this to Charlie or even to his closest friends, he could hardly admit it to a newcomer. He'd sound loony at best, downright nasty at worst.

'It's not you personally. It's more that I'm looking out for this town.'

'Oh yeah?' She rolled her eyes, her incredibly long and thick eyelashes dancing as she did so. 'Because I'm such a terrible threat. I'm a pyromaniac in my spare time, I've been known to shoplift, and I stalk old ladies in the street. Yeah, this town is seriously endangered by my arrival.'

He stifled a laugh, secretly amused by her wry comeback. 'Now you're just being ridiculous.'

'Am I?' She looked narky. It kind of suited her. 'From where I'm sitting, you're the one being ridiculous, and I have no idea why.'

He groaned, louder than he meant to. He knew he should have left hours ago.

She seemed to take the groan as an invitation. 'Listen. You may have lived here for who knows how long – all your life, for all I care – but if you want to make a habit of hanging out in *my* pub, you're going to have to get over yourself, because I'm here to stay. I like to talk and I plan to feel comfortable when I serve someone.'

'You say that now but you've only just arrived. Life's no picnic in the bush, and this is a tough business to take on all on your own.'

She opened her mouth to reply but Charlie interrupted them, coming to rest at the other side of the bar.

'I see you've met my grandson.'

'Your grandson?' Imogen looked at Charlie, her expression incredulous and almost pitying.

'Yep, that he is. My son's boy, Gibson Black.'

'He hasn't exactly introduced himself.' Imogen spoke as if he weren't even there.

Charlie reached out and cuffed Gibson round the ear. 'I've told you to be more sociable. You could at least make an effort to be polite to my new boss.'

'Don't worry, Charlie. I won't judge you on him. You can't choose your family.'

'Hey Charlie,' called one of the blokes from the other end of the bar. 'Got any peanuts? I've got the munchies.'

Charlie tottered off and Imogen returned her focus to Gibson.

'Gibson, hey? As in Gibson's Find?'

'Not in the way you're thinking.' He took another sip of his beer.

'I was thinking maybe your mum was a Gibson.'

'You were thinking wrong. Those Gibsons left town yonks ago, after selling their discovery to the bigwigs.'

'So…?' She eyed his chocolate cake as if she'd start digging in if he didn't.

He pushed it towards her. 'My mum had this thing about naming her kids after the place where they were conceived. I have an older sister called Paris. My parents honeymooned there.'

'Romantic.' She picked up his dessert fork and cut off a chunk. He had to make an effort not to stare as she opened her lips and popped the piece inside.

'Loopy if you ask me.'

She shrugged. 'This cake really is divine. You sure you don't want any?'

He had a stupid urge to lick the icing off her lips. 'I'm sure. I'll just go say goodbye to Charlie.' He stood up. 'Nice meeting you.'

She placed the fork next to the unfinished cake and glared at him, bemusement sparkling in her eyes. 'No need to pretend, Gibson.' She stood as well and he swallowed as he raked his gaze down her peachy-perfect figure. 'I need to go do some work anyway, but you should know, you couldn't be more wrong about me. I know what I'm doing and I can look after myself.'

With those words she stormed off in the direction of the tables and started gathering empty glasses. He watched her for longer than he intended, unable to resist properly checking her out. She got full marks in his head-to-toe assessment, but it wasn't only her physical attributes that grabbed him. There was something else. Something alluring. Something intriguing.

Something he didn't want to think about.

★★★

Despite exhaustion cramping her limbs, when Imogen climbed into bed she rolled onto her side and smiled at the photo of Jamie next to her. When she'd arrived she'd unpacked her favourite photos first, ensuring Jamie's had pride of place in all the rooms.

'Evening gorgeous.'

Some may have found it disturbing that she still talked to him every night, but it was a ritual that calmed her and helped her sleep.

'I had such a great night downstairs. People here are all so welcoming. I hope you're not worrying about me, because I know I'm going to be happy here.'

She leaned her head against the pillow, tucked her hands under her cheek and chattered on about some of the people she'd met, Charlie's idea of a slab party to renovate the place, the new staff who were arriving soon, absolutely everything that came into her head. She imagined Jamie chuckling to himself from wherever he was right now. He'd always said she talked too much, but the gleam in his eye whenever he'd said it had told her he hadn't minded one little bit.

Eventually, when she'd exhausted the day's activities, she blew him a kiss and turned off the light. In the dark she stretched her legs diagonally across the bed – one of many tricks she tried to make it feel less empty. Her eyes squeezed tightly shut, Imogen imagined Jamie snuggling up to her, wrapping his strong, warm arms around her and kissing that little spot just beneath her ear. She didn't have to imagine the sparks his lips would ignite because she dreamed of it every night.

She yawned.

Not long now.

When she slept, he was still alive.

# Chapter Three

Imogen woke early the next morning and pulled on her running shorts, a t-shirt and sneakers.

She hadn't exercised properly since before Jamie died. Truth be told, her health had been the least of her worries, but recently she'd noticed her love handles were feeling extra lovey and her favourite jeans didn't sit right on her hips. She'd hoped all the packing and carrying of boxes might have been enough of a workout, but apparently it didn't negate the comfort-eating. It was time to take drastic measures.

Going on a run would also give her the opportunity to do a proper reconnaissance of the town. Apart from a couple of quick trips to the general store, she'd barely set foot outside the pub since arriving.

After double-knotting her shoelaces, grabbing a bottle of water from the fridge, picking up her keys and slipping them into a pocket, she blew a kiss to the Jamie photo that had the centre spot on her new hall table. If he'd still been around, no way would she have been getting fat. They'd played tennis twice a week in the summer and squash in the winter, not to mention their frequent horizontal activities that burned as many calories as a jog around the block. Apparently.

She paused a moment and pressed her hand against her chest, hoping to ease the pang that erupted at thoughts of Jamie and sex. Although her red-hot dreams were good, they didn't satisfy her like the real thing, and she had to admit her girly bits were getting twitchy. That presented a dilemma, for she'd never seen the appeal of casual sex, and she certainly didn't plan on getting into a relationship.

As seedy as it made her feel, she decided that next time they talked, she would ask Jenna's advice about buying a vibrator. Jenna openly and proudly knew about such things.

That decision made, Imogen took the stairs out of her apartment. When she stepped into the early morning air she breathed in deeply, smiling at the fresh country scent. This was why she'd moved so far away from the city – well, one of many reasons. Fresh air and no pollution – noise or otherwise.

She began to run, turning right out of the pub grounds and onto the main street. The Majestic sat on the corner, just before the sign directing motorists out of town and on their way to Southern Cross.

Next door to the pub stood a couple of abandoned shops. One looked to have been a dress shop in times when there were enough women in town to warrant one, and the other, if the rumours were to be believed, was once a brothel. With the lack of females in Gibson's Find, some of her patrons probably wished it was still in operation. There was no graffiti like you'd see on vacant shops in the city, only weeds forcing themselves up through cracks in the pavement out front. The emptiness was echoed in Imogen's heart.

She was glad to move past the deserted strip to the busier end of the street.

Though it was wide enough for about four trucks to drive parallel to each other, she'd rarely seen more than two cars drive down the main street at the same time. Shops were scattered along one side of the road, and the other was home to an old train station and semi-landscaped bushland dotted with metal-art statues made by locals long ago. On the shop side there was a post office; a cafe that never appeared to have more than two customers at a time; a Holden dealership that looked like it only had three cars for sale; a hardware and farm supplies shed; and a general store with an agency for Bendigo Bank.

The street was empty and, due to the early hour, all the shops were currently closed. Although the wind made the temperature pleasant, a hint of promised warmth already hung in the air. Looked like it'd be another forty-degree scorcher. The last couple of days, her forehead had become a permanent waterfall of sweat, and her shirts were getting stains under her arms and at the back of her neck. Not a good look for the woman in charge.

'Morning.'

She looked round from where she'd been reading the magazine billboards outside the general store and smiled at the owner of the voice. She recognised him as one of the men who'd ribbed Charlie about his mistake that day she'd brought her friends to the pub. He'd been there again last night, but they hadn't been formally introduced. Blonde hair, medium height and reasonably good-looking, she'd put him in his late thirties. His football shorts, sneakers and a t-shirt soaked in sweat told her he'd been exercising as well.

'A group of us get together down on the oval three mornings a week for boot camp, if you're interested,' he said, his grin growing wider. 'I'm Guy, by the way.' He held out his hand but seemed to think better of it at the last minute, pulling it back and wiping his palm against his t-shirt.

She smiled back. 'Imogen. And thanks. I'll think about it.' She took a sip from her water bottle, itching to ask him if any women attended. It wasn't that she minded being one of very few women, not exactly, but she didn't think she'd be comfortable if she were the *only* one.

'Great. Well, I'll see ya round.' Guy waved and jogged across the street.

She read another headline before continuing down the street, walking briskly at first and then starting into a run. At the end of the main street, which wasn't very long, she turned right into the grid of streets that formed the majority of the Gibson's Find township.

As she lengthened her paces, pounding the uneven and cracked pathways, she studied the houses on either side of the road. What struck her as very different from Perth was the mishmash of architecture. Whereas in the city you had a suburb of flash houses or a suburb of shabby ones, here the best and biggest house in the street might be alongside one that looked as if it needed a demolition order.

Jamie would have had a feast in a town like this. So many old places with potential to be turned into works of art. And she'd die to get her thumbs into some of the gardens, or lack thereof. It didn't appear that anyone in Gibson's Find had a green bone in their body. Most of the front yards were desolate and decidedly lacking in colour. No cute gnomes or fairy statues, never mind flowers.

She jogged a little further, pleasantly surprised when she came upon a cute little shack with an abundance of colourful flowers. A middle-aged woman stood in the garden, wielding a hose like she barely had control over the thing. She spied Imogen and waved, hose and all. An icy spray of water fell over Imogen and she jumped back, but not before the front of her top got splashed.

'I'm so sorry,' gushed the woman, screwing off the water, dumping the hose on the grass and rushing forward to greet Imogen over a pristinely kept hedge. 'Can I get you a towel?'

'No, I'm fine.' Imogen pulled the rubber band from her ponytail and shook out her hair. This woman was only the third she'd met in town – Cathy being the first, and the old woman who seemed to sit permanently behind the counter at the general store the second. Granted, she'd barely left the pub, but still, she was beginning to believe the rumours that Gibson's Find was suffering a veritable drought of females. 'No harm done.'

'I'm Karen Davies,' the woman announced as Imogen re-scooped her hair into a ponytail. 'I'm so sorry we haven't met yet, but I work for you. Great way to meet your boss, isn't it?'

'Karen, pleased to meet you.' Imogen grinned at the warmth and embarrassment in the older woman's voice. It went perfectly hand in hand with her appearance. She was round but not obese – her mother would say 'cuddly'. Karen's hair was cropped short around her chin in a practical style and streaked with grey as if she were happy to age gracefully. 'Don't worry about the water. I was hot anyway. How are you feeling?'

Karen had been sick with tonsillitis and therefore hadn't been around yesterday or the day Imogen had arrived, so this was the first time they'd met.

'Much better,' Karen replied with a nod. 'I'm desperate to get back to work but the doc says I need another couple of days' rest. Don't tell her you saw me exerting myself.'

Imogen laughed. 'I won't. But don't overdo it. We'll chat when you're completely better.'

With a quick wave Imogen resumed jogging down the street. If she kept getting stopped by friendly locals she wasn't going to work up much of a sweat at all.

The next few houses were nothing to write home about, in fact some of them looked unoccupied. She was running, lost in her own thoughts and not looking out for traffic when a dirt-covered ute reversed rather quickly out of the driveway in front of her.

She jumped back and grabbed onto a nearby letterbox to stop herself from falling. The ute stopped. A curse sounded inside, and then a dark-haired head popped out the driver's side window.

Her tummy flipped in a traitorous manner. Gibson Black. Just her luck.

'You should be careful how you're driving,' she said before she could think better of it.

He raised his eyebrows, amusement dancing at the corners of his illegally luscious lips as recognition dawned in his eyes. 'And you should be more traffic-conscious when you're running.'

She folded her arms across her chest, noticing it was heaving and that he wasn't being surreptitious about looking. Soaked through from Karen's hose, her white top was now no doubt see-through. Her black running shorts felt ridiculously short and tight and the neck of the water bottle dug into her side, but she refused to look perturbed. 'You're the first bit of traffic I've seen all morning. And anyway, this here's the footpath.'

He shrugged slowly as if he really didn't have the time or inclination to debate with her. 'Maybe you're right, but you're the first jogger I've seen in town in about…' He paused as if thinking this through. 'In forever. You took me by surprise.'

She bit her lip, thinking this was about the closest to an apology she was ever going to get from him.

'What are you doing here, anyway?' She looked past him to the dull-grey fibro house – neater than many of the other houses in the street, but still without much of a garden.

Immediately, she wished she hadn't asked. What right did she have to give him the third degree? Maybe he'd stayed over at his girlfriend's house. There weren't many women in town, but she'd bet money on the fact that if he wanted every one of those few, he'd have them. She tried to ignore the ridiculous resentment that thought invoked. Softening her voice, she added, 'I thought you lived on the family farm.'

He smiled. Well, it was more of a smirk, but his lips definitely lifted. And if his scowl was scandalously sexy, his smile was lethal. Its effects ricocheted right down to her toenails.

'Have you been making enquiries about me?' he asked, in a tone that said he was good-looking and knew it.

She narrowed her eyes and glared. 'No.' She hated that she sounded so aggro, so childish in her reply, probably inflating his ego to mammoth proportions. 'Charlie mentioned it. For some reason, he can't talk enough about you.'

He shrugged and smiled like this amused him as he tapped his fingers on the steering wheel. 'That I do, and I'd best be getting back there.'

'Where?'

He raised one eyebrow and looked at her like she had a flashing Idiot sign on her head. 'My farm.'

'Oh, right.' No wonder he questioned her ability to run the pub on her own. 'Cool.'

*Cool*? Oh Lord. Why couldn't she act normal around this jerk?

'Do you mind stepping back?' He nodded towards the pavement behind her. 'I'm a very careful driver and I don't want any incidents with joggers on my record.'

Damn the man, he was mocking her. She had a good mind to slam her fist through his open window and punch his pretty nose, except she wasn't a violent person. Not usually. 'Sure,' she said instead, gritting her teeth as she took a few steps back. Hell, she should have turned and sprinted the other way, because being in his poisoning presence wasn't doing her any favours. The longer she stood in front of him, practically naked in her wet running clothes, the more stupid she felt.

'Well, I guess I'll see you round,' he said, lifting his hand in a quick goodbye.

'I guess so.' Thinking she hoped not, Imogen mimicked his wave, forgetting that in doing so she was uncovering her wet t-shirt in all its see-through glory. His gaze fell to her chest. All of a sudden her sports bra felt unbelievably tight and wicked sensations danced low in her belly. Sensations she'd thought had been buried with Jamie. Before she could react, he quickly looked away, pressed his foot against the accelerator and all but hooned out of the driveway.

'Oh Lord.' She wished there were a streetlight nearby so she could lean her heavy head against it. Was there something in the water here? It was as if the moment she'd driven past the Welcome To Gibson's Find sign at the edge of the shire, her libido had been awakened from very long and deep slumber. Had to be the fact she hadn't had sex in almost two and a half years. No other reason at all.

Definitely not.

Unable to help herself, she glanced up and scrutinised the house he'd come from. As she looked for any signs of female life, she told herself she didn't actually care but was merely interested if there was a woman around strong enough to put up with the infuriating Gibson Black.

If so, that woman deserved a medal.

★★★

Gibson drove through the large iron entrance gates to Roseglen, his family's 20,000-acre sheep and crop farm, and wished it were seeding or harvest time. As a sole operator – with Charlie's help, when he felt like it, and contracted workers in the busy times – there was always work to do on the farm, but February was his quietest time. He needed to bait, mothball and service the harvester before stowing it away until next season, and there were always fences to fix, other engines to service, stock to feed, water to check and general upkeep. But unfortunately today there was nothing that he really needed to get his teeth stuck into, which – in his current agitated state – was a bad thing.

Not usually the type of bloke to look for trouble, this morning, as he drove down the gravel drive, past the deserted shearing shed, silos, rusty old windmill and hay shed towards the house, he shifted in his seat, half hoping to spot a leaky pipe or a stray sheep in the wrong paddock. The boardies that had been loose when he'd pulled them on this morning now cut into his thighs, and he was glad no one was around to see Imogen's effect on him. The image of her in those tiny, blessedly tight running shorts and that t-shirt soaked with sweat from running her shapely little legs crazy, not to mention her smart mouth, had imprinted itself on his mind. It refused to leave, no matter how many unsexual images he'd tried to conjure on the ten-minute drive from town.

His mother. Curry farts. The smell of old milk. *Cardboard*.

He stopped the car and walked awkwardly towards the house as his two working dogs – twin kelpies called Jack and Jill – bounded towards him.

He rarely stayed in town with Charlie – the old man was more independent than anyone he knew, much to the irritation of Gibson's mother – and the dogs hated it when he did, but late last night Charlie had been in a fluster, unable to find his house keys after his shift, so Gibson had driven back into town with the spares. With Jack and Jill camped out on the front verandah, he needn't worry about his house or his possessions. Friend or foe, his dogs let no one within a hundred-metre radius of his home when he wasn't there. Dogs were the most important things in most cockies' lives. They were easily worth two or three employees and, in his experience, were much less bother than a wife.

'Hey pals.' He bent to stroke them both around the ears. They bounced as if the ground were a trampoline as the three of them headed up the path towards the house. Yes, they were working dogs, but aside from Charlie they were also the only family he had around here anymore. And they were better company than most people, never nagging him about things he didn't want to be nagged about.

The day Serena left the farm had been the day he'd brought the dogs' beds inside. Keeping them close made him feel less alone. The farming rule about working dogs living outside had been the one thing his city-chick wife had really latched on to. Pity she hadn't shown the same enthusiasm towards anything else to do with rural life.

*Ugh*. He shook his head as the door slammed behind him. He didn't want to think about Serena. The divorce had been finalised for near on two years and, as a rule, he harboured thoughts about their short marriage as little as possible. At least thinking of her had succeeded in doing one thing – he no longer had an erection the size of Mt Kosciuszko burning a hole in his pants.

She had that effect. Whenever he thought about his ex-wife his insides grew lead-heavy and he tried to focus on the good things in his life – like the farm, football, Charlie – before the bad thoughts spiralled out of control. He wasn't depressed like Paris had suggested last time he went to Perth for a family lunch. He was simply a little uninspired. Just because his marriage had failed and he didn't walk around with a permanent grin on his face, like his mother and sister, didn't mean he was about to top himself. He simply didn't see the point of trying to keep up appearances.

As he went towards the kitchen seeking breakfast, Gibson chuckled, recalling Paris' suggestion he see a shrink.

He hated how married people couldn't see that there were other ways to live. You didn't have to be coupled off to be happy.

He may have been slightly lonely these last couple of years – a farm was probably the most isolated place a guy could live by himself – but he wouldn't have called his barely twelve months of marriage happy days either.

Grabbing a carton of eggs and a packet of bacon from his fridge, Gibson threw all his pent-up energies into cooking up a feast. In the beginning, he'd put that kind of effort into Serena – making sure his girlfriend was happy. And when she become his wife, his efforts hadn't waned. But no matter what he did, nothing lived up to her idea of how their life should be. He should have known you couldn't pick up a farmer's wife in a nightclub in the city, but he'd found her attractive, they'd got chatting, started dating, one thing led to another, and he'd hoped Serena would help him make the kind of life he always dreamed of. Not the family his parents had created for him, but the kind of marriage Charlie talked about having with Elsie. He wanted a wife who'd be his partner in everything, and that very much included working on the farm.

In the end, he hadn't chosen a wife like Elsie at all; he'd chosen one exactly like his mother.

No one expected marriage to be a piece of cake, but it was even tougher in the bush. Women had to be more than blindsided by love. They had to be tough and inventive, loyal and gutsy, prepared to suffer years of drought, temperamental sheep, isolation and a severe lack of the finer things in life. Serena hadn't stuck around long enough to witness many of these things, but in hindsight, he knew she'd never have coped with any of them.

In his experience, women who fit that definition were few and far between, and Gibson had lost all hope of ever finding one. But instead of dwelling on this fact, he focused all his time and attention on the farm, doing everything within his control to make sure it flourished.

# Chapter Four

Imogen looked around her new office and smiled. Cathy and Trevor hadn't gone yet, but in the last few days Imogen had begun putting her mark on the place. The simple act of Cathy removing her belongings had opened it up from a poky little room into a spacious office. Although she wasn't always immaculate at home, she liked things neat and tidy in the work environment.

The only extravagant items were a few strategically placed photos across her desk – a favourite shot of Jenna and Amy, her sisters and their kids, and one of her parents. She'd made the heart-breaking decision not to include a picture of Jamie. Upstairs, in her apartment, she had almost enough photos to pretend he was still around, but downstairs she wanted to do things differently. She didn't plan on broadcasting her widowed status to anyone. Not that she'd lie – she'd just wait for such a conversation to arise of its own accord.

'Knock knock.'

Imogen looked up to see Karen standing there.

'Hi there.' Karen smiled awkwardly. 'I'm so sorry about the other morning. It was like something off *Funniest Home Videos* – meeting your new boss and trying to drown her.'

Imogen couldn't help but laugh. 'Don't worry about it. A little water never hurt anyone, especially in this climate.'

'Phew.' Karen's smile relaxed.

'Are you all recovered now?'

'Yes. Healthy and raring to go. Cathy mentioned you wanted to see me before I started on the rooms. The log says there were only a couple of guests last night.'

'Yes.' Imogen nodded. 'I imagine that won't take you long, which is kind of why I want to talk to you. Come on in.'

Karen bustled in, the smile lines Imogen had noticed around her eyes crinkled tightly. 'I have to say, it's so fabulous to have a new female face in town, but you'd better watch out. The men around here will be squabbling over you like crows over roadkill. It's once in a blue moon a pretty girl lands in these parts.'

Imogen laughed nervously at the image. 'They can squabble all they like, but I'm not in the market for a relationship.'

'Oh?' Karen's forehead wrinkled. 'A pretty young thing like you? I thought you'd be desperate to fall in love. We've got an abundance of lovely boys around here.'

An image of Gibson Black flashed into her mind, but she shooed it away. He wasn't *lovely*!

Karen continued, oblivious. 'Unless of course some bloke has ruined you already. You're not divorced, are you?' She said 'divorced' like it was a cardinal sin.

'No, nothing like that. I just want to focus on building the business before I worry about relationships.' Imogen hated lying, not that it was exactly a lie. The business part was true, but relationships weren't part of her game plan anymore. She wondered if she should tell Karen the truth – it might be sensible to at least share her past with her employees – but Karen had already moved on.

'Very sensible.' She nodded her head enthusiastically. 'This is a big venture to take on, but I'm sure you're up to it. Tom's told me marvellous things. The town is in desperate need of a revival, and this old place used to be bursting with people of an evening. It would be so lovely to see it come alive again.'

Imogen leaned across her desk and gestured for Karen to take a seat. 'How long have you lived here?'

'Pretty much my whole life. Almost fifty-two years.' The older woman settled in the chair.

'Wow.' Imogen laughed. 'I'll bet a chat with you would be better than reading the local history books, then.'

Karen beamed, obviously pleased with Imogen's analysis. 'You ask me anything you want. If I don't know it, you check with Charlie. If he doesn't know it—'

'It's not worth knowing?' Imogen guessed.

They both laughed.

'That's right,' Karen said with a wry smile. 'Now, I'll bet you've got plenty to be getting on with, so what was it you wanted to talk with me about?'

'I was just wondering if you're happy with your current hours, or if you'd be open to a bit of negotiation.' Imogen kept her voice low – the door was open and she didn't want to offend Cathy or Trevor with her observations. 'I'd like to employ you for longer each day and include the cleaning of the main pub in your duties. Not a huge clean,' she rushed, not wanting to put Karen off, 'but just a quick once-over five days a week, so the dust and grime doesn't get out of hand.'

A knowing smile appeared on Karen's face. She leaned across the desk and whispered, 'Cathy was never much of a housekeeper, and most of the blokes round here don't really notice the dust, but it's nice to know that might be about to change.'

'A wise businessman once told me that you shouldn't change anything in the first three months of business. Well, wise or not, I'm planning on changing a fair bit.'

'Good on you,' Karen chuckled. 'And I can't wait to see the results. That's a yes to the extra work. I'm so bored since the kids fled the nest that even my flowers are getting sick of my company. I'm happy to do some bar work too if the need ever arises. Hell, I'll help in any way I can.'

'Fabulous. I'll keep that in mind,' Imogen promised.

That settled, Karen went to stand up but Imogen raised her hand to stop her. 'You said the town's in desperate need of a revival. What did it used to be like?'

'Ah…' Karen got a wistful look in her eyes and leaned back into the chair. 'Magic. I've never seen the appeal of the city myself, but I guess the folks that pass through here now don't see the place like I do. We used to be a thriving little community – there was even a school until about fifteen years ago.'

Now that she thought of it, Imogen couldn't recall seeing one child since landing in Gibson's Find. She smiled, encouraging Karen to go on.

'Our population used to be triple what it is now. With more women living here, there were kids and community groups aplenty. Fundraisers, balls, bingo nights, you name it. There was never a shortage of social life round these parts. But when the big mine closed, the mining families moved further afield. And that basically left the farmers. With many properties amalgamating in recent years, even the farmers have become few and far between. Some were bought out by big companies, and the managers that live on them now haven't got the link with the history of the community. A lot of them are just here to make a quick buck before buying their own place and settling down. And as you see, there are hardly any women here to give these drop-ins reason to stay. We don't even have our

own football team anymore. The local fellows had to combine with
other towns in the region.' She sighed. 'It's a bit of a chicken-and-egg
situation – whether the women left because things were dwindling
or whether things dwindled because the women left.

'Do you think there's any hope of things ever reversing?' Imogen
asked, her heart saddened at Karen's passionate recounting, and the
fact that she'd impulsively bought a business in what was, in essence,
a dying community.

'I'd like to think so.' Karen nodded, her large breasts lifting and
her whole body getting in on the action. 'Folks are talking about
coming back due to the mining taking off again. Tom thinks I'm
stupid to entertain such hopes, but I look at it this way: the people
who stayed in Gibson's Find are fighters. We haven't let the town
completely die like others around it, so there is a little bit to draw
people back. Ever heard of Black Arrow?'

The name sounded vaguely familiar. 'I think so.'

'Ghost town not far from here. Only thing left is the pub; you
can get a nice meal there though.'

*Phew*, thought Imogen. At least if Gibson's Find did go the same
way, she might be able to survive on passing trade and the reputation she planned to build. But hopefully it would never come to
that. The idea of country towns and their close-knit communities had always appealed to her, and she'd moved here because she
wanted to belong to one. Imogen vowed then and there to help
enthusiastic locals like Karen hold on to the dream.

It might not be much, but she would do whatever she could to
keep *this* small community alive.

\*\*\*

Gibson supposed it was good that he had to head into town occasionally – for supplies, to visit Charlie, to go to ambo training and

the odd Apex Club meeting – but sometimes he wished he could just hole himself up at Roseglen. He felt more than happy in the company of Jack and Jill and his mother's neglected rosebushes, but maybe if he cut himself off totally from human interaction he'd miss it. Then again ... maybe not.

Scratching the back of his neck, he tossed his keys up in the air, caught them again and then jogged down the verandah and the garden path to his ute. This arvo's task was stopping in at the agricultural supplies store to collect some tractor parts, then a quick visit with Charlie before an Apex meeting in the back room of The Majestic at six. Right now his dogs were lying under an old gum tree, no doubt thankful he hadn't called them to work in this scorching heat. They generally loved jumping in the back of the ute and driving round the farm, looking for stray sheep they could exhaust their never-ending energy on, but nobody liked to work in forty-degree temperatures, which is why he made sure he got any outside work out of the way early.

As he approached the picket fence that surrounded the homestead, Gibson eyed the raised patches of dirt where, once upon a time, his mum had tried to grow vegetables. Her enthusiasm for such work hadn't lasted long. He couldn't even recall tasting any fruits of her efforts, but it struck him now that if he had his own veggie garden he'd have to venture into town even less.

No, he shouldn't think like that. It hadn't been a problem until Imogen had arrived and made everyone crazy. Every time he'd been into town since her arrival, every person he spoke to had said something about her.

'See you two later,' he called to the dogs as he climbed into his ute. 'If you're lucky, I'll bring you home a treat.' It was only as he slammed the door that he realised that in future this would mean asking Imogen for something. Trevor often gave him bags of leftovers from the pub, over which Jack and Jill usually went wild, but those days were over. Although Trev and Cathy hadn't left yet on their big adventure, the pub was now officially Imogen's, and no way he was asking her for anything. The dogs would have to make do with Schmackos from the general store.

As he drove down the long, red, dusty drive towards the main road that would take him into town, he studied the paddocks on either side of him – anything to get his thoughts off Imogen and her annoying habit of taking over his mind. The paddocks were dry, stubble still poking out of the ground like someone had come along and planted a load of chopsticks. Although seeding was still a couple of months off, burning would start soon, and then came the relentless prayers of all the farmers in the district for rain. Last year had been disappointingly dry, and although his crop output hadn't been as dismal as some, he was holding out for a much better season this year.

Lord knew the town and its inhabitants needed something to boost morale, other than a new sexy publican, that is. His thoughts drifted to Imogen again and before he knew it, he'd turned into the main street of Gibson's Find. The town had everything he needed, and the only times he ventured further afield were the obligatory trips to see his parents in Perth. Yet he couldn't help wondering what an outsider saw to draw them here. Especially a female outsider with no husband or family in the vicinity.

*Dammit.* He all but slammed his fist against the steering wheel. How did she keep slipping into his head every other second? He simply couldn't get the thought of her in that wet running gear out of his mind. Determined to focus on the task at hand, he parallel-parked outside the agricultural supplies store. When he'd finished inside, he had a good couple of hours before his meeting began, but Lord knew he didn't want to hang around the pub waiting all that time.

Leaving his ute, he ambled down the road, scuffing his boots on the pavement like a schoolboy trying to be late for class. As he entered the general store – where he planned to do more strolling down the narrow, sparsely filled shelves – he spotted Charlie near the bread and, for one short second, entertained the thought that maybe he wouldn't have to pop into the pub at all today. Then, dammit, he remembered his Apex meeting.

'Hey Charlie.' He sidled up to his granddad, glanced into the man's basket and then frowned at the contents – fishing line, bicarb of soda and a packet of Fishermen's Friend.'

'Gibby.' Charlie's face lit up. He shifted his basket in one hand and scratched the side of his head, just beneath his hat, with the other. 'Just doing a bit of shopping for Imogen.'

'What does she want with the fishing line?'

Charlie grimaced and dug his hand into his trouser pocket. 'That's just it, I've lost the list she gave me and I can't remember everything she needed. I'm sure there was something about fish on there.'

Charlie looked woebegone by this fact and Gibson found himself irritated that she'd sent his grandfather out shopping. She had two legs, why couldn't she use them? Cringing at what he was about to do, he dug his mobile phone out of his pocket and dialled the pub.

He let out a relieved sigh when Karen answered the call.

'Hi Karen. Gibson Black here. I'm with Charlie at the store and he's lost the list Imogen gave him for shopping. Don't suppose you could ask her what was on it?'

Karen chuckled. 'I can do better than that. I can read it to you – I just found it.'

'That's definitely better.' Thankful for his good memory, he took a mental note of the five items and then disconnected the call. 'You can keep the bicarb,' he told Charlie, pointing into the trolley, but it's fish sauce she wanted, so the other two can go back. We also need a packet of envelopes, some sticky tape and a packet of plain biscuits. Let me help you.'

Charlie's smile returned and his mood lifted as they walked the store gathering Imogen's requirements. Gibson then gave him a lift to the pub, deciding that he might as well cut his losses and go inside early. He could get a meal, sit in the corner and read the local rag or something.

As they drove the short distance, Charlie spoke. 'You won't tell your mother about my forgetfulness back there, will you?'

Gibson frowned. He'd not thought for a moment that Charlie forgetting a shopping list had any significance, but now he saw his granddad's fear that it could be used as ammunition in the fight Gibson's mum had started recently.

'Course not. Why would I? If I even remember to write a shopping list, I forget to bring it with me more times than I remember.'

'Thanks,' Charlie answered tersely. 'Moving back to the city – into one of those nursing prisons – would kill me. Especially now trade has started to pick up at the pub.'

That was Gibson's cue to ask after the new owner and her ideas, but he purposefully didn't take the hint. He hoped she'd be a fad that didn't last long. Luckily, their conversation was cut short as Gibson turned the ute into the pub.

'You coming in for one last meal cooked by Trevor?' Charlie asked.

Gibson nodded. 'I've got an Apex meeting later, so I'll get an early counter meal.'

\*\*\*

Gibson gave Charlie his meal order and then slunk away to the far corner of the dining room to wait. Imogen had been bless-edly absent when he'd arrived and yet as he sat, he found himself glancing towards the bar every few minutes. Was he hoping for a sighting? He shook his head, determining that he was simply hungry and hoping Trevor wouldn't take long to cook his burger.

About five minutes after he arrived, Guy and Wazza came in. They didn't see him, but headed to the bar and ordered a drink from Charlie. He said something and then Gibson's mates turned, grinned and waved. Once Charlie handed over their beers, Guy and Wazza approached.

'Great minds think alike,' Wazza said, slumping into a chair. He took a long gulp and let out a satisfied sigh. 'We wanted to have one last burger before Trev deserts us.'

Guy chuckled. 'I think it's less about Trevor's cooking and more about Wazza wanting to check out the new publican. *Again*.'

Warren narrowed his eyes at Guy. 'Hey, I'm not the only one.'

*Just great*. So much for a quiet dinner.

A shadow fell over the table. 'Evening boys.'

Gibson didn't need to turn his head to know the voice belonged to Imogen. It washed over him like a long soak in the tub – even her shadow appealed.

'One Majestic burger with the works,' she said chirpily.

As a plate almost completely hidden by hamburger landed in front of him, Gibson knew he had to look up into her eyes. He did it quickly. 'Thanks.'

'You're welcome,' Imogen replied, but she didn't go.

It was the first time they'd spoken since he'd interrupted her morning run a few days ago, and he couldn't think of one damn thing to say. Guy and Wazza appeared too tongue-tied to get a word out either.

Imogen didn't seem to have their tongue paralysis. 'Are you all here for the Apex meeting?'

'Aye aye, captain.' Wazza actually saluted and Gibson cringed.

Guy nodded. 'Sure are. Why don't you pop in and meet everyone if you have the time? We're always looking for good ideas to throw the club behind.'

'Sounds great.' Imogen ran her hand through her hair and glanced at the bar. Gibson took the second to glance down her body, his breath catching at the sight of her skinny-fit, black trousers.

'I suppose I'd better be getting back,' she said. 'You boys just holler if you need anything.' She met Gibson's eyes briefly, making his insides feel as if someone had struck a match against them, and then they both quickly looked away.

'Oh, we will,' Warren promised, his eyes wide as he nodded. Gibson resisted the urge to swat the side of his friend's head. When Imogen was out of earshot, Warren blew air between his lips. 'Wow. Ain't she just the best thing that ever happened around here?'

Gibson wasn't sure about that, but he did know this: as long as she *was* around, he wasn't going to get any peace – unless he battened down the hatches at Roseglen and stopped coming into town altogether.

# Chapter Five

The day before Cathy and Trevor were due to set off on their big adventure, a backpacker barmaid and Imogen's chef from Perth arrived by bus and car respectively.

Pauli, the chef, had worked at the Subiaco wine bar when Imogen first started there all those years ago. She hadn't seen her in a long while, but a mutual friend put them back in contact when he'd heard Imogen was looking for workers. Pauli had recently been through a messy divorce – Imogen vowed not to mention this to Karen – and also wanted to escape the city and all the nasty memories there.

The backpacker was more of a lucky dip, but Imogen liked her immediately. Caliopa was a tall Mexican beauty who, although only twenty-one, was almost entirely covered in tattoos and looked like she'd been a body builder in a previous life. Within seconds of Imogen trying to pronounce her name properly, she told her not to bother because she always went by Cal.

After Imogen showed her new employees to their rooms, she welcomed them in the pub with a drink. She'd asked Charlie and Karen to join them as she'd planned on conducting her first official team meeting. It was about three o'clock in the afternoon and the only other person in the pub was a contractor currently staying at the hotel. He nursed a lone beer at the end of the bar and stared listlessly ahead at the rows of alcohol, as though he had the weight of the world on his shoulders. Cathy and Trevor were still around, so Cathy promised to man the bar while Imogen talked to her new staff.

'Thanks so much for coming, everyone.' Imogen smiled around the table. 'I want to welcome Cal and Pauli to Gibson's Find and thank Charlie and Karen for standing by a newbie. I want to be a fair and fun boss, and I hope you'll all feel like you can come to me with suggestions or concerns at any time.'

'I'll drink to that.' Charlie raised his glass of orange juice and took a sip. Everyone followed suit.

'Thanks Charlie.' Imogen placed her glass back on the table. 'I'll be making a few changes over the next few months – updating the decor, renovating a bit, and we'll also be reinventing the menu.' She looked to Pauli. 'I've worked with Pauli in the past and I guarantee her cooking will make you all drool. The menu will be pretty much her domain, but I know Pauli will be open to suggestions. My vision for the food is hearty, home-style meals like you used to get at Grandma's, but with Pauli's modern twist.'

'Sounds like the best of both worlds.' Karen grinned.

Pauli nodded. 'That's what we're hoping for.'

'It's great that we're all on the same page.' Imogen consulted her mental checklist and continued. 'My main focus is going to be customer service. I want us to offer the kind of service that keeps people coming back and gets them talking.'

'Sounds good to me,' Cal piped up. 'Talking is my greatest talent.'

'Fabulous.' Imogen smiled at her youngest but very enthusiastic employee before continuing. 'As well as serving the locals, I also hope to widen our clientele to include more travellers, and for that reason we'll be offering a larger lunch menu. I'd like to get some events off the ground too – things like quiz nights and bingo – that might bring different people through the door. In time, I hope we'll have to hire even more staff.'

'I'll drink to that.' Charlie lifted his glass and they all followed suit again.

'Anyone have any questions?' Imogen looked to each of her employees.

'When do we start?' Cal asked with a grin.

Everyone laughed and Pauli leaned close and whispered something to the new barwoman. Imogen took another sip of her drink and let out a satisfied sigh. It was all falling into place.

\*\*\*

Early the next morning, the five of them waved goodbye to Cathy and Trevor, then immediately turned back inside, rolled up their sleeves and began spring-cleaning the building which Imogen guessed hadn't had a proper scrub in over a decade. Pauli wasn't rostered on until later in the day but she insisted on starting early.

'I've already visited all the shops in the main street,' she said, raising her hands up in the air. 'What else am I supposed to do?'

Imogen understood where she was coming from – Gibson's Find didn't exactly offer an abundance of leisure activities. She hoped her two out-of-town employees wouldn't up and leave before the ink had dried on their contracts.

Pushing that worry aside, Imogen focused on her long to do list.

About two hours later, Pauli appeared in the doorway between the bar and kitchen. 'Can you come and have a look at the menu?

If you approve, I'll have Cal print them off and laminate them ready for this evening.'

Imogen glanced up from where she was wiping the skirting boards around the bar. 'Is there taste-testing involved?'

Pauli laughed. 'Not this time.'

'Pity.' Her stomach rumbled in disappointment. 'I'm on my way.'

Tonight would be their first true night of business. As lovely as Cathy and Trevor were, Imogen hadn't felt like this was real until she'd seen their caravan fading into the distance. They had run the pub without a changing anything in fifteen years, and she couldn't wait to get stuck in.

She smiled at the delicious aromas that hit her as she entered the kitchen. 'Are you sure there's no tasting necessary?'

Cal, who stood at the stainless steel counter chopping vegetables, piped up. 'Sorry, I've been official taster today. I know it's not in my contract, but I'm more than happy to suffer for the greater good. And Pauli's pasta sauce is definitely good.'

Imogen pretended to pout. 'Fine, show me these menus, then.' She leaned over a clean, clear bench and read over the menu Pauli had placed there. Tempura fish and hand-cut, triple-cooked chips with aioli; vegetarian wellington with sweet potato mash; 8oz sirloin steak with hand-cut chips, confit field mushroom and béarnaise or pepper sauce; rigatoni with pork and fennel sausage; gourmet stuffed potatoes; bitter chocolate tart with homemade vanilla bean ice-cream … the delicious list went on. It was exactly the kind of food she wanted – hearty meals with an original flair. Something hardworking country men would be happy to get their teeth into. She had complete faith in Pauli's ability to make it happen.

She only hoped they'd get a few more bodies through the door that evening and wouldn't have too much wastage.

As if reading her mind, Pauli glanced up from the menus. 'Any idea of numbers for tonight?'

'Nope.' She hoped they'd have the kind of numbers she'd seen the evening Cathy and Paul had surprised her with the cake. But as much as she hated to admit it, most of those men had come for a stickybeak. There hadn't been such a full house since.

Imogen planned to change that, and she planned on Pauli's sensational cooking playing a major part. From what she could tell, there was only one reason (apart from beer) why the ramshackle pub had any patrons: Trevor had provided delicious meals which – due to the lack of females in town – not many of them were getting at home.

'Have you thought about themed food nights?' asked Cal, putting down her knife and coming to stand beside them. 'I'd be happy to oversee a Mexican night.'

'Can you cook?' Pauli asked.

'I can cook you a Mexican soup that will have your eyes rolling in the back of your head. In a good way.'

Pauli chuckled. 'That I'd like to taste. And maybe, if it's a success, I'll get my mum up here to help run a Croatian night.'

'I love it.' Imogen felt the heaviness that had been sitting in her stomach all morning start to lift. With such fabulous staff on her team, how could she fail? 'Let me talk to Charlie about it. He'll know if it's something the locals would go for.'

Charlie may as well have lived in the pub for all the time he spent there. He was technically only a part-timer, but he always seemed to be there when something needed to be done or Imogen needed a listening ear. And as much as the patrons ribbed him for his forgetfulness and the terry towelling hat that appeared to be glued to his head, she knew they all adored him. Such a smiley, happy man; so different to his grandson.

She paused at the door and looked back. 'Oh, and the menus are perfect. Print away.'

She found Charlie in the dining room in a precarious position at the top of a ladder, re-hanging the curtains she'd taken down and washed yesterday. She rushed forward, imagining the stern words Gibson would have for her if he saw Charlie at such heights.

'You don't have to do that.' She sounded harsher than she'd meant to.

'I know I don't, but…' He looked down at her as if he'd forgotten what he was going to say. He swayed a little.

'Charlie, come down right now. We'll get someone else to do this later. Right now I need to pick your brain.'

Her heart rate slowed when he began to descend the ladder. At the bottom, he studied her for a moment and then smiled wistfully. 'You remind me of my Elsie, you know?'

It was the first time she'd seen something akin to sadness taint the sparkle in his eyes. She took his arm and led him over to a quiet table in the corner. Cal, now finished in the kitchen, had the broom out and was about to give the floorboards in the bar a once-over.

'Do you mind bringing two coffees in here?' Imogen called.

Cal smiled. 'Of course, right away.'

As she settled in the chair opposite Charlie, she asked, 'Was Elsie your wife?'

He grinned as if a match had struck and lit him all up inside. 'Ah yes, and what a darling ball-and-chain she was.' This time his eyes glistened and Imogen recognised his heartbreak, because it mirrored her own.

'When did she die?'

'When she was twenty-five.'

Imogen blinked. She hadn't been expecting that.

'She died giving birth to Gibson's father, Harry. If we were in the city maybe someone could have saved her, although maybe not. Sixty years ago, medical miracles weren't as common as they are now.'

A lump formed in Imogen's throat. She wanted to reach out, squeeze Charlie's hand and tell him about Jamie, share it with someone who would understand her pain more than anyone else she knew. But something stopped her. She didn't want to make this about her when Charlie so obviously wanted to talk.

'What was she like?' she asked instead.

Charlie grinned again. 'She was a firecracker – in looks as well as personality. Her hair was even redder than yours.'

Imogen absentmindedly twisted some strands around her index finger.

'I came to Gibson's Find as a young teacher, full of ideals about moulding the next generation. Elsie was a cocky's daughter through and through. She had two young sisters at the school, and although she believed in their education – or so she said – the farm always came first. Her mother died young – giving birth to the third sister – and Elsie became a surrogate parent.'

He paused and smiled wistfully before continuing. 'Often she'd get her sisters to school late, sometimes she wouldn't even bother at all. She thought they were needed more on the farm. It really bugged me.'

'So, it wasn't love at first sight, then?'

Charlie snorted. 'It was pure irritation as first sight, that's what it was. She'd waltz into the schoolroom in trousers and boots and a man's shirt like she owned the joint. I wanted to have words with her about her lack of regard for her sisters' education, but I'd barely ever seen a woman in pants before. Got me tongue-tied and flustered every time I saw her. I hated her for it.'

He blushed a little at the recollection and Imogen smiled, waiting for him to share more.

'One Friday, after the girls hadn't been in school all week, I decided to go out to Roseglen – that's the family farm, named after Elsie's parents – and have it out with her.'

'Good for you. Education is important.'

Charlie snorted again. 'I guess it is, but Elsie quickly changed my views on a lot of things. By the time I rode my bike out there

– fifteen k's, mind you – I was sweaty and aggro and ready to have words with her.'

He paused while Cal delivered two mugs filled with steaming coffee to the table. Imogen thanked her and then wrapped her hands around the mug, eager to hear more. Jenna had called her a soppy, hopeless romantic on more than one occasion, and there was more than a little truth to the accusation.

While Imogen sipped, Charlie continued, almost as if he were reminiscing to himself.

'I arrived at the homestead to find Elsie bent over the rear end of a sheep, her hands stuck up its backside, tugging away like the animal had eaten a gold nugget and she needed to pull it out.'

Imogen giggled at Charlie's description.

'It was a pet sheep, apparently.' He shook his head. 'Somehow it had gotten in with the rams and gotten itself pregnant. Elsie's little sisters were running back and forth from the house bringing cold cloths to lie upon the ewe's head. It was as bizarre a sight as ever I'd seen. Elsie was talking to the old girl like she was a human in labour.

'Well, I just stood there like a stunned mullet – I'd completely forgotten why I'd come and was mesmerised by the first birth I'd ever been privy to. After a while, she looked up, sweat covering her rosy-cheeked face. She blew some tearaway hair out of her eyes and glared at me. "If you're going to stand there staring, the least you could do is lend a hand. Lord knows there aren't many uses for a man, but this baby's stuck and I could do with a bit of strength to pull her out."' Charlie chuckled to himself.

Imogen could almost guess what was coming next.

'We got it out too,' Charlie said, pride shining through his words, even all these years later. 'Elsie checked the wee lamb over and when she was satisfied it was breathing, she laid it down next to its mother. Then she turned back to me, placed her bloodstained hands against my clean-shirted arms, leaned forward and kissed me. On the lips!'

Charlie turned the colour of a fire engine, all the way up his sideburns.

'Ooh,' said Imogen, tickled by the thought. She couldn't imagine his grandson ever getting so flustered over a woman, especially not decades after the event.

'And when she'd finished – kissing me, that is – she looked right into my eyes and said, "Well, I may have just found another good use for a man." Then she kissed me again.'

Imogen pressed her hand against her heart. 'So it was love at first kiss, then?'

'Aye, it definitely was.' Charlie sighed. 'Once I'd experienced the magic of those lips, nothing else seemed to matter anymore. And I certainly didn't want any other man laying a claim on her.'

He dug his wallet out of his pocket and opened it to a black-and-white photo of the most naturally beautiful woman Imogen had ever seen. She was incredibly tall and wiry, and freckles spattered her cheeks, which she could tell, despite the lack of colour in the photo, were as rosy as beetroots. Imogen had never seen the resemblance between Gibson and Charlie and now she understood why. Gibson was the image of his grandmother – same eyes, same wry smile, even the same stance.

'I haven't got many, but this one's my favourite.'

Imogen took her time to admire the photo. 'She's beautiful.'

She thought of her photos of Jamie – placed strategically throughout her apartment so she'd never have to go more than a few hours without seeing him. Her eyes stung with threatened tears. Would she be the same as Charlie when she was in her eighties? Fifty years was a very long time to be alone.

She had to think of something else to say before she became a blubbering mess. 'So, when did you give up teaching?'

Charlie had already told her he spent most of his adult years on the family crop and sheep farm, only moving into town a few years back when the homestead grew too small – whatever that meant.

'I handed in my notice within two weeks of Elsie's kiss. After that I worked with Elsie on the farm and it just felt right. Like what I was born to do. Her sisters married other local farmers, her dad died of his broken heart and we worked together as partners. She didn't even slow down when she got pregnant with Harry.'

He paused for a moment and Imogen saw him swallow.

'I never imagined childbirth would take her. Losing her was the biggest shock of my life.'

Imogen closed her eyes and sucked in a breath. 'I know,' she whispered, without meaning to.

When she opened her eyes, Charlie was staring at her, a hundred questions lingering in his eyes. 'Who did you lose?'

Her turn to swallow, but no amount of swallowing would eliminate the golf ball in her throat. 'My husband, Jamie,' she said eventually. 'The love of my life, too.' Maybe it sounded dramatic but it was the truth. She knew Charlie understood.

'When?'

'Two and half years ago.' She didn't offer the exact calculations, even though she still ticked each day off in her mind. 'He was a firefighter. He died rescuing a young girl during a bushfire.' She shuddered – there was no way she'd ever get over the horror. 'But I don't want anyone here to know,' she added, emerging from her reverie. 'Please don't tell anyone, not even Gibson.'

*Especially* not Gibson. She couldn't bear him changing his grumpy tune and forcing niceties just because he felt sorry for her.

'Coming here was my fresh start,' she explained. 'I need to be my own person and I don't want everyone thinking they already know me. It may sound crazy, but it's the way I want it to be.'

Charlie nodded. 'Your secret's safe with me.'

A slightly awkward silence reigned between them for a few moments – as if they were both unsure whether they should have shared so much – then Imogen remembered why she'd sought Charlie out in the first place.

'Cal and Pauli had an idea and I wanted your thoughts.'

Charlie adjusted his hat and cocked his head to one side, waiting.

'Themed food nights,' she announced. When his expression remained blank, she elaborated, explaining everything her staff had proposed.

He pondered the idea a while, then leaned forward and clasped his hands together. 'I think it could work. Lord knows the blokes round here like a good meal. But how about we do a trial run?'

She hoped he wasn't about to suggest Gibson as one of the taste-testers.

'Have you thought any more about my idea of a slab party?'

Imogen bit her lower lip. 'Yes, I just don't feel very comfortable asking people. And I do have money, it'll just take time to organise and schedule tradesmen.'

Charlie dismissed her reasoning with a wave of his hand. 'This is the country, woman. People in the bush like lending a hand. And if you offer free food and booze to a select group – I can help you sort out the riffraff – then you don't need to feel guilty. You're giving them something in return.'

She glanced around the pub, cataloguing all the jobs that needed to be done – jobs that could be done quite easily and quickly with a few tools and willing bodies. Then she could leave her funds for the bigger renovations. 'You think people would go for that?'

'Honey, the boys round here will be running each other down in their utes to help you.' Charlie grinned and his eyes almost twinkled. 'You just say the word and I'll get the ball rolling.'

It was a win-win situation. Pauli and Cal could test out the new food, and once the work was done, it'd be free drinks for everyone.

'The word,' Imogen said, thinking this was something she didn't need to think about at all.

She and Charlie chose a weekend – two weeks away, to give everyone plenty of notice – and started planning which VIP handymen to invite. Charlie rattled off names, most of which were unfamiliar, telling her who would be useful to have around and to whom they'd need to give the easy jobs. Apparently Gibson was very good with his hands, and Charlie seemed to think he'd be more than willing to help out.

Imogen didn't want to think about Gibson's hands and she didn't like to burst the old man's bubble either, but she'd bet The Majestic on the fact his beloved grandson would rather pick lice off sheep with a pair of tweezers than lend her a hand.

***

That night, Gibson hit the bar at his usual time.

Imogen noticed him the moment he walked in the door. His eyes sought hers, then quickly looked away. She wanted to kick something. While her hormones had a happy party without her every time he came within twenty metres, Gibson appeared to find even being in the same space as her suffocating.

Aside from his irritating good looks, dedication to his grand-father was the only good Imogen could see in Gibson Black. She'd spent more time than she cared to admit trying to work out what the hell his story was. And whether he had a girlfriend stashed away somewhere. She could ask Charlie, but she didn't want him to think she was interested. Which she wasn't. Curiosity just happened to be her middle name, and Gibson was a mystery begging to be solved.

As Charlie made a beeline for his grandson, the breath she hadn't realised she'd been holding eased out. He clearly looked forward to these daily visits, and she knew Charlie was the only reason Gibson ever came in. The times he talked with Charlie were also the only times he bothered with a smile.

To take her mind off *him*, Imogen took the chance to ring her friends while Gibson sat at the bar and Cal and Charlie held the fort.

Tonight, Jenna was even more excitable than normal because she'd been doing serious research. 'Hey babe,' Jenna answered. 'Did you get my email?'

Imogen glanced towards her computer screen from where she was, leaning back in her swivel chair. 'When'd you send it?'

'Oh, only about half an hour ago. I've been looking into our little problem and I think we can get you a real good deal, delivered to your door. I sent you a selection.'

After a few days of deep consideration, and those irritating urges whenever Gibson Black ventured into the pub, Imogen had finally solicited Jenna's help with The Vibrator Acquisition.

Barely able to believe what she was contemplating, and with Jenna still on the line, Imogen opened her email and her eyes boggled – not only at the prices but also the colours, shapes and sizes.

'Well?' Jenna asked after a few moments' silence. 'See anything you like?'

'Um…' Jenna would be disappointed if Imogen backed out now. 'I'll have to give it some thought.' Quite frankly, it was hard to imagine sharing her bedroom – never mind her bed – with any of those things. 'Anyway,' she said, changing the subject before Jenna could nag her to make a hasty decision, 'you know how you and Amy have been talking about coming up for a weekend before the baby arrives?'

'Uh-huh.'

'Are you free the first weekend in March? Amy says she's in if you'll drive.'

'Hell yeah,' Jenna replied, adding a whoop. 'I'll make sure I'm free. But I hope you've ordered in some better champagne since we were last there.'

'Of course,' Imogen said, feigning indignation. 'Just don't get a manicure the day before; this is going to be a working weekend.'

'What do you mean?' Jenna asked.

'I'm throwing a slab party.'

'A what?'

Imogen laughed. 'That was my reaction too when Charlie first mentioned it. Apparently it's a party where everyone brings a slab of beer to celebrate a new house or something, but his idea is a little different. We're going to ask the locals to help with some of the pub renovations, and in return I'll provide the beer for a party at night. Sound like fun?'

'That depends on your definition of fun,' Jenna replied.

Imogen laughed again. 'Hopefully, by the end of the weekend, most of the minor tasks will be done and I'll be able to focus on promoting the pub to a wider clientele.'

Jenna was silent for a moment. 'So there'll be lots of hot blokes there?'

Imogen rolled her eyes but couldn't help smiling. Jenna was nothing if not predictable. 'Yes. Hopefully. With any luck it'll be stinking hot and they may even have to work without their shirts on.'

'Ooh,' Jenna murmured appreciatively.

Imogen pushed aside the thought that immediately jumped into her mind – Gibson Black without his shirt on. Luckily she wouldn't be subjected to that. There wasn't any danger of him joining the party.

That settled, she said goodbye to Jenna, hung up and then peered out at the bar. Gibson was gone, so it was safe. She served a couple of guys and chatted about their work on the mine. One even offered to take her out on his RDO and show her round the site. But as interesting as the idea sounded, she got the distinct impression the guy meant it to be a date, and that wasn't going to happen.

Despite enjoying herself, the night dragged. The stream of men to the bar was steady, but the pub wasn't what you'd call busy. Even Charlie looked weary earlier than usual, so she convinced him to take an early mark at ten o'clock. An hour and a half later, when she and the girls had farewelled the stragglers, collected the dirty glasses and finished cleaning up, Imogen could have curled up under her desk in the downstairs office.

Her limbs ached and she didn't think she had the energy to climb to the stairs to her apartment. Reviving the old place and increasing turnover wasn't going to be as easy as she'd first assumed.

Being her own boss was already taking its toll.

# Chapter Six

If there was one thing more irritating than a female intent on fixing a pub that didn't need fixing, it was a female who refused to leave his head. And Imogen Bates was proving to be one such female.

They'd barely spoken since the morning Gibson had interrupted her run, but that didn't mean they hadn't interacted. Every time he went to the pub they exchanged glances, longer than the average hello-and-how's-your-father, glances that oozed meaning despite their frosty facade. Wherever he went, he thought about her bright eyes, perky physique and feisty personality. He'd never admit it to Guy or Wazza, but he was damn attracted to the woman. He had no intention of acting on his feelings – he could write a book of reasons why he shouldn't – but it didn't stop him anticipating his daily visit.

Once upon a time, Charlie was the sole reason for going there, but he'd be lying if he said that was still the case. Sometimes he spent the whole day checking his watch, counting down the hours until he could head into town for a quick fix of the new publican.

As he moved mobs of sheep from one paddock to another, he pondered his dilemma. When his parents had moved to the city, he promised them that he'd keep an eye on Charlie. For the most part, Charlie didn't need watching, but he had been getting a bit forgetful the last couple of months.

Jack and Jill worked the sheep ahead of him – so competent he barely had to shout any instructions – and a thought struck him. It was his quiet season. He wasn't shearing or crutching, not harvesting or seeding. What was to say he had to visit Charlie in the evening?

When he'd started his visits a couple of years back, evenings had been the obvious option. He'd been seeding at the time and could only fit a visit in after work. Besides, it had been his first year as a bachelor again and going home at night to an empty house – a massive reminder of his personal failings – hadn't been appealing. In the pub's jovial atmosphere, and with the help of the odd beer, it had been easy to forget his woes.

But he'd moved on now. He'd grown accustomed to the quietness and peace at home. Not being nagged about leaving your socks and jocks lying around was only one of the benefits of divorce. Now there was nothing to stop him visiting Charlie at home during daylight hours.

Gibson adjusted his hat, whistled ahead to Jack and Jill and grinned at this epiphany. He laboured harder, hurrying the dogs and the sheep. If he worked quickly, he could have the sheep safely in the new paddock and be in town in time to share lunch with his grandfather.

\*\*\*

'What the hell are you doing here?' Charlie looked up from where he'd been weeding his measly front garden as Gibson stepped out of his ute.

'Brought lunch,' Gibson replied, holding up an esky. 'And a very good morning to you too.'

Charlie heaved himself to his feet and glanced at his watch. 'It's almost afternoon.'

Despite the gruff words, Gibson knew his grandfather was happy about the unexpected visit. 'So it is,' he said, heading for the front door.

He went in ahead of Charlie and began to unload sausages, eggs, bacon and juice from the esky. He hoped there was a fresh loaf of bread lying around for the toast. He'd decided to cook up a typical big breakfast (despite it being well past that time) because Charlie loved that type of food.

'What are you doing?' Charlie asked when he finally entered the tiny kitchen. He frowned at the food laid out on the bench ready to be cooked.

'I told you. I'm making lunch.'

The frown deepened. 'I usually have a Cup-a-Soup and some crackers.'

Gibson feigned a look of disgust. 'Then it's good I'm here. That's no lunch for a grown man.'

Charlie hesitated for a moment, then went to the pantry. He took out a sachet of instant tomato soup and went to boil the kettle.

'You're not going to have that instead of this feast?' Gibson couldn't keep the disbelief out of his voice as he gestured to all his ingredients.

Charlie ripped open the sachet. Gibson noticed his hand shaking as he emptied the powdered contents into an old Scouts mug. 'I'll have that as well,' Charlie finally answered.

'Okay.' Gibson shrugged. Just another one of his grandfather's quirks. While Charlie sat down at the table with his mug and started to blow on the steaming contents, Gibson began to cook.

'What are you doing here, anyway?' Charlie asked, between mouthfuls of soup.

'I wasn't very busy and I thought it'd be nice to have lunch with you.' Gibson didn't look at Charlie as he spoke, choosing to spear and turn the sausages instead. 'Not a sin to spend time with my granddad, is it?'

'No,' Charlie answered tentatively, 'but you'll still be at the pub tonight, won't you?'

Gibson shook his head. 'There's a movie I want to watch on telly.'

'Which one?'

'What?'

'Which movie?'

*Dammit*, why hadn't he planned this better? He hadn't anticipated his grandfather giving him the third degree.

'Can't remember the title,' he said as he popped some bread into the toaster. 'It's had lots of good write-ups though.' He hoped there was a movie on at least one channel tonight. If he told Charlie the real reason he didn't want to go to the pub, he'd never live it down.

Charlie sighed and focused again on his soup, taking tiny but quick spoonfuls until the mug was empty. He stood up, crossed the kitchen and put his mug in the fridge.

Gibson did a double take. 'Do you want me to wash that?' he asked, pointing to the fridge.

'Why would I want you to wash the fridge?' Charlie asked, scratching the side of his head.

'I meant the mug. You just put the mug in the fridge.'

'What?' Charlie's one word was more of a bark. Confusion crossed his face. He retraced his steps and opened the refrigerator.

Gibson's eyes hadn't been fooling him. The empty mug sat on the middle ledge between a tub of margarine and a bag of tomatoes.

'Well, hell,' said Charlie, snatching the mug and all but throwing it into the sink. 'You're flustering me.'

'Sorry.' Puzzled by this uncharacteristic behaviour, Gibson nodded towards a kitchen chair. 'Sit down, Granddad, and let me feed you.'

'I'm quite capable of feeding myself,' he snapped.

'I never said you weren't.' Gibson resisted the urge to throw his hands up in the air. He'd been the only family member to stick up for Charlie when debate raged over whether he should live alone or not. This lunch wasn't going at all how he'd planned. He racked his brain for a safe topic of conversation but the only thing he could think about was Charlie's work at the pub. Not wanting to bring Imogen up, he cast around for something else.

'I spoke to Paris last night,' he said eventually. 'She said Bradley got a merit award at school. Apparently his was the first for this year's kindy class, so she's pretty stoked.' Bradley was his sister's oldest son. Rumoured (by Paris) to be a genius, neither Charlie nor Gibson had seen any evidence thus far. They usually joked about Paris' tendency to talk up everything her kids did.

Today Charlie only nodded and uttered a barely audible, 'That's good.'

Gibson decided to concentrate on getting the meal on the table and work on the conversation after that. He hadn't realised how hungry he was until his nose caught the tempting aroma of cooked sausages and bacon.

'Okay, Granddad,' he said, laying a full plate in front of the old man. 'I hope you're hungry.'

'Sure am,' Charlie replied, a slight smile lifting his lips. 'I haven't eaten anything since breakfast.'

Gibson opened his mouth to mention the soup but thought better of it and chomped down on a sausage instead. As he said earlier, packet soup couldn't be classified as food.

'This is good,' Charlie said after a few mouthfuls, 'but you're still coming to the pub tonight, aren't you?'

Gibson halted his fork and egg halfway to his mouth. 'No, Granddad, I told you I was busy this evening.'

'But you always come.'

'I come to visit you, not the pub, and today I'm visiting you at home instead.' He hadn't noticed his granddad so hung up on routine before. 'That okay?'

'It'll have to be, won't it?' Charlie replied gruffly. 'But you'll come tomorrow night, won't you?'

'We'll see.' Gibson glanced down at his plate so as not to meet Charlie's eye and started back in on his lunch.

\*\*\*

But when tomorrow came, Gibson found that he had to head into town mid-afternoon to buy some strainer posts for fencing. It'd be a waste of petrol to make the trip twice when he could quite easily visit Charlie now. This time he popped into the general store and picked up a packet of Tim Tams to take as an offering. Hopefully with the sweet taste of his favourite biscuit on his tongue, his granddad would be distracted from the fact Gibson had avoided the pub two days in a row.

Charlie was dozing in the rocker out the front when he arrived. Gibson plodded up the wooden steps onto the verandah and Charlie startled at the sound.

'What time is it?' Charlie all but leaped out of the chair. 'Am I late for work?'

'Nope.' Gibson opened the screen door and held it for Charlie. 'I had to come into town, so I thought I'd visit you as well.' He held up the packet of biscuits.

Charlie narrowed his eyes at Gibson. 'You're not coming in for your drink tonight, are you?' He glowered and stormed off down the hallway.

'Not tonight,' said Gibson, trying to keep his voice light as the door banged behind him.

'Another good movie on the telly?' asked Charlie, clearly not believing his excuse at all.

Gibson didn't care. It wasn't as though he was ditching his familial responsibilities – he was still visiting, wasn't he? 'Something like that.'

Charlie reached the kitchen table and sat down on one of the old chairs. 'Never mind. Open that packet and I might forgive you for confusing an old man.'

Happy that Charlie wasn't going to press the issue, Gibson ripped open the foil and shoved the tray across to his grandfather. Then he put the kettle on. Within five minutes they were nursing mugs of tea and discussing the finer points of AFL. Charlie was a Dockers supporter and Gibson barracked for the Eagles. The big West Australian derby was still a couple of months away, but that didn't stop Charlie getting excited. Once that topic was exhausted, Gibson decided he'd better make a move.

As he stood to collect the mugs and ditch the now empty biscuit packet, Charlie spoke. 'I told you about Imogen's slab party, didn't I? I was thinking you could bring your power sander and have a go at the verandah. Imogen reckons people will get splinters from it once she gets the outdoor area functioning better.'

Gibson froze at the sink. 'Slab party?'

'Yes.' Charlie nodded enthusiastically. 'When Imogen told me all the things she wanted to do to the pub, I realised a number of the tasks could be done relatively quickly with local volunteers. That's when I suggested she provide the food and the alcohol and throw a party for anyone who helps her fix up the old girl. The whole town will benefit.'

Yeah, Gibson reckoned the blokes would be lining up for this scheme. 'Um … when is it?' he asked, trying to sound noncommittal.

'First weekend in March. And I'm in charge of organising everyone.'

'That's great.' He tried to sound like he meant it. 'But I won't be able to help. There's a lot happening on the farm right now.'

Charlie raised his eyebrows. 'That's why you can take hours off in the middle of the day, two days in a row, to visit an old man and eat?'

Sometimes Gibson wished Charlie *was* completely off with the fairies like his mum and Paris believed. He had no witty or logical reply. So instead he rinsed the mugs and feigned deafness.

Unfortunately, when his granddad had a bee in his bonnet, he didn't let up. 'Sometimes you're a mystery to me, Gibson Black. I know women haven't been terribly kind to you, but have you got something against Imogen in particular?' When Gibson said nothing, Charlie continued, his voice rising in annoyance. 'You're downright rude to her and now you blatantly refuse to help when everyone knows you're usually the first to lend a hand round here.'

'That's just it,' Gibson said, jumping on this excuse. 'I already do my bit for the town, volunteering for the ambulance and chairing the Apex committee.' Not to mention somehow being coerced into dressing up as Santa Claus at Christmas for the very few children left in the town. 'I'm sorry Granddad, but I just can't do it.'

# Chapter Seven

Imogen watched as Charlie scribbled another name on the list of volunteers that now hung on the wall behind the bar, a list that grew longer by the day.

With only a few days to go until the big slab party, she was beginning to worry that they might have too much help. Thankfully, Amy – a project manager for a major event planning company – would be on hand to oversee things and direct where necessary. Imogen had emailed Amy the list of jobs and the latest list of volunteers, and Amy was going to work out teams and a roster. This task made her feel useful because this late in her pregnancy, she wouldn't be much physical help. Jenna would no doubt prove a good distraction to any men left with nothing to do.

Imogen smiled – she couldn't wait to see her girls.

Then she bit her lip and stared at the list of tasks she'd been working on, wondering whether she'd left anything off. Most of them were minor – moving furniture, hanging the vintage signs she'd sourced from eBay, a bit of gardening in the deserted window boxes out the front – and could be done in less than an hour with only one or two bodies. Then there were some painting jobs – the whole building could do with a new coat – and facelifting the verandah, which would involve some serious TLC. Initially, Charlie had volunteered Gibson to sand down all the rails and posts – apparently he'd renovated the farmhouse at Roseglen a few years back, and the verandah was one of the major improvements. But, of course, he'd declined.

She'd had to force herself not to roll her eyes and scoff when Charlie put in Gibson's apology. He'd offered to lend his sander but was far too busy to lend himself. Well, that was fine with Imogen. She didn't want to put him out.

But Charlie didn't want to leave things there. He'd apologised a number of times on behalf of Gibson, who appeared to have ceased his daily visits to the pub. Mostly, Imogen was happy about this fact. The cranky glare he bestowed on her whenever he sat at the bar made her feel uncomfortable, as did the reactions his mere presence sparked deep down in her core.

She shivered simply thinking of them.

She didn't need grouchy patrons and she certainly didn't need to be distracted by unexplained and unwanted feelings when she was trying her damn best to be professional and make a go of this. But she felt sorry for Charlie, who clearly missed his grandson's visits. Gibson's absence unnerved him and he talked about him much more than before. Worst of all, he felt the need to explain, to justify and make excuses. She supposed it was sweet, but the last thing she needed was a reason to feel sympathy towards Gibson. Unfortunately, earlier that day, Charlie had provided one – touching that kind heart Imogen still needed to harden.

He'd caught her coming out of the office, and just by the gleam in his eyes, she knew he was about to launch into another conversation about his precious grandson.

'I'm a bit busy, Charlie,' she'd said, her arms laden with old account books she planned on storing in a back room. 'Can it wait?'

'Here, let me help.' Charlie put his arms out to take some of her load.

*Great*, now it would take them twice as long to get to the storeroom and back again. 'Thanks,' she said, trying to keep the exasperation from her voice.

Sure enough, as they started down the corridor, Charlie launched into his favourite subject. 'I know you and Gibson didn't hit it off to start with, but he's really not as awful as he makes out.'

'I know he's your grandson, Charlie, but to be honest, I don't waste too much time dwelling on his standoffishness. I have bigger fish to fry.'

Blatant lie – she thought about him much more than she liked. There was no reason she should think about him at all. If she were going to start pondering being with a man other than Jamie – and she wasn't – there were so many that should have been higher up the list than Gibson. Any of the other pub regulars, for a start. All of whom appeared to be kind-hearted, fun, hardworking and, although not quite as jolt-your-insides good-looking as Gibson, certainly smiled more. She liked smiling.

'Good. I'm glad.' Charlie entered the storeroom behind her and put his pile on a shelf. 'But I still want to explain. He's my family and I wouldn't want you to think we raise them grumpy and rude in the Black clan.'

'He hasn't been rude, exactly,' Imogen began. 'More like quiet and reserved.' *Hah!*

'His wife left him a few years ago,' Charlie announced. 'He was a mess.'

'Oh.' Her chest tightened. Why hadn't she expected something like this? No one got to be like Gibson without good reason. But what kind of woman would leave a man like him? Despite the rudeness, the sex would have to set your sheets on fire.

*Argh! Here I am, pondering the horizontal mambo again. What's wrong with me?*

She laid her books next to Charlie's and leaned against the wall. 'I'm sorry to hear that.'

Charlie shrugged and adjusted his hat, as she noticed he did whenever he spoke about something close to his heart. 'Serena was never cut out for country life. Gibson was too blinded by lust to see that.'

'And love?' She couldn't help herself.

'Oh, he loved her all right. Was absolutely gutted when she left.' Charlie sighed sadly. 'It changed him. Believe it or not, before marriage, Gibby was the life of the party round here. The local larrikin.'

She frowned. Could she believe that?

'I'm telling you because I know you'll understand,' Charlie said, folding his arms across his chest.

'How?' She pushed herself off the wall, ready to get back to work. The noise in the bar was growing. Cal was out there but she'd need assistance.

'He's like us, isn't he?' Charlie explained. 'We've each lost the person we loved more than anyone. He's hurting just like you.'

His words felt like a slap in the face. However unfortunate, no way was Gibson's situation anything like hers. She did feel a twinge of pity for him – having the love of your life walk out would definitely be harsh – but what was to say he hadn't treated his wife with the same disregard he showed her?

'I can't believe you can compare us, Charlie. Divorce and death have nothing in common. His loss isn't the same at all, and you of all people should understand that.' She felt the fury building within, raising her temperature. 'Did he ever try to win her back?'

Charlie hung his head. 'Not that I know of.'

'See? I'm sure his pride was hurt, but if he truly loved his wife he wouldn't just let her go. He'd move heaven and earth to win her back. That country verses city stuff is crap. If a woman loves a man, she'll move to Mars to be with him. I would have for Jamie.'

'I'm sorry.' The shock in Charlie's eyes made Imogen realise she'd been overly defensive. 'I just wanted you to know he's got reasons for the way he acts.'

'We've all got reasons, Charlie,' she replied, trying to be a little softer this time. 'And choices. But just because one woman wrongs you doesn't mean you should treat every woman you subsequently meet with such disregard. He'll never be able to move on if that's the case.'

'True,' Charlie answered sadly. 'I really don't know what to do.'

Imogen sighed. This really bugged the old guy – it made her want to drive out to Gibson's farm right away and have it out with him. 'They say time heals everything. Maybe he needs a little more. Or maybe he just needs to meet the right woman.'

'Know anyone?' Charlie looked hopeful for a moment.

She pursed her lips while she thought. 'Maybe.'

Cal was too young and Pauli too adamantly against relationships. The only candidate that came to mind was Jenna. Her friend would be more than happy to scratch any itch Gibson might be harbouring, but physical release was all she would have to offer. Deep down, Imogen imagined Jenna was exactly the same type of woman as Gibson's ex-wife. She was no more likely to settle in the outback than a skyscraper. 'Leave it with me,' she said finally, hoping that promising to help would stop Gibson creeping into every sentence that came out Charlie's mouth.

# Chapter Eight

Early on Friday morning, Gibson did the usual rounds of feeding and checking sheep, all the while umming and ahhing about jumping in his ute and heading to Perth early. He had to go on Sunday to visit his parents anyway, and it wasn't like he had big plans for this evening. Tonight, he'd be alone in his big house, knowing that pretty much every other bloke in town was at the pub, enjoying themselves. The rest of the day loomed ahead and he knew that even if he occupied himself on the farm, his mind would be in town.

He hadn't realised how much The Majestic was a part of his social life – okay, in non-footy season, it *was* his social life – until he'd stopped visiting daily. Aside from Charlie and old Mrs Lorder at the general store, the only conversation he'd had lately had been with Jack and Jill, and he was fairly sure interactions with dogs didn't count. But was driving to his parents' place a few days early going to be any better? He didn't have to be psychic to know his mum would want to talk about Charlie, that she'd try to convince *him* to talk to Charlie and lure him round to her views. And Gibson didn't want to be any more involved in that disagreement than he already was. Even before he'd decided it wasn't an option, Gibson remembered this was his week on the ambulance roster.

As a local St John's volunteer, he did a week on roster once a month – Saturday to Saturday. Most of his call-outs were motor vehicle accidents on the highway and the occasional cardiac problems amongst the older members of the community, but generally they were pretty quiet. He hadn't been needed for over a month. Still, if he chose today to slink off to Perth, Sod's Law said there'd be an emergency.

'Nope, Perth is not an option.'

He only realised he was talking to his dogs again when Jill looked up and cocked her head at him. Jack was wreaking havoc on the paddock of sheep but Jill was the more sensible of the two. She understood that Gibson had bought them for companionship, not to work. She barked at him and her intense stare made Gibson think she wanted to tell him something.

*Don't be ridiculous.* He shook his head and checked the time on his watch. If he didn't want to spend the whole weekend watching the clock and *thinking*, he was going to have to keep busy. Maybe he should swallow his damn discomfort and head into town later to volunteer for the pub renovations. Charlie would welcome him with open arms. Aside from farm work, he hadn't done much manual labour since Serena had moved to Roseglen and they'd made their additions and renovations on the house, but he was good at that kind of work. Liked the buzz you got when a project was finished. A bit like when, after months of stubble burning, seeding, spraying and praying for rain, the crop finally started growing thick and fast. It was those times that made all the hard work and stress of farming worthwhile.

He thought on that a moment and then asked himself why he

really wanted to be involved. The answer was clear. He hadn't seen Imogen for days, but staying away hadn't made any difference. She still invaded his mind on a regular basis, as if she had a right to be there and he had a right to want it.

'Argh!' He let rip a scream from the bottom of his lungs and felt marginally better for it. He didn't want to be a prisoner on his own farm.

He'd been standing in this paddock for who knows how long, and if he didn't make a move soon, the sheep wouldn't get a chance to eat – it took a long while for Jack to tire. He tapped the tray of the ute, indicating for Jill to jump up, and then whistled to Jack. The dog deserted his fun immediately and returned to Jill's side.

'Good dogs.' Feeling determined, Gibson patted each animal on the head and then got back into his ute. Halfway back to the homestead, inspiration struck. While his grandfather and all his mates were working at The Majestic, he'd give himself his own project. Start that veggie garden he'd been deliberating over lately.

*Yes.* Feeling better already, he headed into town, stocked up on seeds and mulch and then returned to Roseglen, determined to keep busy. Soon the garden was taking shape; he was dripping with sweat from the manual exertion and feeling pretty damn happy.

When his mobile rang, he wiped his dirty hands against his dirty jeans and dug the phone out of his pocket. 'Hi Charlie.'

'Gibby. When are you going to bring that sander to the pub?'

Dammit, he'd completely forgotten he'd offered it. 'I'm a bit busy, Granddad.' He surveyed the raised wooden garden beds he'd spent all afternoon knocking together. 'Can you come and get it?'

'Nope. I'm working. Why don't you bring it in and have a drink?'

In other words, *why don't you bring it in, have a drink and sit around while I bend your ear about helping all weekend.*

'Can't do tonight, Granddad. I'll drop it in tomorrow morning before I get stuck into work.'

'Suit yourself,' Charlie grumbled.

Gibson hated disappointing Charlie but on this issue he couldn't allow himself to waver.

It was better for all involved if he kept his distance from the pub, and also from the alluring Imogen Bates.

***

The last few days had been busy. Even before the renovations, the pub was starting to pick up trade in the evenings. Imogen reckoned her exotic young barmaid and her equally attractive chef had a lot to do with it. One night, Cal road-tested her Mexican cuisine by making dinner for the pub staff and they all loved it.

Pauli had been the most effusive in her praise, which surprised Imogen, not only because Pauli undoubtedly cooked better than everyone, but also because the Pauli she knew wasn't the warm-and-fuzzy praise-giving type. Cal, energised by the enthusiastic response, had decided she rather liked cooking for a crowd. She couldn't wait to make a bigger batch on Saturday night, and had been spending a fair bit of time in the kitchen asking Pauli to teach her things. It crossed Imogen's mind that if she wasn't careful she'd have two cooks and be short of bar staff, but in the mood she was in right now, no such worry could really take hold.

Excitement bubbled within her – she couldn't wait for the pub's new look to start taking shape, but even more so, she was dying to catch up with Amy and Jenna at the weekend.

Her best friends surprised her by turning up Friday lunchtime, a good five hours earlier than she'd expected.

'Who are those chicks?' hissed Cal, who was polishing glasses for the night-time rush. Like the locals, the inhabitants of the pub had grown accustomed to the fact that women rarely ventured through the doors.

Imogen looked up from where she was stocktaking to see Amy waddle into the pub wearing a very flattering maternity sundress, and Jenna practically stalk in wearing heels that were high even for her. She dropped her clipboard and rushed around the bar to greet her friends with a hug.

When the embrace ended, she turned her attention to Jenna's shoes. 'I hope you've got some sneakers or Crocs in there as well.'

Amy laughed, her hands resting on her jiggling tummy. 'It's okay. I went through Jenna's suitcase, extracted the stuff I really didn't think she'd need and added in the practical shoes. We're ready to rock'n'roll.'

Jenna pushed her Prada sunnies up onto her head and said huffily, 'She took out my little black dress. I need a drink.'

Imogen showed her friends to the spare rooms in the spacious publican's apartment. She'd had Karen make up the beds that morning. Amy chose to have a nanna nap but Jenna went straight back downstairs to kick off her evening. She insisted on paying her own way, but by the second glass of champagne, it was obvious Jenna wouldn't have to pay another cent – so numerous were the offers from the guys in the pub.

If Imogen didn't know her friend well, or know that these blokes could hold their drink, she'd have been worried that none of them would be fit to report for duty in the morning. As it was, she loved seeing Jenna as the centre of attention.

Amy came down to the bar after a few hours, grabbed an OJ from Imogen and then joined Jenna and her claque of men. Despite not drinking alcohol and having a tummy the size of a large watermelon, the men treated her in the same way, hanging on each woman's every word.

'You go and join them,' said Charlie, sneaking up behind her. 'I'm sure Cal and I can manage for a bit.'

'Of course we can.' Cal wrapped an arm round Charlie and grinned.

Three tables had been pushed together and there was now a rather large group surrounding Amy and Jenna. A couple of men eagerly shoved their chairs aside and pulled another one over to make room for Imogen.

'What are you having?' asked the guy sitting next to Imogen. His name was Warren – though his friends called him Wazza – and he made it into the pub every few nights.

Dammit, she'd forgotten to get herself a drink. She went to stand. 'I'll go grab a Coke. I'm still on duty.'

'I'll get it.' Warren all but rocketed out of his seat and headed for the bar.

Immediately, another bloke scooted over to take his place next to Imogen. 'So, how are you enjoying life in Gibson's Find?' he asked.

'Very much,' she answered honestly. 'I've been really busy but that's the way I like it.'

'But she misses us,' piped up Jenna from across the table. 'Don't you, darling?'

Imogen smiled at her friend and noticed that Guy – the bloke she'd met during her first run – was sitting mighty close. Was Jenna's hand on his knee? The table obstructed her view, but it certainly looked that way. She shouldn't have been surprised – Jenna had always been a fast mover and Guy had Mr Flirtation written all over his face. Good for them.

'Of course I do.' She smiled.

'Given any more thought to joining us at boot camp of a morning?' Guy asked.

'Sorry, but I prefer running. It helps clear my head in the mornings.'

'Suit yourself.' Guy shrugged and turned back to Jenna.

The next few hours passed easily. Imogen loved being back in the company of her friends, and the blokes were easy to get along with. She learnt a lot more about the bachelors of Gibson's Find than she needed to know, but wasn't that one of the perks (and pitfalls) of being a publican? Bottom line was that she couldn't understand why they were all still single. It wasn't as though they had bad body odour or warts growing all over their skin. And Gibson's Find wasn't *that* remote. It was a mystery. She even asked Warren this question.

He shrugged and finished a mouthful of beer before answering. 'It's not just a rain drought we have out here. There's a serious female famine as well. Most of us blokes were born and bred on the land and couldn't imagine living anywhere else. Some of the contractors have sheilas back in Perth, but lots don't. Women in general don't see the appeal of life in the bush. Even the ones raised round here seem to move on eventually.' He paused a second and laughed. 'The few blokes that do have better halves are at home making the most of it.'

'Hmm.' Imogen took a sip of her drink and contemplated this. Reading between the lines, Gibson probably wasn't the only one who'd lost a lover to the city, even if he seemed to be the one most wounded by it.

'What's "hmm" mean?' Warren laughed.

'Just thinking,' she said with a smile. She'd only been in the country a few weeks but so far she liked – no, *loved* – what she saw. The community spirit, the slower pace of life, the wildlife on her morning runs. So there weren't designer boutiques on every corner and the local library (housed in the general store) looked more like the bookshelf in her apartment, but hadn't these women ever heard of online shopping? She wished there were something she could do to fix the famine.

Halfway through this thought, Amy sidled up to Imogen and tapped her on the shoulder. 'Hope you don't mind, sweet, but I'm going to call it a night.'

Imogen glanced at her watch and then stood up. 'I'll come up with you quickly.'

As they passed the bar, she told Charlie and Cal she'd be back before closing time.

Amy took her time climbing the stairs to Imogen's apartment. Her breath seemed laboured and when she reached the front door, she looked like she'd just run a marathon in forty-degree heat.

'Are you okay?' Imogen asked, regretting not giving Amy one of the hotel rooms on the ground level.

'I'm fine.' Amy puffed to catch her breath. 'I just stayed up way past my pregnancy bedtime and the heat's getting to me a little. Nothing a good night's sleep won't fix.'

'Can I get you anything before you go to bed?' Imogen asked.

'A glass of cold water?' Amy said, already on her way to her room.

By the time Imogen returned with the drink, Amy was all tucked up in bed. Imogen perched on the edge and grinned. 'I'm so glad you're here,' she told her friend. 'This is like old times. Remember our sleepovers?'

'How could I forget?' Amy took a long sip of water and then said, 'Although, from what I remember, there wasn't much sleep involved, whereas tonight I'm going to sleep like a proverbial baby. That's if you don't have anything you need to talk about first,' she added quickly, concern evident in her eyes.

'No.' Imogen shook her head, not wanting her very pregnant friend to start worrying unnecessarily. 'I'm all cool. Busy but good.'

'Jamie?' said Amy, not needing to add anything more.

Imogen sighed. 'I think about him all the time, but being here is helping. Having a project is exactly what I need.'

'I'm so glad.' Amy tried to stifle a yawn.

'Go to sleep.' Imogen switched off the bedside lamp and kissed her friend on the forehead. 'Sweet dreams. I'll see you in the morning.'

★★★

When Imogen trekked back downstairs, the crowd had thinned significantly. Cal and Charlie were beginning the end-of-day tasks and Jenna was nowhere to be found. Imogen didn't worry until the pub emptied fifteen minutes later and there was still no sign of her friend.

'Either of you seen Jenna?' she asked her bar staff.

Cal rubbed her lips together and wiggled her eyebrows. 'My guess is Guy is seeing quite a lot of her right now.'

'What?' She shouldn't have been surprised. Jenna had never been short of admirers and the chemistry between those two was obvious.

Cal shrugged and raised her hands as if she didn't know any more. 'I heard her say she'd see him out to his ute about half an hour ago.'

'Thanks.' Imogen locked the front door and sent Charlie and Cal on their way. When there was still no sign of Jenna, she succumbed to the urge to check the car park. She intended to peek quietly but the pub door stuck and when she shoved it, it made a noise, alerting Jenna and Guy to her presence.

'Hi there,' she said as the two lovebirds looked up from a very keen embrace. 'Just checking you're okay, Jenna?'

'She's fine,' Guy drawled. 'Aren't ya, Jen?'

Jenna giggled. 'More than fine.' Then she kissed Guy one more time before pulling back. 'And as much as I'd like to take you up on your offer, Imogen trumps. I haven't had a girly night with her and Amy in a long time.'

Jenna walked towards Imogen as Guy climbed into his ute. 'Can't blame a guy for trying,' he called, before slamming the door shut. He pulled out of the car park and waved. 'See you bright and early!'

'Amy's already in bed,' said Imogen as Guy's ute faded into the night, 'so you lucked out there. If you really wanted to go with him, you should have. He's seems like a nice guy.'

Imogen and Jenna cracked up at the pun, which Imogen hadn't actually intended.

'Well, if he shags anywhere near as good as he kisses, I turned down a very good night, but I don't want to look *too* easy.' Jenna put her arm around Imogen as they walked inside.

'Of course not.' Imogen rolled her eyes.

'Besides,' Jenna began, as Imogen locked the last door and they climbed the stairs to her apartment, 'I have a present for you.'

For a moment, Imogen was thinking of something along the lines of a house-warming gift or maybe a nice piece of art for her office – Jenna was a curator for an exclusive Claremont gallery – but noticing the gleam in her friend's eyes, she guessed exactly what it was. And shuddered.

'Fancy a Milo?' Imogen asked.

'Sure. I'll be right back.' Jenna, still full of life, rushed off to her suitcase – which was ridiculously large for two nights away. Seconds later she returned, placing a bright-pink, rectangular box with a massive silver bow on the bench near Imogen. 'There you go.'

Imogen eyed the pretty box suspiciously. 'Is that what I think it is?'

Jenna nodded, her smile so animated it looked as if it might leap off her face.

Taking a moment to digest this, Imogen stirred Milo into two mugs of steaming milk. She should never have raised the idea. 'You shouldn't have bothered,' she said eventually. She was close enough to Jenna that she could be blatantly honest. 'It was a stupid idea. I really don't think I could get used to using it.'

Jenna refused to be deterred. She picked up her mug and the box. 'Don't be so quick to judge. Let's go sit and open it. Maybe have a play.'

*Eek!* 'I'm not playing with that thing with you.' But Jenna was already on her way to the couch, and whether she heard or not, she didn't comment.

Reluctantly, Imogen picked up the remaining mug and followed her friend. The lounge room was low-lit by a couple of lamps – Imogen had got into the habit of switching them on early in the evening so the place wouldn't be pitch black when she returned. The box, already taking pride of place in the middle of the coffee table, glowed like an alien object. Despite the Milo still being too hot to drink, she took a sip and watched as Jenna slowly undid the bow.

Her drink threatened to shoot back up her oesophagus as she pleaded with higher powers for Jenna not to have brought her one of those tongue-shaped devices she'd seen in her email. Not that she planned on using it anyway. Her request had been made in a moment of insanity.

The ribbon floated to the floor and Jenna giggled with excitement as she removed the lid. Imogen's heart stopped as she watched her friend unveil the present.

'Ta-dah!' Jenna sang as she held up a hot-pink penis-shaped vibrator.

Imogen gulped. At first glance it vaguely resembled her hair straightener, but this thing promised far greater pleasure. Could she really give it a shot?

Jenna must have guessed the workings of her mind. 'Are you intent on never sleeping with anyone else?'

A few months back, she'd have given a resounding yes. Immediately. Now, 'never' seemed like a long time. But she said it anyway and hoped she sounded convincing.

Jenna sighed. 'In that case, this little baby is going to become a very good friend.'

'Okay. Whatever.' Without a thought, Imogen snatched the offending object from her friend and shoved it back in the box. She wanted this awkward conversation over and she didn't want Jenna getting any ideas about giving a demonstration. When the box was shut and safely on the couch beside her, she looked back to Jenna. 'So? Guy? What's the deal?'

Jenna shrugged, that mischievous gleam returning to her eyes. 'You know me. Just having a bit of fun.'

They chatted about the pub and about Jenna's latest scores – both at work and play – for another half an hour, but as much as they could have spent all night talking, Imogen knew they'd need their energy tomorrow.

After saying goodnight to Jenna, dumping the mugs in the sink and listening quickly at Amy's door, Imogen climbed into bed and looked at Jamie's photo. Then she glanced across at the pink box sitting in the middle of her dresser. Jenna had insisted she take it into the bedroom … just in case.

Usually she found it easy to talk to Jamie – looked forward to it all day – but how could you tell your husband you were the proud owner of a dildo? It'd be funny if it wasn't squirmingly embarrassing. If it wasn't her life! She could have said she missed the intimacy between them and explain about the hot flushes she'd been having, but the fact was, she only had those flushes when a certain man was present. To be precise, a certain grouchy and insufferable farmer. These feelings were hard enough to comprehend, never mind finding the right words with which to express them to Jamie.

She never really thought about how he'd feel if she hooked up with another man. When he was alive, they'd been too busy planning their future – a house with a pool, three or four kids splashing in it and a caravan out the back to take the whole family travelling – never imagining that they might not have decades to enjoy each other. Stressing about things that didn't really matter, but never making the most of what they had. When he died, she couldn't imagine the day would come when she'd look at another man and have he's-a-bit-of-all-right thoughts. Now they were sprouting, she didn't know what to do with them and she definitely didn't welcome them.

Perhaps she *should* try the vibrator.

# Chapter Nine

The slab party began with an official breakfast at seven o'clock on Saturday morning. The Majestic would be closed all weekend except to those volunteering, but it seemed to Imogen like Charlie had roped in half the town. Farmers left their properties and live-stock to their own devices and arrived bright and early. Other locals showed up in droves. Karen and Tom turned up armed with tools, paintbrushes and cleaning products. Amy and Jenna sat among the gathering men, going through the plans for the day. The number of volunteers astounded Imogen and she began to think big about what they could achieve by working together, even only for one weekend.

Tormenting smells of cooked bacon, sausages and eggs wafted from the kitchen where Pauli and Cal were in full-swing breakfast mode, singing as they worked. Imogen smiled as she and Karen trekked back and forth from kitchen to dining area, happily serving food to the merry men. Focusing on the pub had undoubtedly been good for her spirits, and it also seemed to have worked its magic on Pauli.

The food was almost gone, the plates were being piled up in the kitchen and Imogen was just about to announce Amy – so she could allocate everyone to their tasks for the day – when Charlie arrived wearing a pair of painter's overalls and his floppy grey terry towelling hat. Imogen almost fell off her bar stool and face-planted the floor when she noticed Gibson behind him. She was surprised to see him here at all, but also shocked at how criminally attractive he looked.

It was obvious that, despite the early hour, Gibson had already been at work on his farm. His brow shone with perspiration, his worn, navy-blue t-shirt clung to his body and his khaki Stubbies gave her a tantalising view of his legs. Tanned, Muscled. With just a nice dusting of hair. Who was she kidding? It was more than nice. His leg hair was turning her on! She caught herself gawping and quickly pulled it together as they approached.

'Hi Charlie. Hi Gibson.' Dammit, she sounded unusually chirpy. She pushed her hair behind her ears and downgraded her smile. 'This is a pleasant surprise.'

'He's not staying,' Charlie announced gruffly. 'He just didn't trust me to carry his precious sander.'

Imogen raised her eyebrows at the power tool in Gibson's grip. He was holding it so tightly that his knuckles were white. She imagined it could pack quite a punch but it didn't exactly look heavy.

'I didn't say that.' Gibson glared at Charlie and then thrust the sander at him. He ran a hand through his hair and looked at Imogen. 'Sorry I can't stay. I hope it's a great success for you.' He bit out the words before turning and striding back out of the pub.

And Imogen – her insides burning up – was helpless to do anything but watch him go.

'Where should I put this?'

She started at Charlie's question, shaking her head and trying to gather her thoughts. What was it about grouchy Gibson Black that had her forgetting simple things like what she needed a sander for in the first place? She didn't like being flustered, especially on an important day like this. It wasn't like she'd never seen a hunk before. Jamie had turned heads in the street too.

Swallowing, she answered Charlie. 'Will it be safe out on the verandah? We'll be moving everything out of here soon.'

'It'd better be safe,' Charlie replied, turning. Over his shoulder, he grumped, 'Anyone steals anything from you and they'll have all these men to pick a fight with, hey boys?'

Shouts of agreement erupted across the room. She smiled at the eager-faced men. It was hard to believe she'd lived in Gibson's Find such a short time. Everyone was so welcoming and friendly and supportive. She felt herself tearing up at the thought. If Jamie was looking down from somewhere, he'd be happy his girl had found a safe haven.

She took a deep breath and gathered her thoughts. 'Okay everyone.' She raised her voice so even the guys at the back of the room could hear. 'Listen up.' The hush of chatter died immediately. She gestured for Amy to stand up beside her and all eyes focused on the two of them. 'Firstly, thank you all for coming. I can't tell you how much it means to me to have you all here. I'd like to introduce you to one of my best friends, Amy Reynolds. Many of you met her and Jenna last night. Like you fabulous lot, they've agreed to devote their weekend to helping turn this place into something absolutely amazing. A pub you're proud to call your local. A pub that attracts people from further afield – hopefully a few extra women as well.' Imogen winked and cheers echoed throughout the room.

'As you can see,' – she gestured to Amy's very pregnant stomach – 'Amy won't be much good for strenuous labour today, so I've put her in charge of organising us all. She's the boss.'

Jenna began handing out Amy's photocopied schedule.

'Hi everyone. Lovely to meet you,' said Amy, clipboard in hand. She was wearing casual clothes like everyone else, but talked in measured tones as if she were in the office. 'I think the best way is to split into groups to tackle each of the major tasks. I've compiled a list of the teams we'll need and soon I'll give you the chance to nominate your preferences.' She took a breath and then began explaining tasks and duties. When she'd finished, everyone was eager to start, but she held up a hand to silence the chattering.

'You'll see from the schedule that we have designated times for breaks. I'd appreciate everyone sticking to these or we'll never get finished. We'll be eating outside in the courtyard, because although I'm sure you're all fast workers, the new dining room probably won't be finished today. Any questions?'

If anyone did have a question, they didn't dare ask it. Imogen guessed it had something to do with Amy's authoritarive tone – not that she was complaining. If anyone could get a pub full of men to achieve, it was Amy.

Finally, Amy gave the word and the men stepped forward to choose their tasks. Within five minutes, the crowd had dispersed into pairs and groups, and despite the warm weather, they all threw themselves enthusiastically into their various tasks.

By mid-morning Imogen could barely believe what had already been achieved. She'd heard no whinging or complaints. The old furniture in the main bar and adjoining dining room had been stacked outside, ready to be taken to the op shop in Southern Cross or simply ditched. Some guys who'd bragged about being clever with hammers were in the courtyard constructing the flat-packed furniture Imogen had ordered to replace the old stuff. She'd gone for very simple stuff – nothing too funky or modern – because she wanted the decor on the walls and the actual building to be the focus of people's attention.

Another couple of blokes had put down drop sheets in the bar, readying it for the mammoth job of painting ceilings and walls. They were now cleaning in preparation for the first layer of paint. Jenna, Guy and a few others formed a team doing the same in the dining room, which was carpeted in the same ghastly, 1970s psychedelic pattern Imogen was subjected to upstairs. Karen, Tom and the majority of the other volunteers had started on the accommodation rooms.

Pauli and Cal were on kitchen duties – taking on the important role of keeping the workers fuelled – so that had left Imogen, Charlie and Warren to start on the verandah. Despite everyone's willingness to help, no one except Warren had been particularly enthused about taking this job, which would mean spending most of the day in the heat. It didn't take long for Imogen to work out that he had ulterior motives.

'Everyone's turning into girls' blouses these days,' said Charlie as he tried to lift one of the heavy outdoor tables on his own.

'Not me,' said Warren, flexing his muscles like a cartoon character. He leaned towards Imogen, offering his upper arm. 'Wanna squeeze?'

'Um, no thanks.' She tried not to sound too crushing. 'Let's help Charlie.'

Between the three of them, they managed to stack all four tables at one end of the verandah.

'Right. Let's get started.' Charlie thrust hard-bristle brooms at Imogen and Warren. When he turned his back and began sweeping, Warren made a questioning grimace at Imogen. She shrugged back. She'd never seen Charlie in anything other than a jovial, chirpy mood, but something had certainly got his goat this morning. She guessed it was Gibson refusing to help, but she wished he wouldn't get so worked up over it. She didn't hold Gibson's absence against him. If anything, they had almost too many volunteers. And for her sanity's sake, it was a good thing Gibson didn't deem her worthy of his help.

For half an hour they worked without a break, scrubbing the old boards and readying them for the sander. When Imogen noticed Charlie getting a little red in the face, she suggested he go inside and fetch them some water.

He dithered for a moment, but when she added, 'Please, Charlie, I'm parched,' and wrapped her hands around her neck to prove her point, he headed inside.

Warren winked at her and sidled closer. 'Good work, babe. Getting us some alone time?'

She raised her eyebrows and gave Warren The Glare. 'I think he's overdoing it,' she said, not taking the bait. Warren might think himself a comedian or a Casanova – she couldn't tell which yet – but she didn't want to give him any encouragement. She took a breather and leaned against the wooden railings. 'Do you mind using the sander if I can convince Charlie to swap to a lighter job?'

'Not at all,' Warren replied good-naturedly, seemingly unfazed by her rebuff. 'But good luck with that. The old dude doesn't like to be told what he can and can't do.'

'Really? I hadn't noticed.'

Warren laughed and then knelt to examine the sander. They were ready to start stripping the first layer off the decking. He put on some safety goggles and Imogen took the chance to slip inside and find Charlie. She wanted to check he was okay. Gibson would never forgive her if she overworked him and he got dehydrated. Hell, she wouldn't forgive herself.

She sucked in her breath as she stepped through the front door. The whole bottom floor of the pub was empty of furniture and the space was much larger than she'd imagined. In the dining room – despite obviously flirting with each other – Jenna and Guy had already starting painting one wall a dark shade of coffee; Jenna had a matching coloured handprint on the back of her tight black tee. Consumed with each other's company, they didn't notice Imogen watching until Amy joined her, the clipboard resting against her tummy.

'They certainly work hard in the bush, don't they?' Amy said, smiling her approval.

Imogen nodded, a little speechless at what was already quite a transformation. Stuff that would have taken her months to do on her own – especially while running the pub as well – was happening before her eyes. 'It's so much better.'

'And this is only the first coat,' Guy said, turning and grinning at her. 'Good colour choice.' He didn't flip her insides like some unmentionable people, but Imogen could see why Jenna would find him a nice distraction.

'Thanks so much for all your hard work, folks,' she said. 'Don't forget to keep your liquid intake up.'

'Yes, Mum,' Jenna and Guy chirped in unison.

She shook her head at them and turned to Amy. 'Have you seen Charlie?'

Amy consulted her list. 'I thought he was outside with you.'

'He came in to get drinks a few minutes ago.' Imogen bit her lip, trying to quell the worry building inside her. There was no reason to start stressing, yet she couldn't curb the feeling. 'I'll check the bar.'

She found Cal and Pauli removing glasses and other objects that might be in the way of the renovators, but no Charlie.

'Are we on track for lunch in half an hour?' Pauli asked.

'Yes, that's perfect,' Imogen replied, distracted. She headed out to the shade of the back courtyard where the furniture construction was in full swing. The tension left her limbs the moment she registered Charlie, bent over a half-made bar stool with an Allen key in his hand. His brow was furrowed and he was poking out his tongue like a young child focusing hard. She tamped down the urge to rush up and give him a big cuddle.

She spoke with the few blokes putting together tables and chairs, complimenting their quick work and thanking them. Then she approached Charlie.

'So, this is where you got to?' She sat in a newly made chair. 'Hmm, comfy.'

He looked up, smiled and then his forehead creased in confusion. 'Just doing my bit.'

'And you're doing a fabulous job, but I thought you were on drink duty? A girl could die of thirst waiting for you.'

His smile morphed into a scowl. 'Drinks? Is that all you think I'm good for? I may be old, but I can work harder than this lot put together.'

Imogen twisted her ponytail round a finger, not sure how to respond. Was the heat making him cranky or was there something more going on? 'Oh, maybe I didn't make myself clear,' she said, pushing the uneasy thought aside, 'but it's hot out here. How about you come inside and help Pauli and Cal organise morning tea?'

'I'm not hot,' snapped Charlie, wiping his brow with the back of his paper-thin, wrinkled hand. 'And I'm fine out here.'

Imogen sighed. 'Okay, I'm sorry. Just looking out for my favourite barman.'

Finally, that got a smile and a tiny blush. Charlie nodded his head at Imogen. 'And you're my favourite publican, so I promise to come in for a drink in a moment.'

Conversation done and dusted, he adjusted his hat and turned his attentions back to the stool.

★★★

By six o'clock that evening, Imogen thought maybe she should call *The Guinness Book of Records* for the most renovations completed in one day.

'It's amazing what can be done when a whole town pulls together,' she said to Charlie, impulsively pulling him into a hug. She popped a peck on the side of his face. 'Thank you for having this wonderful idea.'

Charlie beamed, the tense words they'd exchanged earlier in the day now forgotten. 'I'm not just a handsome face, you know,' he said, leaning against the bar.

'Definitely not. If you were a few years younger, I'd really have to behave myself.'

He was the only man Imogen dared flirt with, and she knew by the grin on his face, he liked it. Unfortunately, his mention of a handsome face got her thinking about Gibson and how he always used to visit his granddad at this time. Stupidly, she glanced at the front door, wondering if he'd come back tonight. The pub was closed to everyone except the workers but she didn't think that would stop him. Gibson Black was the kind of guy who walked round like he owned the stars and did exactly as he pleased.

'Taste this.' Cal laid a platter of Mexican nibbles on the bar – corn chips with homemade dips of guacamole, chilli con queso and green salsa. The divine aromas teased Imogen's tastebuds and distracted her thoughts.

She took a chip and dipped it in the queso, moaning her approval. 'What did I do to deserve such fabulous staff?' she asked Cal, before stealing another one. She finished her mouthful, licked her lips and cleared her throat to address the masses.

'Okay, guys! Time to lay down those brushes, put aside those tools and pick up a drink. The bar is open and Cal's hors d'oeuvres are to die for.' Just to prove her point, she swiped another chip – this time with salsa – before taking her place behind the bar. She'd better keep her distance from that platter or she won't have room for mains, and she'll have to run for double her normal time on Monday morning.

Within seconds, the bar was besieged and her arms – already aching from holding up a paintbrush half the day – got a workout at the beer taps. For a brief moment, Imogen wondered if the alcohol she'd have to supply would end up costing her more than it would have to get professionals in to do the painting, sanding and all the other jobs. But even if it did, it was worth it.

Thanks to these eager men, the interior of the pub now had a whole first layer of paint (including the ceiling), the exterior was looking cleaner than ever and the verandah would soon be polished like a dance floor. Five of the accommodation rooms had been completely done over, with the last three on tomorrow's agenda. All of the new furniture had been constructed and moved inside for the evening's festivities. But quite aside from the physical work achieved, Imogen had laughed and smiled more today than she had in a long time. So much so that her jaw muscles ached almost as much as her arms. With music blaring from the pub's ancient stereo while they worked, there'd been numerous times she'd forgotten about the 'slab' part of the party and simply relaxed and enjoyed it. It had been an amazing day and the night was only just beginning.

As she passed another beer to one of the volunteers, Imogen scanned the crowd for her friends. Jenna and Guy seemed to have disappeared. She rolled her eyes – no surprises there. They'd been carrying on like lovestruck teenagers all day.

And Amy, darling Amy, was weaving through the new tables, talking to the guys as she topped up platters and collected the empty glasses. Despite her smile, Imogen could tell she was tired. When she trekked back to the bar with her latest load, Imogen took the tray and passed it to Cal, before leading Amy over to a chair to sit. Pulling out another one for her legs, she made Amy stretch out. 'What can I get you to drink?'

Amy yawned and Imogen mentally kicked herself. So much for not letting her friend overdo it.

'Are you okay?'

Amy reached out and squeezed Imogen's hand. 'Relax, I'm fine. I've had a great day. I really think you made the right decision coming here.'

'Me too.' Imogen nodded. She'd had the occasional doubt but mostly the pros outweighed the cons.

'And all the guys are really lovely,' Amy continued, taking a quick glance around the pub. 'Not a bad-looking bunch either. Anyone hook your interest yet?'

'Amy!' For a second she wondered if she'd heard correctly.

'I'm sorry, I shouldn't have asked.' Guilt swept across Amy's face. 'It's just—'

'No. You shouldn't have.' Imogen snatched her hand from Amy's, the anger in her voice more for herself than for her friend. Anger because at Amy's ludicrous question, she'd thought immediately of Gibson. 'Orange juice or lemonade?'

'Orange juice, but—' Amy tried to grab Imogen's hand again but she moved quickly out of reach.

'It's okay.' Imogen faked a smile. 'I can't talk about stuff like that now. I'll be right back.'

She knew her brusqueness had hurt Amy, who, as always, only had Imogen's happiness at heart, but she didn't want to move on and she certainly didn't want to start talking about hot guys as if they were still in high school. Taking a deep breath, she headed to the bar.

Halfway through pouring the juice, a shriek rang out behind her: Amy – she'd recognise that shriek anywhere. Dropping the glass and ignoring the mess as it clattered onto the floor behind her, Imogen rushed back to her friend. She fell to her knees next to Amy and grabbed her hand.

'What's wrong?'

'My waters just broke.' Amy pressed her free hand against her stomach. 'At least I think they did.'

Imogen looked down and her heart stopped beating at the sight of liquid trickling from the chair onto the floor. 'Oh God. Isn't it too early?'

'Yes.' Amy's calm demeanour collapsed as a tear slid down her cheek.

*Good one, Imogen. Way to stress the pregnant lady.* Knowing it was up to her to keep it together, she all but cooed, 'Everything's going to be fine.' She looked behind her to see Pauli on the phone, her instructions loud and clear as she requested an ambulance. Charlie stretched up to turn off the stereo. Cal rushed over with a pillow and a large glass of water. God, she loved her team.

But where the hell was Jenna?

'I'm scared.' Amy clutched Imogen's hand so hard it cut off circulation. 'I want Ryan.'

'I know, honey. As soon as the ambulance gets here, I'll call him.' She stroked Amy's head and tucked some hair behind her ear. 'I'm not leaving you until then.'

★★★

'Do you think we should move her some place more comfortable?' Pauli asked as soon as she was off the phone. 'I told the ambulance to park out the back, so maybe we should take her to room 1 while we wait. That's if you think you can walk,' she added quickly, looking to Amy.

Amy nodded. 'Definitely. I feel like a circus clown here.'

Imogen registered the curious eyes of the slab party volunteers peering at the commotion. 'Good idea,' she said. With Pauli's help, she wrapped a towel (for modesty's sake) round Amy's waist and helped her stand. The crowd of onlookers stepped back as the trio headed past the bar and into the foyer, which led to the corridor of lower level hotel rooms.

As they passed it on their right, the store cupboard opened and Jenna and Guy spilled out, giggling.

'Careful,' barked Pauli as Jenna almost crashed into them.

Startled, Jenna's flushed face flashed white as Guy pulled her back out of the way. 'What's wrong?' She shrugged out of his grip. 'Oh my God. Are you okay, Amy?'

'Not sure,' Amy managed, her usually smiley face now etched with worry.

Imogen looked Jenna up and down, raised her eyebrows at the sight of her dishevelled hair and clothing, but stopped short of grilling her. 'Her waters have broken,' she explained.

'Oh my!' Jenna tagged behind them as they made their way into the room. The three women almost fell over themselves trying to help Amy onto the bed.

Pauli looked to Imogen. 'Now Jenna's here, should I get back to the pub to help Charlie and Cal?'

'Thanks,' Imogen said, so glad she had help she could rely on. 'Can you make sure everyone is well fed and watered?'

'Shall do. Good luck.' Pauli smiled to Amy as she left.

Imogen turned back to her friend. 'How are you feeling now?' she asked, puffing a pillow behind Amy's head.

'Like I'm in labour,' Amy answered, cringing. She screwed up her face and let out a sound Imogen had never heard before. She clutched her belly and froze for a moment. 'I think I just had my first contraction.'

'We need to call an ambulance,' Jenna said, patting her skirt as if looking for her phone.

'Already done,' snapped Imogen. *While you were bonking some bloke you only just met.* She didn't know why she felt aggro at Jenna – she should have been used to her friend's antics by now – but she did.

'Excellent.' Jenna glanced back to Amy. 'It's going to be all right, sweetie. Is there anything we can do for you?'

Imogen knelt down on the opposite side of the bed to Jenna and held Amy's hand.

'I want Ryan.' Amy sniffed.

Jenna located a box of tissues and whipped one out. Handing it to her friend, she said, 'I know, honey. I wish he was here too, but can I get you a drink or something?'

'More water.' Amy's words came out on a quick breath before she winced again. A groan followed.

Imogen and Jenna watched in horror as another contraction took hold.

'Should we be timing this?' Jenna hissed.

'Good idea.' Imogen glanced at her watch and made a mental note of the start time.

As if eager to get away, Jenna stood. 'I better go get the water.' When she returned with a glass and a bottle of water, the contraction had ended and Amy gulped the whole lot down in seconds. Imogen and Jenna looked to each other, their eyebrows raised. Imogen guessed she wasn't the only one praying the ambulance would hurry.

As Amy tried to relax into the pillows and find a comfortable position again, Imogen tried for small talk. 'Thank you for everything you organised today Amy, I can't believe—'

'You need to call Ryan!' Amy pleaded. 'Give me your phone and I'll call him.'

But Imogen didn't know what to say. Ryan would go insane with worry, so she wanted to wait until she had a better idea of what to tell him. Maybe these were Braxton Hicks contractions? Maybe Amy wasn't really in labour and the ambulance folk would set everything right. *But what about the waters breaking?* asked an annoying voice inside Imogen's head.

Before she could tell that voice to take a hike, they heard voices down the hallway. Moments later, two men in green St Johns Ambulance uniforms appeared. Imogen had heard stories about ambulances taking forever in the country, and it may have felt that way, but in reality, the Gibson's Find volunteers were quick.

She looked at the first man, an older farmer who'd only been in the pub once. He smiled warmly and she turned her focus to the other man. Her heart jolted in recognition.

*Gibson!* Just her bloody luck. His eyes met hers before he looked away. In those brief seconds, her insides twisted – not unpleasantly – and she had to lick her lips, which all of a sudden felt parched.

As if Imogen weren't even there, he turned his attention to Amy. Pulling on a pair of latex gloves, he knelt next to the bed and took her hand. The other officer stood close behind, carrying a medical bag as if on standby for instruction. She'd heard there was often only one qualified officer and a driver to attend call-outs, and it looked as if Gibson were the guy in charge. His focus locked on Amy and he spoke in a soothing voice Imogen would never have imagined him capable of.

'So, your waters have broken. Any other signs of labour?'

Amy nodded. 'I've just started contractions… Oh fuck!'

Imogen looked to Jenna, who appeared as anxious as she felt. Amy never swore. As their friend screwed up her whole face and rocked forward, groaning as the contraction strengthened, Imogen knelt and offered her hand. Amy snatched it and within seconds Imogen wished she'd offered something plastic instead. She bit her lip, reasoning the pain she felt had to be a fraction of what Amy was feeling.

Finally, Amy's groaning died down and she released Imogen's hand. Imogen shook it out a little and looked to Jenna. 'Your turn next time.'

Catching her breath, Amy said, 'I haven't actually been feeling the best the last forty-eight hours. I had lower back pain a bit today.'

Gibson looked up and glared at Imogen. Guessing his thoughts, she couldn't help but defend herself. 'She never said a word.'

'I didn't,' Amy said quickly, offering Imogen an apologetic smile. 'This isn't Immy's fault. It's all mine. I never imagined I was in labour, I just thought I'd overdone it a bit. Oh God, Ryan will never forgive me if something happens to our baby. I'll never forgive myself.'

'Nothing's going to happen.' Imogen stroked Amy's hair out of her eyes with her still-functioning hand and squeezed her shoulder. And of course Ryan would forgive her – she'd never seen anyone as devoted to their spouse as Ryan was to Amy. It was gorgeous, sometimes sickeningly so.

'Okay. How far along are you?' Gibson asked.

'Just over thirty-six weeks.' Amy clutched her belly and sobbed. 'This is too early.'

'It's okay, we're going to look after you and the baby.' Gibson squeezed Amy's hand and then looked up at the other officer. 'Dave, we're gonna have to call Comms on this one. We'll need a plane.'

Dave pulled a phone out of his pocket and started dialling. While he waited for a response, he indicated to Gibson that he was going to the van to get the stretcher ready. Gibson opened up the oxygen equipment and prepared an oxygen mask for Amy, before taking out a blood pressure cuff and wrapping it around her arm. He glanced at his watch. 'How long since your last contraction?'

Amy glanced to Imogen for direction.

'It wasn't anywhere as intense as that one, but I'd say about five minutes.'

'Okay,' Gibson mused, as if he were searching through a mental training manual, trying to recall what he knew about childbirth.

'The Flying Doctor has been notified and we're a high priority,' Dave announced, returning to the room. 'Stretcher is in the hallway and Comms is calling back with their on-call obstetrician ASAP.'

'Great, thanks Dave.' Gibson turned back to Amy just as the next contraction hit.

'Oh God,' she moaned, positioning herself on all fours. 'Here comes another one...'

'It's all right.' Gibson moved closer to Amy and this time he rubbed her back.

'There now, you're doing a fine job,' Gibson cooed. 'Did you have antenatal classes?'

'Of course I fucking did,' Amy shrieked, turning her head to glare at him. 'Do I look like the village idiot?'

Imogen's eyes widened at Amy's uncharacteristic language and tone, but Gibson didn't flinch, continuing to rub his patient's back. 'Definitely not,' he soothed. 'Did they teach you much about breathing?'

Amy didn't answer immediately – choosing to summon her wild beast side instead. Imogen heard a collective release of air when she eventually quietened and sank back onto the pillows – she hadn't been the only one holding her breath.

'Sorry,' Amy said, sweat dripping off her brow. 'We did learn about breathing. I'd totally forgotten. Maybe I am an idiot.' She sobbed a little and Gibson rushed to contradict her.

'No, you're not. But try to think now. What did they teach you?'

Amy's brow furrowed slightly and then she said, 'Well, first stage of labour, you're supposed to breathe deeply to keep calm and relaxed. How am I doing at that?'

Everyone laughed – even Gibson, which shocked Imogen, because she hadn't realised he was capable. When the laughter died down, seriousness returned to Gibson's face. 'Do you think you might be further along than you think?'

Amy went pale, but before she could reply her contractions started all over again.

Imogen stepped back, helpless, as her friend rocked on the bed, her face contorting in agony.

'Why the hell is this happening to me? I was going to have a fucking epidural. Do you do epis?'

'Sorry, we're not sanctioned to administer drugs.'

'But you've done this before, right?'

Imogen saw Gibson swallow.

'Dave, we need that obstetrician. Now.'

Dave set to dialling again.

'Imogen,' Gibson addressed her, for the first time using her actual name. 'We're going to need towels, more water and some wet flannels.'

'Okay.' Thank God there was something useful she could do. 'We're onto it.'

'Thanks.' Turning his back on Imogen and Jenna, Gibson returned his focus to Amy.

As Imogen and Jenna left the room and hurried down the corridor towards the linen storeroom, Jenna rambled, 'Oh my goodness, I can't believe this is happening. You are going to have a baby born right here in your pub. You might make the news. This is going to be brilliant publicity.'

'If the baby's okay.' Imogen couldn't rid the sense of dread that was building in her gut.

Jenna scoffed. 'Of course it'll be okay. Can't be anything else. Amy's doing a good job so far and those ambo guys know what they're doing. And one of them is totally *hot!*' She bounced on the spot like a cartoon jelly bean.

Imogen rolled her eyes. No points for guessing who Jenna was referring to. 'It doesn't matter if they're good-looking,' she spat. 'For once in your life, can you think with your brain instead of your libido?' They'd arrived at the storeroom. She wrenched the door open and stormed inside.

'Whoa, what's got your goat?' Jenna asked, close behind.

'I'll tell you what's got my goat.' Imogen whirled around, her hands snapping to her hips as fury raged within her. 'Amy scared the hell of me out there. They've wanted this baby forever – five IVF attempts, and she's in labour way before her due date. And while Amy's in need and I'm terrified, where the hell are you? In a cupboard, bonking some bloke you've only just met. That's what's got my goat.'

Nodding slowly, as if Imogen belonged in the looney bin, Jenna began grabbing towels. 'I'm sorry,' she said shortly, red rushing to her cheeks.

*Crap!* Imogen immediately regretted the outburst. Now, not only had she let one friend work too hard today, which had possibly induced early labour, she'd probably alienated the other.

'I'm sorry, Jenna,' Imogen began, grabbing some flannels. 'I don't know what's come over me.' She guessed it had something to do with Amy's mention of Imogen moving on, the thoughts that suggestion had sparked, and then Gibson turning up so soon after. The fact that Jenna was indulging in the exact activity Imogen was trying not to think about didn't help at all. And on top of all that… 'I guess I'm just worried about Amy. I had no right—'

'It's okay,' Jenna said forcefully. 'Let's just get back to her.'

And she was right. Amy had to be their priority right now.

Armed with supplies, they headed back to the room and opened the door to hear an unfamiliar but authoritative female voice on speakerphone. 'Right, as Amy is fully dilated, she can start pushing when she's ready.'

Pushing? Where the hell had that come from? Weren't first babies supposed to take their time? Lots of time?

But the scene in the room told Imogen that this baby was coming now. Amy lay propped up against the pillows, her knees up around her shoulders and her legs open wide. Gibson knelt at the end of the bed, leaning over, his gloved hands probing Amy's privates. The sight made Imogen squirm but Amy seemed beyond caring.

'Have you called Ryan?' she panted.

'I will do, in a moment.' And what the hell was she going to say to him? He'd want to jump in the car immediately, but … would they take Amy to Kalgoorlie or to Perth? Imogen looked to Gibson. 'Is the baby coming now?'

'Looks that way,' he said, without even glancing in her direction.

Amy shrieked her way into another contraction that quickly became a long, guttural groan. 'I. Want. To. Push.'

Imogen dropped the towels on a nearby chair and then knelt down beside Amy. 'Do you need my hand again?' she asked. Anything not to have to watch Gibson do what he had to do.

'Thanks.' Amy took Imogen's hand and smiled.

Things went fast after that.

# Chapter Ten

Gibson had never delivered a baby before. If he'd thought it was even a remote possibility, he'd never have joined St John's as a volunteer officer in the first place, but all the trainers he ever listened to had professed that a woman in labour in a tiny outback town was a rarity. Most went to Perth, or a nearer large town, long before their due date. In fact, this type of emergency was so rare that, despite having monthly training sessions to keep their skills up-to-date, he'd never studied childbirth.

But here he was, just after seven o'clock on a Saturday night – when he'd normally be settling down on the couch with his TV remote – helping a total stranger give birth. Just his luck, he'd scored a woman who'd travelled *away* from the safety of a city hospital. Not that she was *that* near her due date – even he knew human babies incubated for forty weeks. She'd gone into labour a whole month early.

As Amy's perineum (a word he learnt from the on-call doctor) bulged during the contraction, he fought his rising panic and managed to say, 'I can see the top of the head.'

*A head!* If he weren't already kneeling, his legs might have collapsed underneath him. This baby had its own agenda, and that didn't include waiting for the Flying Doctor. Gibson was about to add midwife to his curriculum vitae.

'You can both do this,' came his mentor's voice from the phone's speaker. 'I want you to listen carefully and follow my instructions.'

'Will do,' he replied. This whole thing terrified him but he wasn't about to let it show. Although he'd never anticipated delivering a baby, once upon a time he had imagined being there for the birth of his child – but that was never going to happen now. Maybe he should be grateful he was getting the chance to get this close.

The doctor explained that he should encourage Amy to push during each contraction, but when the perineum started to really stretch, she'd need to pant to allow him to guide the baby's head out.

*Too easy.* Gibson gulped. 'Thanks, doc.'

With a series of instructions that went something like, 'Push, that's the way, Amy. Stop pushing, start panting. Pant, Amy, PANT,' he watched in wonder as the crown of the baby's head slowly grew in size and retreated less after each contraction finished.

Despite her shock at going into labour early, far from home and far from her husband, she did an amazing job. She didn't panic but concentrated on her panting and pushed whenever the listening doctor instructed. Her friends sat on either side of her, providing sips of water, hands to hold and a constant stream of encouragement, despite Amy ranting at them. But as the minutes passed and the contractions increased in strength and frequency, she started to tire.

'I can't do this anymore.' Exhausted, Amy fell back with a sob.

Gibson snapped his head up – she couldn't give up now – but

his gaze met Imogen's instead. She smiled encouragingly, her eyes supporting him even though he guessed she was as terrified as him. Because of her smile, he had the confidence to continue.

'Yes, you can,' he said, looking to Amy. 'You're almost there. I reckon with the next contraction you might have your baby.' He sounded far more confident than he felt, but fortunately Amy didn't know that and neither, he hoped, did Jenna nor Imogen.

Beside Gibson, Dave changed his gloves again and readied towels and blankets for the newborn. Under the doctor's guidance, Gibson pressed two fingers onto the baby's head to keep it in the right position. He was trying to think logically and calmly, focusing on the doctor's initial words that births that happened this fast were usually easy and complication free. Oh man, he hoped so. They had one chance and one chance only to do this thing right.

Like an Amazonian superstar, Amy pushed even harder.

The baby's head was born, and a moment later it turned. As instructed, Gibson carefully ran his fingers around the baby's neck to check the cord wasn't wrapped around it. At his touch, the red-faced, black-haired baby cried, and goosebumps flooded his skin. He had to swallow the lump in his throat to say, 'We're almost there. One more big push.'

And Amy gave it everything. As she pushed, Gibson gently guided the top shoulder out and then lifted the baby so the bottom shoulder could be delivered. The next moment, on a gush of fluid, the rest of the baby slithered out into his grasp. Big, dark-blue eyes gazed up at him as the goosebumps on his skin multiplied. *A new life.* His throat felt tight and he had to blink a couple of times before he could speak.

'It's a boy.'

With a great deal of care, he laid Amy's son on her belly.

'Is he okay?' Amy asked anxiously.

'Is he?' came the doctor's voice on the speaker.

Gibson had almost forgotten her presence, so intent was he on examining his patient. 'Yes, his breathing is excellent. His colour's good. He's amazing.' His voice choked on the last word.

'Excellent. Clamp and cut the umbilical cord when you're ready, and then wrap him to keep him warm,' the doctor instructed, her voice filled with relief.

Dave, ready with more towels and everything they needed, passed Gibson the medical scissors and he took them, every cell in his body working to keep his hand steady. Wasn't this job usually given to the father? Pushing that thought aside, he applied the umbilical clamp and cut down on the surprisingly tough cord.

Following the doctor's instructions, he lifted the little dude slightly and placed him gently on Amy's chest, where she'd pushed her t-shirt up to get precious skin-to-skin contact with her child. As he draped a towel over the baby to keep him warm, the expression on Amy's face was priceless. She gazed down at her little man, counted his fingers and toes and explored his simple perfection.

The lump in Gibson's throat grew to become massive and he quickly changed his gloves, needing the distraction of the simple task.

For the last few minutes, Imogen had been unobtrusively snapping photos with her phone. Shots that would, without a doubt, become favourites in the family album. Jenna now plucked her own phone out of her pocket and dialled. Within moments Amy was speaking tearfully to her husband. While Dave monitored mother and baby, the doctor talked Gibson through delivering the placenta.

And when it was all over, Comms informed them that a plane had been dispatched and would be landing within half an hour. At this news, Gibson breathed a sigh of relief. It had been a hell of a ride so far, but he would be more than glad to hand over to the professionals. Amy and her baby seemed in good health, but he couldn't forget the fact they were dealing with a premmie.

Gibson didn't like to hurry Amy, who looked so serene and

content snuggling her baby, but the Flying Doctors didn't like to wait. 'We've got to get you to the airstrip.'

\*\*\*

Gibson, Dave and Imogen stood side by side, watching the plane as it lifted off into the night sky. When it was nothing but a speck, Gibson sighed and tugged off his last set of gloves.

He couldn't believe it. He'd delivered a baby. Amy was the real hero here – she'd done all the hard work – but he was pretty damn chuffed. The rush of seeing that little face, of hearing his first cry, and knowing he'd had a part in it, was like nothing Gibson had ever experienced before. Keeping the smile off his face would be near impossible tonight. And why should he? This would go down as one of the best, most rewarding days in his life.

'Thanks for everything,' said Imogen.

He looked to her and grinned, the first time he'd let his guard down in her presence. 'Crazy day, hey?'

She laughed, smiling as she blew out air between her lips, making wisps of her thick fringe fly up. The simple gesture showcased her beauty and reminded him of all the reasons he should stay away.

'You can say that again,' she said. And then she reached out and rested her fingers against his arm. The touch – although barely there – was like brushing up against an electric fence. 'Please, come back to the pub and let me buy you guys a drink.'

She glanced at Dave as she made her offer, and her words included both officers, but Gibson felt as if they were just for him. And although he knew accepting would be dangerous, although he knew he shouldn't, he couldn't help himself.

'Thanks,' he found himself saying. 'That would be great.'

\*\*\*

Imogen couldn't believe it. Buzzing from the excitement of Amy's birth, she'd asked Gibson and Dave back to the pub because it seemed the right thing to do, but she never expected a positive reply. Not from Gibson, anyway. He'd even smiled.

She'd felt that smile as heat in every bone of her body, and guessed her happiness was evident in the form of rosy cheeks as well. Oh well, who cared? What was more amazing, more exciting, than watching one of your best friends give birth? And he'd been there.

With Jenna and Amy in the plane on their way to Perth, she wanted to celebrate with someone who'd seen it all happen. The sudden arrival of Amy's baby had been magical, miraculous even, and she thought – hoped – that now they'd shared something so special, Gibson might treat her differently. Perhaps he'd lose the distance and disdain and let her see the real him: the man she'd seen a glimpse of that night, the man Charlie adored.

'I'm afraid I've got an early start tomorrow,' said Dave. 'I'll have to pass.' He looked to Gibson. 'But you go. I'll drop you two at the pub and then clean and restock the van before I head home.'

'You sure?' Gibson looked as if he might be reconsidering his acceptance, and Imogen's heart stopped beating a moment. Which was stupid – she shouldn't give a damn if he changed his mind or not.

Dave nodded. 'Yeah, it's fine. You look like you could do with a drink.'

★★★

Imogen and Gibson stepped inside The Majestic to cheers and shrieks and the best welcoming party ever. Heeding her instructions, Pauli and Cal hadn't waited to serve their Mexican delights. Full of food, the volunteers were in high spirits, the country music was up loud again and the party was in full swing.

Pauli, her chef's hat slightly wonky on her head, greeted Gibson and Imogen at the door. 'Well? Are they okay?'

'They're on a plane to Perth right now. The baby's tiny, but in the competent hands of the Flying Doctors. I think they'll both be fine.'

Imogen tried to concentrate as a warm hand landed on her back, helping to guide her through the crowd towards the bar. Her spine fizzed with the sensation – a feeling she'd never expected to experience again. Without a doubt, the hand was Gibson's. She couldn't believe he was being so chivalrous towards her, but then again, she'd seen a very different side of him today, in the way he'd taken care of Amy. His gentleness and kindness had forced her to look at him in a different light.

Pauli waited until Imogen sat on a stool at the bar before she bombarded her with more questions. 'Well? What happened? I need details.'

'How about you get us a drink first?' Gibson said, his tone dry.

'Aye aye, captain,' Pauli fake-saluted and looked him up and down like she'd only just noticed he was there. More likely, his presence surprised her. But she turned and surveyed the choices anyway. 'What will you be having?' she called over her shoulder.

'Champagne,' Imogen cried, finally finding her voice. 'The most expensive stuff we have.'

Pauli smiled, selected a chilled bottle of Veuve Clicquot and waved it in the air. 'Will this do?'

Imogen nodded, unable to keep a grin from twisting her lips. About to tell them everything, she noticed something. 'Where's Charlie?'

Pauli scanned the room. 'Dammit. I sent him to collect glasses ages ago.' The tables stacked with empties told them he hadn't followed through on the task.

'I'll go.' Imogen slipped off her stool and scanned the room before starting down the corridor. She found him in her office, staring at the roster she'd pinned to the corkboard. 'Charlie?' she said from the doorway.

He turned. 'Hello love. Just checking my roster for this week.'

Imogen frowned and stepped inside. 'I printed you a copy to take home. You said you were going to stick it on your fridge.'

Ignoring this information, Charlie quickly turned grumpy. 'Where've you been, anyway? Cal and I have been run off our feet.'

'Gibson and I took Amy to the airstrip, remember? She had her baby.'

'Oh, yeah, of course.' He scratched the side of his head and sighed. 'Think I'm just a little tired. How is she? How's the little one?'

'It's been a long day,' Imogen said. *Understatement of the year.* 'Let's go get a drink and I'll fill you in.' She led Charlie back to the bar and was careful not to let him see when she mouthed at Pauli not to mention the glass thing.

Catching on, Pauli set out five champagne flutes, filled each one with the fancy champagne and called Cal over. A number of guys pulled their stools closer to hear the gossip.

'Well?' Pauli asked for the third time in as many minutes. 'The full story? I thought first babies were supposed to take days of labour.'

Everyone laughed. Imogen looked to Gibson, waiting for him to tell his story, but he just shrugged one shoulder, lifted his glass to his lips and, without waiting for a toast, took a sip.

'Apparently, not always. It was so fast, my head spun.' Imogen touched a hand to her forehead in recollection. 'And it was magical. I've never seen a more beautiful, healthy, *loud* baby boy.'

'Aww!' Cal and Pauli exclaimed as one.

Pauli quickly wiped her eyes, but not before Imogen noticed the glisten of water. Her chef wasn't as tough as she liked everyone to believe. 'I wish we could have been there too.'

'It was amazing,' Imogen continued, fingering the stem of her champagne glass. 'Gibson was amazing.'

All eyes turned to him.

Charlie glowed. 'You delivered a baby?'

Gibson shrugged again. 'It isn't really as difficult as it looks.' His eyes gleamed wickedly as he looked to Imogen. 'Amy should take most of the credit.'

It was the most natural thing in the world to elbow him good-naturedly in the side. And Imogen did.

He looked surprised. Clutching his side, he feigned pain and then grinned back at her. 'So, you tell the story then.'

'Amy did do the hard stuff,' Imogen conceded, 'but Gibson supported and encouraged her. He was incredible.' She didn't look at him when she said this, not wanting him to see the newfound respect and admiration in her eyes. She didn't want his head to swell any larger than it already had. 'Here, do you want to see pics?'

'Yes please!'

As Cal and Pauli leaned over her phone and Imogen clicked through baby photos, Charlie and Gibson struck up conversation and the lingering blokes returned to their beers. In Imogen's experience, men could only look at baby photos for so long, whereas women – even those who swore they'd *never* be clucky, like Pauli – could look for hours. Cal and Pauli served a couple of blokes in between, but it seemed like they'd been scrolling through the shots for hours when Imogen's phone rang in her hand.

'Jenna!'

'Ugh, I feel terrible,' came Jenna's voice seconds later. 'I'm never riding in a small plane again. How are things there? Tell Guy I'm sorry to have run off on him like that.'

Imogen glanced across the room to where Guy was playing pool. 'Will do. How are Amy and the baby? Has Ryan seen him?'

'Yes. But only briefly. He's got to spend the night in the neonatal ward because he has low blood sugar and low body temp.'

'Oh no.' The anxiety Imogen had experienced when Amy was first in labour returned. 'Is he going to be okay?'

'Oh, yes, fine,' Jenna rushed. 'They're feeding him through a tube for now to get him strong, but apparently he's one of the healthiest babies in there. He's a fighter.'

'Thank God.' Imogen hated being so far away. 'Does he have a name yet?'

'They're discussing possibilities. Personally, I thought they'd have a better idea by now. I mean, I know he's early but surely they have *some* preferences. Anyway, I wanted to ask you about my car. I'm going to need it on Monday, and obviously I can't just get a cab out to Gibson's Find to pick it up…'

'I'll drive it,' Imogen decided there and then. 'There's a bus from Perth tomorrow afternoon, so I'll catch that back.' She'd have to cancel the second half of the slab party, but on the scale of importance, friends' babies came before renovations. There'd be other weekends, or maybe she'd just hire tradies to finish the job.

'Sorry,' Jenna said. 'If there was any other way… It's just I really need my car for work.'

'I know you do. It's fine. I want to have a cuddle with the baby before he gets too big, anyway. Will that be possible?'

'I'm not sure,' Jenna replied. 'I guess it depends how he goes overnight. At the moment, only Amy and Ryan are allowed to see him.'

'Oh.' Imogen couldn't hide her disappointment. 'Never mind, I want to see Amy and you, anyway. Our weekend together was cut short.'

'For the bestest ever reason.'

'Of course, but still. How about I meet you at the hospital tomorrow about twelve to give you your keys and visit Amy?' Imogen asked.

'Sounds like a plan.' Jenna yawned. 'Sorry Im, I'm going to have to go. I'm exhausted. I'll see you tomorrow.'

'Can't wait. I doubt I'll be able to sleep tonight. See ya.'

Imogen ended the call and looked up to find Cal, Pauli, Gibson, Guy and Charlie all gathered around, staring at her, wide-eyed and open-mouthed. It seemed she wasn't the only one invested in Amy and the baby now, and that warmed the cockles of her heart. After relaying everything that Jenna had said, Imogen glanced at the clock and realised it was past closing time. She rang the closing bell to get the boys' attention.

'Thank you so much everyone. It's been one hell of a day and I really appreciate all you've done for me. Unfortunately, I'm going to have to postpone tomorrow's work as I have to head to Perth to be with my friend and her baby.'

Whoops and cheers erupted around the room and then people started standing to leave. Imogen didn't expect hugs from each and every attendee, but she welcomed them nevertheless, glowing in the warm congratulations offered by her new friends. When the men had left, only Gibson and her staff remained. He'd stayed to see Charlie home but mucked in with the rest of them, collecting glasses, wiping tables and even taking out the rubbish.

They'd barely spoken since entering the pub, so it surprised her when he grabbed her elbow as she passed him in the saloon. 'Do you have a moment?'

She nodded, wondering what he could possibly want to say to her and trying to ignore the delicious vibrations ricocheting up her arm.

'I'm going to visit my folks in the city tomorrow – Sunday lunch once a month.' He rolled his eyes before continuing. 'Seems silly for you to catch the bus when I'll be driving back here anyway.' He shrugged. 'What do you say? Want to catch a lift back with me?'

# Chapter Eleven

Gibson woke early. Despite the late night, he leapt from his bed with more enthusiasm than he had in a long time. But it wasn't the prospect of driving to Perth and having lunch with his family that put a spring in his step and a smile on his lips. It was the adrenalin still pumping through his veins after yesterday's events. He'd delivered a baby!

Like a stamp at the front of his brain, the look on that baby's face went with him as he downed coffee, showered, brushed his teeth and made sure Jack and Jill had food and water for the day. That magic expression, at being plucked from the womb and thrust into a brand new world, stayed with him as he began his journey. Was it shock? Horror? Excitement? Amy's baby had his whole life in front of him, everything new and waiting to be discovered. So much potential.

Gibson found himself wanting everything for that child, and he felt a weird yearning to protect it. He was glad he'd arranged to collect Imogen from the hospital, and couldn't wait for lunch to be over so he could go and see the baby.

As he neared Perth and his parents' house, thoughts of the baby took a back seat as thoughts of Charlie and his mum's disagreement took precedence. Sure enough, the moment his mother opened the front door, she started.

'Gibson!' A breath of pause, not to smile at him but to summon more irritation. 'Where's Charlie?'

'Nice to see you too, Mum.' He leaned forward and kissed her on the cheek before waving at his dad, who stood behind. Debbie wore her Sunday best, whereas Harry wore a chambray shirt, jeans and boots. You could take the man away from the farm but you couldn't take the farm out of the man. 'Are Paris and the kids here yet?' he asked. He'd never spent much time with his niece and nephew, but he liked them, and today, playing *anything* with them would be better than sitting with the adults.

'They couldn't come,' Debbie sighed. 'There's a family function on at Steve's work.' The scowl on her lips told Gibson her exact opinion of this so-called excuse.

Normally their absence wouldn't bother Gibson, but today was the first lunch he'd been to since his mother had raised concerns about Charlie's mental health. The first lunch he'd been to without Charlie. Without grandkids or Paris' chattering to distract her, his mum would not be deterred from discussions of Charlie. She could be a very persistent woman when she wanted to be.

Unless… He stepped inside the house and before she could start up again, he said, 'You'll never guess what I did yesterday.'

His dad's eyes lit up and he closed the door behind them. 'Bought a new tractor?'

'Sorry Dad, this isn't farming related.' He paused for anticipation. 'I delivered a baby.'

'You what?' His mum steadied herself against the hall table.

Gibson caught her arm. 'Why don't we go through, get a drink and I'll tell you all about it?'

Seemingly speechless, Debbie let herself be led into the kitchen-dining room, where she flicked on the kettle and then placed three mugs on the bench in front of her. Gibson took the milk from its little jug in the fridge, handed it to his mother and then sat at the table with his dad.

'Whose baby?' came his mum's first question.

He took a breath, and then began the tale of what Amy was doing in Gibson's Find and how he'd come to deliver her baby. At the end of his story, he got out his phone and showed his parents a picture he'd snapped of Amy and the child not long after the delivery.

'Oh, he's so sweet,' his mum cried, tears welling in her eyes. 'I remember when you and Paris were that big. What was it like? Delivering the dear little thing?'

As Debbie patted at her eyes with a tissue, Gibson struggled to find the right words. 'Incomparable to anything.' He couldn't help his massive grin. 'Amazing. I never imagined I'd ever do anything so meaningful.'

'Good on ya, son.' Harry, sitting beside Gibson, clapped his hand down on his shoulder in a show of masculine congratulations.

Debbie picked up her Royal Doulton cup (only the best for visitors and Sundays) and then put it back down. She stared at Gibson so he felt her eyes boring into him, forcing him to meet her gaze. 'I understand that it was special, but there's nothing like having your own child, you know, seeing your own baby born.'

Gibson tried not to flinch. *Would she ever let up?* He felt like Charlie. Ambushed. 'I can imagine, Mum.' He kept his voice light, but firm. 'But my focus is the farm; another relationship isn't on my agenda.'

She made a scathing tsk with her tongue. 'You can't stay in that big house all alone forever.'

That's exactly what he planned to do. 'I'm not thinking of forever right now, Mum.' Another lie. 'I know you think I've had long enough to get over Serena, but please just leave it. I don't want to fight about this. It's my business, not yours.'

'Suit yourself.' Clearly annoyed, Debbie pushed her chair back, abandoning her cup of tea as she yanked open the oven to check the roast. As usual, Gibson spied a chicken far too big for only three of them.

He smiled weakly at his dad and got a similar smile back. They both drank tea. When the cups were finished and Debbie was still fussing about – Gibson knew better than to volunteer catering assistance – Harry asked, 'This friend of the mother, the one that's bought The Majestic. What's she like?'

'Imogen?' All the words that came into his head he immediately dismissed as inappropriate. 'She seems all right. Hardworking. Charlie likes her and she says she wants to get involved in the community.'

Debbie couldn't resist joining the conversation. She paused in the task of whisking gravy over the hot plate. 'It doesn't sound right to me. A single girl managing such an establishment. What's she going to do if a six-foot gentleman gets rowdy one night?'

'He'd hardly be a gentleman if he gets rowdy, now, would he, Debs?' Harry commented.

Debbie shot him a practised glare. 'That's not the point, Harry.'

And the bizarre thing was that Gibson wanted to stick up for Imogen, despite the fact that he was guilty of exactly the same thoughts. He smothered this strange urge. 'I don't know, Mum. None of my business.'

'Well, of course it's your business. Charlie's working there and it's your local watering hole. If things go bad, you'll be reeled in to it all. Case in point: whose friend's baby did you have to deliver yesterday?'

'Mum!' Gibson scoffed at the absurdity of her argument. He didn't even know why they were having this conversation. Why she cared.

'Debbie. Is the lunch ready? Let's eat,' Harry suggested in a rare moment of authority.

'Yes, let's.' Gibson couldn't agree more. The quicker he downed lunch, the quicker he could make his excuses and leave the stress-zone. As if he didn't have enough on his plate right now.

As usual, lunch was superb. Debbie still cooked like it was Christmas every Sunday: a roast meat that varied depending on what the butcher had on special, a ridiculous assortment of veggies, stuffing *and* Yorkshire pudding. Gibson didn't know anyone who made Yorkshire pudding like his mother – hell, he hardly knew anyone who made Yorkshire pudding – which meant his tastebuds always rejoiced in the monthly lunch, even if his blood pressure didn't.

Somehow, they managed small talk while they ate. Harry mentioned he was thinking of putting in a fish pond out the front. Debbie said she'd joined a quilting club and was going to make a special quilt for each of her grandchildren. She stared pointedly at Gibson, but he refused to take the bait.

Then, when lunch was over, the table cleared and a massive apple crumble was about to be served, Harry turned the conversation to farming. 'What are your plans for this year, son? Does Charlie get out to the farm much?' Seconds after mentioning his father, Harry cringed, and rightly so. Debbie grabbed back on to the topic like a puppy with a new chew toy.

'Yes. How is Charlie? I know you think I was overreacting last time I was there, but I know what I saw. Your father was with you out at the farm most of the time, so he didn't notice how scatter-brained Charlie has become. I'm seriously worried.'

Gibson's jaw tightened and he mentally counted to five before responding. 'I know, Mum, and I've already said I'll keep an eye on him. But you didn't expect him to welcome your announcement that you thought he had Alzheimer's, did you?'

Debbie slapped a serving of apple crumble into a bowl and pushed it towards Gibson. 'I've never seen any point in beating around the bush.'

Harry didn't say a word, just scooped a spoonful of dessert into his mouth and chewed. Suddenly Gibson didn't feel like his favourite pudding. He put down his dessert fork. 'Look, Mum. We'll have to agree to disagree about this. But I promise you, I'll look out for Charlie. Just go easy on him, please.'

Debbie sighed. 'Okay. I don't want to be right, you know.'

Gibson wished he could believe her. But instead he chose to change the subject. 'Tell me more about these quilts.'

The next half hour or so passed with as much tension as if Charlie were actually in the room with them. Gibson listened to his mum explain in minute detail the first quilt she was making, and all the while he sat there seething at the fact his father hadn't said a word in Charlie's defence.

At least there was one good thing about never being in a relationship again – he'd never be forced to leave the land he loved like his father had been.

***

Imogen met Jenna in front of King Edward Memorial Hospital for Women just before midday. Wearing large black sunglasses, skinny jeans and a silky tee accessorised with heeled sandals and a matching tote bag that looked to have the latest issue of *Marie Claire* poking out the top, Jenna looked like she'd just stepped off a Paris catwalk. In contrast, Imogen looked exactly like she'd spent the last three and a half hours sitting in a car, fretting about what the hell she was going to talk about during the drive home with Gibson Black. She could almost feel the worry lines etched into her forehead.

'Hey there,' she tried to inject enthusiasm into her voice, waving as Jenna closed the gap between them.

'I'm so glad to see you,' Jenna said, embracing Imogen in a hug. 'We need to talk. Visiting hours aren't for a while, so why don't we grab some lunch. I know a cafe round the corner.'

Jenna seemed more effusive than she should have been, considering that Imogen had all but accused her of being a slut yesterday. She wasn't normally one to hold a grudge, but still.

'Jenna,' Imogen began as they pounded the pavement towards the cafe precinct, 'I'm sorry about yesterday. I should never have said those things about you and Guy, it's just—'

Jenna shook her head. 'It's forgotten. And you're probably right, but with all that testosterone in one room and that gorgeous man practically begging me to make him smile, I couldn't help myself.'

'I totally understand. How do you think it is being surrounded by it *all* the time?' Imogen asked before she could censor her words.

'Tempting?' Jenna suggested, slowing down and wiggling her eyebrows suggestively. 'I imagine that's why you asked me for the vibrator?'

'Shh, someone might hear you,' Imogen hissed, quickly scanning the area and pulling Jenna onwards. 'And that request was made in a moment of insanity.'

Jenna laughed. 'They're not illegal, you know. Neither is being attracted to someone other than Jamie.'

Imogen's chest tightened. 'I'm not looking for another relationship. When I made my marriage vows, I meant them.'

Jenna stopped outside a cafe but didn't make to go inside. Instead, she turned to Imogen and took both her hands, shaking them slightly as she stared into her friend's eyes. 'You said, till death do us part, not till you die too.'

'I don't know.' Imogen sighed, anger rearing its head within her. Anger at Jamie – a hero to the world, but the man who ruined her life by leaving her way too early. She believed in one true love, in fate and living happily ever after. If Jamie had been The One – and she was damn certain he had – then how could she possibly fall in love with anyone else?

As if reading her mind, Jenna said, 'You know you don't have to love someone to have fun with them. This is the twenty-first century, people sleep together without a contract in place.' She shrugged as she pushed her hand against the cafe door. 'I'm just saying, it's something to think about.'

And as they ordered a meal and wine (hey, she wasn't driving again), Imogen thought about precious little else. But she wasn't like Jenna. She couldn't get her head around having sex with someone simply to scratch an itch. She was glad when the waiter took away their menus and Jenna pulled out the *Marie Claire*. 'Business time,' Jenna said, opening the magazine at a bookmarked page.

Imogen raised one eyebrow and peered down at the page. Jenna swivelled the mag around so Imogen could read the heading: 'Stuck in a Man Drought? Look no further than rural Australia's little reservoirs of untapped men!' She began reading but Jenna launched into conversation before she'd even finished the first paragraph.

'I was thinking about all those lovely, gorgeous, *horny* men you have in your pub when I woke up this morning. And then over my coffee, I flicked to this article. It must be fate. See,' she tapped a beautifully manicured nail in the middle of the page. 'You could run one of these weekends in Gibson's Find, at The Majestic.'

Imogen glanced up at Jenna and then back down to the article.

Jenna took this as a cue to keep talking. 'I'm more than happy to do my bit for the boys in the bush, but there's only so much one girl can do. I reckon that barmaid and chef of yours may have eyes for each other rather than the patrons, so I was thinking perhaps we should share.'

Giggling inwardly at Jenna's fervour, Imogen held up her hand. 'Can you just let me finish reading?'

The journalist had written about a number of Aussie towns that could have been Gibson's Find – small pockets where men vastly outnumbered women; places where, when farmers talked about drought, they weren't just referring to the weather. And then the focus switched to Australia's cities, where women in their late twenties and early thirties lamented the shortage of available men. One of the women they interviewed said she was 'on the lookout for a country bloke with a big heart and a big you-know-what.' She claimed that nice guys in the city were few and far between, that most of them were full of airs and graces and believed themselves God's gift, spending more money on skincare and fashion than women did.

As if to prove the magazine's point, a guy in a suit strolled by and bumped into Jenna and Imogen's table. He didn't bother to apologise, apparently too consumed with something on his smart phone.

Imogen thought of the men in her pub who probably didn't even own a suit, who spent their days in Stubbies shorts and Blundstone boots, but would fall over themselves to apologise if they even nudged a woman by accident. She thought of Gibson, whose daily skincare routine probably extended as far as a block of soap, a bit of warm water and his hairbrush. A razor on the days he had the time or inclination to shave. But who just happened to be more attractive than all the men in this cafe.

She looked back at the page and focused on finishing the article. A woman in a Victorian town had started running weekend events to bring city chicks to the outback to meet potential husbands – like *The Farmer Wants a Wife* but without the television cameras.

Imogen could see the value, not only for her male and horny (as Jenna put it) patrons, but also for her as a businesswoman. This kind of program didn't seem too difficult, but it had the potential to increase her income *and* to revive a dying town. There was merit in every angle she considered.

And perhaps if she focused more on other people's relationships, she wouldn't have time to ponder the lack of intimacy and companionship in her own life. She looked back up at Jenna as the waiter delivered two massive chicken caesar salads. 'I love it. Would you help me? You've got loads more experience organising things like this.'

'Will I help you?' Jenna practically shrieked. She lifted her wine glass, indicating Imogen should do the same with hers. 'I'm counting on being your right-hand gal. Besides, I need a good excuse to see Guy again, and this one seems as perfect as any.'

Both smiling, they toasted their plan and then dug into their salads. They were eager to get to Amy, see the baby and tell her their grand idea.

\*\*\*

Five minutes before visiting hours began, Imogen and Jenna were outside the postnatal ward, giggling with excitement.

Ryan met the girls at the door of Amy's room and the look on his face plucked at Imogen's heartstrings. 'Proud Dad' didn't even begin to cover it. He lifted his index finger to his lips. 'Come on in ladies, but keep the noise down. Gibson's sleeping.'

'Gibson?' Imogen looked past Ryan to Amy, who was lying on the bed cradling the baby in the nook of her arm, looking as pleased as her husband.

'Uh-huh,' Amy nodded, smiling as she gestured to the plastic visitor chair. 'Come sit.'

After the first round of oohing and ahhing and careful hugs so as not to crush the baby, Imogen perched on the edge of her very uncomfortable chair and asked again, 'Gibson? You're naming the baby after *him*?'

'Of course.' Amy laughed as if this were the most ridiculous question ever.

Ryan sat beside her on the bed and gently caressed the baby's head. 'Seems more than appropriate. Amy told me he was a rock during the birth. I can't wait to shake the guy's hand and buy him a drink. We'll be heading your way for a weekend as soon as possible.'

'You won't have to wait that long,' Jenna piped up from her spot at the foot of the bed. 'He's picking Imogen up in about an hour.'

'Oh, is he?' Amy acted as if Jenna had just announced Hugh Jackman's imminent arrival. She even made to straighten her wonky nightgown.

'Yes,' Imogen said brusquely. She'd managed not to think about him during lunch, but now the anxiety barrelled back with a vengeance. 'He happened to be coming to Perth today, so it made sense to get a lift with him, rather than take the bus. I'll get home quicker that way.'

Amy, Ryan and Jenna all raised their eyebrows and Imogen realised she'd been too effusive in her reasoning. Why did she feel she had to explain a perfectly logical, reasonable and innocent lift?

'Anyway,' she adopted a let's-move-on tone, 'When do I get a cuddle with the little guy?'

Happy to have the conversation back on her child, Amy beamed. 'You can take him now, if you like, but you have to disinfect your hands with that lotion first.' She pointed to a pump bottle attached to the wall. After Imogen had rubbed the disinfectant all over her hands and halfway up her arms, she sat back down.

Ryan lifted the baby from Amy's arms and carried him round the bed like he was bearing the Crown Jewels, before laying him in Imogen's waiting arms. 'We're lucky he's able to come out of the neonatal nursery during the day. He's doing really well but not breastfeeding properly, so they have to top him up by tube after each feed. But it's just so wonderful for him to be with us some of the time.'

Imogen's arms shook as she adjusted Gibson (she wasn't sure she'd ever get used to *that* name belonging to *this* baby) in her arms. 'Should I even be holding him?'

'Yes,' Amy replied. 'I want you to.'

At the sound of his mother's voice, Gibson made a sweet noise in his sleep and wriggled as if positioning himself comfortably. Everyone laughed at his antics and Imogen stared down, taking in every tiny detail. One hand had escaped the muslin cloth he was tightly wrapped in, and she gently counted each miniscule finger. Miniscule but perfect. A red smudge – the baby's stork mark – rested between his brows, but she resisted the urge to touch it, not wanting to move a muscle in case she woke him and broke the moment.

*This was it.* This was as close as she was ever going to get to a newborn of her own. Before the accident, she and Jamie had been trying for a baby for a couple of months – still enjoying the process, not yet at the stage where they worried they might not be able to conceive – and the day he died she'd been waiting for her period. Desperately hoping and praying it wouldn't come. When a couple of his colleagues and a police officer arrived at her house and delivered the dreadful news that Jamie wouldn't be coming home, being pregnant – having his baby – became even more important. The arrival of her period only hours later had been like a double whammy of grief.

Two of her most precious dreams had died that day: the dream of spending the rest of her life with Jamie and the dream of becoming a mother, of having a family. Moving to the country and buying the pub had been a symbol of moving on and making new plans, new dreams, but holding little Gibson now brought all the emotion and devastation of her loss flooding back. As if sensing her sadness, he twisted in her arms, opened his eyes, looked up into her watery ones and let out a wail. Less than a day old and already he only had eyes for his mum.

Like a seasoned mother, Amy tore her concentration from the conversation and held out her arms. 'He's hungry. I need to feed him.' She pressed the buzzer beside the bed and called for a nurse.

'Of course.' Imogen checked her hold was firm and then stood to pass him over. Amy lifted her top and nuzzled the baby close against her chest. Imogen watched as Gibson moved his head, rooting around for his afternoon tea. He found the milk tap, attached himself and within seconds let out tiny satisfied mewls.

It was beautiful, but the emotion of watching her best friend doing something so natural, something she herself would never have the chance to do, made her chest physically ache.

A knock at the door interrupted her melancholic thoughts. She looked up to see Gibson (the big one) standing in the doorway and her chest ached in an altogether different manner. At the sight of him her bones turned to mush. Wearing snug-fitting, faded jeans and a pale-blue shirt that had the crisp, fine quality that only comes from an extremely high thread count weave, he looked like an advertisement for enhanced virility, and she felt the effect in her loins. He looked straight at Amy and his namesake and grinned, evoking a nasty bout of jealousy from Imogen. The feeling gave her the grumps worse than she already had. What kind of person begrudged a baby attention?

'Congratulations,' Gibson said, leaning over the bed and kissing Amy on the cheek. 'I didn't really get the chance to say that yesterday.' He leaned down towards the baby, and then snapped back to a stand as if he'd been slapped. 'Oh God, sorry, I didn't realise.'

A gorgeous flush came over his face as it dawned on him he'd just been peering at a naked breast.

Amy giggled, shifting her bundle slightly. 'It's alright; you've already seen more of me than anyone aside from my husband, so there's no need to be embarrassed.'

Gibson let out a relieved sigh and then turned to Ryan. He held out his hand. 'You must be the father.'

'G'day mate.' Ryan shook Gibson's hand and then pulled him into a hug. 'I can't thank you enough for everything you did. Lord knows what would have happened if you weren't there. Amy's been singing your praises all morning.'

Gibson looked a little uncomfortable in the embrace, but he accepted it and Ryan's thanks gracefully. 'You're welcome,' he said, stepping back. 'I'm so relieved the little guy is okay.'

'He's going to be grand.' Ryan beamed at the baby. 'My only regret is I wasn't there to welcome him into the world, but I'm glad they were both in good hands. And thanks for picking up Imogen too. I hope you didn't have to travel down especially.'

'Nah, I had to see my parents anyway.'

'They live in Perth, then?'

Gibson nodded. 'Yeah, moved here a few years back.'

'But they were farmers before?'

Imogen stilled at Ryan's question. He'd always been such an open and friendly guy – in direct opposition to Gibson – but now his questions sounded prying. To her surprise, Gibson didn't appear to notice.

'Yes.' He leaned back against the wall as if settling in for a long conversation. 'My farm has been in Dad's family for a couple of generations, but Mum is a city girl. She's glad to be back amongst the shops and the restaurants.'

Ryan chuckled. 'Must be great being your own boss, working the land. I love working outdoors, but it's not quite the same in the city.'

'Guess not.' There was a slight pause, then Gibson added, 'Next time you visit Imogen, you're more than welcome to come out to my farm and have a look around.'

'Really?'

Imogen resisted rolling her eyes – you'd think Gibson had just offered to *give* Ryan his property. The thought immediately irritated her. Why did she become uncharacteristically narky whenever Gibson was around? As she tapped her feet against the linoleum, it slowly dawned on her that perhaps Gibson wasn't a grumpy, rude person all the time, but only when it came to her. There was no mention of her joining Gibson and the new parents when they visited his farm, and she felt the snub deeply.

Baby Gibson tired quickly, and the neonatal nurse took him away to finish feeding by tube. A tear trickled down Amy's cheek as they all watched Gibson go.

'Do you want to go with him?' Ryan asked, taking her hand.

Amy sniffed. 'No, I'm okay. I want to chat with these guys and I know he's in good hands.' She took a moment to blow her nose, then tucked her hair behind her ears and smiled at her visitors. She focused on Imogen. 'I'm sorry for ruining your renovation weekend.'

Imogen waved her apology away. 'Don't be silly. There'll be plenty of time for fixing up the pub later.'

After that, the conversation did the rounds of babies, farms and day jobs. An orderly came in to leave Amy her menu choices for the following day and everyone helped her make decisions about what to order. A croissant-versus-porridge debate erupted and the croissants won. About an hour later, when Amy started to get restless, Imogen suggested it was time for them to leave.

'You must want to get back to Gibson,' she said, leaning over the bed to give Amy a hug and a kiss. 'Congratulations again. He's perfect.'

'Thank you,' Amy whispered, her voice once again choked with emotion.

Jenna and Gibson offered their goodbyes and before Imogen knew it, they were all heading for the hospital elevators. In a matter of minutes Jenna would step into her Mini Cooper, leaving Imogen and Gibson alone.

Imogen could hear her heart pounding in her ears. She hated uncomfortable silences, and if their conversational efforts so far were anything to go by, this would be a very long three and a half hours. She should have made a mental inventory of things to talk about. The baby? His visit to his parents? Um…

'Well, this is me.' Jenna slowed in front of her silver car. 'Thanks for driving it back, Immy.'

*Already?* Imogen did a double take. She must have been in some kind of trance, for she couldn't recall even leaving the hospital. 'No worries,' she managed above the ridiculous nerves that were churning up her insides. She hugged her friend, all the while reminding herself that this wasn't a date, it was a car pool. If the silence got awkward, she could read the magazine Jenna had lent her.

'Bye Gibson. Nice meeting you again.' Jenna leaned forward and pecked him on the cheek. Imogen wondered what it would feel like to brush *her* lips up against his skin. And then she wanted to scream. Why couldn't she control these unwelcome thoughts?

'You too,' Gibson replied, his voice warm and good-natured. That figured. Jenna had all the guys eating from the palm of her hand. 'I guess I might see you round.'

'Bye Jenna,' Imogen said firmly. She didn't want to hang around and watch Jenna work her magic with yet another male. Especially the unworkable Gibson. 'We've got a long drive ahead, we should get going. I'll call you soon about our plans.'

Jenna winked. 'Can't wait.'

Imogen turned to Gibson and said, a little too eagerly, 'Right, let's go.'

'Sure,' he replied.

Together they walked to his ute, which was parked only a short distance away. Gibson looked relieved when he opened the door for her, no doubt as eager as she was to get the uncomfortable journey over.

# Chapter Twelve

'That was a heck of a weekend,' Gibson said as he and Imogen clicked their seatbelts into place. 'Probably not exactly as you'd planned, though.' He added a chuckle for good measure.

Although not much of a chatterbox at the best of times, he was determined to make conversation with the publican over the next few hours. He wished he hadn't offered to drive her, but Charlie had known about the visit to his parents in Perth and his granddad would never have forgiven him if he hadn't at least offered. Charlie was always yabbering on about chivalry and the need to be a gentleman.

Glancing in the rear-view mirror, he saw her lush lips twist into a smile as she relaxed into the passenger seat. 'And I bet delivering a baby wasn't on your to do list either,' she retorted.

'Not this weekend,' he said as he turned the key in the ignition, 'but at least now I can tick it off my bucket list.'

'Satisfying.' She shuffled in her seat to face him. He kept his focus forward as he navigated them out of the busy hospital car park and onto the even busier road. 'Do you really have a bucket list?' she asked.

He shrugged. 'Sure, doesn't everyone?'

'I've never really thought about it,' she admitted. Then, 'Delivering a baby wasn't really on yours, was it?'

'No. But it was a thrill, and now I've done it, I think it's something everyone should experience.'

'Like having kids,' she mused. He thought he detected a hint of sadness in her voice. 'Typical bucket list stuff, really.'

'Actually, that's not on mine,' he admitted. Of course, he wouldn't tell her that he'd rewritten his list (metaphorically speaking) the day Serena had packed her bags. He turned onto the highway that would take them out of the city and home.

'Do you mind if I open a window and turn off the air-con?' she asked. 'I sometimes get carsick and need fresh air.'

'Sure.'

Imogen pressed the button and lowered the automatic windows; he did his to match. She gasped in some air, then flicked her hair back and stared out the window. He didn't know if he was imagining things but she seemed intent on not meeting his gaze. Probably a good thing. Lord knew he didn't need the temptation he'd felt those few times he'd been close enough to look into her eyes.

'Shall we draft your bucket list?' he said, clutching at straws for something to fill the awkward silence.

'What?' She sounded amused.

'Hey, this is quite a drive and I'm distressed by the fact that you don't have a bucket list. You must be one of the only people I know who hasn't thought about this.'

'That's ridiculous,' she said, turning to look at him. 'You're the only person *I* know who's ever admitted to having one.' But he could tell by the tone in her voice she was coming around, probably already ticking over her innermost dreams and desires.

'You know you want to.'

She let out a derisive snort. 'Okay. I want to go fishing.'

His turn to laugh. 'That's it?'

'What's so funny?' she said, and he wondered if she'd whack him playfully again like she did last night at the pub.

He cleared his throat. 'I'm talking big ambitions here – stuff like, you want to sail the world solo, be the youngest Australian Prime Minister, learn to speak Japanese.'

'I'm sorry to disappoint, but fishing's number one.'

'You've really never been fishing before?' Although he hadn't fished for years, his memories of summer holidays – of the whole family heading down to Hopetoun, and Granddad and him spending all their mornings in the threadbare dinghy throwing lines – were as strong as ever. Once upon a time, he'd dreamt of taking his own family there for holidays.

Oblivious to his thoughts, she explained, 'I grew up in an all-girl family. Dad was mostly working but the time he did have off, he'd take us to the movies or to shows. Outdoor pursuits weren't really his thing.'

'But you want to?' He chomped down on the urge to offer to take her some time. The last thing he needed was a weekend away with a pretty girl. Not this pretty girl, anyway.

'Definitely.' She nodded. 'It'll probably bore me senseless – I'm not one for sitting still for long – but I'd like to be able to say I've done it.'

'Fair enough,' he said, 'what next?'

'Hmm…' She fiddled with a plain gold ring while she pondered. It looked a lot like a wedding band but she wore it on the wrong hand. 'Gamble in Vegas, skydive, learn to ride a motorbike, be an extra in a movie – preferably in Hollywood – go on a spontaneous road trip.' She stopped and bent forward to rummage in her handbag.

'What are you doing?'

'Well, now you've got me started, I'm on a roll. I need to write this stuff down.'

They spent the next hour brainstorming their bucket lists. Laughs were loud and long, and as the roads got wider, the houses became fewer and the paddocks less green. The tense time at his parents' place became a distant memory as they competed against each other over who could think up the most ludicrous ideas. Imogen wrote his list down too, which was a good thing, because he'd lied about actually having one. The first half of the journey flew by and Gibson found himself wanting to know more about her. These days, most women he came into contact with – usually at the odd party he attended in Perth – bored him stupid, reminding him far too much of Serena and their futile years together. But Imogen was different. Part of him was curious about the girl Granddad and all his mates couldn't get enough of. But part of him knew it wouldn't be wise to get any closer.

When they stopped midway at a servo for sustenance, he resisted the urge to ask if she wanted to take a break at the adjoining park and eat their hamburgers and chips in the fresh air. It wasn't wise to prolong the journey. She insisted on paying for his dinner since he'd gone out of his way to collect her from the hospital and had already forked out for the petrol.

'It's not that out of the way,' he said as they trekked back across the car park to his ute.

She turned and tossed him a sceptical glare. 'Didn't you say your parents live in Scarborough?'

'Yeah.' He nodded as he beeped his ute unlocked.

'I wasn't on your way.' She smiled, balancing her meal on top of the vehicle as she opened her door. He should have opened it for her. 'Not that I don't appreciate it. So, was there a special occasion today? Or… Oh, you said you visit them every month, don't you? Does Charlie ever go?'

They were in the car now, had clicked their seatbelts into position and he'd turned the ignition on, but before he could answer, she went on.

'I'm sorry. It's none of my business.' She plucked a chip from its bucket and took a bite.

Normally, he'd agree. He wouldn't normally talk about his family with anyone, but for some reason he didn't want her to feel uncomfortable. 'No, it's fine,' he said, turning onto the open road. With one hand he began unwrapping his burger. 'Charlie and Mum aren't seeing eye to eye at the moment. He usually comes with me every month, but not this time.'

'Here, give me that.' She leaned across and took his burger, unwrapping it and placing it on top of the paper, back on his lap, so he could more easily eat and drive. Her fingers brushed his groin when she returned the burger and he almost leapt out of his chair. Seemingly oblivious to his reaction, she continued, 'Do your parents ever come back to the farm? To Gibson's Find?'

He was silent, still recovering from the accidental encounter with her fingers, but also pondering the answer to her question. He didn't want to paint his mum in too bad a light – she was how she was. She'd lasted on the land more than twenty years longer than Serena, and when it came to Charlie, she only had his best interests at heart, or so she thought. But her visits were rare and the last one had created such a storm he almost wished she hadn't bothered. Imogen read his silence as reluctance.

'I'm sorry, too many questions. Jamie always said I should have been a journalist.'

'Who's Jamie?'

'My husband.' Her voice cracked slightly on the confession. 'Charlie didn't tell you?'

*Whoa.* He was silent again, turning over the idea that she too had a dud marriage under her belt. 'No,' he replied eventually. 'Are you still married?'

'No.'

So much sadness dwelled within that one word. So much that he felt uncharacteristically compelled to share his disastrous divorce with her. He hadn't thought they had anything in common but it looked like he'd been wrong.

'He's dead,' she uttered, so quietly he almost missed it.

But he couldn't miss the vibe that hung in the air. Gone was the easygoing mood of their journey so far. *He's dead!* And what the hell should he say to that? 'Sorry' didn't seem to cut it, but he *was* sorry. Serena hadn't died, she'd left. He couldn't imagine losing a partner when you thought you still had the rest of your lives together.

'You don't know what to say, do you?'

'No,' he admitted.

'It's okay,' she said, 'I've heard a number of variations but none of them help ease the pain. It's why I hadn't planned on sharing my past with anyone in Gibson's Find. I wanted a fresh slate.'

'I won't tell anyone.'

She chuckled lightly. 'But you still want to say sorry, don't you? I don't need your pity.'

'Hell, Imogen.' He overtook a beat-up Toyota that was treating the wide road like a narrow English lane. 'I wouldn't have a heart if I didn't feel something. How old are you? Twenty-five? That's too young to lose a husband.'

'I'm thirty,' she informed him. 'I was twenty-seven when he died but I don't think there's ever a right time to lose a partner. For whatever reason,' she added.

Whether she meant it that way or not, Gibson heard her underlying meaning loud and clear.

'Charlie told you, didn't he?'

'He may have mentioned something in conversation.'

Gibson snorted. 'So how did Jamie die? Or would you prefer not to talk about it, like I'd much prefer not to talk about my ex?'

'I don't mind talking about it. It hurts but it's getting easier every day.' She took a sip of her Coke and sucked in a breath then puffed it out again as if psyching herself up. 'Jamie was a firefighter. He was based in Perth, but they often went further afield when a bad fire took hold in a country area where there weren't many local firies. Do you remember those terrible fires a few years back, down south, near Margaret River?'

'Yeah.' It had been all over the papers and the news.

'Jamie rescued a little girl from a burning two-storey house. They're still not entirely sure what happened. He threw the little girl down to his colleagues and was supposed to jump after her – they couldn't go back through the house, the ground floor was already consumed by flames. But he never jumped.' She paused a moment and he swore he heard her intake of breath. 'The floor collapsed, and by the time his mates got to him, it was too late.'

'I think I remember the headlines,' Gibson said, racking his mind for something worthwhile to say. 'They crowned him a hero.'

'He *was* a hero,' Imogen said forcefully. 'He always cared more about other people than he did himself. Everyone adored him.'

*Okay, okay*, thought Gibson, *I get it. Jamie the hero*. And then he realised how ludicrous his thoughts were. *What am I? Jealous?*

'I'm guessing that just because he died saving someone else, doesn't make it any easier for you.'

She sighed deeply. 'I think it might have made it even harder. For a while, I truly wished he hadn't gone into that house. I would rather some parents have lost their daughter than me go through the pain of losing my husband. What kind of person does that make me?'

'Normal,' he said, the agony in her voice making him uncomfortable.

'No,' she replied vehemently. 'It makes me someone I don't like. I've just seen my best friend give birth. I can barely begin to imagine the pain she and Ryan would go through if anything happened to little Gibson.'

'Would you change the past now if you could? Not stop the fire, but swap Jamie for the little girl.'

'No,' she said again, the fervour of her earlier reply gone. 'Of course not. That would have killed Jamie, anyway, if he'd failed at saving her.'

Neither of them said anything for a while. The burgers were finished, the chips and drinks consumed, another twenty or so kilometres travelled. When he couldn't stand the silence any longer, he asked her something they'd only touched briefly on before.

'So why a country pub? Why Gibson's Find?' He got that she wanted to move away, go some place where everyone didn't know her history, but it was a massive commitment.

She tapped on her empty Coke can, and in the rear-view mirror, he saw her smile again. 'Does it sound strange to admit that I've always had a thing for the outback watering hole? Dad's a cop, so we lived in a few country towns over the years, until we moved back to Perth so my older sister could start high school.'

'Really?' When he'd first seen her with Amy and Jenna, he'd never have guessed she'd spent time living rural.

'Yes,' she said, as if it were a stupid question. 'Not just WA either. But anyway, the pubs… Wherever we went, whether we stayed or were only travelling through, the first thing I always noticed was the hotel. I just loved them. Their wide verandahs, decorative awnings, Aussie beer signs, dusty exteriors, even their names. I've actually got a photo album full of the pubs in all the country towns I've ever lived in or visited.'

'You're kidding?'

'Nope. At one stage dad worried that I might turn into an alcoholic.'

'Still, it's a big step from taking photos of pubs to buying one. And in a place where you know no one.'

'That was part of the appeal,' she said. 'And I know what you're thinking: How did I afford it? What makes me think I have the wherewithal to make a success of it?'

All those questions had crossed his mind at some time in the past few weeks; right now they didn't seem as pertinent. 'You're doing a good job so far, it seems.'

'It seems?' She snorted. 'Was that almost a compliment, Gibson Black?'

His heart flipped over at the undeniable flirtation in her voice. And dammit, he wanted to flirt back. But that wouldn't be right.

'So, how did you afford it?' he asked instead. 'I know Cathy and Trev were hanging out to go, but it couldn't have been that cheap. And you've done a lot of work there already.'

'Jamie had good life insurance,' she explained. 'My parents tried to get me to invest it in shares, but where's the sense of adventure in that?'

'Nowhere,' he agreed, realising that her spark and sense of adventure were two of the things he liked about her. She wasn't afraid to get stuck in, to get dirty – he'd seen that yesterday when he turned up in the ambulance and saw all that she'd achieved in a day.

'As for experience,' she continued, 'I've worked in a flash bar in Subiaco almost since I finished high school, managing it for the last four years. I haven't got any theoretical training in hospitality or business, but what I don't know, I reckon I can learn. Any further questions?'

'I think I'm satisfied for now,' he said, trying not to smile.

'Good.' She adjusted herself in the seat, angling her face towards him. 'Because you were about to tell me about your family and why Charlie and your mum aren't on happy terms.'

'I was?'

'You were.'

'All right, all right.' They still had an hour's drive ahead of them, she'd spilt her heart, and he certainly didn't want to talk about Serena. 'About a month ago, Mum came for a visit and tried to convince Charlie to go with them to Perth.'

'To live?'

He nodded. 'Yes. And taking Charlie away from the bush would be like taking chocolate away from a woman with PMT. He told them exactly this, but Mum was adamant. She was staying with him for a few days and said she was worried about him living on his own, that she thought he was getting forgetful. She managed to convince Dad and Paris, and they all jumped on the bandwagon, trying to convince Charlie that he'd get a lot out of moving into one of those retirement homes. They totally ambushed him.'

'Ouch. No wonder he doesn't want to visit. I can't imagine anyone telling Charlie what to do.'

'No, and as you can imagine, he didn't take kindly to being told they thought he was past it. He was already forced off the farm and into a place in town when Mum wanted to turn the house into a B&B and use his room for guests. That idea didn't take seed, but he'd moved by the time she changed her mind. No way was he going to move again. After raising a son, and then sharing the house with a daughter-in-law and eventually two grandchildren, he realised he liked living alone. Then Mum mentioned Alzheimer's and he really lost it.'

'Oh.'

'What's "oh" supposed to mean?'

She hesitated a moment, bit down on her lip before saying, 'Well, it's probably nothing. It's just—'

'What?' He cut in before she had a chance to continue. Discussions about Charlie's health set him on edge. If he were wrong and Charlie was going downhill, his mother and Paris would never let him forget it.

'Relax, I'm trying to explain.' She leaned forward and switched off the radio that had been playing low. 'I don't know anything about dementia but I can't help but notice that Charlie *is* very forgetful.'

'He's old. He's supposed to be forgetful.' He forced himself to keep the annoyance out of his voice. She was beginning to sound like his mother.

'Do you want me to go on or not?'

His turn to sigh. He stared at the road ahead. 'Sure. Go on.'

'It's just little things and not all the time,' she explained, 'but I often have to give him instructions more than once. And occasionally I'll give him a job to do and have to go looking for him because he gets distracted and starts on something else. They're not big things, but they're adding up.'

'Charlie loves working at the pub.'

'I know,' she rushed, 'and I'm more than happy to keep him on as long as his forgetfulness doesn't get out of hand. But I do wonder if there isn't more to it than old age.'

'Nah.' Gibson shook his head, refusing to believe it. 'I'm no Alzheimer's expert, but he's pretty together for his age. He pays all his own bills, keeps his house clean, does his own shopping. He's practically a walking encyclopaedia of general knowledge. He still remembers people and always cooks for himself.' He pushed aside the recollection of how flustered Charlie got that day Gibson had arrived and cooked him lunch – or the time in the shop when he'd forgotten Imogen's shopping list.

'Yeah, you're probably right. Both sets of my grandparents died young, so I haven't had much experience with old age.'

'But I appreciate your concern,' he said, not looking at her as he spoke. Since his parents had moved to Perth, the responsibility of looking out for Charlie had fallen solely on his shoulders. Although he didn't mind, and certainly didn't see it as a chore, it was good to know Imogen also cared about him. She seemed like the kind of woman who cared about everyone she came in contact with.

The kind of woman who, once upon a time, would have been just his type.

★★★

When Imogen and Gibson turned off the highway and into town later that night, the main street was deserted. Security lights glittered in the few shops and dull streetlights struggled to illuminate the road, but the pub was lit up like a Christmas tree. Shadows moved in the windows and a Lee Kernaghan tune blared through the open door. Lights along the verandah showcased bunches of blue balloons on every pole.

'What's going on?' Imogen asked as Gibson slowed the ute in front of the building.

'The balloons are for Amy,' he said, smiling. 'It's a country tradition. Whenever someone in town has a baby, pink or blue balloons are hung outside their workplace to spread the good news.'

'Aww, that's really sweet.' Imogen sighed as he parked. 'I wonder who organised it?'

'Probably Karen,' he predicted. 'Your new female staff wouldn't know about the custom – and I can't see any of the blokes getting it together.'

But he was wrong. When they entered the pub a few moments later, they almost tumbled over in shock at what they saw. Heads swivelled to greet them with full-face smiles. Charlie, Cal and Pauli stood among the punters, lifted their glasses and shouted, 'Surprise!'

Not only was the painting finished, the floors were polished to the perfection of a diamond, the new furniture was in position and the vintage signs she'd spent weeks hunting down were now hung around the walls in the exact positions she'd anticipated. Someone must have found her plan. Imogen pressed her hand against her chest, trying to take it all in. Words eluded her.

'Here, come sit down.' Cal rushed over, took hold of Imogen's elbow and led her to a stool. Charlie reached across and placed a tumbler of something yellow in front of her. She gulped it down, grimaced at the taste and then took another look around her.

'Wow.' It really was the only word for it. 'I thought I said to leave the work till I came back.' She glared at Cal and Pauli, but in an appreciative, happy way.

They held up their hands and Pauli nodded to Charlie. 'It was all his idea. He rallied the troops early this morning, filled them all with caffeine, and they've only just knocked off. He also organised the balloons out front. Did you seen them?'

'Yes. Thanks.' Imogen smiled at Charlie, finding it hard to get even two words past the grateful lump in her throat. Perhaps her fears about his mental health were unfounded after all.

Everyone looked at her expectantly. Despite feeling like she could curl up in bed right this second and unsure if she could string together a coherent sentence, she wanted to say a few words.

Instinctively, she looked for Gibson, but he'd already taken a position at the other end of the bar, far away from her. Her heart sank. They'd shared such easy camaraderie during the journey home that she stupidly thought all his standoffishness would be over, that maybe they could be friends. But one look at him now and she knew she'd thought wrong. He couldn't even meet her gaze. He hadn't said much since she voiced her worries about Charlie. Maybe he didn't appreciate her interference. Maybe he was angry.

Pulling herself together, she straightened her shoulders and stood. Cal whistled to get everyone's attention, which wasn't really necessary. Imogen cleared her throat and silently prayed for inspiration.

'Thanks. I wish there was more I could say, but you are all amazing. I can't thank you enough for giving up your weekend. The place looks fabulous – far better than I imagined – and so perfect for a top secret idea I have.'

Her staff looked at her with intrigue and Wazza shouted, 'Tell us! Don't be a tease!' She sensed Gibson looking as well, but she resisted the impulse to turn and check.

'I've got a few things to investigate before I can tell you more, but let's just say, I'm hoping all this hard work will reap *you* some rewards as well.'

With time for one more round of drinks, Imogen forced herself off the stool to take over from Charlie, who deserved a break. For a change, he didn't resist, instead making a beeline for Gibson. They sat at the very end of the bar, a visual distance from everyone else, Charlie grinning as Gibson talked. Imogen tried not to stare, ignored the desire to buzz about and eavesdrop on their conversation, but it was like ignoring a full block of chocolate in the fridge. If she was curious about Gibson before, now she felt like she could burst with the desperate need to know more about him.

In almost four hours of solitude they'd talked about practically everything under the sun – she'd shared her painful story about Jamie and they'd discussed Charlie at length – but he'd given nothing away about his ex-wife and their divorce. She shouldn't care; there was no logical reason for her to give a fig why his wife had left him, but dammit she did. Had she always been this nosy? Or had landing in a small town where everyone was supposed to know everything about everyone else sent her over the edge?

The other men in the pub were an open book – one she could write herself if she had five minutes to do so. Warren was a larrikin, desperate to have fun and get laid; Guy was similar, but she got the impression that deep down he longed for something more serious. Then there were the others: farmers, farm hands, guys that worked in the nearby mine. She could take one look at any of them and pretty much guarantee what they were thinking, but all her woman's intuition flew out the window when it came to Gibson Black.

It irritated her that she cared, so she was almost relieved when he finally pushed off his stool and said goodbye to Charlie. She feigned busyness, wiping the bar with a vigour it didn't need, her heart pumping all the while as she wondered if – stupidly hoped – he'd stop and say goodbye to her, acknowledge what they'd shared. She got a goodbye, albeit a brief one, which included Cal and Pauli in the equation.

'Night girls.'

He waved as he swaggered towards the exit, looking absolutely dapper despite sitting in a hot ute for the last four hours. As a hot flush swept over her, Imogen found herself helpless to do anything but stare.

'See ya. Bye.' Cal and Pauli tossed careless farewells in Gibson's direction, yet Imogen couldn't even manage one word. How could they not be affected?

She wanted to run after him. She wanted to grill him about whether he'd resume his daily visits to Charlie now, to ask him all the questions she'd neglected to ask in his ute. She wanted to *do* things with him, and although she would never admit it to anyone else, she could no longer fool herself. Where Gibson Black was concerned, Imogen was losing a battle.

That night, she again found it difficult to talk to Jamie.

# Chapter Thirteen

Gibson had always been a sleeper. His mother happily told anyone who'd listen that when he was a boy, she'd barely have left his bedroom after kissing him goodnight before he started to snore. In reality, Gibson was pretty certain he didn't snore – neither Serena nor any of the other women he'd been with had ever complained in that department – but he humoured his mum because the rest was true: he did love to sleep, and usually he was gone within a few seconds of laying his head on his pillow.

But the past few nights, sleep had proved near impossible. Even on Sunday, following an eight-hour round trip after being up before dawn to check the sheep, he spent the night tossing and turning and wishing he'd had longer with Imogen to chat. He didn't care to analyse this fact and was glad that pretty soon he'd start seeding on Roseglen, giving him something to focus his energies on other than things that weren't meant to be.

He glanced at his digital alarm clock again and groaned. Four-thirty.

If he got up now, he'd have most of his jobs done before the sun even rose. But what would he do with the rest of the day? While pondering this quandary, a brilliant idea popped into his head.

*Boot camp!*

Wazza and Guy had been hassling him to join their crazy exercise regime since they started it, just before Christmas, supposedly to keep the football team fit during the off months. He'd never seen the appeal before – believing that those who worked on the land got enough exercise going about their daily routines and didn't need structured fitness drills – but lately he'd begun to look at boot camp in a whole other light.

Staying away from the pub hadn't done the trick, cold showers weren't working, and counting sheep was a joke. Gibson needed to put his body through something harsh, something that would tire him out and put an end to the fantasies he knew he shouldn't be having.

Glad to be doing something proactive, he got out of bed with a new spring in his step. As he entered the kitchen, Jack and Jill peered sceptically at him from their beanbag – he swore a look of anxiety flashed between them.

'It's okay, sooks,' he told them as he filled the kettle and then flicked the switch. 'Go back to sleep. I don't need you this morning.' He bypassed breakfast and took his cuppa into the study to start on some bookwork. He churned through the invoices he'd been putting off for almost a month and then updated his records on Agrimaster. Finally, when the sun was just nudging the horizon, he turned off the computer and put on his footy shorts, a t-shirt and sneakers.

He didn't see another car as he drove into town but when he turned into the oval there was already quite a crowd. Chris – who led the bootcamp – Wazza, Guy, a couple of other farmers, some shearers and the local cop were assembled in the middle of the field doing stretches.

'Well, well, well,' Guy called as Gibson got out of the ute. 'Never thought we'd see you here.'

'You rabbit on enough about something, I have to come test it out,' Gibson replied, scratching the side of his head and hoping desperately that this would work. He joined the rest of the group and dropped into a thigh stretch. The guys were a few seconds into the next stretch – a hammy – when the three men in front of him looked up and let out low whistles of surprise.

Chris' mouth dropped open. 'Holy shit.'

Of course Gibson turned to look, but the words that almost slipped from his lips were much harsher than 'holy shit'. He balled his fists at his sides and resisted the childish urge to kick the near-dead grass. What was *she* doing here?

'Looks like it's our lucky morning,' said Guy under his breath, so that only Gibson could hear him.

His chest tightened at Guy's words for a number of reasons, 'lucky' not being one of them. While the blokes around him practically tripped over their sneakers in the rush to go forth and welcome Imogen, Gibson hung back. Despite the obstruction of the men in front of him, the visual of Imogen jogging their way was impossible not to appreciate. She was wearing those tiny shorts again, and a top that wasn't wet like that other time but may as well have been thanks to its minuscule fit. His imagination ran away with itself as he stood there like a cardboard cut-out, unable to control the thoughts rushing through his mind and sending messages south.

'Must be the morning for newcomers,' said the local cop. 'Something in the air?'

'Oh? Am I not the only newbie?' Imogen asked, sounding pleased by the fact.

Like the Red Sea folding back, the blokes in front of Gibson stepped aside, and before he could school his expression to one of nonchalance, Imogen looked up and met his gaze.

Somewhere to the side of him, he thought he registered one of the guys speaking – 'This is Gibson's first time too' – but he couldn't be a hundred percent sure, because it was taking everything he had to concentrate on breathing.

'Really?' Imogen grinned, but he fought the desire to smile back. 'What a coincidence.'

A damn nuisance was what it was. How the hell was he supposed to rid his body of the tension she was solely responsible for creating with her parading around half-naked alongside him? He should just go, suddenly recall an urgent job that had to be done on the farm. But right about now that elusive cat had his tongue clamped tight.

Something had shifted between them during their drive from Perth. They'd talked – really talked – and he could no longer write her off as a city chick with fanciful ideas she'd soon get bored with. But now, he realised, it'd be easier if she were. He liked and respected her, and found her attractive too, which complicated things.

'You've missed the stretches,' Chris told Imogen.

She shrugged. 'I jogged here, so I'm warmed up already.'

Not as warm as him, Gibson bet, and not as warm as her other fans either.

'Let's form a couple of rows,' Chris went on. Before he'd finished the instruction, the other men were scrambling to be one of the lucky ones on either side of Imogen. Not Gibson. For self-preservation, he chose the row in front of her and at the opposite end. He threw himself into the push-ups, trying to block out his surroundings and just exert himself.

All was going swimmingly until Chris announced they should all turn the other way. Next on the agenda were lunges across the oval and it couldn't have been more torturous. But it wasn't the agony of Gibson's thigh muscles contracting with each move that tormented him – that kind of exertion was why he'd come – it was the hell of watching Imogen's already tight butt contract each time *she* made the move. The agony of knowing, no matter how much he longed to make another kind of move, it wouldn't be right.

Somehow he made it through the hour, doing his best not to drool like the other guys. Did Imogen notice their attention? Did she care? She trained with equal vigour as the men, pushing herself further with each excruciating exercise. When they were done, she mentioned popping to the public conveniences and he grabbed the chance to leave before she came out.

As he stooped to pick up his water bottle, Wazza and Guy came up alongside him. Guy slapped him on the back. 'Did she tell you she was coming this morning?' he asked with a grin.

Gibson flinched and straightened to a stand, leaving the bottle at his feet. 'No. Why would she?'

'I've been thinking about our bet,' Wazza said, before taking a sip from his own water bottle. He swiped his mouth with the back of his hand, then added, 'I think Guy should be out, and I was wondering if you'd like a little wager?'

'What are you talking about?' Gibson said, irritated and pretending he had no recollection of his mates' stupid bet.

Guy was only too pleased to remind him. 'Remember Waz and I had that bet about who could bed Imogen first? Well, apparently I'm out.'

Wazza made a scoffing noise and elbowed his mate. 'He's out because he's gaga over Jenna.'

Guy shrugged and smiled smugly.

'Besides,' Wazza continued, 'there's the Female Friendship Code of Honour to consider.'

'The what?' Gibson looked towards the toilet block, not wanting Imogen to overhear this crass conversation, and wondering if his buddies were ever going to grow up.

'Guy's ruined his chances with Imogen, hasn't he? Even if he were still interested, there's no way she'd ever sleep with him after he did the deed with one of her BFFs. Seriously, it's how women think. So I was thinking maybe *you'd* like to take up the challenge? What do ya say?'

Gibson grimaced and shook his head. 'I say you need to grow up and start treating the woman', he couldn't bring himself to say her name in this context – 'with a bit of respect.'

Wazza and Guy raised their eyebrows at the reprimand but he didn't plan on sticking around to explain himself. He might not always agree with them, but generally he found their antics amusing. Not today.

Despite the sweat swimming on his skin, the morning's exertion had not been the success he'd hoped for. He still felt tight and strung up in all the wrong places. He stooped again, this time snatching his keys and water bottle. Without a goodbye to his friends, he strode across the grass to his ute.

***

In the ladies' bathroom, Imogen splashed water on her face and then looked into the mirror, silently congratulating herself for getting through an hour of exercise with Gibson sweating in close proximity. He was the reason she'd finally decided to give boot camp a shot, but she'd never in her wildest imagination considered he might be part of the group. He didn't seem the sort – yes, he had a great body; yes, she'd noticed – but it looked the type you achieved through hard manual labour, not structured exercise.

The way he achieved his sixpack didn't matter, but the fact he'd been invading her thoughts since the night she returned from Perth did. It had been one hot fantasy after another, with Jamie's face constantly interchanging with Gibson's in the sordid dreams that came every night.

She'd heard men joke about taking cold showers and throwing themselves into physical chores to tame overzealous hormones, and in the early hours of this morning, boot camp had seemed the nicer option. Now she wished she'd just stood under the shower and let the cold tap work its magic.

She'd never felt so strung up in all her life.

She sighed and stared again at her reflection, wondering what was happening to her. Before coming to Gibson's Find, she'd had to deal with grief and worries about how to direct the rest of her life, but she'd never contemplated having to face this kind of quandary. She'd adored sex with Jamie – loved the way he always made her feel so cherished – and they had a healthy sex life, but usually he was the one that initiated. Just her luck, her libido had come into its own when she no longer had a sparring partner, when she no longer had the option to crawl into someone's arms and lose herself.

Telling herself she couldn't hide in the bathroom all day, she took a deep breath and ventured outside. Yet as soon as she exited the conveniences, her whole body jolted at the sight of Gibson only a few metres away, striding towards his ute.

'Hi there,' she called, wanting to reclaim some of the ease that had flowed between them on their trip back from Perth.

He stopped, turned slowly and gave her a look that made her wish she hadn't said anything at all.

'Have I done something wrong, Gibson?' She folded her arms across her chest, determined to get a straight answer. 'I thought we were friends now. Why are you giving me the cold shoulder again?'

'Leave it,' he practically growled. His eyes narrowed and a storm looked to be brewing in his pupils.

'No.' She let her voice rise. 'What is it with you? Is it because of your wife? Is it me? Or are you like this with everyone? I thought we got on well the other day, why can't you—'

He clamped his fingers around her arm and tugged her round the side of the building, out of view of everyone else. At the skin-on-skin contact she lost her train of thought. She found her back up against the bricks with him standing in front of her, still holding her wrists and oh-so-incredibly close. Their eyes met for one brief second and she didn't know whether to scream or to lean forward and touch her lips against his.

Before she could make her decision, he took it out of her hands.

One moment she was contemplating a kiss, the next his mouth was on hers and she was melting. All the anger, all the tension that had been building up these past few days – weeks even – evaporated at the taste of him. It had been so damn long, yet instinctively her body knew how to react – her hands found their way to his neck and up into his hair. She revelled in the feeling as she pulled him closer to deepen the kiss. He groaned, but didn't break away, slipping his tongue inside her mouth and, in doing so, turning her insides upside down. She clung to him, not wanting the moment to end, not wanting real life to intervene when this fantasy was perfectly delicious. But eventually they needed air.

As quickly as he'd come to her, he pulled away. Wiped his lips, rolled his eyes, shook his head, tried to thrust his hands into pockets he didn't have. The whole caboodle of regret. She stood there in pleasant shock as he clamped his hands behind his head instead.

'That's why!' He all but glared at her. 'That's why I've been keeping my distance.'

'Huh?' She could barely think, but his words made no sense.

'I'm attracted to you, dammit.' He quickly peeped around the corner to check they hadn't been sprung. 'Happy now?'

A rush of endorphins flooded her. She let his confession sink in. Pushing aside the image of Jamie that snuck into her head, she instead thought of Jenna's advice and how marvellous she'd felt only seconds before. Unfortunately, her friend was right – her libido hadn't died alongside her husband and she couldn't ignore the joy that ignited inside her at Gibson's admission, the rush that came from his kiss. The encounter fuelled the illicit thoughts she'd been harbouring. Scared, hopeful, anxious, she finally found her voice. Smiling up at him, desperate to soften his scowl and maybe score a replay, she tipped her head to one side. 'Is that such a problem?'

'Yes.' He sounded exasperated.

'Why?' she asked, trying to get her head around his declaration.

'Because I've been married before and there's no way I'm going to let it happen again.' His tone told her that was it – case closed, debate over before it had even begun – but she wasn't giving in that easily. Not now the idea was starting to take root.

She smiled, courage building within. 'That makes two of us.'

'Good.' He nodded, then seemed to realise she'd agreed with him. A frown creased his brow. 'Um…'

'I'm not in the market for another relationship either.' She rushed to continue before he could say another word. 'I've always believed in The One and Jamie was it. There isn't room in my life for another love, and Lord knows right now I should be focusing all my attention on my new business. But,' she shrugged, 'I'm only human. I can't help the fact I really want to jump your bones.'

'Imogen!' She didn't think he was the type of guy to shock easily, but there was a gorgeous blush of red spreading across his otherwise tanned cheeks. She'd surprised herself too. She'd never in her life been so forthcoming about sex.

'Yes, Gibson?' She fluttered her eyelashes in a most uncharacteristic manner, resisting the urge to play dirty and lean in for another kiss.

'Are you propositioning me?'

She thought he did very well to keep a straight face, but the twitch at the side of his neck told her he wouldn't take too much convincing.

'Yes.' She hadn't thought this through, but she answered before doubt had a chance to take hold. 'It's the perfect solution. You don't want another relationship and I'm still in love with my husband, but there's something between us. Something I'd like to explore. And I think you'd like to as well.' She looked into his eyes, daring him to disagree.

He closed them and sighed, but the words that left his mouth moments later were a symphony to her ears. 'Don't say another word.' He lifted his index finger to cover her lips. With one more glance round the side of the building, he turned back to her. 'Make like you're heading home, but meet me round the corner.'

Imogen nodded and then shivered as he turned away from her and hurried to his ute. She took a moment to collect herself, to ensure that when she stepped into view of the boot camp crew, they wouldn't be able to tell what had happened by the expression on her face.

She waved across the field as she stepped into the guys' line of vision. They waved back at her – happy and merry – and she hightailed it off the oval before any of them could get ideas about following her, or worse, offering her a lift home.

It was then, when she ran through the big metal gates of the oval, that the enormity of what she was about to do sank in. There'd been no misunderstanding – she and Gibson were about to do the deed, and right now she couldn't summon any hesitation. She pounded the bitumen, pheromones running riot in her veins as she looked ahead for Gibson's ute. And when she saw it, pulled over on the side of the road a couple of hundred metres from the oval, she called on energy reserves she didn't think she still had and sprinted to meet him.

When she was about ten metres away, he leaned over and pushed open the passenger-side door. 'What took you so long?' Even before she saw his face, she could tell he was smiling. Knowing he used his smiles sparingly made her smile even more.

*Rachael Johns*

She slid into the seat beside him and tried to look disapproving as she said, 'Some of us had to run.'

He laughed, stretched across her to pull the door shut and seized the opportunity to kiss her. Normally uncomfortable in confined spaces, she found the pressure of Gibson up against her anything but. Her breasts felt deliciously tight and heavy as his chest rested against hers and she met his lips with the same enthusiasm he showed for her. At the sound of a car approaching, they sprung apart. They both turned at the sound and then slumped into their seats when they ascertained the driver wasn't a local.

'No one can know about this,' Imogen told him. She didn't want word getting around and the locals thinking she was easy. Not when she'd worked so hard to appear professional and keep her distance.

'Agreed,' Gibson said, turning the key in the ignition. 'I don't give a damn what people think, but I don't want Charlie getting ideas.'

'Ah, yes.' She thought back to the conversation where Charlie had voiced his hopes that his grandson would find love again. Guilt visited briefly but she banished it, telling herself that Gibson was a grown man and *he* wasn't looking for love, so she was in no danger. 'Where are we going?' she asked.

'Not far.' He pulled onto the road and put one hand onto her knee. A few minutes out of town, he turned down a gravel road that looked as if it hadn't seen travellers for decades. Dust flew as he tore up the road and then swerved quickly into a driveway.

'Your place?' she asked, her voice husky, all her attention on the hand inching up her thigh.

'Uh-uh.' He swerved again, bringing the ute to a stop under a couple of old gums. 'It's a deserted property. Bert's place – old mate of Charlie's. His kids are fighting over what to do with it.'

'Oh. Good.' From the inside out, every nerve ending in her body was burning with desire. She wanted what lay ahead more than she'd wanted anything in quite some time, and patience had no part to play.

Gibson chuckled as he killed the engine, leaned towards her, unclicked her seatbelt and began to take delicious liberties with his hand.

'Oh, I don't mean "good" because his family's fighting, I mean—'

'Shut up, Imogen!' His voice had an edge as his fingers slipped under the cotton of her shorts and her heart shuddered in her chest. Her knees fell apart of their own accord and she didn't think herself capable of further speech anyhow, but he made certain, leaning in to finish the kiss they'd started at the oval.

She opened her mouth, welcomed him, met him, teased him, teased herself. She caught her hands in his hair, explored the skin at the bottom of his neck and found she needed more. Much more. They were twisted to face each other, the gearstick rammed up between them. Discomfort didn't enter the equation but she needed no obstructions. Shooing his hand away for a second, she climbed across the shifter and positioned herself on top of him.

His erection was obvious against her thigh, pressing into her, sending her wild with lust as she imagined it inside her instead. As she leaned close to resume their kiss, he tugged a lever under his seat and pushed it back, taking her with him, so they were almost flat and she was lying on top. He touched her chin, forced her to meet his gaze.

He was smiling – the brightest, biggest, most natural smile she'd ever seen on him. The closest was when he'd delivered Amy's baby, but that smile hadn't been for her.

His grin was like an aphrodisiac, not that she needed anything of the sort. Unable to play coy or control her hormones any longer, she boldly slipped her hands under his t-shirt. His sensational stomach muscles contracted beneath her touch. He sucked in a breath. 'I'm sorry, I'm all sweaty.'

'So am I and I don't give a damn.' She yanked his top hard, tugging it up and over his head, ditching it on the passenger seat before pressing a kiss to the hollow at his neck. He whistled low. She kissed lower, exploring every inch with her hands. Licking his skin, tasting salt, never imagining sweat could be so enticing. And then his thumb was on her chin again as he gently lifted her head and forced her to look at him once more.

'Are you sure you want to do this?' he asked, his voice low and strained.

'What?' She focused her eyes back on him, anxious for a moment. 'Yes. Do you?'

'Stupid question.'

And then he lowered his hand, easing it down her neck, raking his fingers over her breasts, making her nipples rock hard. Just when she thought her veins would explode with the need pulsing through them, he ventured lower. Overdosed on anticipation, Imogen's insides clenched as he reached the waistband of her shorts. And then she couldn't think anymore.

Somehow, despite the confines of the cab, they managed to rid each other of every scrap of clothing. His fingers slipped between her thighs again, cupping her crotch, and she almost collapsed against him. Need crept into her bones, right to the marrow.

'Steady there,' he said into her ear, before starting things that didn't steady her at all.

As the first wave of orgasm reared up inside her, Imogen gave herself over completely to the delicious sensations that had been absent from her life for far too long.

# Chapter Fourteen

*Was this how it felt to be alive?* As Gibson drove back towards the pub, he glanced over at Imogen. She met his eyes and her grin lit a face still flushed from their shenanigans. He wanted to pull the ute off the bitumen and kiss her all over again. *More.* He couldn't recall his heart beating so fast and he thought he could survive on the euphoria of their encounter for days.

The silence wasn't awkward, but he wanted to talk to her, only, he couldn't think of anything to say.

As they neared town, she ran her hands through her hair. 'Can I borrow the rear-view mirror?' she asked, angling it towards her before he could reply.

'Jeez. I look terrible.' Her eyes widened in horror, but he didn't see what she saw.

So her hair looked like a bird's nest and her face like she'd just run a marathon; all he saw was energy and beauty. The fact he was solely responsible for the look made him feel cocky, not apologetic.

Still, he wasn't a complete cad. He pulled over to the side of the road and leaned across to dig around in the glove box. He retrieved an ancient comb and a packet of fresh wipes his mother had given him so long ago that they'd probably dried out.

'You look beautiful,' he said, offering her his finds, 'but these might make you feel better.'

She smiled wickedly. 'Oh, I feel just fine, but the bed-hair look has never suited me.'

'I dunno.' He lifted his hand and ran it through her hair, his fingers jamming in the beautiful mess. 'I think you could be the poster child.'

She snorted and proceeded to attack her hair with the comb. 'You know, when we met, I'd never have imagined you had such cheesy pick-up lines.'

'Cheesy?' He pressed his hand against his heart. 'I must be out of practice.'

She giggled and then turned back to the task of fixing herself up. Smiling, he turned back onto the road and drove towards the pub. Parking out the front meant he couldn't lean over and kiss Imogen goodbye, but a simple 'bye' didn't seem adequate.

'I'll see you later,' was what he finally settled on.

'I'll look forward to it,' she promised as she opened the ute's door. 'See you soon.'

He didn't watch her walk inside, wanting to drive off before anyone caught him looking, but that didn't mean she left his thoughts.

★★★

Gibson drove back to the farm, showered, shaved and checked on his sheep, but no matter how he tried, he couldn't stop thinking about Imogen. The way she'd flirted, the feel of her skin against his, the look in her eyes when they were done. It was obvious she'd enjoyed being with him as much as he had with her, but the more he went over it in his head, the more he realised what a massive step she'd taken.

He was the first person she'd slept with since her husband died. Was she really okay with that?

Suddenly unsure, he reached for the phone to call her and then realised he didn't have her mobile number. He couldn't phone her at the pub. That would start tongues wagging in a way neither of them wanted.

Maybe it was just that he wanted to see her again, but he couldn't ignore the unsettling feeling growing inside him. Grabbing the keys, he got back in the ute and headed back to town, figuring he could get some lunch while at the same time checking she was okay.

***

Despite none of her employees seeing her return, Imogen felt like a teenager slinking back home after a naughty night out. Fifteen minutes after Gibson dropped her off, she stepped out of the shower and the reality of what they'd just done together hit her like a cold fish to the side of the head. Realisation slammed her conscience as a zillion emotions swirled and crashed in her stomach. If her body wasn't still thrumming from his touch, she wouldn't have believed it had happened. She wasn't the type of girl who had sex in cars, especially not with men she'd only just met. Okay, so technically it was a *ute*, and she'd known Gibson a month or so, but what was she thinking?

Trembling, she pulled the towel tight around her body and walked straight past the mirror, not daring to look into it for fear of what she'd see. Of whom she'd see looking back.

Last night she'd been a faithful widow. This morning, she was someone who'd just had animalistic monkey sex with a virtual stranger. And she was mortified.

Her sordid actions repulsed her. But walking out of the bathroom and into the bedroom wasn't any better – smiling at her from the bedside table was Jamie. For the first time ever, the sight of his carefree, boy-next-door smile made her feel physically ill. Clutching her stomach, hoping to ease the sensation that someone had planted a brick there, she dropped onto the bed and stared at the blank ceiling.

How could she face Gibson after this? What would she say if he expected an encore? If only she could think of a way to turn back time.

Minutes passed, and then her mobile phone began to buzz from its position next to Jamie. At the sound, Imogen startled so much she banged her head on the back of the bed. 'Ouch.' When usually she'd simply curse and whine at being such a klutz, this time tears spouted. Rubbing her head, she leaned over and peered down at the caller ID: Jenna.

Ignoring the call, Imogen rolled over, peeled back her doona and snuggled underneath. In a way, this was all Jenna's fault. She'd encouraged her, put the thought into her head that sex could be kept separate from anything else. Jenna would scream and giggle on the other end of the phone. Jenna, who viewed sex on a different level to Imogen – *that* Jenna would see this situation as fabulous.

But there was one thing Jenna didn't understand. Having never been in love herself, she didn't know that true love lasted a lifetime and surpassed all sorts of boundaries, including death. She didn't understand that although her body might be craving intimacy with a man, Imogen didn't *want* to feel such things. Because what did that say about her love for Jamie?

She only realised the phone had stopped ringing when it started up again. Assuming it was Jenna, she went to press the button that would signal her as busy and saw it was one of the staff calling from downstairs. Frowning – they'd never called her mobile before – she wiped her eyes, sucked in a deep breath and pulled herself together enough to answer it.

'Hello?'

'Are you getting a cold?' Cal's accent made her immediately recognisable.

'No,' Imogen replied, and then decided that was a better idea than further questioning. 'I mean, yes, I think I might be.' She sniffed for effect. 'What's up?'

'Oh, sorry, I hate to bother you when you're sick, but the truck hasn't turned up with the grog delivery.'

'The alcohol?' Gathering her towel around her again and holding it with one hand, Imogen forced herself out of bed.

'Yes,' Cal said.

*Damn.* Imogen rushed to her tallboy and picked up her watch. It was almost midday. The pub would be opening any second, her delivery was supposed to have been here over an hour ago, and where had she been when she should have been downstairs getting ready? Frolicking on some deserted farm with Gibson Black. Shameful heat rushed to her cheeks. She'd barely been in Gibson's Find a month and already she was allowing distractions to take precedence.

'I'll be down in a minute.'

'I'm so sorry to have bothered you. Karen's here cleaning. She and I can open up. And I'll call the delivery company and see what's happening. Go back to bed if you're sick.'

Cal was a sweetie. But her kind heart was misdirected here. Imogen didn't deserve sympathy. 'I'm fine,' she told her. 'See you soon.'

After disconnecting, Imogen threw herself into the task of dressing. Following black trousers and a dusky-pink shirt, she carelessly applied a layer of foundation and lip gloss, and then hurried downstairs.

The next half hour was spent ear to phone as she tried to find out why her fortnightly delivery of alcohol had gone AWOL – apparently to some pub up north instead of to her – and what the transport company was going to do about it. What would usually be a disaster – she didn't want to be the proverbial pub with no beer – became something to throw her energies into, something to keep her mind from fretting over other things.

'It's all sorted,' she announced, feeling pleased with herself when she came back into the bar following the phone calls. The words had been for Cal, but Cal was nowhere to be seen. It was Gibson standing behind the bar – a picture of self-confidence, oozing happiness and sex. He glanced sideways at her and winked as he leaned over a beer tap, pulling a glass for a patron she didn't recognise.

A chill shot down her spine. Didn't he have a farm to run? More to the point, what was he doing behind her bar, serving? Imogen closed her mouth and gritted her teeth, not wanting to grill him in front of the customer. Not wanting to think about the feelings his mere presence erupted deep inside her.

'There you go,' Gibson said, handing the man his beer and taking a ten-dollar note in return. He passed the money to Imogen who, still on edge, entered the sale into the cash register and conjured the change.

She was both glad and annoyed when the man took his glass and wandered off towards the pool table. Glad because she wanted to confront Gibson alone; annoyed because her hormones couldn't be trusted. Flummoxed by both emotions, she turned away. Maybe if she went about her business and pretended he wasn't here, he'd get the message and go. Childish, yes, but she didn't know what to say or how to face him. How could she have acted so wantonly? How could she have enjoyed it when the only person she'd ever slept with before him was Jamie? It should have been awkward, uncomfortable, but … oh Lord, it was anything but!

She had to do something to make it up to Jamie, to ease this feeling that she'd betrayed him, and if that meant ignoring Gibson Black, so be it. He'd managed to do a perfectly good job of ignoring her the first few weeks of their acquaintance.

That decision made, she could have kissed Cal when she sauntered back into the bar from the direction of the restrooms a few moments later. Surely Gibson wouldn't say anything suggestive with one of her employees present.

'Thanks Gibson.' Cal smiled at Gibson as if he'd rescued her from a deserted road on a cold, stormy night, then she looked to Imogen. 'When a girl's gotta go, a girl's gotta go. Luckily, Gibson walked into the bar at just the right moment.' Cal beamed at him again. Imogen glared.

He shrugged, but his smile dimmed as he registered her expression. 'Happy to help. I've watched Granddad do it enough times.'

Dammit, she was going to have to thank him otherwise Cal would start to wonder what was wrong. 'Thanks,' she all but grunted. *Thanks for leading me astray and luring me places I didn't want to go.*

'No worries.' Gibson toyed with the watch at his wrist and stood there lamely, as if he didn't know what to say or do next. Well, that made two of them.

As if sensing their unease, Cal glanced between the two of them, frowned and shook her head before turning and charging towards the kitchen.

'Look, Imogen,' Gibson stepped closer the moment Cal was out of earshot.

She jumped back and held up her hand to stop him, widening the distance between them as if he were a physical threat. 'Please. Don't.' Talking about what they'd done would make it even more real. Simply looking into his eyes brought all the memories rushing back and right now, she couldn't handle them.

'But Imogen, we have to…'

'No,' she said firmly. 'We don't.' She fought the urge to put her hands over her ears so she wouldn't hear anything else he might say. She could barely bring herself to look at him, but hearing his voice – so calm, so gentle, so different from the tone he used to use with her – made everything even worse.

He stilled, his eyes searching her face, sadness and resignation eventually reigning while hers remained blank and cold. 'Okay,' he said. 'We'll talk later.'

'Maybe,' she managed to reply, although the word was barely audible and her whole body trembled with the effort. Maybe she'd be able to talk about this in time, but right now all she could focus on was self-loathing and regret.

\*\*\*

It took all Gibson's willpower to turn away from Imogen and walk out of the pub. The way she was acting right now – as if she couldn't bear to look at him, never mind be in the same room – told him everything he needed to know.

Regret was plastered all over her face.

And the realisation made him feel like the flystrike he'd been checking his stock for. Dammit, he should have steered clear, stayed firm in his resolve not to touch her. But when *she'd* propositioned *him*, he hadn't been able to help himself. He swallowed at the recollection. Considering he'd just experienced the best sex of his life, Gibson had never felt so crap. He wanted to turn back, to reach out to Imogen again and try to fix his mistakes, but the way she'd flinched from him moments earlier stopped him.

How could things go from so right to so wrong in a matter of hours? He wanted to push it. He wanted to make her talk about the feelings that were troubling her — he'd bet top dollar that number one was guilt, which she had no need to feel — but he didn't want to widen the gap between them any further.

For a short window of time, he'd been on top of the universe, thinking he'd found the perfect woman — one who wanted his body, wanted the pleasure he could offer, but didn't want commitment he couldn't give. Of course it was too good to be true. He had to accept that Friends-With-Benefits were fictional things. In real life, you couldn't have sex without complications. At least, women couldn't.

Although it killed him to go, he accepted that Imogen needed time and space. He'd give it to her today, maybe even tomorrow if she still insisted on it, but he wouldn't be a stranger in the pub anymore. He wouldn't change his plans, wouldn't alter his visits to Charlie just because being near him made her uncomfortable. Avoidance hadn't worked the first time round and he could see no reason it would work better now. Gibson's Find was a tiny town and, despite his initial assumptions, neither of them were going anywhere fast.

They'd have to learn to live with each other, but truthfully, Gibson wanted more than that. In Imogen Bates, he hoped he'd found a friend, and he didn't plan on letting outstanding sex get in the way.

# Chapter Fifteen

Imogen spent much of the next week on the telephone, pulling together her first matchmaking weekend. She'd run the idea past Charlie, Karen, Pauli and Cal after her return from Perth, and they all agreed it was a fabulous one.

After much brainstorming, her team came up with a name for the weekend. Imogen worried it was a little corny, but Jenna assured her it had the catchy vibe they needed in order to attract women from the city. Thus, the first Man Drought weekend was scheduled for April.

A PR friend of Jenna's had drafted up press releases and was eagerly helping spread the word. They'd even set up a Facebook page. Each day, more people phoned, faxed, emailed and even wrote letters requesting information about the event. Half the tickets were booked before they'd officially gone on sale. Imogen could barely believe it.

She didn't know who was more excited by the idea: herself, the local boys, or the girls she'd spoken to from the city. The whole town got behind her and from every direction she had offers of help and suggestions. The few residual members of the CWA had offered to help with the catering and some locals had offered beds for accommodation once The Majestic's rooms were filled. As word spread, offers had been coming from further afield, and as a result, she managed to book two bands (one for each night) at a fraction of the cost she budgeted. With tickets almost gone, Jenna already had ideas about a second event.

Happy for the diversion from thoughts of Gibson Black, Imogen embraced the busyness. Although she went out of her way not to talk to him, Gibson resumed his visits to Charlie, spending most nights perched on a stool at one end of the bar. She steered clear of that end – leaving the service up to Cal or Charlie – but she couldn't help but overhear snippets of conversation. And Cal, who now thought Gibson's grouchiness a hoot – much to Imogen's irritation – insisted on passing on exactly what he thought of her Man Drought ideas.

He'd apparently christened the venture a joke, telling Cal, Charlie and anyone who'd listen that the lure of food, wine, partying and men would not attract the kind of women who'd ever want to make a life out here in the bush.

Imogen disagreed. Almost all of the women she'd spoken to so far seemed genuinely to be looking for a change of direction in their lives and were excited about the prospect of visiting the country. She desperately wanted to tell him so, but in the name of self-preservation, she refused to take his bait. She had the feeling his ribbing was solely for the purpose of getting her to break her silence. Yes, he may not have loved the idea as much as everyone, but he wasn't usually this vocal about anything. He seemed to have loosened up since their lapse of judgement – that was how she tried to think of it – but it could just have been her imagination.

He stole glimpses of her as he chatted with the bar staff and his mates. She saw because she unwittingly found herself doing the same, then flushing hot when he caught her.

And tonight, the flushes were coming fast and furious. He'd arrived at the bar an hour or so later than usual – she'd been checking her damn watch – and it was immediately obvious he'd come straight from the shower. She was collecting glasses when he strode past, offered the briefest nod of acknowledgement and continued to the bar before she had time to contemplate a response. His hair was wet and he left a tantalising aroma of clean male in his wake. His stubble told Imogen he hadn't taken the time to shave and she wondered why he was in such a rush. Was he meeting someone?

She hated that she cared, but couldn't deny that she did. If she didn't want him, was it fair to hope that no one else had him either? Annoyed at herself, annoyed at him, annoyed at the world, she checked that Cal and Charlie had everything under control at the bar and then went into the storeroom under the guise of stock-taking. Really, she needed a moment (or ten) to calm herself. This constant edginess whenever he stepped into her world drained her energies when she had so much else she needed to focus on.

Switching on the light, Imogen immediately got to work, rearranging cartons of beer in order to see what needed restocking. As she lifted the third carton, she sensed movement behind her. Although she didn't feel threatened, as such, she gripped the carton against her stomach, ready to react. As she twisted, a tall, dark figure came into view and every reflex in her body slowed. The man she'd been avoiding for days stood centimetres away, every bit as impressive as her body remembered. Her conscience simply had no idea what to do with him. Still frozen, she could do nothing but watch as his hands reached out and came to rest on hers over the box. Her skin tingled at his touch and she sucked in a detrimental breath – detrimental because it filled her head with his arousing scent.

'Here, let me help,' he said, trying to ease the carton from her grip.

She held on tight and yanked the box back against her, grateful for its presence between them. 'No, I'm fine. Really.' *Yeah, that's exactly how you sound.*

While her heart stampeded, his hands dropped to his sides, but he didn't step away and she was up against the wall so she couldn't go back any further. He peered right into her eyes, as if wanting access to her soul. His close proximity made it almost impossible to look anywhere else. For a few long moments she wished that things were different, wished she could be like Jenna and simply live life to the full, simply enjoy Gibson, without guilt.

'This has to stop.'

Blinking, she gulped and shrugged one shoulder. Did he mean her body's ridiculous reaction to him? 'What does?'

He sighed, took the box while her guard was down and placed it on top of the pile beside them. She folded her arms, hoping he'd read her body language and wouldn't try anything on. The faint noise of country rock drifted from the bar, reminding her how far they were from anyone. How alone. Her traitorous stomach tumble-turned at the realisation.

'This denial.' His voice was low, seductively so, and she took a second to get her brain back to the conversation. 'We need to talk about what we did. Please?'

The desperate plea in his voice sent her gaze snapping to his. Her mouth went dry at what she saw. Gone was the cockiness he usually wore like a shield and in its place was raw hurt. Desperation. Holy shit, she'd been a complete bitch. If a man had treated one of her friends like she was treating him, she'd have chopped him up into little bits. And this wasn't even his fault. She dropped her head, shame making it heavy, as she sunk down onto a carton and flopped her hands into her lap.

Gibson smiled a slightly victorious grin and went to shut the door. As it clanged into place, she almost demanded that he open it again. But he wasn't dangerous, not exactly, and being alone with him had to be better than risking someone overhearing their conversation.

For a few moments, silence reigned, as if he were expecting her to go first. It should have been easy, because she'd hardly thought of anything or anyone else for the last few days. Despite the pub business cranking and her need to focus on the Man Drought event, Gibson and the guilt he summoned inside her had never been far from her mind.

'I wanted to apologise, but you haven't given me the chance.' His words penetrated her thoughts as he smiled slightly, perhaps trying to erode the pained expression she noted in his eyes. 'I'd be forgiven for thinking I smell.'

*Anything but*, she thought, immediately breathing in the fragrance she'd been desperate to ignore. His scent could be funnelled into a bottle and labelled Aphrodisiac. She swallowed and shook her head. 'I'm the one that should be apologising.' Her throat felt clogged as emotion rushed there. It wasn't an easy conversation, which was why she'd been avoiding it. 'I just…'

'I understand. You weren't ready.' Regret laced his words as he knelt down and reached out to hold one of her hands.

His touch was comforting, and although he stroked his thumb against her skin, she understood he wasn't aiming for seduction.

'And it's okay,' he continued, 'but please don't ignore me. We're adults, so we slept together…' He wiggled his eyebrows in good nature and she shivered at the recollection. 'Yes, I'd like to do it again,' he admitted, with a wry grin.

She winced inwardly, but thankfully, he went on before she had to respond.

'But I respect that you don't feel the same.' He paused a moment. 'At least, that's the vibe I'm getting.'

She opened her mouth to speak, but shut it again when she realised she didn't know what to say. It wasn't that she didn't *want* to do it again, she just couldn't.

Eventually, she managed, 'I should be the one apologising. I've treated you terribly. I overreacted.' Her cheeks burned at the thought of how childish she'd been. She hung her head, unable to meet his gaze. 'It was good, Gibson – really good – but I can't deal with this right now. I'm not ready. I know you're not after a relationship,' she rushed to add before he could remind her he wasn't looking for one, 'but Jamie's still my man. And I know he's dead, I know that, but I can't betray him.'

He nodded. 'I get that, I do. Jamie's one lucky guy.'

She squeezed his hand and whispered, 'Thank you.'

'I'm man enough to deal with rejection.' He released her and laughed before his look turned serious. 'But I don't want you to ignore me anymore. I want us to be adults and move on.'

She nodded. His idea sounded good in theory, but she had no experience dealing with a guy after they'd slept together. Except with Jamie, but obviously that was different.

'I don't know about you,' Gibson said, pushing into a stand, 'but I really enjoyed the trip back from Perth. You're a cool chick, Imogen, and I'd rather have you as friend than foe. What do you say? Can we give friendship a red-hot go?'

Imogen found herself staring at his long, sexy legs – recalling them pressed against hers in the heat of passion – and for a second, wondered if she was insane for writing off the option of more. Then she stood, forcing her eyes upwards and her thoughts back to the present. She could handle it; she'd make sure she could. And with Jenna and Amy miles away, she'd be stupid to ignore the friendship of a good, kind man. 'Yes, I'd like that.'

'Awesome.' His lips curled into a slow, easy smile.

They stared at each other for a few moments and she wondered how they were going to go about this so-called friendship. How she was ever going to ignore the attraction.

'Imogen!' A shout from the corridor had them both turning to look at the closed door.

'Charlie,' Imogen hissed to Gibson. She flushed at the thought of what he might think, finding her alone with his grandson like this.

He nodded and they both froze as the door handle twisted.

'You in there, Imogen?' The door swung back and Charlie appeared in the doorway. His eyebrows shot up and he looked from Gibson to Imogen and then back again. 'Sorry if I'm interrupting anything,' he said gruffly.

Gibson smirked like he thought the situation hilarious, but Imogen didn't want any of her employees thinking badly of her. Unlike some, she'd never had sex in a stockroom, and wasn't about to start.

'No, of course you're not,' she said, perhaps a tad too emphatically. She swallowed, trying to inject moisture into her dry throat. 'Gibson was just helping me move the heavy stock.'

'I see.' The disapproval written on Charlie's face told her he didn't believe her.

'Anyway, is there a problem, Charlie?' She hoped to distract his thoughts. 'Why'd you come looking for me?'

Charlie scratched the top of his head, which was usually covered by his terry-towelling hat. 'Um. I … I'm sorry, I can't remember.'

'Never mind.' Imogen took a quick breath and smiled at him. 'We'd best get back out there to help Cal.'

Without another glance at either man, she headed out for the bar, silently praying that Charlie's on-again-off-again memory didn't choose to stick on this.

# Chapter Sixteen

Gibson's hand froze on the spanner as he listened from his position underneath the seeding rig. He'd been replacing knife points, but at the sound of a vehicle approaching, he cocked his head to try and hear better. He recognised it instantly as Charlie's beat-up old Holden – the one he'd always vowed to restore but never got round to doing. It was a mystery how the old girl still started, but it wasn't a mystery why Charlie was putting in an unscheduled visit. From the moment Charlie found him in the stockroom with Imogen last night, Gibson had been expecting this.

He dropped the wrench and slid out from under the big machine. He pulled his sunglasses down from their resting place on top of his head and watched as the car approached.

'You slacking again?' Charlie chuckled to himself as he got out of his car and wiped his hands down the front of his pants.

Gibson shrugged. 'It's what I do best.' Which they both knew was a lie. He closed the distance between them and slapped his hand on Charlie's back. 'So, what about you? To what do I owe the pleasure?' If he knew Charlie, there'd be at least ten minutes of bush-beating before he got to his point.

'Haven't been round for a while. Thought I should come out and check everything's in order. I see you're servicing the rig.' Charlie nodded towards the farm vehicles in the shed.

'Yeah. I want to start seeding early this year. They're predicting rain.'

'Good boy,' Charlie mused, which proved he was distracted, because usually he chose teasing Gibson over flattery any day.

Rather than raising the topic of Imogen – which was presumably the reason for the visit – Gibson opted for diversion tactics. 'Granddad, come for a drive with me. I'd like your advice on a couple of things.'

'Sure.' Charlie straightened his hat and turned towards Gibson's ute.

As they drove towards the far end of the property, Gibson outlined his cropping plans for this season and the next. Charlie offered a few suggestions, but agreed overall that Gibson had the right ideas. Then all of a sudden he leaned forward and switched off the stereo, which had been playing an old Cold Chisel CD.

Gibson's gut churned slightly – here came The Talk.

'I was thinking you could offer Roseglen for the Man Drought weekend,' Charlie said, breaking the silence.

Gibson blinked. 'You thought what?' This was not the lecture he'd been expecting.

'You heard me. Imogen's struggling to find a property to hold her farm visit – all the blokes round here want in on the weekend, and that precludes them offering their farms.'

'Granddad, you know I think it's a big joke right? And all the girls that'll flock here will be jokes, as well. Why would I want to be part of that?'

'For Imogen,' Charlie answered sternly. 'And not all women are like Serena, Gibson. It's time you got that through your thick skull.'

As Charlie continued, Gibson fought the urge to turn the stereo back on. He'd heard this spiel one too many times. The fact was, women weren't really the problem. Granddad didn't know the full truth about why Serena left, so Gibson would likely have to listen to this tired speech a hundred times more. Maybe he should just have told him, but something always stopped him. It wasn't the easiest thing to talk about, especially with a bloke you'd always admired and looked up to.

'And I'd say Imogen is worth ten Serenas put together,' Charlie finished.

'You've got that right.'

'So, you *are* seeing her.' Charlie clapped his hands together, and Gibson realised he'd been lured right into the trap.

'No, I'm not.' Despite this being the truth, he felt the muscle at the side of his neck twitch as if it were a lie.

'Are you sleeping with her?'

Charlie's direct question threw him, and he almost lost control of the ute as he careened round the corner of a paddock. He stopped alongside a fence that really needed to be replaced and turned to his granddad. 'No.'

'Oh really?' Charlie raised his eyebrows and his forehead creased in the way it always had when he'd known Gibson was lying as a child. He never got away with fudging the truth with Charlie.

'It was just once,' he admitted, discomfort forming a ball in his gut at the fact he was talking sex with his granddad.

Charlie swore and slammed his hand on the dashboard. Gibson flinched. 'I expected more of you than that, Gibson Black. We're not quick, wham-bam-thank-you-ma'am types of men. Us Blacks treat women right.'

'Granddad,' Gibson spoke loudly to interrupt Charlie's tirade. 'She doesn't want to again.' And he couldn't blame her, the way he'd acted. Although she'd been as hot for him as he'd been for her, he hadn't treated her right. He should have thought things through. Maybe if he'd taken the time to woo her – taken her to a *bed*, at least – she would have had time to come to her senses.

Charlie wasn't listening; he barrelled right on through Gibson's protest. 'I may not have known Imogen long, but she's a sweet girl and I won't have her taken advantage of. She's been through hell the last few years and she deserves better than that.' He yanked the hat off his head and scrunched it in his hands. 'Your grandmother will cuff you round the head if you're lying!'

Every muscle in Gibson's body contracted, and the guilt at how he'd treated Imogen dispersed for a moment. Had he heard correctly? 'Granddad,' he said seriously, 'I never met Grandma. She's dead. She died before I was even born.'

Charlie blinked and shook his head slightly. He wrung his hat between his fingers like it were a wet cloth, and then snapped. 'I … I … I know that,' he all but shouted. 'I meant, metaphorically. Not a sin to chat to a dead woman, you know, not when you love her like I loved Elsie. Every time I visit her gravestone I tell her about you, about Harry, Paris and your mum. Elsie was as open-minded as they come, but she'd agree with me on this one. You don't mess around with a lady.'

Gibson let out a long breath. 'Granddad,' he began slowly, 'I promise you I don't want to hurt Imogen. What happened was a mistake. Like me, she doesn't want another relationship, but…' *Man, talk about awkward.* 'I'm hoping we can be friends instead.'

'Hmm.' Charlie frowned. 'I loved your grandma more than I ever thought I could love any woman, but it's lonely without her. I sometimes wish I'd found someone else to warm my toes in bed. You two shouldn't be so quick to write off more.'

'Look, Imogen's still hung up on her husband, and she knows I'm not looking for another wife, so we're good. Trust me.'

'Hmm,' Charlie said again, popping the hat back on his head and shifting in his seat a little. He looked as if he were deep in thought. Gibson's gaze darted round the paddock as he wondered what Charlie was thinking about. Finally, he put the ute back into gear, and that's when Charlie hit him with it: 'If you're friends, then you'll be happy to help her out.'

'How? Is she having another slab party?'

Charlie laughed. 'And people say *I'm* forgetful. No, the Man Drought farm visit. I'll tell her you'll be happy for her to come out here for a look-see.'

Gibson resisted the urge to let his head hit the steering wheel. This was Charlie – was he ever not going to get his way? 'All right, if she wants this place, she can have it.'

'Hah.' Charlie chuckled to himself and Gibson looked into the rear-view mirror to see his enormous grin.

The Talk over, his arm truly twisted, Gibson drove his granddad to Elsie's grave. His grandmother had been buried on Roseglen in the days when it was still legal to have a private graveyard. She rested alongside a sister, a number of family pets and both her parents. After paying quick respects, Gibson retreated to his ute to read the latest issue of *Farm Weekly* while Charlie knelt beside the now-decrepit headstone, pulled the weeds from the dirt around it and settled in to talk to Elsie about who knows what.

Gibson and Imogen, most likely.

# Chapter Seventeen

Early on Friday morning, Imogen waved goodbye to Karen, who was mopping the bar area, and headed out to her car to drive to Gibson's farm. To her employee, she appeared cool, calm and together, but inside she was quaking.

She'd delegated the job of finding a farm for the Man Drought weekend to Charlie, and somehow he'd conned Gibson into offering Roseglen.

They planned to head out there on Saturday so the girls who'd signed up could experience a taste of farm life. She wanted as many opportunities as possible for them to try their hand at farming – driving a tractor, fixing a fence, maybe even shearing sheep – and she needed a farmer willing to cooperate. There weren't a zillion other offers because most of the other bachelors had registered as participants.

Despite her reservations about Gibson's commitment to the project, Imogen couldn't wait to see his farm. She hadn't been on a working property for a long time. One of the few times her father took time off work to holiday while she was young, they'd spent an amazing vacation on a cattle station way up north. Her sisters had spent ten days moaning and groaning about the dirt and dust, but she loved every moment. When they went home, her seven-year-old self refused to take off the pair of Blundstone boots – her first – which her parents bought her for the trip. She even took them to school for show and tell.

They lived in a few country towns after that, and she was the only one disappointed when they moved back to Perth the year she started high school. The older girls were over the moon to be within walking distance of shops, movie theatres and a greater pool of boys, but she'd loved living in the sticks. Still, if her father hadn't been transferred to Perth, she'd likely never have met Amy and Jenna – or Jamie – so she couldn't be disappointed.

Holding her bag with the hand-sketched map Charlie had given her in it in one hand, Imogen shook her head as she opened her car door. She'd been caught up in memories when what she needed to focus on was the morning ahead. A morning in which her excitement about pulling on boots and trekking over paddocks was slightly dimmed by the trepidation in her heart at just how she'd cope seeing Gibson again.

She took a deep breath as she slid into her seat and tugged the seatbelt over her. Thank God Charlie would be there too. She didn't know whether to thank her old barman or berate him for arranging this. She turned the key in the ignition and took another quick glance at Charlie's map. It appeared a fairly straightforward route – take the highway out of town towards Southern Cross for ten kilometres, turn left at the gravel road with the mural-painted wheat silo on the corner, another five kilometres on the gravel and Roseglen would be on her right. Apparently, the farm gate was impossible to miss.

She turned her radio on full blast and pulled out onto the main street, happily listening to the country tunes on the local station. Jenna would have hated it, but it was already starting to feel normal to Imogen.

As she drove, she silently counted rusty windmills and old eucalypts in the sparse, dry paddocks alongside the road. For this far into the Wheatbelt, the scenery was surprisingly picturesque. The drive went quickly; she spotted the silo and turned sharply onto the red gravel road. Not used to navigating unpaved roads, she gripped the wheel tightly and drove like a granny, scared to pick up speed in case she lost control. Gum trees grew on both sides, their branches meeting over the road to create a peaceful, country feel. After a few kilometres, she started to relax and increased her speed to just below the limit. Glancing in the rear-view mirror, she smiled when she saw red dust whirling up behind her car like some sort of outback storm. This was exactly what she wanted for her city-born, country-bound girls.

A fox bounded across the road in front her as the Roseglen gate loomed into view. Charlie was right: there was no way anyone could miss it. She slowed as she turned the car and then stopped at the wrought-iron gate. Unable to help herself, she paused for a minute to admire the intricate craftsmanship and then dug her phone from her bag. She switched it to camera mode, stepped out of the car and snapped a photo. Old and rustic, the border of welded roses added a feminine softness to the gate. If only farm gates were still made this way – the name of the farm welded into the gate, giving it character and charm.

According to Charlie, who would talk about his beloved family farm 24/7 if you let him, Gibson's great-granddad, Glen, had designed the gate as a wedding present for his beloved wife, Rose – Elsie's mother. Glen and Rose also built the current homestead, which Charlie spoke about with the same enthusiasm. She wondered if the old house still had touches of generations past.

Imogen's hopelessly romantic heart sighed at the thought, although she knew that must have been close to a hundred years ago now, and it was doubtful the house still looked how the young lovers had envisioned it. Two more couples had called it home since then – three, if you counted Gibson and his ex.

A magpie swooped down from a nearby eucalypt, perched on the gate only metres away and stared beady-eyed right at her, bringing her thoughts back to the present.

'Shoo,' she shouted and waved her arms, hoping to scare it, hoping it didn't have offspring somewhere it wanted to protect.

It seemed to glare at her for a few moments before flapping its wings, shrieking and tossing itself into the air. Imogen puffed out a breath of relief and went forward to tackle the gate. She'd heard some farm gates were almost impossible for city slickers to open, so she smiled when this one swung back easily. She got back into her car, drove through and stopped on the other side to close it again. No way would she be responsible for letting all Gibson's livestock out onto the public road.

As she travelled slowly down the long driveway, Imogen's pulse picked up speed. It was as if her hormones knew they'd see *him* again in a moment.

*Settle girls. Don't go getting any ideas. This visit is purely professional.*

She passed paddocks of sheep, fields of bare stubble and a huge, old corrugated-iron building which she guessed to be the shearing shed, before a white picket fence came into view. Moments later, her eyes set on the vision behind the fence.

She sucked in a gasp. Before her was a perfectly kept, circa 1900s homestead with wide verandahs, all surrounded by a gorgeous cottage garden – one that had to struggle under the high temperatures and water restrictions. She never imagined such a paradise could exist in the dry heat of the Wheatbelt.

How could Gibson's wife have left it? What the hell had he done?

It had to be something terrible to send a sane woman running from this blissful setting. Not to mention running from him. Consumed by these thoughts, Imogen almost missed the man himself waving from off to one side. *Almost.*

But the moment her eyes took in the sight of him, messages shot from her brain to every feminine spot in her body. Feelings she'd barely been able to control before she slept with him were amplified now. She swallowed, trying to return moisture to her dry mouth as her nipples peaked and that spot at the apex of her thighs grew needy and tight. Her body hated this denial, but every time she contemplated changing her mind and propositioning him again, all she had to do was think about how she felt after the first time. Her mind couldn't handle the post-sex agony a second time, so her body would have to chill.

She glanced at the house again, took a quick breath and then looked back to see two hyperactive black-and-white dogs heading towards her. Putting her car into gear, she killed the engine and silently prayed that the morning wouldn't be too awkward.

★★★

Jack and Jill danced at Gibson's feet as if they knew Charlie was on his way. They'd heard the distant sound of an engine before he did and had raced towards the noise.

But when Imogen's miniscule silver Toyota came into view, Gibson frowned, surprised that Charlie hadn't insisted on driving after all the effort he'd gone to in arranging this. He shuddered at the thought of what lay ahead. To say he was having doubts about a bunch of city women trekking all over Roseglen in their high-heeled sandals was an understatement – and he held Charlie and his power of manipulation responsible.

Still, he stepped forward and forced a wave as Imogen brought the car to a stop under an old gum tree. His mum had spent years lobbying his dad to chop it down, but Charlie loved that tree, because he'd first kissed Elsie underneath it, and he'd threatened to chain himself to the trunk if his daughter-in-law ever came good on her threat to call in the tree loppers.

Speaking of Charlie, where on earth was he? His frown grew as he registered Imogen's empty passenger seat. Jack and Jill bounded forth and, knowing they'd show his guest no mercy, he followed them.

'Dogs! Come!' he hollered as she opened her car door. As usual whenever a visitor was concerned, they paid no attention, instead scrambling over each other to be the most enthusiastic member of the welcome party. Jack jumped onto Imogen's lap before she could escape her car, but the giggles from inside told him she wasn't worried by the canine attention.

'I'm okay,' she shouted as Gibson grabbed Jill by the scruff of her neck. Times like these a collar would have been handy, but he'd never seen the need living out here. 'I love dogs.'

'In that case…' He released Jill. 'I promise they'll lose interest in a moment. They've just got to get it out of their systems.'

'It's fine.' She welcomed Jill onto her lap as well, all the while holding her head high to avoid being kissed. After giving both dogs neck rubs that made the skin beneath *his* collar shiver, she finally emerged. His mouth fell open at the sight of tiny denim shorts as she leaned back into the car to fetch a bag. Her legs, as shapely as any he'd ever laid eyes on, looked like they'd go on forever, and he followed them down, rejoicing at the sight of the Blundstones on her feet.

A memory came unbidden to him, of the first day he brought Serena out to the farm. Whereas Imogen was wearing boots, cut-off denim shorts and a baggy t-shirt with Little Miss Chatterbox on the front, Serena had dressed like she was going to the races. With hindsight, it should have been a red alert, but at the time he'd stupidly chosen to ignore it.

He blinked, realising he was comparing Imogen with his ex when he had no reason to. The differences didn't matter, because they were never going to go there. And that suited him fine, because when she eventually got over Jamie, he guaranteed she'd be looking for the kind of relationship he wasn't capable of giving. She had 'Marry Me and Make Me a Mum' written all over her pretty face.

Imogen turned and caught him gazing. Awkwardness ruled for a brief second and she raised an eyebrow.

'Where's Charlie?' he asked, pulling himself together as she slammed the car door.

Her brow puckered. 'I thought he'd already be here. He told me he was coming out early to watch the sunrise with Elsie.'

If Gibson didn't know that sitting beside Elsie's grave early some mornings was one of his granddad's rituals, Imogen's statement would have been worrying. 'I haven't seen him.'

'Oh.' Imogen flicked her hair behind her shoulders in a way that tightened every muscle in his body.

*Charlie. Focus on Charlie.* 'Shall we go inside and give him a call?'

She nodded, absentmindedly stroking Jack's floppy ears. *Lucky little bugger.*

Gibson forced his eyes to the house, and dodging the still semi-bouncy dogs, they headed for the gate in the picket fence. Opening it, he gestured for her to go ahead through the modern-looking garden arbour – one of Serena's modifications – and up the cobbled path towards his house. In doing, so he copped a perfect view of Imogen's pert behind as she sashayed along. If he didn't know better, he'd think she meant to torment him.

She jogged the few steps onto the verandah and then stopped to slip off her boots. He'd stopped bothering with such things not long after Serena left, but on this occasion he did the same with his in-dire-need-of-replacement Blundies to distract himself from the view. When they were both barefoot, Gibson pushed open the front door and welcomed her into his house.

He didn't get many visitors out here, and the few who did come were mates who'd been there a thousand times pre- and post-Serena. They were mostly blokes who knew where to find the beer fridge but never took any notice of the interior decoration. Hell, he only knew the word because Serena had been so hung up on modernising the place.

He watched as Imogen did a 360. A look of distaste flashed across her face but she covered it quickly. He chuckled.

'What's so funny?' She looked to him tentatively, unease evident in the corner of her eyes.

'The look on your face. Don't you like my castle?'

'It's not that…' She stumbled, and he could tell she found lying difficult. 'It's just not what I expected from the outside.'

'My ex-wife fancied herself a designer, and she never bought into the whole country chic thing.' From the beginning, Serena's interior choices had been at odds with the setting. It was as though she'd tried to transplant a modern penthouse apartment into an outback homestead. Everything from the furniture to the couch and rugs was white and sharp angles. Except for the large-screen TV and stereo system, which Serena would also have purchased in white, if possible. He didn't know how she'd planned to baby-proof the house when the time came, despite her desperate noises to start a family.

'You don't like it, then?'

He snorted. 'No.' For almost three years, he'd been vowing to undo everything Serena had done. The house felt cold, as his marriage had, even before the final nail was hammered in the coffin. And it was so big – built for a family he was never going to have. If it weren't for Jack and Jill, he'd hate being here.

'Why did Serena leave?'

Although he'd invited his ex-wife into the conversation, Imogen's question caught him off guard. Recovering, he rattled off his well-rehearsed answer. 'She had crazy notions of what being married to a farmer would be like. When it didn't turn out the way she'd imagined, when I worked long and often late hours, she started to miss the city – her friends and the designer boutiques – and she decided marrying me was a very big mistake.'

'That must have been tough.'

He shrugged; Serena's decision to go hadn't been the toughest bit. 'It's not one of my best memories, but I'm glad she had the guts to leave. If there's one thing I never wanted, it was to marry someone who didn't find happiness in the same things I did. We should never have gotten together in the first place.'

Having said enough on the subject, he walked further into the house, heading to the phone hanging on the kitchen wall.

Whether Imogen's curiosity was satisfied or whether she simply wasn't that interested in his past, he didn't know, but she let the topic go and stayed silent while he dialled Charlie's number.

The phone rang out and Gibson wondered if he dialled the wrong number in haste. He tried again without success. Charlie didn't have a mobile, and he didn't have voicemail or an answering machine at home either, so their options were slim. He hung up and shook his head at Imogen. 'He's not answering. Might be running late but already on his way. Want a coffee while we wait?'

'Sure.' But her smile didn't reach her eyes. She looked nervous, as if she were scared he might try to seduce her while they were alone.

He liked to think he was a man with impeccable restraint, but the way he'd acted in his ute showed otherwise. 'Or we could just head out and start the tour. Charlie knows this place better than me anyway. He'll find us.'

'Yes. Good idea.' She'd already turned and headed for the front door.

He found her on the verandah, tugging her boots back onto pink-socked feet and at the same time inhaling deeply. Her eyes were closed and a kooky grin stretched across her face. 'What are you doing?'

She blushed a little. 'Trying to imprint this smell on my memory.'

'You like it?' Instinctively, he sniffed too. All he could smell was the sheep manure he'd thrown on the garden beds last week, and the stink of the chicken coop mixed with early-morning heat. Smells he took for granted; smells his mother and Serena called 'farmyard' before turning up their noses and rushing inside to douse themselves in perfume.

'Definitely.' She nodded. 'It's one of the many reasons I'm happy to be back in the bush. The fresh smells motivate me to get up and exercise in the morning and I'm never disappointed. In the city, I hated it; here, I'm desperate to get up and out. Only yesterday I saw a kangaroo bound across the road on my morning run.' Lifting a hand, Imogen shaded her eyes from the blazing sun and surveyed the land just past the picket fence. 'Where to first, Farmer Black?'

'Back inside the house to bed,' was his first thought, but damn, if they had any chance at friendship, he needed to drag his mind out of the gutter and keep it out. He swallowed, knowing this wouldn't be an easy task. Everything about her surprised and refreshed him. 'We'll go get the quad bike from the shed. When Charlie does turn up, he'll need the ute to find us. I don't trust that piece of shit he calls a car on the farm terrain.'

With the dogs at their heels, they walked to the shed that housed the majority of his machinery.

'Do we need helmets?' Imogen asked when she eyed the red four-wheeler he planned on taking out.

'Nope.' He shook his head. 'We're tough in the bush. Besides, I promise to go gentle.'

She raised one eyebrow at what he realised may have had an

insinuating tone. He couldn't help himself – when dealing with an attractive woman, what man wouldn't throw in a little flirt?

Still, he inwardly kicked himself and wondered where the hell Charlie had got to. It'd be easier to be normal – or at least restrained – with him buzzing about.

'Thanks,' she said eventually. 'Let's get going, then.'

That had to be the best idea anyone had suggested all day. Once he focused on showing her round the property, they'd both be distracted by the need to work out an agenda for her silly weekend, and not by another kind of need altogether. He stepped up close to the bike and swung his leg over, settling into position.

★★★

Climbing on the back of the quad bike, Imogen didn't know if she trusted herself sitting so close to Gibson, but he appeared to have no qualms and she didn't want to put any ideas into his head.

Taking a breath to keep her hormones under control, she positioned herself behind him, unsure whether to rest her hands on the back of the seat or wrap her arms round his middle. Her fingers twitched and her ovaries quivered at the mere thought of touching his muscled midriff again, so she clamped her fingers onto the seat behind her and prayed he'd stay true to his promise to ride gently. *Where the hell was Charlie?* Damn his tardiness and the fact it had forced Gibson to leave him the ute. If they were in there now, at least there'd be a gearstick between them … not that it had proven much of an obstacle last time.

Where Gibson was concerned, her hormones took on a life of their own – and she didn't like it one little bit.

'You ready?' He twisted his neck to look at her, and his tone said this wasn't the first time he'd asked.

She tried to answer in the affirmative, but when sound struggled to make it past her tonsils, she nodded. He smiled, faced forward again, turned the key in the bike's ignition, revved a little and took off.

He rode fast over bumpy terrain, through rocky paddocks, ditches and dips, but she kept her grip tight on the back of the seat, refusing to give in, no matter how dangerous the track or how much of an argument her hormones offered.

It took a while, but eventually her racing heart slowed to a normal beat, her nostrils focused more on the smells of the land than the manly aroma in front of them, and she started to make mental notes about Roseglen. He rode to the furthest part of the property before killing the ignition and asking if she'd like to stretch her legs.

'Sure.' Standing and stretching out her fingers, which stung from being so tightly curled, Imogen took the chance to look around her. 'Wow.'

They were at a high part of the property. The paddocks of Gibson's farm stretched out for kilometres in front of them, and in the distance she could just make out the town.

Gibson grinned, straightening up after getting off the bike himself. 'Impressive, isn't it?'

'Will it be impossible to get everyone up here for a look?'

'Tricky, but not impossible.'

She took another few moments to stare out across the horizon.

'It's our unofficial lookout,' he explained, pride oozing from every word. 'The top of this hill is not only the highest point of Roseglen, it's also the highest in the region.'

She well believed it. From what she'd seen so far, there was barely a speed bump in the flats surrounding Gibson's Find.

'We could try to get your city girls to hike out here, of course, but it's unlikely that many of them would make it.'

She folded her arms. 'Well, if we can't bring everyone up here, what else does Roseglen have to offer?'

'You mean aside from my four-poster bed?'

Her knees quivered, but he uttered this question as if he hadn't meant anything suggestive, so she pretended she wasn't at all affected. *Who needs a bed when we're the only souls around for miles?*

'Aside from that,' she said, banishing that unhelpful thought.

He cleared his throat. 'We're the second biggest farm in the region. Where many others have suffered from the drought, we've managed to maintain our crop yields and continue to produce good quality merino sheep. If the weather's still warm, I have the pool, and if you're lucky, we may have a few lambs by then. In my experience, women like lambs.' He shrugged. 'But, if you've had plenty of other offers…?'

He damn well knew she hadn't. She rolled her eyes at his sexist generalisation. No way would she admit she loved the idea of tiny lambs and their soft, still snow-white wool. 'See, you hate the idea of a matchmaking weekend.'

'Hate's a strong word,' he said, rocking back on his heels. 'I love your enthusiasm and I'm sure you're sincere about wanting to revive the area, but I'm a bit of a cynic and I don't have high hopes for its success.'

She sighed, taking another long look at the simply splendid view, trying not to think about how perfect his place was for her requirements. 'So you don't have ulterior motives? You won't sabotage the weekend and make me look like a total failure?'

He stepped towards her and her heart froze. For a second, she wondered if he was going to touch her, but he shoved his hands in his pockets and stopped short of invading her personal space. 'I don't want you to fail, Imogen. I promise. Charlie said most of the blokes who have suitable farms registered for the weekend – and that makes them ineligible.'

She nodded.

'I guarantee I won't be registering, and despite what you think of me, I'm really quite a nice guy. I'd like to help you if I can.'

He had no idea what she thought of him, or rather, how conflicting her many thoughts were. 'Thank you.'

'Great. Now that's settled, do you want to tell me exactly what you need from me, or shall we finish the tour first?'

The view was too perfect to leave just yet, and she didn't trust herself back on the bike either, not after he'd shown her his softer side. 'Let's sit.' Without waiting for him, she plonked down on a patch of surprisingly green grass and stretched out her legs.

He strode back to the quad bike, retrieved a bottle of water and came to sit beside her. Proving God had bestowed him with some gentlemanly genes as well as the excess of good-looking ones, he offered her the bottle first. She drank it down greedily, desperate for water to not only quench her thirst but also cool her body temp. When she handed the bottle back, he drank quickly and then spoke, 'What time will your ladies come out here?'

She rattled off her plans for Saturday morning, which included a stroll down the main street. 'Pauli will make a gourmet picnic for everyone and we'll bring it out here mid-morning. The blokes will make their own way, but Tom's going to drive the community bus for the girls. Is there a good spot for a picnic, aside from up here?'

He nodded. 'The yard in front of the shearing shed's as good as any. There are a few trees, and if it's too hot or raining, we can eat inside. I'll even hose the shed down before you bring your ladies.'

'Thanks. That sounds perfect.'

'So what else will be on the agenda, aside from lunch?' he asked.

'If you agree and don't think it's too difficult,' she began, picking up a leaf off the ground and twisting it between her fingers, 'I'd like to offer some real farming experiences. Maybe they could try to drive a tractor, have a go on the quad bike… Charlie mentioned the possibility of getting a few sheep in and demonstrating some shearing.'

She bit her lip, resisting making any further suggestions while she waited for his reaction. Running the farm entirely on his own made Gibson a busy man and she didn't want to push her luck.

'I think we can manage all that,' he said. 'I'm guessing that they'll be back in town for the evening.'

'Yes. That'll be a less formal get-to-know-each-other night than the Friday. Pauli has planned a special menu and Just a Bunch of Cowgirls are playing.'

'Wow.' He didn't hide his surprise. The Cowgirls were an up-and-coming band, currently garnering loads of positive publicity. 'You're really going all out.'

She shrugged, inwardly pleased at his approval. 'Jenna's got a friend with contacts. The Cowgirls are passionate about reviving outback towns and they see this as a very good cause.'

'That's great. Maybe you'll prove me wrong about this venture.'

'Maybe. Now, tell me, did you always want to be farmer?' It had been something she'd been wondering – not specifically about him, but also about the other young farmers in the region.

'Yep. Always.' The grin that stretched across his face told her this was the absolute truth. 'I can't remember a time when I didn't want to be outside, chasing sheep, digging up dirt. I helped Dad fix my first fence at five years old and knew then that this was my calling. That probably sounds cheesy.'

'Not at all. Was your dad the same?'

'Yeah, at least he used to be. Mum's continual whinging about the life of a farmer's wife got him down. She's much happier in the city and he puts up with it.'

'Your mum didn't like it out here?'

'Nope. The moment Paris got married and moved away, Mum started making plans to follow. When I got engaged, she badgered Dad into handing the farm over to me, and he took early retirement. I know he misses the farm but he's thrown himself into other things. Me? I don't think I could be happy anywhere but here.' He took a breath. 'Sorry, I'm probably boring you senseless. How'd you get into the hospitality business? Was that a calling too?'

'You're not boring me at all.' But maybe he didn't want to talk about himself anymore. 'I had no idea what I wanted to do when I left school. I read a brochure on a hospitality course and thought it sounded fun. I liked the social aspect. So I went to TAFE and got a job at the wine bar. I finished the course and stayed there. It's a pretty straightforward story, really.'

'Did you like it?'

'I did for a while, but the last few years felt like I was putting my everything in and not getting anything out. I worked so hard, but for what? I always harboured this dream of having my own restaurant or cafe one day.'

'What did Jamie think about that? Were you working towards it?'

A lump landed in her throat. She realised she'd never even told Jamie. His career had always been their primary focus and they'd wanted to start a family, so she didn't see how becoming a business-woman would ever work. Knowing this, she'd never raised it – it was one of those pie-in-the-sky fantasies, like winning Lotto and moving to Hawaii or something.

As if sensing her discomfort, Gibson glanced at his watch, reminding her they both had jobs to get back to.

'It was always something to look forward to in the future,' she lied, then pushed herself up off the ground. 'I guess we'd better move on.'

'Yeah.' He echoed her action. 'I've got grumpy, pregnant sheep to check on. In fact, you can help me on our way back.'

'Oh, can I now?'

He laughed at her fake incredulity, and for some reason the ride down the hill wasn't as torturous to her libido as the ride up had been. She was still aware of Gibson's fabulous body only centimetres from her own, the muscles of his thighs moving against the fabric of his jeans, but she wasn't so on edge. The easiness of their conversation made her begin to think she really might have found a friend.

As promised, they stopped in a nearby paddock and Gibson looked over the sheep. They all stared dumbly at her as if wondering who the hell she was.

'Can I pat one?' she asked.

Gibson laughed and shook his head. 'You can try.'

She climbed off the bike and took a step towards the flock, but where they'd been frozen seconds earlier, they scattered in all directions as she approached. They were a lot faster than what she'd expected given their rotund bellies. Rather than making a complete fool of herself, she stepped back, admitting defeat.

'Come on,' Gibson called from back on the quad bike, his tone betraying his amusement. 'I'll see if I can find you some leftover wool in the sheds.'

'Thanks, but there's no need.' She laughed, turning back towards the bike and climbing on, her stomach only dropping a fraction as her legs brushed against his. 'I'd much rather pat your gorgeous dogs. At least they have the good sense to tell friend from foe.'

\*\*\*

Gibson didn't want the morning to end. Chatting with Imogen and learning more about her past was as natural and easy as breathing. She showed a genuine enthusiasm for his land and livestock – something Serena never had.

But he had to stop comparing the two women. It was probably a good thing she had to get back into town. He had a list of menial tasks that would keep him busy till well after dusk, and if he spent too much time in her company he might start thinking thoughts he shouldn't: thoughts of getting her into bed, maybe more.

He rode carefully over the paddocks, trying to ignore the temptation of her body crashing into his as they flew over bumps. About a kilometre from the house, he felt a tap on his back and slowed the bike so he could listen.

'What's that?' Imogen asked. He followed her finger to an old drywall hut, a long-forgotten garden and a few unevenly placed gravestones not far way.

He killed the engine. 'That was the first building on Roseglen, built by my great-grandparents. Next to it is our family cemetery.'

'Can we have a look, or…' Her voice drifted off.

'Sure. Charlie's the only one who really comes here anymore.' Gibson climbed off the quad and fell into step beside her as she approached the historic site.

'This is amazing.' She froze not far from the first decrepit headstone and stared at the beaten-up cottage, more than weathered by almost a century of harsh conditions. 'What's it used for?'

'Nothing anymore. My great-grandparents started their married life in this shack. It's pretty run-down now, but Charlie still comes here quite a bit – apparently he and Elsie used to escape here to get away from her father and sisters. And she's buried just over there.' He pointed to the newest (but still ancient) gravestone. The flowers Charlie had laid there a couple of days ago were still fresh and vibrant.

Imogen turned, walked forward and then leaned down to read the inscription. Her forehead furrowed in concentration and a few strands of runaway crimson fell across her face. He resisted the urge to invade the moment and brush them back.

'He really loved her, didn't he?'

At her near-whispered words, he straightened, not wanting to be caught staring. 'Yeah. He did.'

'I think it's beautiful,' she mused, standing and glancing towards the shack.

Not wanting to talk or think about such love – the kind he'd never experienced – he said the first thing that came into his head. 'Would you like to take a look inside?'

Her eyes widened and a smile lifted her lips. 'You don't think Charlie will mind?'

'Course not. Charlie adores you. I think he'd let you do absolutely anything.'

Pink blossomed in her cheeks and she glanced down at the sparsely covered ground, as if embarrassed. 'In that case, I'd love to.'

The uneven wooden door creaked as they pushed it open, but thankfully didn't fall off its primitive hinges. They stepped inside the tiny two-room house and Gibson could almost see the thoughts rushing through Imogen's head – the tiny, cosiness of a space where a whole family had once lived. No inside toilet, no luxuries.

He hadn't been inside here since he was a teenager, but nothing much had changed. An old table and two chairs had pride of place in the immaculately clean room, and the broom he guessed Charlie used to sweep the place rested against one wall. That was it.

Imogen lifted a hand and ran it gently along one wall. 'It always amazes me, looking at places like this. Nowadays we take so much for granted, but what kind of hardships did the native Aussies and then those people who first settled here go through?' She was silent for a moment, then she smiled at him. 'You're lucky to have such heritage on your doorstep.'

His heart clenched at her words. Lucky? For as long as he could recall, his mother and then Serena had been barking in his ear about what was lacking out here in the middle of nowhere, yet here was someone who looked at the world through different coloured glasses. A woman who appreciated life and history, nature and people. He had to get out of this confined space before *he* did something she'd regret.

'Thank you,' he managed, taking a step towards the open door. 'If you think this is something your girls would like to see we could check with Charlie. There's ample room for picnicking outside and it's not as far a walk as the lookout.'

She followed him out onto the tiny porch. 'I think this would be perfect, but we have to make sure it's okay.'

Gibson rolled his eyes. 'As I said earlier, you only have to smile and he'll agree.'

They'd spent longer than expected out touring the farm, so they headed straight back to the homestead and Imogen's car. Imogen played with Jack and Jill while he popped inside to get her handbag, and then that awkward moment came upon them where they stood beside her car, facing each other in order to say goodbye.

'Thanks for having me. And for letting me use your farm for the weekend. I really appreciate it.' She stared past her car, across the property. When she looked back to him, there was a pensive smile etched across her face. 'For what it's worth, Gibson, I think Serena must have had a few roos loose in the top paddock.'

Their gazes held for a few moments and her words sent his heart soaring ridiculously. He grinned, knowing she chose the silly colloquialism so her words didn't seem too serious. 'Thanks,' he said, not needing her to elaborate. He understood she meant him *and* the farm – that she couldn't comprehend how Serena could have left either of them.

For one second, that was enough. The knowledge that Imogen thought highly of him – *liked* him – sent the blood surging through his body as if she'd breathed life back into his soul. At that moment, for what it was worth, he was glad Serena had left. Just having Imogen here amplified how wrong his marriage had been. Experiencing her joy was almost worth the pain that had gone before.

She'd burst into his world, snuck deep under his defences and become someone he couldn't get out of his head. He couldn't take his eyes off her, standing upright and beaming beneath Charlie's old eucalypt. The branches swayed above them and the shadows of the leaves swept back and forth across her face, making her seem almost ethereal. Pesky cockatoos screeched above them but nothing could break the moment. He felt an almost magnetic pull, drawing him towards her. Unable to look away from her lips, he imagined them mashed against his, her body heat one with his once again, and he didn't know if he were man enough to resist.

He took a step closer, and just as he was about to cross the line that would ruin their fragile friendship for good, the dogs started barking.

'Charlie,' he breathed, his eyes still glued to her.

'Finally.' She smiled, turned in the direction of his approaching car and started waving, apparently unaffected by their near-moment.

Gibson puffed out a breath of relief. This was for the best; he had no right to fantasise about anything more. Despite this truth, every muscle in his body remained trip-wire tight as Charlie's car stopped a few metres in front of them.

Why did life have to be so damn unfair?

# Chapter Eighteen

This was how Saturday nights at The Majestic should be. Cal and Charlie were busy serving drinks at the bar and Imogen was run off her feet delivering food to tables. But instead of the ache that used to linger in her calf muscles after a long shift at the wine bar, she had a spring in her step and an uncontainable smile on her face.

Life certainly hadn't turned out how she'd planned, but it was true what they said about time healing wounds, and she'd been more than ready to embrace this new direction. She still didn't know if they'd succeed at this *being friends* business, but she'd de-stressed immensely since Gibson made her confront the issue. Despite a few awkward moments, the visit to his farm had been a triumph, and she was determined to be a grown-up and move on.

She laid a plate of Pauli's to-die-for sweet-potato wedges on a table in front of Wazza and his mates, and noticed his regular sidekick was absent. That was odd, especially for a Saturday night.

'Where's Guy tonight?' she asked, starting to collect their empty glasses.

The men at the table exchanged boyish grins.

She glared at them. 'What's going on?'

'You mean you don't know?' Warren's eyes widened. 'So much for females telling their friends everything.'

'If you don't tell me right away,' she threatened Warren, perching her hands on her hips, 'I'll put a halt to your drinks for the rest of the evening.'

'Woman, don't blaspheme.' Warren pulled his beer towards him and then held up his hands in surrender. 'He's gone to the big smoke to stay with Jenna, hasn't he.'

'What?' She'd been on the phone to Jenna up to three times a day this last week, pulling all the details together for the Man Drought weekend, and not once had she even mentioned Guy. A second date? Or a first, if she wanted to get technical. 'No way!' It didn't compute. Jenna *never* had second dates. It wasn't in her make-up.

'Yes way,' confirmed Warren with a grin. 'He left this morning, actually.'

'Well … thanks for the information,' she said, making the decision to call Jenna the moment all her staff finished their tea breaks.

She absentmindedly collected the last couple of glasses and as she turned back to the bar she saw Gibson sitting there, leaning on one elbow as he chatted away to Charlie. Her belly did the obligatory flip – one she needed to breed out – and she had to work hard to keep hold of all the glasses. How the hell had he managed to sneak in without her noticing? She took the glasses into the kitchen and then served another couple of patrons at the bar before edging along to him.

'Busy tonight?' He smiled and she willed her body not to react.

Swallowing in an attempt to give her throat some much-needed moisture, she nodded. 'Just the way I like it. Can I get you a drink?'

He frowned and gestured to the glass of beer in front of him.

'Oh.' She licked her lips. 'Sorry.'

He smiled briefly but it wasn't as raw as the one before. 'I'd have another but I'm driving.' Gibson nodded towards Charlie at the other end of the bar. 'Did he ask you about dinner yet?'

Charlie had proposed the idea of cooking them dinner to apologise for not making the farm tour.

'Yes,' she answered slowly. 'I told him it sounded nice, but that he didn't need to make it up to us.'

'You're not horribly opposed to the idea?' he asked with the hint of a smirk. 'Charlie has a reputation as a bit of a matchmaker.'

'Really?' She raised an eyebrow. 'I think we can handle him. Besides, I haven't had a night out in forever, and he's been raving about this dish he makes since he asked me this arvo.'

'Let me guess...' He rolled his eyes, but she could tell it was in good spirits. The initial bubble of lust between them had eased and they were settling into friendly conversation. 'Elsie's shepherd's pie?'

'That's the one. Is it really any different from normal shepherd's pie?'

'Oh yeah, it really is.' His eyes kind of glazed over as he nodded.

'That good, hey?' She licked her lips at the thought.

He nodded. 'Until you've tasted Elsie's shepherd's pie, you haven't lived.'

'I guess it's settled then. We'll go play with Charlie.'

He smiled what she knew was grateful thanks but he needn't have bothered. These last few weeks, she'd spent more time with Charlie than almost anyone else at The Majestic. He made her and the other girls laugh on a regular basis, but he also looked out for them, and she'd seen his serious, sentimental side with every mention of his late wife. Charlie was like the grandfather she'd always wanted. And because of his loss, he understood her like no one else did. She'd already do anything for him.

She bent down and grabbed a bottle of water from the bar fridge, then took a sip while glancing over to the table with Warren and his mates.

'What's up?' Gibson asked, following her gaze. 'You seem a bit distracted tonight.'

'More like confused,' she admitted.

'Anything you'd like to share?' He lifted his glass and took a sip.

She contemplated for a moment, not accustomed to having someone here she could air her worries to. 'I … um … it's Jenna.'

'Care to elaborate?' He took another sip of his beer and waited. When she still didn't say anything, he added, 'I'm not a mind-reader.'

She took a quick breath. 'Warren told me Guy has gone to Perth to see Jenna.'

'I see. And that's a problem because…?'

She groaned. 'I don't know… Because she didn't mention it to me. And because it's just odd. Jenna *never* has relationships. She flits from one guy to the next, never spending more than a night or two with each, and she never told me Guy was going to visit her. Letting a man stay the weekend at her place is serious.'

Gibson laughed. 'And you're *worried* about this? You're worried she's going to fall head over heels and move to the middle of nowhere for the sole purpose of shacking up with Guy?'

'Yes,' she all but shrieked, and then quickly corrected herself. 'No. I'm not worried about it, it's just … I don't know, odd.'

She couldn't quite explain why Jenna getting into a relationship would bug her. And she could be blowing it out of all proportion, but after years of accepting that Jenna was how she was, Imogen always assumed her friend would be single – and there for her. When Jamie died, she could always call on Jenna, knowing she wasn't interrupting a cosy couple's existence. Amy was great – possibly better at sympathy than anyone – but she had Ryan, whereas Jenna would blow off any guy to eat ice-cream out of the tub with Imogen.

'Relax,' Gibson said, interrupting her thoughts. 'It won't happen.'

'What won't?' She shook her head slightly, wondering if the conversation had moved on without her.

'This'll just be another one of Jenna's flings,' he said matter-of-factly. 'She'll never settle out here. She's just like all the rest.'

Imogen didn't take kindly to her friend being bundled up so negatively with Gibson's ex-wife. The fact he put all women in the same small box infuriated her

'I'll have you know, Jenna can handle anything she puts her mind to. If she falls in love with Guy, she'll move out here.'

He scoffed at that, but she'd drifted into her own little bubble, a lightbulb going off inside her head. *That was it!* Jenna hadn't called to brag about a dirty weekend with Guy because it meant something. Something more than she'd ever experienced before. Maybe Jenna had finally found The One. Imogen grinned at the thought.

Gibson took another sip of his beer. He swallowed, then wiped the froth from his lips with the back of his hand. 'Jenna might move, but she won't stay.'

'Not all women are like Serena,' Imogen snapped, slamming her bottle down on the bar and spilling water all over her fingers. She'd had it with his attitude.

His face lost all expression as he carefully placed his near-empty glass on the bar. 'That's where you're wrong,' he said, before pushing slowly off his stool. 'All women are.'

Unmistakable sadness flashed across his face, but he covered it quickly. She bit down on the urge to apologise, because she hadn't said anything which overstepped the mark. She wasn't in the habit of keeping quiet about her opinions, just as he was happy to convey his. And as she watched him wave a seemingly carefree goodbye to Charlie, she fought another urge entirely. The urge to go after him and offer make-up sex.

Appalled at such wantonness, when she'd so adamantly told him she didn't want him, she sighed deeply, took a final sip of her water and then forced her focus back to the bar and the patrons. For the next few hours she served drinks, collected glasses and chatted on autopilot, unsure whether Charlie's curious glances were a figment of her imagination or if he'd witnessed the altercation with Gibson.

And when the time came to turn out the stragglers and bid her staff goodnight, Imogen was more than ready to fall into bed. Or so she thought.

Lying on her side in bed, Imogen couldn't find the right words for what she wanted to say to Jamie. She wanted to talk like they used to, to tell him how confused and utterly bereft she felt. Confused about her feelings for Gibson, confused and upset about Jenna, or rather, Jenna's lack of communication with her. Since their first day of high school, she, Amy and Jenna had told each other every little pesky detail of their lives. When it came to her encounters with the opposite sex, sometimes Jenna shared a bit too much, but Imogen would choose too much detail over silence any day. Sure, Jenna hadn't exactly been silent – but the fact that they talked every day and emailed back and forth as well and she *still* hadn't mentioned Guy really hurt.

Did Amy know? She glanced at the alarm clock beside her bed – too late to call her, even if she'd likely be up feeding the baby. And what if Amy *did* know about Jenna and Guy? Were they keeping it a secret from her on purpose? She could see no reason why they would, but then again, she hadn't told them about Gibson. Her traitorous belly flipped at the mere thought of him and an ache pounded the front of her skull. If it weren't for the thin walls and the fact that Cal and Pauli's rooms were just below, she'd have screamed, because right now Gibson Black was infuriating her something chronic.

Quite aside from the attraction that simmered between them no matter how much she tried to ignore it, his woe-is-me, all-women-are-the-same record was getting boring. So he was divorced. Big deal! Half the adult population have divorces under their belts, but that didn't mean they all turned into bitter hermits who refused to think one nice thought about the opposite sex. She knew he wouldn't have touched her with a barge pole if she'd been single and on the pull. Ironically, her dead husband made her an attractive option.

And right now, that made her want to vomit.

Imogen sighed and snatched up the photo of Jamie, holding it and shaking it in frustration. She hadn't spoken to him for a couple of days. Guilt hit her like a kick to the gut.

She clutched the frame against her chest. 'Oh Jamie. Life would be so much less complicated if you'd let someone else be the hero… The pub is going great guns, better even than I imagined, but each day without you is still a huge learning curve. And I don't know if I'm doing it okay or doing it all wrong. I…'

A tear trickled down her cheek and she stopped rambling because she didn't even know what she wanted to say.

She was all over the place tonight and she hated it. She hated having secrets from her best friends and she hated the way one quick bonk with Gibson had made her feel fabulous and terrible all at the same time. She didn't want to need him, but she was beginning to wonder if such feelings were out of her control. But how could she tell any of *this* to Jamie?

Tearing back the bed covers, she got up and thumped across the room. As crazy as the notion seemed, she needed to get out into the fresh air and run. She knew running in the middle of the night was insane, but life had thrown her curveballs and she didn't know how to process them in any other way.

***

Gibson kicked off his boots at his front door and barely stopped to ruffle the excited heads of Jack and Jill before heading for his fridge and grabbing a beer.

He took a hasty slug of the drink he'd wanted to have at the pub but couldn't because he had to drive. He thought briefly of the many drinks he could have had if he and Imogen hadn't agreed to stop at one episode of good – no, make that *great* – sex. But they had, he couldn't, and it was a good thing.

They were nothing more than friends – acquaintances, really – so why did he feel so damn lousy about fighting with her?

He grabbed another beer and headed out to the verandah with both bottles, planning to drink them in quick succession so legally, he couldn't drive back into town and apologise. Logically, he knew he owed her that. He'd been short-tempered and dismissive of her feelings when she'd talked about her friend. But he just didn't want Guy to fall into the same trap he had. Okay, strictly that wasn't true. It was unlikely that Guy and whomever he seduced to the sticks would have the same problems Gibson and his ex-wife had.

If he were honest, he realised after her visit to the farm that he was getting in deep with Imogen. She'd become a constant player in his mind, to the point that he found it tricky to think about anything else long enough to get things done. He'd been desperate to see her again, but had he thrown that barb about all women being the same because deep down he needed to put barriers between them?

He flopped into the surprisingly comfortable wicker outdoor sofa said ex-wife had purchased from some exorbitantly priced furniture shop. He'd tried to tell Serena the combination of white and padded cushions wasn't practical out here, but would she listen? Hell no. By that time the cracks in their marriage were more than evident, and she'd thrown herself into the decorating in an attempt to distract herself from their growing number of other issues.

Glancing at the unopened bottle of beer, Gibson sighed, moved to stand again and then stopped himself. *Don't go!*

He just knew that if he did go back to town, if he did offer Imogen the apology she deserved, she'd take one look at him and know that there was something else, that the throwaway comment about all women being like Serena was something she'd want to pry into. As independent as she was, she was a woman, and that meant *talking things through*, going over and over them until you both wondered what actually started the discussion in the first place. They may have agreed to be friends, but he had no intention of sharing with her what was at the root of his disastrous marriage.

He swore to himself – on the day he learned the truth, and then again on the day Serena packed her bags and sped up the gravel drive in that ridiculous Audi convertible – that nothing – not Charlie, not another woman, not torture by foreign spies – would induce him to reveal his secret. He was man enough to live with it, to change his life, to moderate his ambitions, his dreams, but that didn't mean anyone else had to know. It didn't mean he had to put up with their thoughts, suggestions, *opinions* of what he should do to remedy the situation. As if he hadn't thought of them anyway. What did they *think* he'd thought about, lying in his empty four-poster on those cold, lonely winter nights after Serena had gone? How the hell could he have thought about anything else?

# Chapter Nineteen

On Monday evening, Imogen lifted her hair straightener, closed the tongs around a chunk of near-dry frizz and groaned at her reflection in the mirror. She hadn't dressed up in an age and she was out of practice.

All this effort – a flimsy pink sundress, lots more make-up than she usually wore, heels and the hair – was for Charlie, to thank him for going to the effort of making dinner. Yeah, right… She'd never been much of a liar, and lying to herself she had about as much chance of success as she would if she tried to teach her parents' blue heeler to sing opera. Buckley's.

Fact was, she'd barely thought about anyone or anything else but Gibson since Saturday night. She was angsty over the way he'd departed, worried that there was something going on that she – as a friend – should try to help him with. Her anger waned in the early hours of the morning as she'd run – she reasoned that his actions and his opinions had to be rooted in deep pain

– and she couldn't deny that she missed him. Even the Jenna-Guy dilemma had taken a backseat. Despite a good crowd in the pub on Sunday night, it had felt empty to her. A truckie had spent the evening glued to Gibson's bar stool. Some of the local boys made an effort to engage her in conversation and she'd tried, dammit, she'd tried to be attentive and friendly, but she feared she'd failed miserably. More than one patron asked her if she was okay and she sensed Cal, Pauli and even Charlie had been walking on eggshells around her.

No matter what she tried, she'd been unable to snap out of her funk until today, when she'd woken up knowing there were only hours until she'd see *him* again. And that made her feel better – a fact she didn't want to analyse too closely.

Her mobile phone buzzed from the bedroom, and she was so deep in thought that she almost dropped the hair straightener. She saved the fall but managed to burn herself in the process.

'Youch.' Shaking her hand, she dashed out of the en suite and across the room to answer the phone. According to Sod's Law, the phone stopped ringing just as her non-burnt hand closed around it. 'Dammit.'

She glanced at the screen and uttered a harsher curse as she registered the name of her missed caller: *Jenna*. It was her first call of the day, the first since last week, and the first since she'd learnt of Guy's weekend in the city. Desperate to talk to her friend, Imogen rang back, but the busy tone only caused more frustration.

Her hand throbbed, reminding her of what the call had interrupted; reminding her she didn't have all night to faff about. Deciding to call Jenna first thing in the morning, she stepped back into the en suite to finish.

★★★

Judging by the reception when she went down to the pub half an hour later, she hadn't done too badly at all.

'Wow.' Cal wolf-whistled and paused in the process of pulling a glass of beer. 'Charlie is one lucky guy.'

Of course, Imogen blushed. As far as she could tell, no one knew Gibson had also been invited to Charlie's special dinner. Pushing that thought aside, she revelled in the lovely attention she received not only from Cal, Pauli and Karen, who'd volunteered to fill in for the evening, but also from the blokes scattered around the pub.

Their compliments made her wonder why she'd shoved fashion and make-up aside for so long. Perhaps paying more attention to her presentation was the key to feeling better about herself?

'Are you sure you'll all be okay tonight?' she asked, fiddling with the strap on her shoulder bag, ready to yank it off and throw herself into work if required.

'Go.' Paulie made shooing motions with her hands. 'We'll be fine.'

'You've got my mobile number, just in case?'

Cal rolled her eyes, but she was smiling. 'Your mobile is programmed into all of ours, but even if it wasn't, you've plastered it all over the bar, office and kitchen. We'll probably all have it memorised by the end of the night. Go!'

'Okay, okay, I get the message.' Imogen grabbed a bottle of wine from behind the bar and then started towards the door before someone decided to pick her up and throw her out. The fact they cared and thought she deserved the break warmed her insides as if she'd just indulged in a hot chocolate with all the trimmings. Once outside, the balmy evening wind hit her cheeks, and she received another round of compliments from the guys at the outdoor tables. She made small talk for a few moments about the upcoming footy season, and then politely excused herself. Not wanting to arrive hot and sweaty, she slowed her steps as she walked the back-streets to Charlie's house. Lost in thoughts about what his cooking would be like, she didn't hear Gibson's ute approaching until he'd almost caught up to her.

'Evening.' At his greeting through the open car window her insides melted. Just for once she wished she could be prepared for her body's reaction. She took a quick breath before turning towards him and smiling. She'd already decided if he didn't mention their altercation over Jenna and Guy, she wouldn't either. She didn't want anything to spoil Charlie's special dinner.

'Hi,' she said, offering a silly little wave.

'Hi yourself. Can I give you a lift?' Even from the distance she was at, she noticed Gibson's Adam's apple moving up and down as his eyes roved down her body. That body reacted as if his eyes were fingers, touching every inch of her intimately. The appreciative looks of the guys in the pub had been fabulous for her self-confidence but they were nothing like Gibson's gaze. Their stares hadn't sparked a heat in her core that his long, lusty looks did now. She suddenly felt so weak she didn't know if she could walk the tiny distance to his ute.

Somehow she managed and he leaned over and pushed the passenger door open. As she slid into the seat, her traitorous mind imagined he might kiss her, but he remained the perfect gentleman.

'Did you have a busy Sunday?' she asked, almost swallowing her tongue at the sight she hadn't noticed while standing in the dusk light. She wasn't the only one who'd made an effort. Was that cologne? Imogen wanted to lean over and smell his neck where it emerged from the top of a crisp grey shirt, to run her fingers through his hair, which once again was still wet from the shower. Instead, she gave her eyes permission to look down. Smart black chinos and shiny black shoes had replaced his workwear and dusty boots. She didn't know which side of Gibson she liked better: the rugged cowboy, Akubra hat and all, or this polished man of the world. Then again, maybe she didn't care. Maybe where he was concerned, she wasn't actually all that fussy.

*Oh Lord!*

Just before they reached Charlie's house, she realised he'd been answering her question, telling her about his day, and she hadn't heard a word of it. She didn't want to look rude, so she made a few interested noises and breathed a sigh of relief when Gibson turned into Charlie's drive.

Getting out and traipsing up the garden path alongside Gibson felt somewhat awkward. Did he feel the same way? As the path narrowed near the porch, her hand accidentally brushed his and she pulled it back in embarrassment, immediately regretting her haste. She felt like a teenager on a first date, which was preposterous on so many levels – the main one being the fact they'd already done the deed together, and both agreed it wasn't going to happen again.

They took three steps up onto the porch and then stopped in front of the door. She waited to take her lead from Gibson, thinking he might just head inside. But whether he would normally do so or not, today he lifted his sexy hand – gosh, why did she have to notice this kind of stuff? – and rapped on the wooden door. Imogen took the few moments to glance up and down the porch, smiling at the ancient rocker and the abundance of pot plants. When Charlie didn't answer after what seemed like a reasonable amount of time, even taking into account the way he shuffled, they both glanced at each other awkwardly. Imogen saw her own anxiety reflected in Gibson's eyes.

'Maybe he's got the music up loud?' she suggested, with a hopeful shrug.

Gibson shook his head. 'He likes silence while he cooks.' Creases tainted his usually smooth forehead but she resisted the urge to reach out and smooth them.

'Oh.' And now that she listened, the house did sound silent. 'Well, what should we do?'

In reply, Gibson slipped his hand into his pocket and conjured a lone key. She nodded as he slipped it into the lock and pushed the door open. He stepped inside and headed down a short corridor. Imogen closed the door behind them and followed him into the living room. They found Charlie sitting peacefully on a two-seater tapestry couch with a tea towel over his head.

Imogen gasped, and for a second contemplated the worst. Gibson acted quickly, stepping forward and yanking the tea towel off his grandfather's head.

Charlie startled, opening his eyes. He blinked and then struggled to his feet. Gibson reached out to steady the old man as they both eyed each other suspiciously. Soon, Charlie's attention shifted to Imogen and she smiled as he scrutinised her. He looked back to Gibson. 'You two off some place fancy?'

Gibson's brows knitted together. He obviously had no idea what to say, or what to do next, and unfortunately she didn't have the answers either. 'Granddad, you invited us for dinner tonight. Don't you remember?'

An awkward silence hung over them. Imogen could almost see Charlie's brain ticking over. He looked back and forth between them again and then his nostrils flared and his cheeks grew red. As if hit with the clarity bug, he snapped, 'That was supposed to be tomorrow.'

'I don't think so, it's Cal's night off tomorrow,' Imogen said, and immediately wished she hadn't.

Charlie looked angry, almost like a stranger. 'Must have been some misunderstanding,' Charlie decided, his lower lip pushed out considerably further than his upper one.

'That's fine, Granddad, our mistake,' said Gibson quickly. 'How about I go get some takeaway from the pub and bring it back here? We can still have a nice evening.' He looked to Imogen for assistance.

She nodded. 'Oh yes, Pauli's chilli-and-paprika-crumbed cutlets are on the menu tonight.' She rubbed her tummy. 'Great idea.'

'No.' Charlie's voice was like a gunshot. 'I said I'd make dinner for you and that's exactly what I intend to do, even if you did turn up twenty-four hours early. Sit.' He pointed at the tiny sofa.

Like two naughty kids, they scuttled to the couch and plopped down. Even with them sitting at the ends, Imogen could practically feel Gibson's thigh against her own. Suddenly desperate for a glass of wine, she remembered the bottle she'd brought. One glance at the stricken look on Gibson's face told her he could do with a drink too. She held up the bottle while Charlie bent to pick a remote off a coffee table scattered with old farming magazines.

'Can I interest you in a glass, Charlie?' She made to stand. He all but snatched the bottle from her grip and gestured for her to stay put.

'Lovely,' he said shortly. He tucked the bottle under his arm, and aimed the remote at the kind of stereo she hadn't expected to find in an old man's house. Immediately, soft – undeniably romantic – jazz filled the room. 'You two make yourselves comfortable while I get the drinks. Back in a moment.'

He padded out of the room and Imogen and Gibson's eyes met in shared concern. 'Let's not jump to conclusions,' she said. 'Maybe we really did just cross wires.'

He nodded and half smiled. 'Maybe,' he said on a sigh. She desperately wanted to talk this through with him, but with Charlie only a room away she didn't want to be overheard. The old man's feelings were of paramount importance to her and she knew Gibson felt the same.

When Charlie returned, his famous smile was back in prime position. 'Here y'are.' He flourished two crystal champagne glasses at her and Gibson. The colour, bubbles and fruity aroma she smelled as she took her glass told Imogen it wasn't filled with her mediocre offering but with the finest sparkling wine. She thought back to her talk with Charlie about how he wanted Gibson to find happiness again and guessed the wine was one step of a wicked plan. However misguided, she couldn't help but find his attempts at matchmaking sweet.

'Aren't you joining us?' she asked, looking to Charlie as her fingers caressed the stem of the beautiful glass.

'Not yet. You kids enjoy yourselves.' With that directive, he turned and left the room, shutting the door behind him.

'Maybe you're right.' Gibson visibly relaxed as he leaned back into the couch. He smiled at her as he gestured around the room and held up his glass. 'Expensive champagne, seductive music; I'd say Charlie knows exactly what he's doing. If we'd turned up tomorrow he'd no doubt have had the kitchen table decked out with a fancy cloth and candles and the meal all ready.' He took the first sip of his champagne.

'I think it's sweet. He just wants you to be happy.'

'And you.' Gibson tipped his head towards her. 'He thinks you're the duck's nuts.'

She laughed. 'And that's a good thing?'

'Oh yeah, that's a very good thing.'

A delicious shiver flooded her body at the way he said these words. Not wanting to feel such things, she focused on savouring the deliciousness of the wine instead. 'Has he done this before?' She was curious whether this treatment had been offered up to someone else before her.

'No. He's made suggestions, but … this is new.'

An embarrassing thought struck her. 'Does he know we've…' Heat rushed to her cheeks as she gestured between them, unable to bring herself to say the words out loud.

'He knows.' Gibson's lips formed an undeniable smirk.

She wanted to slap him. 'Gibson, it's one thing flapping your jaws about your conquests to mates, but to your *grandfather*?'

'I would never talk about you or anyone I've slept with to the boys. Or Granddad. Never. Charlie confronted me about it.'

Shame rolled over her and the burning sensation in her cheeks increased. What must Charlie think of her? She took a much-needed sip of her wine and groaned.

Gibson drank again too and then, as if he had a direct line to her thoughts, said, 'Don't worry. He doesn't think badly of you. It's me he wants to stone. This is probably his way of showing me the proper way to woo a woman.'

She smiled a little, because that was cute. Gibson hadn't exactly wooed her in the ute, but then again, she hadn't exactly been complaining. This recollection demanded another sip of champagne. At this rate, she'd be drunk before dinner, which wasn't a good idea. She needed to keep all her wits about her around Gibson Black.

She was about to ask him about his day again, to tell her more about the farm, anything to fill the weighted silence, but he got in first.

'So, tell me about your family.' It was small talk to ease them away from the current topic of conversation and that suited her just fine. 'You said your dad's a cop and you're part of an all-girl family. How many girls, exactly?'

Family was a safe topic. She adored her sisters and could talk about them till she bored him. 'Too many. I have three sisters and each of their stories is pretty much the same. They married young, had kids and are busy living happily ever after in various parts of Australia.'

'Lucky women,' he said. She detected a hint of sarcasm in his tone, although not enough to call him on it. She didn't want to start another debate about women and love. 'How young were you when you got married?'

'For your information, I was twenty-five, which is older than all my sisters.' She drifted off for a moment, smiling wistfully as she recalled that magical day. Blue skies, the foreshore of the beautiful Swan River, lots of family and friends. Forever ahead of them. 'Jamie and I were high school sweethearts, but we broke up for a while in between. I guess the fact we eventually drifted back to each other shows that it was meant to be.'

He simply nodded and took another sip of his champagne. He leaned a bit further back into the couch and looked about to stretch up and rest his arm along the back of it, but seemed to think better of it and, at the last moment, put his spare hand on his knee instead. 'So if they're all scattered about, you must miss them.'

'We talk a lot on the phone, but because they don't live in Perth, I didn't see them much anyway. I do miss Jenna and Amy though. I love it out here, but it can be lonely.' Realising what she'd just confessed – she didn't want him to think that she was having doubts about the move – she added, 'Thank the Lord for phones and emails.'

'Ah, Jenna.' He hung his head a second before turning to her and offering an apologetic smile. 'I'm sorry I was a bit insensitive about her and Guy the other night. I was out of line.'

'Thanks. Apology accepted.' It surprised her that he'd brought it up, but she was glad he had. She liked that he was man enough to say sorry. 'I'm sorry too, about what I said about Serena. I was out of line as well. I didn't know her and I don't know why you split up.' *Hint, hint,* she thought as she toyed with the stem of her glass and waited. When Gibson didn't comment, she swallowed before elaborating. 'It's hard to believe it was just the city-country thing. Surely no woman is really that shallow?'

He smiled knowingly at her and she swore her heart actually stopped for a moment in anticipation of what he might divulge.

She hadn't realised until that moment how much she wanted to know. Sure, she was curious – that was a woman's prerogative – but it was more than that. She wanted to *know* him, to find out what had shaped him and what made him tick. She wanted to be a true friend.

'There is more,' he finally admitted, and Imogen had to rein in the urge to punch the air in victory. 'But I'm not going to talk about it.' He spoke kindly, yet his tone said there'd be no use arguing. He downed the dregs of his champagne and frowned as he looked towards the closed door. 'Should we check on Charlie?'

It was an obvious attempt at changing the subject, but the banging and clanging coming from the kitchen told Imogen this might be a good idea.

'Is he usually this noisy while cooking?' she asked, also staring at the door.

They both cringed as another loud crash sounded.

'No,' said Gibson. 'He's not.' He slapped his glass down on the coffee table. It tipped over but he ignored it, already on his way out of the room.

★★★

Imogen put her glass down, righted Gibson's and then followed. It was only when she entered the 1970s kitchen that she noticed the absence of cooking smells. Usually when she went to dinner somewhere, she revelled in the delicious aromas. Tonight she'd been so distracted that she hadn't noticed their absence.

Charlie turned and spotted them both standing in the doorway. All the overhead cupboards were open, and pans had spilled out from the lower cupboards onto the linoleum floor. Yet beyond the mess, there was a small round table with a pretty floral cloth and candles all waiting to be lit.

Gibson cleared his throat and surveyed the disaster zone. 'You okay, Granddad? Anything we can help with?'

'I'm fine,' Charlie replied, the sheen of sweat on his face telling them he was anything but. 'I just can't find the recipe for your grandma's shepherd's pie.' He turned around and started on the drawers. She guessed the strength in his arms came from years working on the farm and more recently carrying slabs of beer, but couldn't help but feel sorry for the drawers as he yanked at them one by one. 'Your mother probably moved it when she visited last. When she tried to have me committed.'

'Granddad!' Gibson's voice was loud and firm as he stepped over a frying pan and some barbecue tongs. He stooped beside his grandfather and stilled him.

Imogen watched, her heart in her throat; she felt like an intruder but didn't want to leave either of them in what was clearly an hour of need.

'Granddad,' Gibson said again, his voice softer now. 'You don't need a recipe for Elsie's pie; you've been making it for years. Hell, I could probably make it.'

'It's not *that* easy, lad,' Charlie snapped.

An uncomfortable silence filled the air. Gibson looked to Imogen and all she could do was bite her lip and shrug. Finally, he turned back to his granddad. 'I'm sure you're right and it isn't easy. We'll help you find the recipe, but how about we just make something simple tonight. Shepherd's pie takes a while to prepare, and even longer to cook.'

Charlie looked up at Imogen in a way that made her feel as if she were a stranger. He wasn't acting himself, but she guessed it was out of his control. She smiled at him, stepping further into the kitchen. 'Do you mind if I cook something?' she asked, her heart thumping in her ears as she waited for his answer, wondering if he'd grouch at her as well. 'I don't get the chance much anymore.'

After long moments of tension-filled stillness, Charlie slumped against the kitchen bench. His head fell into his hands as he let out a gut-wrenching sob. 'I just don't know what's wrong with me,' he admitted. 'Gibson's right, I've been making Elsie's pie for years. But tonight I just couldn't get it together.'

'It's fine,' she said, closing the distance between them and squeezing Charlie's shoulder. She swallowed the lump in her throat and blinked away threatened tears. 'We all have days like that. I've been working you pretty hard at the pub.'

'I always told you women were slave drivers,' Gibson added. He was trying to lighten the mood, but Imogen could hear the worry in his voice, see it in the creases round his eyes.

And she knew that tonight they had to move on. It was no good for either of them to stand here worrying about the strange way Charlie was acting. She'd talk to Gibson about it later if he'd let her. She didn't pretend to be an expert, but she was beginning to think that his mother's concerns might be legitimate.

'Okay,' she said, turning to open the fridge. She surveyed the contents and retrieved an onion, some mince and some tomatoes. 'Let's make spaghetti.'

'My favourite.' Gibson smiled, moving to sit down at the kitchen table.

'It's everyone's favourite,' she said. A red-checked apron hanging on a hook caught her eye. She scooped it up and tossed it to Gibson. 'And don't think you're just going to sit there and have me wait on you hand and foot. Onions. Now.'

Chuckling, Gibson stood and surprised her by wrapping the apron round his waist. Warm shivers stirred her belly, but it could have been because Charlie had an electric fan-heater on unnecessarily. Wiping her brow, she surreptitiously switched it off and turned to Charlie. 'Now, how are you at grating cheese?'

Within a couple of minutes, Imogen had located a CD of old

sixties music, put it on the player in the lounge, and had both men following her orders. Gibson even cried over the onions.

'No woman ever made you cook before?' Secretly, she thought it kind of sweet. 'They're not *that* bad, you know.'

'Which is why you gave them to me, of course.' He rubbed his eyes with the back of his hands and then presented her with a plate of beautifully chopped onions. She took them and tossed them in with the mince she was frying. As well as the fresh tomatoes, Charlie had a tin of tomato soup in his cupboard and a jar of crushed dried garlic that didn't look as if it had been opened for years. She sneezed at the dust as she opened the garlic, but still tossed a pinch into her impromptu bolognaise sauce. The aroma as she stirred made her stomach rumble.

Charlie visibly relaxed after that. They refilled their glasses of bubbly, and while they waited for the sauce to simmer and thicken, Gibson and Imogen listened happily as Charlie told stories of Elsie and his early days at Roseglen. They didn't sit down to eat until nine o'clock, but had a lot of fun in the meantime, and Imogen found herself and Gibson slipping into an easy, playful banter. The dish smelled surprisingly delicious and Charlie had enough fresh vegetables for them to throw together a chunky Greek salad as well.

At the table, Charlie lifted his glass before tucking into dinner. 'To Imogen and Gibson.'

She raised her brow and Gibson shrugged. He seemed to believe it safer to lift their glasses and join in. She guessed he didn't want to upset Charlie, but an uncomfortable feeling swirled in her gut as she and Gibson said in unison, 'To us.' She'd have to seek Charlie out tomorrow and make sure he understood that no amount of matchmaking would change her mind about a new relationship – even if his grandson was a bit of a hunk. *Understatement of the century!*

Gibson downed his whole glass of champagne. Then, while she echoed the action – well, quite a few gulps anyway – he changed the subject.

'Footy season's not far away, Granddad.'

A sparkle only equal to the one he got when he talked about Elsie lit Charlie's eyes. He finished his mouthful of pasta and then said, 'Bring it on.'

'Yeah, I can't wait to see the Eagles flog the Dockers again.' Gibson started in on his meal, twisting the spaghetti strings around his fork.

'Watch it, boy.' Charlie lifted his fork and jabbed it in Gibson's direction.

Gibson shrugged back with a mischievous grin. 'Only telling it how it is.'

A smile threatening on Charlie's face, he lowered his fork. 'You'll eat your words soon, Gibby, mark mine.'

Shaking his head, Gibson looked to Imogen. 'Who do you go for?'

She shrugged. 'My parents were basketball fanatics, so footy didn't really make it onto the radar.'

'What about Jamie?' Gibson asked, before embarking on another mouthful.

'Um … he went for Carlton. He grew up over east.'

Charlie glanced at Imogen, his expression confused. 'Who's Jamie?'

She almost choked on a piece of cucumber. Gibson frowned and neither of them said anything for a few long moments.

Finally, Imogen cleared her throat, wondering how many times she'd have to have this conversation with Charlie. 'He's my husband,' she said, and then added quickly, '*was* my husband, I mean. He died three years ago.'

'Oh, that's terrible,' Charlie said, real sympathy filling his eyes as he reached across to pat Imogen's hand with his old papery one. 'Do you mind me asking what happened?'

It seemed he had no recollection of their conversation. Taking a deep breath, she quickly filled him in, her heart breaking all over again at the connection they shared.

'That's just awful.' Charlie dropped his fork into his half-finished dinner and sighed. 'Here I've been going on all night about my precious wife, when you'd probably like to talk about your husband too.'

'It's fine,' she said, taking *another* quick sip of wine. She vowed to switch to water soon. 'I love listening to your stories.' Although he was a generally happy person, Charlie positively came alive when he spoke about his wife. And despite the fact they'd only had a few years of marriage, he and Elsie had clocked up a lot of funny experiences in that time.

It was stupid, but in a way she felt jealous of Charlie's memories. She and Jamie hadn't had long together either, but Charlie and Elsie appeared to have fit so much more into such a short time. And unlike her and Jamie, Charlie and Elsie had a legacy, in Gibson's father and Gibson. For Charlie's sake, Imogen hoped that one day Gibson would find someone he wanted to do more with than simply have sex.

'Nothing like a good love story. Was it love at first sight?' Charlie asked.

'Kind of,' Imogen mused, recalling the first time she saw Jamie. She generally just said they met in high school, but Charlie (and probably even Gibson) would see the humour in the truth. 'I was thirteen. It was our first day of high school and Jenna dared me to run through the boys' change rooms when they were getting dressed for P.E. So I did. Most of the boys were already putting their sneakers on, but Jamie was standing there in nothing but black jocks. I don't know who was more embarrassed – him or me. I couldn't look him in the eye for months after that, but nor could I get him out of my head.'

Charlie snorted with laughter and even Gibson smirked. After that, she and Charlie exchanged more stories of their lost spouses. She was less effusive than he was, and neither of them asked Gibson if he wanted to talk about Serena, but where it was uncomfortable on one level, she somehow knew that sharing memories was exactly what Charlie needed. And Gibson seemed to get that too, for when the talk started to wane, he suggested the family photo albums.

Leaving the dishes for later, they migrated to the lounge room. While Charlie and Gibson dug out the albums, Imogen stepped out onto the front porch to call the pub and check everything was fine.

'The Majestic,' Cal answered chirpily.

Imogen smiled at the sound of background music and chatter. 'Is everything okay there?'

'Imogen.' She could almost see Cal rolling her eyes. 'We're fine, and you're supposed to be out enjoying yourself. Everything going well there?'

'Yeah fine,' Imogen said, deciding not to say anything about Charlie's strange behaviour. It wasn't her place. 'Are you sure you don't need me to come back and help close?'

'Positive. Now if you don't mind, I have thirsty men to serve. And I'll see *you* in the morning.'

'Okay, okay.' Imogen disconnected and headed back inside. Gibson gestured for her to sit on the tiny couch next to Charlie and he perched on the armrest beside her as Charlie opened a big photo album across his lap. Shivers shot down her spine and she couldn't tell whether it was the proximity to Gibson again or the specialness of the black-and-white photos before her.

'That's Elsie.' Charlie pointed at a twenty-something girl in plain trousers, an oversized man's shirt and pigtails. 'Her farm uniform.' Adoration shone through every word. 'Although her town clothes weren't much different. She was a tomboy through and through. I've never been able to pinpoint exactly what it was about her that got my heart beating and my tongue in a knot, but she had a spark not present in most women.'

'She sure looks like she had spunk,' Imogen said, staring down at the photo.

Over the next hour, they flicked through the pages and the years. Where the photos of Elsie and the early days of their marriage were sparse, there were a few more images of Gibson's parents and entire albums devoted to Gibson and his sister Paris. Gibson cringed and groaned beside her as Charlie ran through practically every embarrassing incident in his childhood. She couldn't get enough of the stories.

'That's my favourite,' Imogen decided, pointing to a photo of Gibson, around two years old, butt naked except for a pair of white rollerskates.

'He loved those skates,' Charlie chuckled. 'For some reason he had it in his head that skating had to be done starkers. We never could get him to put clothes on when he was wearing them.'

Imogen laughed until she wept. Charlie was about to launch into another story when Gibson glanced at his watch. 'I suppose we'd better be going soon.'

'Yes.' Despite having a ball, she was exhausted and guessed Charlie probably felt the same. She wiped her eyes and stood. 'Let me clear some of the dishes first.'

'I'll help,' Gibson offered.

'No, no.' Charlie made to stand up, but Imogen and Gibson told him to stay put and enjoy his photos a little longer. In the kitchen, Gibson filled the sink and Imogen located tea towels. They talked in hushed voices while charging through the washing up.

'I suppose I can't ignore it any longer, can I?' Gibson didn't need to tell Imogen what he meant.

'I really don't know. He does seem a little forgetful.'

'A little? You'd already told him about Jamie, hadn't you?'

She sighed and nodded. 'Yes. But then, he's so together in other ways. I'm not a doctor and I just don't know. Maybe forgetfulness is normal at his age.'

Gibson scrubbed a couple more plates. 'You're right. I shouldn't overreact. One of the blokes I went to high school with is a doctor. We're still good friends. I'll give him a call tomorrow. And maybe I'll just make a bigger effort and spend more time with Charlie.'

'You already do so much. Maybe your family need to make a bit more effort.' When she'd first arrived she'd looked down on Gibson for only stopping in to see his grandfather once a day, but now she understood she'd been unreasonable in her judgement. He did more for Charlie than most grandchildren did.

'Yeah, maybe.' But she got the impression he'd prefer to handle this without their help. 'Thanks for coming tonight,' he added, taking the plug out of the sink and turning to face her. Despite his hands still being sopping wet, he wrapped his arms around her and drew her close. 'I love the way you are with Charlie. It means so much to him to be able to share Elsie. Thank you for listening.'

She froze, terrified that this was more than a friendly hug. Her treacherous stomach fluttered at the thought. 'I understand him.'

'Yes, I know.' His words were so low she wouldn't have heard them if they weren't so close. Then he pulled back, slipped his hands into his pockets and looked into her eyes. 'You know you can talk to me about Jamie whenever you want to. I mean it about being friends and I'm more than happy to listen.'

She pursed her lips because tears were threatening and she didn't want him to see how his words affected her. She hadn't realised until he said it, but she really did need a friend out here.

'Thank you,' she said, pulling herself together. 'And the same goes for you. I'm more than happy to listen about Serena if there's anything you'd like to share.'

He laughed. 'Nice try.'

***

Gibson forced himself to step away from Imogen. He'd felt her tense at his hug and knew he'd probably overstepped the mark, but he wanted to show his appreciation for her understanding with Charlie. It hadn't been about sex – well, not until he felt his body react despite his best intentions. But it was hard when she smelled and felt so damn good against him.

He reflected on the way she'd spoken to Charlie about Jamie and in seconds the stirrings of his erection died.

He cleared his throat. 'Guess we'd better go check on Charlie, say goodnight.'

She nodded and glanced at her watch. 'I can't believe how late it is. I hope the girls were okay closing the pub.'

'They'll have been fine,' he said, starting towards the living room. 'But thank you for taking the leap and leaving the pub tonight. I know that must have been hard.' She'd done it for Charlie, because she cared about his grandfather as well. That knowledge both comforted and unnerved him.

Imogen followed, and they stopped at the door to the living room when they saw that Charlie – photo album still spread open on his lap – had nodded off on the couch. Gibson's chest seized at the sight.

'Sweet man,' Imogen said, almost too quietly for him to hear.

He stepped up to his grandfather, gently pried the album from his grasp and laid it on the coffee table. He didn't know whether to wake him or leave him. The couch was small, but Charlie wasn't a giant anymore – in fact, for the first time ever he appeared almost frail to Gibson. He pushed the unwelcome thought out of his mind and stooped down to tug off Charlie's boots. He recalled a time when Charlie had done such things for him. As a boy, he'd never imagined the time might come when Charlie needed Gibson more than the other way around.

'Anything I can do?' Imogen's question jolted him from his thoughts.

Charlie hadn't stirred while Gibson had taken off his shoes, so he said, 'No thanks. I'll just cover him over, drive you home and then come back to stay with him. I don't want him to be alone tonight.' He tugged the old crocheted rug from the back of the couch and tucked it around Charlie as best he could, all the while wondering if he should try convincing his grandfather to move back to the farm.

'I agree. But you should stay with him,' Imogen said, already picking her handbag up off the coffee table. 'It's not far, I'll be fine walking.'

And Gibson was torn. He swept his hand through his hair, contemplating the decision. Part of him didn't want to leave, but another part knew his grandfather would never forgive him if he let a lady walk home alone in the dark. Imogen was a strong, independent and capable woman, but it was late.

'No, I'll drive you,' he insisted. 'Charlie will be okay for a few moments.'

'Thanks.'

Then she chipped away at his defences even more by crossing the room and bending down to Charlie. She placed a gentle kiss on his forehead and whispered, 'Thanks for a special night.'

Gibson shook the neckline of his shirt, loosening the top few buttons. The room felt stuffy. It had been a stressful night in many ways, and he could do with a few moments of fresh, near-midnight air.

He locked the door behind them and gestured for Imogen to go ahead down the garden path. Just before they got to his ute, he passed her and opened the passenger door. When she slid into the seat and her dress inched upwards, he scored a tantalising glimpse of bare thigh. He sucked in a breath and closed his eyes, trying to ignore the temptation. And when he got in beside her, he all but glued his hands to the steering wheel because he didn't trust himself, not when he was all over the place with worry about Charlie.

# Chapter Twenty

The streets were quiet, dark and empty so there wasn't time for talk – small or otherwise – on the way to the pub. When they stopped in the back car park and looked up to see a light glowing in her apartment, he found that he didn't want to leave her just yet. As if sensing his unease, she turned and smiled at him. 'Do you want to come up for a few moments? I make a mean Milo.'

He knew she was offering an ear to listen, but he couldn't help teasing. He needed to lighten the mood before he suffocated. 'Aren't you supposed to offer me coffee?'

Her lips broke into a smile that went all the way to her eyes. She shook her head, laughing. 'Yes, except this offer isn't a euphemism. Just friends, remember?'

'Damn!' He hit the steering wheel with the heel of his hand theatrically.

'Come on,' she said, her hand already on the door handle. 'I can be a good listener too.'

He well believed it. He just hoped he could trust himself alone in her house. The morning at his farm on the quad bike with her had been pure torture; being on the couch at Charlie's a severe test of his willpower… Putting the temptation out of his mind, he yanked the key out of the ignition and undid his seatbelt. She didn't need to tell him to tread quietly as they crept across the car park and into the building. He didn't want to be the one responsible for tarnishing her reputation, especially when nothing was actually happening. The empty pub seemed odd without its music and jovial chatter. They passed through the bar and into the corridor that led to the stairs and her apartment.

Neither of them made a sound as they walked by the staff quarters, and the carpeted stairs muffled their steps as they trekked upstairs to her rooms. He stopped behind her at the door, waiting while she located her key in her bag and then pushed the door open. She stepped inside and he followed, automatically scanning the open-plan apartment, which was low-lit with lamps scattered throughout. A couple of shelves rested against the back of the lounge room, both chock full of books. An eclectic mix of art and photo frames decorated surfaces and walls. Coffee cups and discarded clothes littered the floor.

'Sorry about the mess, I've been focusing more on downstairs,' she said, dropping her handbag near the door. 'Aside from Amy and Jenna, you're the first guest I've had. Make yourself at home. I'll be back in a moment.' While she walked off to put the kettle on, he accepted the invitation to snoop.

He turned his head this way and that as he perused the various works of art, but it was the photos that captured his interest. There were a few photos of people he guessed to be her parents and sisters and a couple of her, Jenna and Amy, but there was a definite theme: Imogen plus Jamie equalled happiness. Every second photo was of them. And in every shot she glowed, her hand always touching him in some way. Jamie looked liked the cat that had scored a packet of never-ending mouse, his chest permanently puffed up. Imogen smiled more than anyone Gibson had ever seen anyone smile. He couldn't help but wish she'd smile *that* smile at him.

By contrast, all his photos of him and Serena looked posed, as if they'd been waiting for a professional photographer to take a snap. Serena had certainly never looked at *him* that way. But could he blame her? As he stared down at a solo photo of Jamie in his fire-fighting gear – didn't all girls like a guy in uniform? – one word came to mind: virile. *You could never compete with someone like that,* he warned himself. Even if he planned to … which he didn't.

'Here you are.'

He swung round at the sound of Imogen's soft voice to see her walking towards him carrying two steaming mugs. She'd changed out of her dress into stripy pyjama pants and a beer t-shirt. On her feet she wore the fluffiest slippers he'd ever seen. He couldn't help but smile.

'Nice outfit,' he said, taking a second glance up and down her body and pushing thoughts of her dead husband far from his mind. He took the mug she offered, soaking in the warmth as he wrapped his fingers round it and sniffed. The delicious aroma of malted chocolate was much better than coffee.

She pointed one foot out in front and grinned downwards. 'Those heels were really uncomfortable.'

'Maybe so, but they were damn sexy.' He hadn't been able to take his eyes off her legs all evening. 'Sorry,' he rushed, 'I didn't mean to overstep the mark. I'm trying like hell not to.'

'I know.' She smiled and sank down into an armchair. 'I appreciate it.' She gestured to the couch behind him.

He stepped back, sat down and took a sip of the sweet drink, before placing it on the coffee table. His hot feet twitched in his boots and he wanted to take them off, but didn't think he should be making himself comfortable. In theory, he was here to talk about Charlie, but now – alone in her house – wayward thoughts threatened to take over.

'I should spend more time with him,' he said, focusing.

'No.' Imogen laid her mug on the table and came to sit beside him. She squeezed his shoulder. 'You do so much for him. You visit every day and he appreciates it. He loves your visits, can't talk enough about you. Please don't beat yourself up. That's the last thing he needs.'

She was so close, it'd be easy to lean forward and kiss her, but he somehow summoned restraint. 'Has he ever told you about Bert?'

She shook her head, removed her hand and retrieved her drink. She settled on the couch beside him, taking sips as she listened.

'He was his best mate from the time he moved here. They were mates for decades. He died a year ago.'

'Oh.'

'Granddad was okay before Bert went, at least I think he was.' Gibson paused, finding it difficult to actually admit his grandfather might not be okay anymore. 'Bert was a widower too. They did everything together. He and Bert used to come out to the farm a lot, and they'd go into Southern Cross to play bowls twice a week. His life was full. Then Bert died – heart attack on the bowling green – and Granddad took on more shifts at the pub, I think so he didn't feel so lost. He also started talking more about Elsie. Seriously, I'd never heard so many stories about her until these last few months. Now she seems to be all he wants to talk about, that and…' *Fixing Gibson up with a nice girl.*

He took another gulp of his Milo, but despite all its settling qualities he wished for something stronger. He turned his head to Imogen, shrugging because he didn't know what else to say.

She smiled, edged closer on the couch and took his hand – one friend supporting another. 'We'll look after him,' she said earnestly.

'Cal, Pauli and I, we already adore him. Not to mention Karen and Tom. He's not alone out here. And neither are you.'

Her touch might have been lethal but it was her words that really affected him. His throat grew thick and his eyes felt scratchy. Gibson couldn't remember the last time he cried, and he didn't want to now, because whatever she said, he *was* alone. Always. Imogen might support him with Charlie, they may even be able to get past the chemistry and embrace friendship, but in all the ways that really mattered, he'd always be alone.

'Thanks.' He swallowed, squeezed her hand quickly to show his appreciation and then extracted his. He made a show of glancing at his watch. 'I'd better get back to him.'

'Yeah.' Imogen stood and escorted him out of her apartment, down the stairs and to the back door of the pub.

He stood there like an awkward teenager at the end of a first date. But after all she'd done for Charlie and him tonight, it felt wrong to leave without some sort of acknowledgement. Shaking her hand would be naff. A hug would have them up close and personal again. Not allowing any more time for contemplation, he leaned forward and brushed his lips against her cheek in the briefest of pecks. He hoped she took it for the platonic kiss he meant it to be, even if his body was screaming at him otherwise.

\*\*\*

As Imogen closed the door behind Gibson, her hand rushed to her cheek where his lips had fluttered only moments before. How could a mere peck on the cheek invoke so much reaction? She turned and almost collapsed against the back of the door; part of her wanted to scrub her face clean and part of her never wanted to wash that spot again!

For a fleeting second she fantasised about what might have happened had she pulled Gibson in when he'd kissed her, instead of standing as straight and lifeless as a fence picket. But what kind of mixed signals would she be giving the poor man then? She'd told him she didn't want to be more than friends and she meant it. They'd done a good job of it tonight; she'd tried so damn hard. It wasn't her fault her hormones were taking a little longer to get with the program.

At the raging battle between logic and lust, her head began to throb, the telltale first signs of a headache. But it wasn't only her feelings towards Gibson Black causing anxiety; it was also worry about Charlie. She sighed a deep sigh that flicked hair out of her eyes. Gibson had finally opened up, finally admitted that Charlie might have a problem. She hoped that in the light of day he'd still be willing to talk, because as much as he liked to be a sole operator, Charlie *was* her business as well. She couldn't bear it if something were to happen while he was working for her.

A yawn escaped her lips. It was now after midnight, well past her usual bedtime. She yawned again and glanced ahead up the stairs to her apartment. They could have been Mount Everest for all the enthusiasm she could summon to climb them. Tonight had been emotionally draining in more ways than one, and it was only the thought of bed and the oblivion of slumber that forced her tired legs to work.

Once in her apartment, she locked the door behind her, made a lame attempt at brushing her teeth and then flung herself under the covers. Despite the still-warm weather, Imogen drew the doona up under her chin and tried to get comfy. She'd speak to Jamie tomorrow. Blowing his photo a kiss goodnight, she leaned over and switched off the bedside light. Lying flat on her back, she squeezed her eyes shut, waiting for sleep to come.

But of course it didn't.

Her body felt as taut as freshly tuned violin strings, and she groaned as she listened to every creak and squeak the old building made. She'd never noticed the noises before, and for a second or two it sounded as if someone were creeping around downstairs. Had she forgotten to lock the back door in her haste to get rid of Gibson? Her heart stammered and only the thought of Cal and Pauli not too far away comforted her.

*Gibson would be better. No one would mess with him.*

And dammit, she couldn't get that thought out of her head. The noises ceased but it was too late. The fantasy had returned with a vengeance: what would have happened after she'd pulled that big, muscular body into her embrace, where they'd have ended up, the way their limbs would have twisted and tangled blissfully in the act.

She flung the doona back, no longer in need of comforting but of something else altogether. Beads of sweat swam across her brow, between her breasts and in other unmentionable places. She stormed out of the bedroom and into the kitchen, almost yanking the fridge door off its hinges in her rush for ice-cold water. Drink it or toss it over herself? That was the question. She opted for drink, feeling the cool liquid spreading through her body, but unfortunately doing nothing to quell the fire that raged within her.

*Arousal.* There was no other word for the intensity she was feeling. Discarding the jug of water on the kitchen bench, she trekked back to her room. She almost resorted to the vibrator. Almost, but not quite. Oh, she knew plenty of people used them – had never judged Jenna for her love affair with hers – but she just couldn't bring herself to take that step. Wrongly or rightly, she felt that bringing the pink battery-operated boyfriend out of its box would be like admitting defeat.

Imogen needed to be able to control her physical feelings towards Gibson without artificial assistance, and she swore she'd win this battle if it killed her.

# Chapter Twenty-one

Having remembered to turn the alarm off on her mobile when she went to sleep, Imogen was shocked at the time when she woke only a few hours later. Whether she liked it or not, her body clock had become adapted to early morning exercise. Unable to get back to sleep, she decided to get up and go with her usual run.

Not wanting a repeat of that embarrassing incident where she'd almost been run over by Gibson, Imogen had altered her running route after that. But today, without making a conscious decision, she found herself heading back that way.

\*\*\*

Gibson woke in the hard single bed in Charlie's spare room, his mind flashing with episodes from the previous night as he tried to recall why he was still there. He stared at the ceiling for a few long moments before recollection dawned. He rolled onto his side and groaned, not only at the shocking psychedelic wallpaper (the kind that was briefly fashionable in the seventies) but also at the hard decisions that lay ahead of him regarding his granddad.

Should he confront Charlie about his worries? Should he call his parents and risk an earbashing from his mother? She'd likely have Charlie summoned to some institution in Perth. Or maybe he could just monitor the situation a little longer. Times like this he wished he believed in all that new-age craziness his sister Paris constantly rabbited on about, because right now, calling a psychic and asking for direction seemed like a mighty fine plan.

Noise from the kitchen jostled Gibson from his thoughts. He sprung from the bed, grabbed the pants he'd shucked off when he returned from Imogen's in the early hours of the morning, pulled them on and headed out to greet his granddad, dreading what kind of confusion he might find. Yawning, he stepped into the kitchen and smelled freshly brewed coffee. Just the medicine he needed.

Charlie turned from where he'd been opening the curtains to let in the dawn and grinned at Gibson. He glanced to the empty champagne bottle on the table and chuckled. 'Had a big night, did we? That's why I zonked it on the couch and you couldn't drive home. You did see Imogen home first, didn't ya?'

Gibson blinked away the recollection of seeing Imogen home – the torturous thoughts he'd had for half the night after finally leaving her. 'You remember Imogen was here?'

Charlie stared boggle-eyed at Gibson, like he were the one who needed his head tested. 'Course I remember. I didn't drink that much. We had a bonza dinner and then looked at the old photos. I didn't drone on too much, did I?'

'Not that I recall.' Gibson's head ached, trying to work out what Charlie knew and what he didn't. In lieu of painkillers, he took two steps across the linoleum, picked up the pot of coffee, poured a mug and drank it as quickly as if he were sculling a beer. As he slapped the empty mug down on the bench top, a knock came from the front door.

Charlie frowned as they glanced at the time on his microwave – 7:00 a.m. 'We're probably safe to open the door,' he decided. 'I don't think the Jehovah's Witnesses are early risers.'

Gibson refilled his mug and then, curious, he followed Charlie down the short hallway. As his grandfather peeled open the door, he caught a flash of soft red hair before his brain registered the owner of the locks. Where his mind was slow, his body more than made up for it. His groin tightened as he took in the vision of Imogen wearing those illegally tight running shorts again. He'd managed to sit by her on the couch and keep his hands to himself while she wore PJs, for crying out loud, but a pair of shorts threatened to snap his control. And how the hell did she look so fabulous after so little sleep?

It appeared he wasn't the only male affected. 'Good morning, gorgeous,' Charlie flirted. 'You're looking mighty fine this morning. If I was only a few years younger, you'd be in serious danger.'

Imogen laughed. 'If you were a few years younger, Charlie, you'd be the one in danger. How are you feeling this morning?'

'Fine, fine,' he said, seemingly oblivious to the look of concern that Imogen gave Gibson.

Gibson shook his head behind his grandfather's back, trying to tell her that Charlie had been acting normal so far.

'So, what can we do for you?' Charlie asked Imogen. 'Not that this early morning visit isn't delightful, but—'

'Gibson and I arranged to go running,' Imogen announced, looking to him to corroborate her story.

He glanced at her running gear again – muscles all over his body contracting at the sight – and tried to nod. 'Um, yeah.' He patted his almost-flat abs. 'Mum reckoned I was getting a bit of a paunch last time I saw her, so Imogen invited me to go running with her.'

Charlie peered down at Gibson's gut. 'Hmm, she may have a point, for once.'

*What?* Gibson pressed his hands to his stomach, looking for evidence of a spread. Imogen smirked and coughed, her hand rushing to her mouth to cover her amusement.

'But you can't go running in those pants.' Charlie pointed at them accusingly. 'You can borrow something of mine.'

Before Gibson could argue, Charlie turned and shuffled down the hallway. Gibson glared at Imogen. 'Couldn't you have thought of a different excuse? Running isn't really my thing.'

She raised one obviously amused eyebrow. 'Really? Then what was boot camp?'

'You know what the hell boot camp was,' he replied dryly.

She blushed, then leaned forward and whispered, 'Has he really been okay this morning?'

Gibson glanced quickly behind him to check Charlie was still digging around for workout clothes and then nodded. 'He seems completely with it. I don't know what to think, but I'm definitely going to talk to my friend about it ASAP.'

'Hmm.' Imogen brushed some hair off her face. 'I suppose there's no need to worry your parents unnecessarily. Maybe your friend could suggest a way to confront Charlie without getting him offside.'

Gibson nodded, inwardly shuddering at the thought. He'd have to tread carefully, because whatever happened, he didn't want to risk alienating Charlie the way his mum and dad had.

Before they could say any more, Charlie reappeared, holding a massive pair of brown, holey shorts and an oversized purple t-shirt like they were a whopper fishing catch. Gibson cringed even before Charlie thrust the items at him, and his nose twitched at the smell of mothballs. The smirk on Imogen's face told Gibson the odour hadn't gone unnoticed by her either.

'These'll be perfect,' Charlie said. When Gibson didn't make a move, he nodded towards the bathroom. 'Well, go get your kit on. Don't keep the lady waiting.'

Scowling, Gibson balled up the clothes and went to get changed.

Charlie and Imogen were chatting about the Man Drought weekend when he finally emerged, holding the waistband of the shorts so as not to have them fall around his ankles. 'All right. I'm ready,' he said. If they had to do this, he wanted it over quick smart.

'What about shoes?' Imogen looked down towards his naked feet, obviously trying to smother a giggle.

'I've only got the ones I wore last night,' he said, glaring at her, 'and they're not exactly made for running.' Nothing he was wearing felt made for exercise, but if he wanted any chance of keeping up with her, he'd have to go barefoot.

She shrugged. 'Suit yourself.'

They waved goodbye to Charlie, and Gibson grudgingly followed Imogen down the garden path.

'Are you always so chirpy in the morning?' he asked as they turned onto the footpath.

'Oh yeah. Especially when I start the day with exercise. Are you always so grumpy?'

'Yep. There's only one type of exercise I believe in starting the day with.' He hitched up the waistband of the enormous shorts again.

'I see.' He thought her voice sounded slightly strangled as she strode ahead of him, her long legs eating up the pavement with each graceful step.

He averted his gaze. It was hard enough keeping pace with her when he had to keep a vice-like grip on his shorts, never mind with his libido distracting him. He couldn't get the image of spending a whole night with Imogen out of his head. The thought was like drinking a sixpack of rum-and-cola on an empty stomach. It'd be an incomparable rush while it happened, but he couldn't bear the regret and discomfort that'd take root afterwards. Not when they were finally moving on from the last time.

'Hey slowpoke!'

He tore himself from his thoughts to see Imogen a good few metres ahead of him.

'I actually want a workout,' she said, cockily. 'If you can't keep up—'

'Course I can keep up. It's these damn pants. Would be easier if I was running naked.'

She stumbled on a crack in the pavement, but saved herself from falling by grabbing on to a nearby letterbox.

'You okay?' he asked, catching up and reaching out to help her.

'Fine. I just can't…' She stopped and clutched her stomach. Close up, he realised she was laughing – tears in her deep-green eyes. 'It's the visual,' she said, gasping for breath. 'You running in Charlie's shorts was bad enough, but naked? All that…' – her eyes flicked down to his package – 'flying free.' And then she burst out in another episode of giggles.

Feeling the need to stick up for his nuts, and trying to stifle a laugh himself, Gibson put his hands onto his hips. The instant he let go of the dysfunctional elastic waistband, it dropped towards the pavement as if the ground had a magnetic force. A whoosh of warm morning wind blasted his privates as he stood there in nothing but Charlie's old shirt and his own black jocks.

And Imogen lost it. If she'd been fighting hysterics a moment ago, now she could no longer control herself. She doubled over, her ponytail bouncing on top of her head as she laughed.

Gibson stood motionless, knowing he needed to bend over and pull up the shorts, but unable to do so because he'd finally seen the funny side. Laughter bubbled from deep within him and erupted into something he couldn't control. They stood there in the middle of the path, literally trembling with amusement like a couple of crazy kids.

The wall of defence she usually kept firmly around her crumbled and he realised he was getting his first glimpse of the real Imogen. More real even than when she'd trembled in his car and screamed his name in release.

And damn it felt good.

The sound of a vehicle registered somewhere at the back of his brain. He tried to pull himself out of this madness, but one glance at Imogen sent him over the edge again. He couldn't recall the last time he'd laughed so much, and judging by the tears streaming down her face, she felt the same. His arms shaking, he reached out to touch her face, to wipe her tears with his thumbs. And that's when the vehicle pulled up beside them.

'Well, well, well. What have we here?' Wazza stepped out of his ute and looked over the top. The sweaty shearer's singlet he wore indicated he'd just come from boot camp.

Guy leaned out the passenger-side window and wolf-whistled. 'Looks like debauchery to me, mate. The kind of depravity we ought to report to the local copper.'

Gibson stopped laughing as suddenly as if his mates had thrown a bucket of icy water over him. He yanked up the granddad pants and instinctively stepped in front of Imogen.

'Ah ... maybe,' Wazza said, and Gibson didn't like the tone of his voice. 'But I say we only report them if Gibson doesn't pay up.'

'Oh, yeah, the bet.' Guy grinned even more and winked at Imogen.

Gibson kept a grip on his shorts, resisting the urge to take to the road and pummel both his mates.

'What bet?' Imogen asked, her chest still heaving as her breathing finally began to calm.

'Never mind.' Gibson glanced quickly behind him.

Laughing, Wazza slid back into the ute. He shouted across Guy, through the open window, 'I'm sure Gibson will fill you in.' With that, Wazza hooned the ute down the street and out of sight.

'What bet?' Imogen asked again. Why did women have to be so damn persistent?

'Waz and Guy's stupid bet,' he said, deciding to come clean. He'd never wanted any part of it anyway. 'They haven't grown up yet, and when you first arrived they had a bet about who could get you into bed first.'

A combination of horror and amusement flashed across her face. 'And how much did you bet?'

'Don't be ridiculous, you know I didn't bet anything at all.' He ran a hand through his hair and sighed. 'I didn't *want* to get you into bed. I couldn't help myself.'

***

'What the hell have you been keeping from me, girlfriend?'

Imogen balanced the phone between her ear and shoulder as she secured a towel around her body. Her phone had been buzzing when she'd stepped out of the shower following her run and she hadn't had time to check the caller ID, but she recognised Jenna's irate voice immediately.

It didn't take long to work out what she was on about. The bush telegraph had grown wings and flown to the city.

'I've been meaning to ask the same thing,' Imogen said to her friend.

There was a silence at both ends of the line.

Eventually, Imogen found her voice. 'I'm guessing you had a call from Guy this morning.'

'Well … yes,' Jenna finally admitted. 'He's been calling quite a lot, actually.'

'So I heard.' Imogen couldn't help the frostiness in her voice. 'How was your weekend?'

'Really good,' Jenna said on a sigh. 'I ... I'm sorry I didn't tell you. Guy rang me the night after the slab party and we've phoned every night since. I've never talked so much to a man in my life. Like, really talked. And then when he wanted to come visit me, I didn't know how I felt. I figured I'd probably get sick of him and be desperate to send him back, and I didn't tell you or Amy because I didn't want you to read into it more than was there.'

'Okay.' Imogen could never stay angry at Jenna for long and she sounded so genuine – genuinely confused. If there were one thing Imogen could empathise with at the moment, it was confusion. 'And did you get sick of him? He's obviously still on your radar.'

'Oh Imogen, there's never been anyone more on my radar. I can't think about anything else, never mind any*one* else.'

Imogen's tummy flipped at Jenna's words. She related completely; it was exactly how she'd felt about Jamie. He'd consumed her so that everything around them seemed insignificant. The fact Jenna had found someone that made her feel these things both pleased and surprised her.

'Men come into the gallery,' Jenna continued. 'They smile and try to flirt with me, and they're good-looking blokes – the type I'd usually have a thing for – but I feel nothing. At all. It's really quite scary.'

'So what are you doing about it?'

'I'm coming up on Friday. The weekdays are long, but at least Guy isn't *that* far away. It's not a long-term solution though; we're going to talk about our future this weekend.'

*The future?* Already? Imogen and Amy had all but given up on Jenna ever settling down with anyone. 'That's wonderful! I can't wait to see you. I'll get the spare room made up,' Imogen said, excited at the prospect of catching up with her friend so soon. Hanging out with Jenna would also help distract her from other things, like Gibson admitting that he hadn't *wanted* to sleep with her but couldn't *help* himself.

'Uh…do you mind if I don't stay with you?' Jenna asked. 'We've kind of got plans.'

Imogen tried to keep the hurt from her voice. 'Of course not. We'll do lunch or something.'

'Definitely.'

Imogen recognised that Jenna was so caught up in the bliss of new love she wouldn't recognise another's pain, and she felt upset at herself for feeling it anyway. Wasn't this what she and Amy had always wanted for Jenna? To find what they both had in their marriages? And, despite his childish bet, Guy was a nice bloke.

'Now, what's this I hear about you and the divine Gibson Black? What's happening?' Jenna asked, bursting into Imogen's thoughts.

Her pulse skipped a beat. Technically, nothing was happening. Not anymore.

'Nothing, we're just friends,' Imogen said, because it was the truth. 'We went for a run together this morning.' No one in the world was less likely to judge her for having a quickie in a ute than Jenna. But the truth was, she still didn't know how she felt, and she didn't need any more encouragement to go back for more.

'That's not what Guy reckons.'

Imogen told Jenna about Gibson borrowing Charlie's clothes and how Guy and Warren had driven by at exactly the wrong moment. She left out the bit about the bet, but couldn't help the giggles that came with just thinking about Gibson struggling in Charlie's clothes – she hadn't laughed that hard in a very long time.

Jenna laughed too, but only half-heartedly.

'I think it's one of those had-to-be-there moments,' Imogen said, biting her lip to try and quell her amusement. 'Anyway, how's Amy going? Have you seen much of little Gibson?' she asked, trying to steer the conversation away from the other Gibson.

'Oh yeah, he's so cute.' Imogen could hear the smile in Jenna's voice. 'Did Amy tell you she and Ryan are coming up this weekend too?'

'No.'

'Oh shit, maybe it was supposed to be a surprise, but Ryan's really excited,' Jenna explained. 'It's his last weekend before he goes back to work and Amy says he's driving her mad with talking about seeing Gibson's farm.'

Why did every conversation have to lead back to Gibson? As a shiver slid down her spine, Imogen forced that thought out of her head and chatted with Jenna for another five minutes, making plans for the weekend and thrashing through some more ideas for Man Drought. Perhaps it was a good thing Jenna was now partnered off. It meant she might be more actual help on the weekend and less likely to be distracted by the men on offer.

# Chapter Twenty-two

If there were ever a lovesick puppy contest in Gibson's Find, Guy would take out the gold, silver and bronze.

On Friday night, he rolled into the pub a good hour earlier than usual, ordered a beer and perched himself on a chair as near to the entrance as possible. Imogen tried to make conversation with him at first, and then Cal gave it a go, but for all the response they received, they may as well have been talking with the local livestock. From his vantage point by one of the wide front windows, Guy could see right up the main street, and Imogen knew exactly what (or rather whom) he was watching for. She couldn't wait to see her friends either.

It had only been a few weeks since she'd sat at Amy's bedside in the hospital, gaping down at that precious baby, but it felt like a century. So much had happened since then, and her life in Perth felt like an alternate reality. She hadn't shopped in a supermarket or a speciality store since coming to Gibson's Find, and the strangest thing was she didn't even miss it. Until Jamie had died, she'd always thought she enjoyed working at the wine bar, but she didn't miss that either. Being out here in the bush, running her own business, making a new life all felt so right. But it also added to the guilt.

How could she be so settled, so at peace, with Jamie no longer a part of her life?

'What's a guy have to do to get a drink round here?'

Imogen startled at the voice. Her stomach tumbled and she had to catch her breath. Somehow her new *friend* had slipped into the pub without her noticing. She forced a breath through her lungs as she turned to smile at him.

As if reading her mind, Gibson said, 'I came in the back door with Charlie.'

Briefly distracted from Amy and Jenna's imminent arrival, she asked, 'How is he?'

They'd both tried to get him to relax since the night of the dinner, and Imogen even suggested he cut back on his hours, work fewer late nights. But stubborn as anything, he'd adamantly refused. Everyone was walking on eggshells around the old man, who'd now made too many mistakes for it to be coincidence. The problem was, without coming straight out and telling him they were worried about his memory – which Gibson didn't want to do for fear of upsetting him – they couldn't push the point. He'd been unable to get through to his doctor friend yet, but after both Cal and Karen questioned Charlie's forgetfulness, Gibson had agreed to Imogen discussing the matter with the other employees. They were all now keeping an extra eye out for any issues.

'Yeah, great, it seems. And I've decided to take him to the football next Sunday afternoon. Will you be okay without him?'

Imogen nodded as she got Gibson a schooner of his favourite brew – sadly, the day would probably be easier and less stressful without him. 'That's a brilliant idea. He'll love it.'

He closed his fingers around the glass and took a long sip. 'When are your friends arriving?'

'Any minute.' She snuck another glance towards the door and nodded towards Guy. 'Your mate's set up a vigil.'

Gibson chuckled, but it was only half-hearted. 'Good for him.'

Imogen raised one eyebrow at his distracted statement. 'What's up?' she asked, filling some bowls with pretzels and nuts.

'I finally spoke to my friend about Charlie.'

Imogen paused in her task and looked up, waiting for more. 'And?' She always had to work so hard to pry any information out of him.

Gibson sighed and ran a hand through his hair. 'Daniel thinks I should talk to my parents, and that we should confront Charlie together about him having preliminary dementia tests. Apparently, they can be done by a GP, and then if anything shows up, he'll be referred to a gerontologist for a full assessment.' He screwed up his face. 'But how can I do that to him? I saw how upset he got when Mum suggested he move into a place where he would be looked after, one of those "communities".'

Although he kept his voice down, Gibson became more and more agitated. He was letting down his guard, showing emotion he'd previously kept under lock and key. Instinctively, she wanted to reach out and squeeze his hand; better still, trek round the bar and hug him tight … just a friendly embrace for support and encouragement, the kind she'd give Jenna or Amy if they needed it. But her mind filled with images of the peck on the cheek last Monday night and she didn't trust herself to do either.

She opened her mouth, choosing to offer comfort in words when a shout sounded from the front of the pub.

'She's here!'

Imogen and Gibson's attention was jolted towards the door at Guy's excited announcement. She saw the look on the man's face

– total adoration – and in that second she knew that Jenna had found the guy she'd spend her life with. Or at least as long as fate allowed. Her heart squeezed at the thought.

Jenna stepped up onto the verandah and dropped her bags, running towards her new man.

'Aren't you going to go over?' Gibson took another long sip of his beer as Jenna flung her arms around Guy. Amy and Ryan entered the pub behind her, Ryan pushing a mammoth pram-shaped obstruction.

Imogen shook herself, rubbing her arms to get rid of the goose-bumps. 'Yes. Of course. Back in a moment,' she called to Cal and Charlie as she headed around the bar towards her friends. The three of them huddled in the middle of the room as if this were the first time they'd seen each other in decades. Jenna let go of Guy long enough to embrace Imogen tightly. She pulled back and looked into Imogen's eyes, scrutinising her.

'You used it?' Jenna hissed.

Imogen was momentarily confused. 'What?' Then she realised. *The vibrator.* 'No! Shh. Later.' She flushed bright red. It had been ages since she and Gibson had slept together – even if she still thought about it on a regular basis – but Jenna had always been expert at picking these things. For once, she wished her friend had also been schooled in the ways of tact.

Slipping out of the huddle, Imogen turned to get a look into the top-of-the-range pram. 'How is he? When do I get a cuddle?'

'As soon as I've fed him,' Amy assured her. 'He's been fretting the last half hour but Jenna didn't want to stop.'

Imogen peered down at little Gibson. He looked up at her, wide-eyed but placid. He didn't appear to be fretting, but what did she know about babies?

'Okay, good.' She stepped back so Ryan could ease the pram further into the building. 'Do you want to go somewhere quieter to feed him? There's the office or my apartment, if you'd be more comfortable there.'

'Thanks, that'd be great.' Amy leaned over the pram and scooped her little man up in her arms. The smile she gave the baby before resting his down-covered head upon her shoulder was akin to the one Guy had given Jenna.

Imogen was happy for her friends and all their glee, she really was, but she couldn't help feeling a little sorry for herself.

'Will you be okay without me, hon?' Ryan asked Amy as he glanced towards the bar.

'Sure.' Amy smiled. 'You go chat with Gibson.'

*Chat with Gibson!* The directive sounded so natural, as if Amy and Ryan had known Gibson their whole lives.

Ryan didn't need to be told twice. He dropped kisses on his baby and his wife and then made for the bar.

'I'll stay with Guy, if you don't mind,' Jenna said.

*Hell, you're already sitting on his lap!*

'Enjoy yourself.' Amy wiggled her eyebrows at Jenna and shifted Gibson a little in her arms.

Jenna leaned into Guy's chest and toyed with the buttons of his shirt. 'Oh, I *will*.' Her words positively dripped with wicked intent and, if it were possible, Guy's goofy grin stretched a little further.

'Yeah, have fun.' Imogen forced a smile to show she meant it. Then she grabbed the rail of the pram and wove through the tables to the back of the pub. She glanced at Gibson as she passed, that strange twisting feeling grabbing hold inside her again as she watched Ryan land on the stool beside him. Perhaps it was because Ryan and Jamie had been best friends, and it felt weird to have her husband's mate socialising with the man she'd had a fling with. Well, perhaps fling was a bit of an overstatement, but would Ryan be so keen to 'buy' Gibson a drink if he knew what she'd done with him?

Her heart beat fast, so fast she swore she could hear it thrashing in her ears, as she worried Gibson would let something slip.

'Isn't that a turn-up for the books,' Amy said when they entered the corridor that led to the landlord's residence. 'Jenna smitten.'

'Um, yeah…' Imogen parked the pram at the bottom of the stairs and removed the enormous nappy bag which hung over the rail. She winced as she hooked it on her shoulder – what did babies have that was so damn heavy?

'I wouldn't believe it if I hadn't just seen that greeting with my own eyes.' Amy giggled. 'For a second there, I thought you were going to tell them to hire a room.'

'Really? Did I look that put out?' Imogen paused before launching up the stairs.

'I thought you were going to hit someone.'

'Sorry.' Sharp shots of pain stabbed into Imogen's forehead. 'I'm really happy for Jenna, and I'm so excited you guys are here, but I've got a lot on my mind at the moment.' She slipped the key from the chain that hung around her neck and unlocked the door.

Once inside, Imogen relieved herself of the bag and gestured for her friend to park herself on the couch.

Amy said, 'Some people thought we were crazy coming this far with a newborn baby – especially when he was premmie – but the doctor said he was fine to travel and I wanted to see you. I know you're busy thinking about the Man Drought weekend, but you'd let me know if there was anything more the matter, wouldn't you?'

'Yes. I would, but I'm fine, honestly.' Imogen smiled at her friend and forced a natural breath through her lungs. Maybe she should just tell Amy and Jenna the truth about Gibson, because right now keeping such a big secret from her best friends was eating a chunk inside her. Maybe later … when they were all together.

Amy sunk onto the couch. Then, like she'd been doing it her whole life, she leaned back, flipped up her top, unhooked the front of her maternity bra and manoeuvred baby Gibson into feeding position. She watched for a couple of minutes, mesmerised by the tiny sucking sounds.

'Can I get you a drink?' Imogen finally asked. 'I've heard breast-feeding makes you really thirsty.'

'You've no idea,' Amy snorted, absentmindedly stroking little Gibson's head as he suckled hard.

*No, I don't, and I never will.* Of course, Imogen forced a smile and went to fetch a glass of iced water. Amy hadn't meant to hurt with her comment.

When she returned, Amy was swapping the baby to the other breast. Imogen handed her the water and watched as she gulped it down. 'How long does he take to feed?'

'Not long, only about five minutes on each side,' Amy told her, leaning over to put the empty glass on the table. 'Apparently, that's quick for newborns. Guess he takes after his dad.'

They both laughed.

When Amy's baby fell asleep at her breast, she looked up at Imogen. 'Would you like to change him before we go downstairs?'

Something squeezed around Imogen's heart. 'Yes please.' Most people wouldn't rush to change someone else's baby's dirty nappy, but Imogen wanted to be as much a part of this child's life as possible. She'd probably never experience breastfeeding herself, never snuggle a child and know it had grown from almost nothing in her womb, but she would jump at anything Amy let her share.

Amy handed Gibson to Imogen and took everything she needed from the nappy bag: wipes, a new nappy, a tiny plastic bag, rash cream. They laid the little guy on a clean towel on the couch and Imogen carefully peeled back the two sticky strips on the nappy.

'He's so tiny,' she exclaimed, feeling as if Gibson's little legs might break as she slid the old nappy out from under him.

'He's grown a lot already,' Amy stated, then added, 'Be careful, he can be lethal with that thing.'

Only just in time did Imogen realise what her friend meant. Her reflexes quick, she had the new nappy up and over him just in time to save her uniform from getting squirted. 'I guess we need another nappy now,' she said when he'd finished.

Laughing, Amy retrieved one and handed it to Imogen.

'So that's why that bag's so heavy,' Imogen said, still giggling. 'Reinforcements.'

'Exactly,' Amy replied, gazing down at her little boy.

'Take two.' Imogen put a new nappy on Gibson and scooped up the bundle of sweet-swelling baby, clutching him close against her chest and sniffing his hair. He was warm and soft and snuggly in her arms. She wanted nothing more than to curl up on the couch with him and cherish his tinyness, but Amy was eager to get back downstairs to Ryan, and Imogen had a pub to run.

'Can I take him down?' Imogen asked, not wanting to give him back just yet.

'Sure.' Amy nodded. 'He won't feed again for another few hours, so I might even be naughty and have a little drink.'

As they left the apartment, Imogen descended the stairs as if she were carrying the heir to a throne. Cal stopped her at the edge of the bar for a look, and even Pauli – who had never given the impression of having a maternal bone in her body – did her share of oohing and ahhing.

'I could just eat him up,' Cal said, leaning close and stroking the baby's cheeks. 'Nom nom.'

Pauli laughed dryly and poked Cal in the side. 'You could eat almost anything.'

Finally, one of the patrons, a local farmer who was very rough around the edges but whom Imogen had learnt was all bark and no bite, hollered, 'A bloke could die of thirst in this pub.'

Cal rolled her eyes and went to serve him, Pauli returned to the kitchen, and for the first time since coming downstairs, Imogen looked past the baby in her arms and saw Gibson. He'd migrated from his usual stool by the bar to a table in the corner where he sat, seemingly quite at ease, in the company of Guy, Jenna and Ryan.

\*\*\*

Gibson wasn't alone for long after Imogen went to meet her friends. Charlie ambled over and offered him another drink and even before his grandfather had rid the bottle of its top, Ryan was perched on the stool alongside him.

'Hey mate. Great to see you again.' He held out his hand and nodded towards the beer bottle. 'Next one's on me.'

'Thanks.' Gibson shook Ryan's hand. For a city bloke, he had a strong handshake and his hands were rough and callused. It made him wonder what Amy's husband did for a living. He didn't think Imogen had ever mentioned it. Most of their conversations lately focused on the pub, Charlie, the farm or friendly arguments about the futility of her Man Drought mission.

He was actually coming round to the idea now, although of course he'd never tell her that. The way she described it, the day sounded like a B&S Ball for thirty-somethings, and he had ripper memories from his B&S days.

Gibson had begun to drift into his own little world when he heard Charlie introducing himself to Ryan.

'Hi there,' his grandfather said, offering his hand across the bar. 'You the wee baby's father, then?'

'Yep, that's me.' Ryan's grin stretched from ear to ear as he took Charlie's hand. 'Ryan Reynolds. Pleased to meet you.'

'You too.' Charlie tipped his head. 'Charlie Black. Can I get you a drink?'

'Thought you'd never ask.' Ryan dug out his wallet, which Gibson noticed already boasted a photo of baby, mum and dad. He looked to Gibson. 'Another one of these?'

Charlie went to fetch the beers and Gibson nodded a quick thanks, tearing his gaze away from the perfect picture. 'So, how was the drive?'

'Oh, yeah, great,' Ryan said, snapping his wallet shut and shoving it back in his pocket. 'It's not really that far once you start driving. The girls were desperate to come and I'm really looking forward to having a look round your farm – if we're still on.'

'Uh, yeah, sure.' Gibson had completely forgotten about the offer he'd made in the rush of the moment at the hospital. Ryan had expressed genuine interest in the farm and he'd just named his baby after him, so it had felt like the right thing to do. 'That'd be great. Will you be bringing Amy and the baby?'

Charlie delivered their beers and then shuffled to the other end of the bar to serve someone else. Ryan lifted his bottle and pushed the other one to Gibson. 'Nah, she'll probably want to hang in town and catch up with Imogen. The girls aren't used to such long periods apart.'

While Ryan took his first sip, a funny feeling washed over Gibson at the mention of Imogen. She constantly occupied his mind now, but when someone else mentioned her name, he had to force himself to appear nonchalant, when what he felt was anything but. He did his damn best to be impeccably behaved in her presence but it wasn't easy and there were a lot of cold showers involved.

'Did you meet Imogen and Jenna through Amy?' he asked.

'Kind of. We all started high school together. Me, Amz, Jenna, Im and Jamie.' Ryan suddenly looked horrified. 'Jamie is, um ... *was*...' He took a breath and started again. 'Has Imogen told you much about her past?'

'It's all right,' Gibson said. 'It's not common knowledge but a few of us know about Jamie. She's a strong woman.'

'That's for sure. We all miss him like mad, but I can't imagine losing Amy, can't imagine the pain Imogen feels. Must admit we thought she was insane when she said she wanted to buy a pub, but Jamie would be glad she's found something to focus on. Something to live for.' Ryan went quiet for a moment, then turned slightly and nodded towards Jenna and Guy. 'Listen, do you want to come over and join us?'

Jenna and Guy looked so enthralled with each other, Gibson didn't think they'd either welcome or notice company, but he knew for a fact that the chairs they sat on were comfier than the bar stools. 'Sure, why not?' He guessed Imogen would navigate there when she returned with Amy and he couldn't help wanting to be near her.

It struck him that his daily visits to the pub were now as much about her as they were about Charlie. But where that thought would once have scared the hell out of him, would have spurred him to make excuses and head home, now he pushed it out of his mind and picked up his beer. He and Ryan headed towards the corner table and, surprisingly, Jenna and Guy looked up and welcomed them. Gibson settled into a chair by the window and found the conversation easy.

He learned that Jenna was a curator in some gallery. The way she spoke about art with such passion made him realise she wasn't the ditzy blonde he'd pegged her as. And he had to admit, she and Guy seemed well suited. In looks they were as striking a duo as you could get, and they were already finishing each other's sentences like an old married couple. Although, he couldn't imagine how they'd manage if they decided to make some kind of long-term commitment. Like Gibson, Guy didn't view farming as a job, but a lifestyle. One he'd been born and bred into, one he lived and breathed. He couldn't see Guy packing his bags and heading to the city.

Ryan was the type of bloke who never stopped smiling. He had that easy way of making everyone he talked to feel important. He asked Gibson and Guy lots of questions about farming and almost seemed surprised when they returned the favour, asking him about his job.

He shrugged. 'Ah … I'm just a landscape gardener. Always liked working with my hands.'

'Do you do private gardens or public ones?' Gibson asked, thinking that being outdoors suited Ryan's personality and also likely accounted for why being in the country appealed to him.

Ryan began to explain, but his words died away as he looked past Gibson and his smile grew even more. On instinct, Gibson turned and his heart jolted at the sight. Not at Amy, not even simply at seeing Imogen, but at the way she walked towards them, gently swaying her luscious hips as she clutched Ryan and Amy's baby against her chest, as though he were the most precious thing in the world.

*She'll make a brilliant mother.*

He hadn't taken a sip of his beer for a good few minutes, but he almost choked on that thought. What the fuck did it matter what kind of mother she'd make? Was he getting in too deep? Friendship was supposed to be easier than sex, but right now, it wasn't only teasing his balls, it was taking its toll on his heart as well. He should have got the hell out of there.

The balls of his feet already pushing into the ground, he made the fatal error of meeting Imogen's gaze. They were almost at the table now. She looked straight at him and smiled, but it wasn't her usual wide-lipped grin, the smile he'd been treated to more and more lately. There was something lacking, and as she lowered herself and the baby into the chair across from his, he noted something akin to sadness in her eyes. This was odd, considering she had her two best friends near, and it made him reassess his decision to go. She'd gone beyond the call of friendship this week, listening endlessly to his worries about Charlie, not to mention looking out for him at work. The least he could do was stick around to see if she needed support in return.

'I hope you're looking after my guests,' she said, looking to him and Guy and visibly trying to stretch her smile. 'I want them to come back.'

'You won't be able to keep us away,' Ryan said, pulling Amy onto his lap.

Gibson became acutely aware that he and Imogen were the odd couple – the only pair in the group who weren't actually a couple.

'So, said Imogen, tell us more about this Man Drought weekend,' Ryan asked. 'It sounds like a hoot. I'm almost disappointed I'm a married man.'

Amy punched him in the shoulder and he feigned severe injury. Everyone laughed, because they all knew Ryan wouldn't swap his wedding ring for anyone or anything.

Offering a smile that looked more genuine by the second, Imogen glanced at Gibson. 'Maybe I should let him fill you in. He seems to think he knows best about the situation.'

Gibson raised his eyebrows and took a slug of beer.

'Yeah,' Guy piped up, grinning knowingly, 'tell us what you think about it all.'

'All right.' Gibson leaned back, getting comfy in the seat. Everyone leaned forward in anticipation, but he let them wait a moment. 'I think it's a fabulous idea.'

'Liar!' Imogen only realised she'd shouted when baby Gibson stirred and started to cry. The others laughed – even Amy as she offered to take her baby back.

'Good one,' Gibson said, shaking his head in mock-disgust. 'Upset the baby, why don't you?'

The look she gave him made him think she might whack him like Amy had Ryan.

'If you'd told the truth, I wouldn't have raised my voice,' she spat, still smiling good-naturedly.

'Well, I seem to be outnumbered. Everyone else can't wait, so…' He shrugged. 'If you can't beat 'em, join 'em, right?'

Jenna couldn't hold back after that. She took it upon herself to outline every angle of the Man Drought weekend and why it would be fun as well as positive for the town.

'Even if only a couple of matches are made, the word-of-mouth advertising will mean other women will be starting to trek this way of their own accord. The pub and the town will soon be a hotspot on the Western Australian map,' she concluded.

Gibson pitied anyone who walked into her gallery just to browse – at her animated spiel the excitement was building even in his gut.

'Will you and Amy be making the trip?' he asked Ryan.

'Nah,' Ryan shook his head. 'It's back to work for me on Monday, and although we'd love to come, it doesn't really sound like the kind of thing you can bring a baby to. I'm sure we'll hear all about it from Imogen and Jenna though.'

'Damn straight,' promised Jenna. 'And I'll take a zillion photos.'

After that, they ordered dinner. Gibson hadn't been planning on a late one in town, but he found himself choosing from the menu anyway. Imogen ate with them and then spent the evening flitting back and forth between the bar and the table. Even when she wasn't with them, he could sense her exact whereabouts in the pub.

Arriving late, Wazza joined them halfway through the food. He stole chips from Guy and Gibson's plates and then – typical Wazza style – ordered a meal of his own when everyone else was done. Cal and Charlie joined the conversation on their breaks and the evening flew by. Gibson couldn't believe the time when Cal rang the closing bell. He'd avoided late nights out for a long time, and could count the number of nights he been out with his mates since his divorce on one hand.

He'd deliberately withdrawn from the limited social life there was in Gibson's Find, but all of a sudden he couldn't recall why. He'd forgotten how enjoyable it was just tossing back a few beers and having a good meal with mates. Imogen and her friends had reminded him of this, and he found himself really looking forward to the weekend.

He should have taken a leaf out of her book – life may not have taken the path he'd always imagined it would, but that didn't mean there wasn't another path that could be just as fulfilling. It was time to stop wallowing. Time to reassess and adjust his life goals.

# Chapter Twenty-three

'Woohoo!' Jenna punched the air as Guy's ute drove out of the pub car park with Ryan happily riding in the front seat. It was nine o'clock on Saturday morning and the boys were on their way to Gibson's farm for some bloke time. She turned to Imogen and Amy, who was carrying Gibson in a baby sling. 'Let's play.'

Imogen raised an eyebrow at her friend and couldn't keep the amusement from her voice. 'Getting bored in paradise already?' she asked.

'Not at all,' Jenna said, happiness glowing all over her face. She stepped between Imogen and Amy and wrapped one arm around each of them. 'Last night was amazing. Every day with Guy keeps getting better and better, but that doesn't mean I don't need my girl time.'

Imogen understood exactly what she meant. Ryan had been up at the crack of dawn, pottering round Imogen's kitchen like a kid at Christmas, eager to get the day started. She'd been just as excited.

Having arranged the roster so she wouldn't be needed until late afternoon, she had big plans for a day inside: eating chocolate, flicking through the magazines Jenna had brought from the city, watching favourite romantic comedies, painting each other's toenails, simply talking… They hadn't had a day like this in far too long.

'Amen to girl time,' Amy added. 'Although I hope you don't mind one man present.'

Jenna laughed and Imogen pressed a kiss against baby Gibson's forehead. 'Since he can't talk and spill our girly secrets, we'll make an exception just this once.'

Once inside the apartment, Amy commandeered the couch to feed Gibson, Imogen headed to the kitchen for snacks, and Jenna emptied what she called her 'bag of tricks' all over the coffee table. Neither Amy nor Imogen had ever been *girly* girls, but whenever Jenna was around they played along. Once in a while, they quite enjoyed the whole princess act of facials, manicures and pedicures.

Such luxuries were usually accompanied by chocolate and champagne, but today they decided to go easy on the latter since Amy was breastfeeding and Imogen had to work that night. In theory, Jenna agreed to this, but her actions told a different story. She pulled a bottle from the bottom of her bag, held it high and popped the cork just as Imogen returned with a tray of heated pastries.

'So sue me,' she said with a grin, as Amy and Imogen glared at her. 'I feel like celebrating.'

'Celebrating what?' Imogen asked, taking a bite of a mini chocolate croissant.

'Hmm … let's see, good sex? No, make that fabulous sex, the meeting of like minds and … um…' She glanced around the apartment as if looking for inspiration. 'More fabulous sex.'

Amy shifted Gibson to the other side and shrugged. 'Sounds as good a reason as any to me.'

Starting to blush at the topic of discussion, Imogen headed back to the kitchen, stole a few moments to pull herself together and returned with three champagne flutes. She held each one up as Jenna did the honours, and then passed a glass to Amy.

'To fabulous sex.' Jenna held her glass high and then clinked it in quick succession against Amy's and Imogen's. She collapsed into an armchair and took a sip.

Amy held her glass in her free hand and stared longingly at it. 'I'm not sure I should be drinking this.'

'Surely a tiny sip won't do you any harm,' Imogen said. Now that she could smell the fruity aroma in her own glass, she was rethinking her decision to go easy. What was a girly weekend without champagne?

'That's not what I meant.' Amy snorted. 'I was too uncomfortable during the last month or so of pregnancy to make love with Ryan. I feel like we haven't touched each other in ages.'

Although Amy tried to make a joke of it, you couldn't miss the sadness in her voice. She missed the intimacy with her husband and boy-oh-boy could Imogen relate. The romp with Gibson hadn't been in the same ballpark as what she'd shared with Jamie, but it had at least fulfilled a need. Not wanting to think about that or *him* right now, she took a sip and tried to think of something to say to Amy. Unfortunately, she couldn't find any words of comfort.

Amy read her silence in totally the wrong way. 'Oh, Imogen,' she rushed, leaning forward and almost crushing the baby as she placed her glass on the table. She edged along the couch so her thigh was touching Imogen's and put the arm that had been holding the glass around Imogen's shoulders. 'I'm sorry. That was so insensitive. Here I am, gushing about not having sex for a couple of months, but at least I've still got my husband.'

She pulled Imogen into her side, but Imogen resisted – she didn't deserve this kind of sympathy. The mood in the room had switched from lighthearted and carefree to dark and heavy in a heartbeat. This weekend wasn't supposed to be about tears. Lord knows they'd shed enough of them in the past. Imogen glanced at Jenna, hoping her friend would do her usual trick of saying something funny to clear the air.

'Maybe you should lend her your vibrator, Imogen!'

Imogen winced. Not that, *anything* but that.

'Your what?' Amy's eyes widened as she stared at Imogen.

Reluctantly, she filled Amy in, surprised that Jenna hadn't already told her. By the end of the story, Amy was laughing so hard she had to hand Gibson to Imogen. 'I … have to … see it.' She clutched her belly, only just managing to get the words past her giggles.

'No. Don't be silly.' Imogen stared down at little Gibson's angelic face. 'Mummy and Aunty Jenna are being silly, aren't they, little man?'

'It's not silly, it's hilarious.' Amy took a deep breath. 'I've never needed a *vibrator*, but that doesn't mean I'm not curious. Please get it out.'

'Really? You've never even seen one?' Jenna was incredulous. 'I have failed you both. You should have said something. I'd have been more than happy to show you my collection.'

'This is stupid.' Imogen rolled her eyes, but in the end she relented. She knew her friends: once they were stuck on something, there was no moving on until they got it out of their systems. Rattling off the position of the pink box, Imogen gave Jenna permission to get it from her bedroom.

Amy bounced on the couch in anticipation. Rolling her eyes, Imogen turned Gibson's head against her shoulder to protect his innocent eyes from his mother's depravity.

'Ta-dah!' Jenna appeared back in the lounge room, whipping the fake penis out of its box like a bunny from a magician's top hat. Imogen couldn't help but smirk, imagining Jenna as the assistant to an 'adult' magician.

'Oh! My!' Amy thrust her hand over her mouth. 'It actually looks like one.'

Jenna snorted. 'Honey, if you've seen one that size, Ryan deserves a prize. Guy's is good, but not that good.'

Amy and Jenna succumbed to hysterics again, but Imogen rocked Gibson quietly off to one side. Her cheeks and forehead burned with the sordid thoughts rushing through her head. From what she could recall of Gibson's … um … appendage, it more than measured up to the battery-operated imitation. Jamie had been well-hung, but Gibson, well…

'What's it like?' Imogen glanced up to see Amy turning the vibrator in her hand. 'Go on, spill,' Amy pleaded.

'I haven't used it,' Imogen replied, snuggling the baby close and pushing aside the thoughts she'd been harbouring seconds before. She didn't know why this fact mattered so much, but it did.

'Bull. Shit.' Jenna shook her head. 'I don't care how much you rabbit on about life out here agreeing with you, you don't get that glow in your eyes from country air. You've been getting good release from my present.'

'Shut up, Jenna.' Imogen blushed. With her free hand, she picked up her glass and went to take another sip before realising it was empty. So much for not drinking too much. 'You have no idea what you're talking about,' she added instead.

'Girls, girls, stop.' Amy put down the offending item and held up her hands. 'We're here to relax, have fun and enjoy each other's company. Not bicker about unimportant things. I want to hear all about Imogen's adventures out here. And then,' she turned to Jenna, 'I want to hear exactly what you plan to do about this thing you have going with the farmer.'

The mention of Guy had Jenna beaming ridiculously again. She glanced to Imogen. 'Sorry, I didn't mean to upset you.'

'It's okay. I know.' Imogen wanted to explain why she'd snapped, why she felt so on edge, but the whole vibrator episode hit a nerve. More and more she'd thought about using it these last few days, but each time she'd decided it wouldn't live up to what she'd experienced with Gibson. The man's namesake murmured a baby noise in her arms, and she peered down at his sweet perfection.

It would have been so much easier if she'd had her moment of insanity with a passer-by – one of the travellers who booked a room for one night and then continued on – instead of the grandson of one of her staff. Instead of a local who insisted they could be friends.

'You and Gibson were pretty chummy last night,' Amy mused. 'He seems like a really nice guy.'

Imogen stiffened. Swallowed. Once again wondered if Amy had a direct line to her thoughts. This was her chance to come clean, and part of her really wanted to. If she couldn't discuss her guilt with her best friends, who could she turn to? She shrugged. 'He's only here for Charlie.' Her friends raised their eyebrows – she hadn't meant to sound so defensive.

'That's nice of him.' Jenna selected a pastry from the tray and started to nibble. 'And what's his *story?* Married, divorced, gay?'

*As if!* 'How should I know?' Imogen snapped.

More raised eyebrows, an exchange of meaning-filled stares, and then, 'I don't know, Imogen, you tell us,' from Amy.

With that one statement Imogen knew she'd been caught. She dropped her head, wanting to catch it in her hands but unable to do so because her hands were full of newborn. Instead, she pulled the baby closer, glanced first to Amy, then to Jenna, then to the ceiling.

'Okay, okay, I slept with him.'

Silence filled the room at her announcement. You could have heard a sheep bleat in the next shire. Imogen kept her eyes trained on a Victorian ceiling rose that was wasted in the publican's apartment, and waited for someone to say anything. Already she felt relieved, like a pin had popped the bubble of tension in her heart.

'Wow,' breathed Amy eventually.

'I knew it! Guy was right,' Jenna added. 'And was it fabulous?'

Imogen laughed, when she felt like crying.

Amy stood, picked up her baby and took him across the room to lay him in the pram. When she returned, she sat down next to Imogen. Jenna had already plonked herself on the other side. The two-seater couch was really too small for all of them, but Imogen felt her friends arms close around her. She leaned into their group hug and sobbed.

For a long time, there were no words. Just tears, back rubs and someone stroking her hair. She'd always loved people playing with or brushing with her hair – it relaxed her and her friends knew this. She was so damn lucky to have these fabulous women in her life and she wanted to talk about what she'd done, how being with Gibson had made her feel, but where the hell was she supposed to start?

Sniffing, she pulled out of their embrace. 'Thanks guys. I just miss him so much.' She meant Jamie, although she hadn't been able to get Gibson out of her mind since that fateful day either.

'That's totally understandable,' Amy said. At her voice, the baby made a noise in the pram and she stretched out her hand and started to rock it.

'We miss him too,' Jenna added quietly, 'but you are allowed to move on.'

Her heart stampeded at the mere thought. 'Moving *here* was about moving on, starting a new business, making a new life, but it was never about finding a new man and it *definitely* didn't include sleeping around.'

Jenna let out a snort of disbelief. 'Unless there are other men you're not telling us about, I hardly think you can call it sleeping around. How many times have you slept with him?'

'Once,' Imogen admitted, unable to meet her friend's eye. 'But that one time was in the back of his ute, at the side of a road.'

'No way.' Amy sounded surprised, impressed and also a little disappointed.

'I know.'

Jenna clapped her hands and shrieked, 'You go, girl.'

Imogen glared at her.

'Sorry.' Jenna shrugged apologetically. 'But was it really that terrible?'

There wasn't a straightforward answer to that question. 'If I'm going to talk about this, I'm going to need more poison. Sorry Amy.' Imogen picked up the bottle and shared the remnants between her and Jenna's glasses.

'Go for it.' Amy waved her hand in front of her face. 'I'll just overdose on water.'

After a long sip of liquid courage, Imogen finally felt ready to talk. 'The actual act wasn't terrible at all.' She took a deep breath and shared with her friends everything that had happened since she met Gibson. The feelings of desire she hadn't experienced in years, the way Gibson had been distant and downright grumpy at first, and how she'd still found herself attracted to him. His admission of lust and the magic they'd experienced straight after. She was generous with her detail, so much so that it almost felt as if she were sharing someone else's story. Jenna was on the edge of her seat throughout and Amy fanned her face a number of times.

'God. It sounds so hot,' Jenna sighed. 'Although I could have told you that simply by looking at the man. I have a sixth sense about these things, you know.'

'And so you should,' Amy said with a smirk. 'How many guys have you slept with now?'

Jenna poked her tongue at Amy. 'That's beside the point. Now I've found Mr Right, my playtime is over, but Imogen's is just beginning.'

'It is not,' Imogen objected. 'I don't want to *play*.' The connotations made her feel sick. 'I had my playtime with Jamie. Now I … I don't know what I want.'

'Don't get angry at me for saying this,' Amy began, in a tone that made Imogen wonder if she should poke her fingers into her ears and hum, 'but maybe you want more than play. What you had with Jamie was more than some people ever find, but it doesn't mean you can't or won't ever find it with someone else. For you to take the major step of getting intimate with Gibson, there had to be something special there. I know there did. So maybe you should open yourself up to the possibility of more … with him.'

Imogen hadn't allowed herself to entertain that possibility for a number of reasons. Every time she started to think about merely sleeping with Gibson again, the guilt of how she felt after that one time came rushing back. She couldn't deal with that on a daily basis. But there was another massive roadblock – one she now realised had never been far from her mind.

'This is all a moot point anyway,' she told her friends, 'because even if I was willing to consider it, he doesn't want a relationship.'

★★★

Out at Roseglen, the blokes were having a ripper of a day.

They'd started by taking Ryan on a jaunt round the property and making him feed the sheep. Gibson was impressed by Ryan's questions – the city bloke wanted to know everything from what the sheep ate (mostly lupin, which was high-protein and high-energy) to what crop would be sown where over the next few months (a bit of wheat, a bit of canola). Although they came from completely different backgrounds, the three men clicked, and Gibson found himself making plans for catching up with Ryan and Amy in Perth some time, maybe taking in a football game or something.

They enjoyed a man's lunch of bacon, eggs and beans – their one token vegetable – and then Gibson suggested to Guy they take Ryan stubble-burning for the remainder of the day. He had fences to fix and hadn't planned on starting burning until next week, but it was definitely more exciting than fencing, which – although it sorted the boys from the men – was as boring as batshit.

For a brief moment after he suggested it, Gibson thought he may have made a massive error of judgement – like, how could he forget the guy's best mate died fighting a fire? But he let out a breath of relief when Ryan's eyes lit up in anticipation.

Luckily, the wind was neither too strong or too weak, so it was perfect burning-off weather. The men hauled a chilled sixpack of beer and the fire unit onto the back of the ute, and as they drove out to the paddocks, Guy gave their city visitor the lowdown on burning off.

'We do this every year before seeding. The aim is to reduce the weed and straw burden left over from the previous year and get the paddock ready. It's not rocket science,' he explained, 'but the fire can get away if you're not careful. One minute it's burning gently, the next minute, bam! But it does add a bit of excitement.'

Ryan smirked. 'These fires sound a bit like women, just when you think you've got them under control, they prove you wrong.'

'Amen. Exactly like that,' Guy agreed.

The blokes laughed as they approached a paddock that had held canola last season. Guy opened and closed the gates as they passed through, and when they arrived at their destination, Gibson parked the ute alongside a rickety fence and they all tumbled out.

His hands on his hips, Ryan surveyed the dry paddock before them. 'The stubble's a lot thicker than I imagined.'

Guy nodded. 'That's why we want to get rid of as much as possible before seeding. The burning should also kill any weed seeds. See this thing?' he said, holding up a green stripy sphere.

'It's called a paddymelon.' The paddock was covered in them. 'It's a weed from South Africa. Pain in the arse.'

Gibson walked to the back of the ute and retrieved the drip torch: a long metal stick with the handle and fuel container on one end and a wick on the other. Charlie occasionally helped him burn stubble, but he mostly did this job alone since his parents moved to Perth.

One thing about farming was that it often left farmers with far too much time to contemplate. Many men liked this, joking that they spent longer on their tractors than was strictly necessary because it was better than heading indoors and being nagged by the missus. Gibson had been one of those men during those last few months with Serena. He shook himself, hating every time she came into his head. Today, he was happy for the company. Happy not to contemplate any of the issues that currently took up his headspace.

Drip torch in hand, he headed back round the ute to where Guy was giving Ryan a potted history of Western Australian farming. Guy could talk the leg off a piece of furniture, and if he didn't interrupt, they'd never get anything done.

'Do you want to do the honours?' he asked, holding the torch out to Ryan.

'Really?' Ryan looked as if Gibson was holding out a python. 'You sure?'

'Yeah, definitely.' He turned to Guy. 'Do you want to follow us in the ute?'

Nodding, Guy headed back to the vehicle. Trying not to offer a long-winded explanation, Gibson gave Ryan a quick explanation. They'd work round the edge of the paddock first, testing the conditions before going back up and down the middle. The idea was to light up the header trails, where the majority of the rubbish was spat out from the machine during harvest. If he were on his own, he'd have lit the fire by leaning out the side of his ute, but he wanted to give Ryan the chance to get up close and personal, to see the stubble wilt and the blasted paddymelons blow and pop.

Ryan was a quick learner, and before long the outer border of the paddock was alight. Gibson left Ryan and Guy with a beer each at the gate, and then took the ute, lighting up and down the middle of the paddock. When he'd finished, he headed back to his friends, satisfied a good job had been started.

Guy cracked open a beer, handing it to Gibson as he joined them at the gate.

Ryan held up his bottle. 'If this is the life of a farmer, I'm seriously in the wrong job.'

Gibson laughed, biting down on the impulse to tell him that this was a luxury. Instead he took a quenching sip of his own drink. Yeah, beer found its way into many farming activities, but sitting idle was rare. Usually, he'd make sure the fire was under control and then head off to the next paddock or another job on the never-ending list of tasks that needed to be completed.

All three men watched the stubble, sipping beer and waiting for someone to break the comfortable silence. Gibson wondered if the other two were thinking about Amy and Jenna, because Lord knows he couldn't get Imogen out of his head.

As if he was a mind reader, Ryan spoke. 'So guys, man to man, how's Imogen really coping out here?'

Gibson shifted uncomfortably against the fence as his grip tightened around the bottle. Guy glanced over.

'Must admit this move surprised us all,' Ryan continued. 'It's hard, her being so far away. A single woman alone in a pub; she's the perfect prey for undesirables. I worry about her.'

'Um…' Gibson hesitated. If Ryan knew the truth, maybe he'd consider *him* one of those undesirables. Or maybe he already knew.

Guy jumped in before Gibson had the chance to work out what the hell he planned on saying. 'She's awesome, mate. I wouldn't worry. Aside from running with Gibson, I don't think I've seen her talk to a bloke for longer than five minutes. I'm sure she can hold her own. Besides, she's one of us now. We'll look out for her.'

Gibson nodded, hoping Ryan wouldn't ask about the running.

'Thanks,' Ryan said, then turned to Gibson. 'So you've been seeing a bit of her, have you?'

Gibson realised that even if Imogen had told her friends anything, Amy hadn't passed it on. He aimed for a nonchalant shrug, when his feelings towards her were anything but. 'We went for a jog once. I agree, she's a great chick – we'll make sure none of the blokes take advantage. Hell, she's being so great with my granddad, I'd do anything for her.' He held his breath when he'd finished, wondering if his promise had been a little over the top. It was true, though. He *would* do anything for her.

'Thanks.' Ryan nodded his appreciation. 'It's good to know she's doing okay. She's had a rough time and she needs friends around her.'

'Jenna said Imogen's husband died.' Guy said.

'Yes.' That one word was jam-packed with choked emotion. 'It was a shock for us all. Jamie was one of those guys who everyone thought was invincible, he had so much life ahead of him. He'd have made an awesome dad. May sound a bit corny, but I couldn't wait for us to have kids together. You know, play footy with them, take them camping.'

'Yeah,' Guy replied, and took another sip of his beer. 'So, mate, what's it like being a dad? Having a rugrat?'

Ryan grinned. 'The absolute best. No greater feeling than holding the little dude, having him look up into your eyes and smile – even though Amz says it's just wind at this stage. I already live for him.'

Gibson tried to speak but nothing could push past the lump in his throat. After a few silent moments of contemplation, he tried to redirect the conversation, but every thought that entered his head revolved around Imogen. 'So, do you think Imogen will ever move on? Find someone else, maybe settle down?'

Ryan twisted his beer bottle between his thumb and index finger, a pensive expression on his face. 'You know, I wouldn't be surprised if she didn't. She's strong and independent, and although I'd like to see her happy again – and it's definitely what Jamie would have wanted – I just can't imagine who could replace him. It'd even be weird for us, accepting someone to fill his spot.'

'Yeah, right.' Ryan's words shouldn't have made Gibson feel like they did. He stared ahead, noticed a flame that had jumped off-track. It didn't look like a serious issue, but he grabbed the chance to get away. 'Just going to check that out,' he said, pointing in the direction of the errant flame and launching into a jog. He guessed Guy would be raising his eyebrows at his paranoia, but he didn't care.

By the time he returned to the gate, the second beers were almost finished. The conversation had moved on to football and Ryan and Guy were making bets about which AFL teams would get through to the grand final.

The afternoon sun was slowing fading. Ryan would likely have stayed on the farm for a couple more hours but Guy was eager to get back to Jenna. And although Gibson wouldn't admit it, he felt the same about Imogen. The boys packed up the fire gear and headed back to the house. After making plans to meet at the pub, Ryan and Guy drove off to get cleaned up. Gibson fed the dogs, had a lightning-quick shower, took longer than he normally would agonising over which clean shirt to wear, and then drove back into town.

Part of him knew it would be safer to stay away, but Ryan had voiced his hopes that Gibson would be at the pub again tonight, and he wasn't strong enough to pass up the opportunity of another evening near Imogen.

***

The Saturday night crowd hadn't yet arrived at the pub, so Cal pushed Imogen in the direction of her friends. 'How often do you get to hang out with them?' she asked. 'Go and have fun. I'll call if I need help.'

Ryan had come back from the farm that afternoon, beaming and full of stories about their day. Somehow Amy had shut him up long enough to push him into the shower to get the smell of smoke out of his hair. Jenna had gone to Guy's place for a few hours, but now they were back, settled at the same table they'd occupied the night before.

After a brief hesitation, Imogen relented and approached the table with a tray of drinks. Gibson wasn't there, and as she handed round the glasses, she bit down on the urge to ask the guys whether he was coming in tonight. If she mentioned him, Jenna and Amy would toss knowing smiles her way, and she wouldn't be able to stop the spread of red up her neck and all over her face. She wasn't sure whether she wanted him here or not – last night had been awkward enough with them the only two not coupled off – but her friends knowing she'd slept with him would take awkward to a whole other level.

Still, she did want to see him. His wry grin, which took a lot to elicit, had become more frequent in the pub. When it wasn't making her knees weak, it made her feel comfortable – safe, somehow.

She tried to concentrate on the conversation going on around her, but her mind was snagged on one thing: *Am I willing to consider a relationship?*

As much as she didn't want to contemplate this question, she couldn't stop. Doubts had been planted from all directions – Jenna, Amy, Charlie, even simply watching other couples interact. She missed that. She missed the intimacy – not sexual, although that would be an added bonus – you had with a boyfriend, a husband, a lover.

When she curled up in bed at night, she still talked to Jamie, but she didn't need their nightly conversations to keep her going anymore. Once, they'd been the highlight of her day, but now there was something else, *someone* else she looked forward to even more.

That was Gibson Black.

*Oh Lord!* Rarely feeling the inclination to swear, Imogen suddenly thought of a number of words she wanted to shout out loud. And they were all words that would have her mother washing her mouth out with soap.

Of all the men she could have chosen, she had to fall for – if that's what this was – one who swore black and blue he was never getting married again. Not that she'd gotten as far as contemplating marriage, but she was a traditional kind of girl. Casual sex might scratch an itch, but in her opinion, sex was overrated unless it came in a package alongside friendship, a future and love. Sex without strings hadn't worked for her. Was Amy right? Was it because deep down she wanted more?

Her heart skipped a few beats at the thought. She'd come to Gibson's Find alone, relishing the chance to be independent, to show her friends and family that she could make a new life for herself. Could it be that new life would involve something she'd never imagined possible?

'What are you smiling at?' Guy asked, before taking a long sip of his beer.

'You two,' she said, thinking quickly and gesturing to the new lovebirds. Maybe she wasn't crazy about Gibson, maybe it was simply loved-up Jenna and Guy and gorgeous little Gibby playing havoc with her emotions. 'It's hard not to.'

Guy grinned as he pulled Jenna even closer. Both men seemed to accept this excuse, but Jenna and Amy scrutinised her. She ignored them, staring into the pram at their side. 'Can I have a cuddle?'

'Sure.' Amy lifted baby Gibson out of the pram and handed him to Imogen. Conversation flowed – everything from the boys' day out at Roseglen to the Man Drought weekend and Jenna's latest exhibition – until Ryan lifted a hand to wave at someone who'd just walked in the door and Imogen's whole body seized up.

She had all of three seconds to prepare before Gibson folded himself gracefully into the chair beside her and greetings were exchanged all around. She couldn't even look at him, so scared was she that Amy and Jenna would be watching her every move and analysing each tiny flutter of her eyelashes. Her hands began to shake and she tightened her hold on the baby. She was happy she'd told her friends – getting *that* off her chest felt like a heavy load had been lifted – but it meant they'd be watching her and Gibson like hawks.

Conversation ebbed and flowed around her, but Imogen couldn't have relayed what was discussed. She remained quiet, subconsciously rocking along to the background music as her gaze constantly flicked to the bar, looking for an excuse to escape. After about half an hour, the pub began to fill and Imogen stood. Likely Cal and Charlie had everything under control, but she wouldn't be taking her role seriously if she didn't make sure. She passed baby Gibson back to Amy and fled to the bar.

'Need help?' Imogen asked Cal.

'Actually, yes, sorry.' She sounded unusually flustered. Imogen followed her employee's gaze to see Charlie with a long line of untouched drinks on the bar in front of him.

She frowned. 'Problems?'

'You could say that,' Cal sighed. 'He's getting everyone's drinks mixed up. The locals are being tolerant, but those contractors we have staying are starting to get pissed about it. If you could just help me clear the crowds, then I should be able to handle it again.'

Cal could handle it on her own, but she shouldn't have to. Imogen served one man who was tapping dirty fingernails on the wood of the bar and then scooted along to Charlie.

'Hey mate,' she began, racking her mind for the most tactful words for what she needed to say. 'Do you mind going and entertaining my guests? Ryan would love to hear your farming stories – he's had enough of Gibson and Guy's.' And even if he hadn't, he'd have to put up with it. Imogen couldn't afford mistakes on her busiest night of the week.

Charlie seemed to be deliberating, so Imogen batted her eyelashes for effect. She let out a sigh of relief when he headed to the table armed with another round of drinks and the dinner menu.

She'd have to talk to Gibson about him again, but was it wrong to be happy about his forgetfulness just this once? Wrong to use it as an excuse to get away from the awkwardness she'd felt sitting there with Gibson and her friends? Whatever the answer, she knew one thing for sure.

She wanted her friends back in the city so she could have Gibson all to herself again.

# Chapter Twenty-four

It was Friday morning, exactly seven days before the Man Drought weekend. Although the days were crazy busy, Imogen found time to nurture her little crush. It had taken a while to get her head around it – there'd been a few tears and much staring at Jamie's photo before she'd admitted it to herself – but now she was getting used to the idea. She was ready to move on. Really move on.

Maybe there wasn't just *one* perfect person for everyone.

Once that thought had seeded itself in her head, there was no going back. Gibson consumed her thoughts, so that she had to make a mammoth effort to focus on other things. The times he swaggered into the pub, smiled his country-boy grin and ordered a beer had become the highlights of her days. And the best thing? He'd popped in a couple of times when Charlie wasn't even rostered to chat and check that Imogen had everything under control for the weekend. He'd even offered his help as an extra barman. Talk about a turnaround! Not that she was complaining. Not. At. All.

Over coffee, they'd discussed everything from Charlie to their parents, their favourite movies, and foods they wouldn't eat if they were paid to. Time in his company flew by and she felt as close to him as she did to Jenna and Amy, yet she hadn't garnered the courage to confess her feelings. He'd sleep with her again in a second – of that she was certain – but she didn't believe he could offer more. If only she could get to the bottom of his marriage issues.

'Penny for them?' Pauli passed through the bar on her way to the kitchen ready to start her shift.

'Just wondering what you were making for lunch,' Imogen lied, rubbing her tummy for effect.

Pauli's eyes lit up. 'Cal gave me the recipe for her Mexican soup. I thought I'd give it a try alongside the usual lunchtime pies.'

'Give what a try?'

Imogen and Pauli turned. As if her thoughts had summoned him, Gibson stood in the doorway looking his usual version of ruggedly handsome.

'It's a secret, good-looking.' Pauli wriggled her eyebrows before continuing on her way.

'Wipe that smile off your face.' Imogen pretended to be stern. 'She only said that because you shower her with compliments about her cooking. Now, what can I do for you today?'

'Actually, it's what I can do for you. Charlie said there was a wobbly post on the verandah, and, well,' he held up his hands, 'I had a few moments to spare.'

Of course she smiled. He had that effect. 'Fabulous. Thank you. I'll bring you out a coffee.'

While Gibson got busy with nails and a hammer, Imogen switched on the coffee machine. She made his usual long black and made herself a latte. Despite having a load of paperwork to get through, she couldn't see the harm in one drink with the handyman.

Carrying two takeaway cups outside, she paused as she stepped onto the verandah. He was at the other end, tool belt wrapped around his torso as he reached up to steady the top of the post.

She found herself fantasising again. An image popped into her head: a sweet boy (or girl, she wasn't fussy) with her eyes and his dark-chocolate hair. If only she could thaw his frosty heart, they'd make beautiful babies. The thought caused her lips to lift and her heart to flutter, until reality landed. She'd always had a terrible habit of getting ahead of herself.

'Do I get to drink that coffee before it gets cold?' he turned to look at her.

'Not if I throw it over you first,' she said, walking to join him and give him the coffee.

'Settle Gretel,' he growled, but his lips twisted into a smile.

They sipped in silence for a while, and then he mentioned that the rest of the posts could probably do with replacing too.

She groaned. 'I'll add it to the list.' By now she should have been used to the fact that where old buildings were concerned, there were always more things to be done. The slab party volunteers had done a fabulous job, but most of their work had been surface stuff.

'I'm starting seeding soon, but after that, I'm happy to do it. It won't take much.'

'Thanks, I'll pay you for it.'

He waved her suggestion away with his hand. 'Don't be silly. But speaking of payment, I know Charlie's not been the best employee lately and Karen mentioned you might be looking for an extra staff member.'

She nodded. 'But it's not only because of Charlie,' she rushed. 'We're getting busier. I want the safety net in case any of us get sick.'

'Can you afford the extra staff member?' he asked.

They both knew she wouldn't let Charlie go if she could help it, but she'd decided to make sure there were more bar staff rostered on at the same time as him, just in case.

She tried for a carefree shrug. 'I think so. Business has really picked up lately. I was thinking about it anyway.'

He took another sip of his coffee, then said, 'Let me pay Charlie's wages for the time being.'

'No.' Her objection was loud. 'I don't need—'

He held his hand up and cut her off. 'Please. Let me do this. Just until I've got him to the doctor and we know what's happening. I want to help.'

She frowned, but she could see his point. 'Okay.' She downed the rest of her coffee and heard the paperwork beckoning. 'Guess I'd better do some work. Yell if you need anything.'

As she turned, he reached out and touched her arm. Her heart jolted at the contact. 'Thanks for understanding,' he said, looking seriously into her eyes. 'And Imogen?'

'Yes.' Her mouth went dry.

'Please don't tell Charlie about our arrangement.'

Her heart sunk. He was stuck on Charlie – rightly so – where she still had her head in the clouds.

'I won't,' she promised. 'And you're so welcome.'

★★★

Gibson listened to the Sunday morning radio show on ABC Radio as Charlie dozed in the passenger seat beside him. They were headed to Perth for the AFL game – Dockers versus Eagles – and his heart was light with anticipation. He hadn't been to an actual game in years. The road was long and straight, giving him plenty of time to think, much like the long hours on a tractor during seeding and harvesting.

He glanced at Charlie. Although he was still a strapping, bulky man, he'd appeared frailer lately. What Gibson couldn't tell was if this was real or whether Charlie's strange behaviour was making him look at his grandfather differently. He thought of the man he used to be – always on the go, taking Gibson and Paris out to football games or camping up on Lookout hill. Most of his childhood memories involved his grandfather in some way. When Charlie was gone – and he knew this would happen eventually – that was the man he wanted to remember. Today was about creating new memories on the strong foundations of old ones.

As they got closer to Perth, his thoughts drifted from Charlie to his parents, then to the farm, and finally came to rest on Imogen. *Imogen!* Even her name made him feel good – a simple rush to the head: better than beer, better than a rollercoaster, better than sex. No, not better than sex with her. That one episode topped the charts where his sex life was concerned. Maybe it was because she'd been the first after a long drought, but something told him otherwise.

When he thought of Imogen now, sex wasn't the foremost thing in his mind. Thinking about their interaction yesterday, he couldn't help but grin at the way she'd threatened to throw his coffee all over him. He almost wished she had. Then he'd have had a stellar excuse to throw her over his shoulder and spank her. But that episode wasn't unique – things were always like that between them now. Sparks flying, but both of them too conscious of the boundaries to follow through.

*Yes. Boundaries, Gibson. Hold on to those boundaries.*

Charlie stirred and Gibson pounced on the opportunity for conversation. 'Good sleep, Granddad?'

'I wasn't sleeping,' Charlie said gruffly. 'Just closing my eyes to block out the sun.'

'Of course.' Gibson chuckled. He loved that Charlie would never admit to any human weakness – not that sleeping was a weakness – but he knew this character trait might cause issues soon. Maybe he should have broached the subject of the doctor now, while they were in the car and Charlie couldn't escape.

Before he had the chance, Charlie said, 'You're not thinking of taking me to see your parents, are you? Wouldn't want to spoil a good day.'

Gibson blinked. A visit to his folks hadn't crossed his mind. 'Course not. This day is about you and me.' He decided not to say anything else. If he told Charlie his fears, the day would be over before it had even begun.

Charlie smiled and looked out the window as the city came into view.

***

Soon they'd parked the car and were trekking towards Subiaco Oval, joining the hordes of excited supporters all decked out in brightly coloured fan-wear – purple and white for the Dockers, and blue and gold for the Eagles. Gibson stayed close to Charlie, making sure he wasn't knocked over in the rush to get through the gates and up into the stands.

Gibson had supported the Eagles since the eighties, as had his grandfather. But when the Dockers were founded in 1994, Charlie switched his loyalties, saying that Fremantle had always been in his blood. Gibson was only a boy at the time, but already believed that you chose a team and stuck to it. The rivalry had been a sore point between them since.

When they found their seats, they seemed to be the only pair that had come together that were wearing different coloured scarves. Charlie leaned forward in his plastic seat and rubbed his forehead.

'You all right, Granddad?' Gibson asked.

Charlie sat up straight. 'Fine. What's the time? When's the game start?'

Like a child, Charlie didn't see why they should wait for the stadium to fill or for the official start time. They were here, and as far as he was concerned, that was all that mattered. He was really starting to get agitated when the siren finally sounded. Relieved, Gibson flopped back into his chair, amped to watch the game.

The Eagles scored the first four goals, but then the Dockers came into their own. By the end of the first quarter, the score was a rare equal.

'Come on!' Charlie screamed when the Eagles repelled a promising attack early in the second quarter, and a first-gamer smothered a kick to stop a certain goal. His neck veins bulged as he shook his fists in the air, but the intent look on his face and his all-out grin when the Dockers finally scored again told Gibson his granddad was having a blast.

The score was neck and neck and both teams were playing the best they'd played for a long time, so Gibson couldn't believe it when, five minutes before halftime, Charlie insisted he fetch him a pie.

'What? Can't it wait?' Gibson's eyes remained on the field where two opposing players were in a tangle over the ball. This was like asking him to go get popcorn during the climax of a movie.

'I'm starving,' Charlie replied. He rubbed his belly. 'Starting to get dizzy.'

That had Gibson leaping out of his chair. The last thing he wanted was Charlie fainting in the middle of an overcrowded stadium. Grumbling under his breath, he squeezed past angry fans to get to the exit.

When he emerged, the area that housed the restrooms and refreshment stands was deserted except for the stadium staff and a pregnant woman coming out of the ladies'. As he and the woman approached each other from opposite directions, he glanced her way, intending to offer a friendly smile, but stopped short in his tracks.

'Serena?' Whether he'd meant to say her name aloud or not he didn't know, but she stopped and looked up from where she'd been typing something on a mobile phone. One hand went to rest on her belly.

'Gibson! So good to see you.' She sounded happier to see him than he was to see her. She stashed the phone in her bag and rushed forward to give him a hug. The embrace was uncomfortable, not least because of the massive bump protruding between them.

Finally, she stepped back slightly, her hands still on his arms as she looked him over. 'You're looking fabulous,' she said, as if they'd barely been more than acquaintances and hadn't seen each other since high school.

Grudgingly he told her the same, because pregnancy did suit her. Even if you removed the designer maternity outfit from the equation, she glowed in the way all pregnant women were supposed to.

She finally let him go. 'So, how's the farm? How's your family?' Her smile was forced and her tone full of fake enthusiasm.

'Fine,' he replied, not wanting to encourage her. 'I see you're doing well.'

'Ah. Yes.' She rubbed her bump, the glow in her cheeks deepening to a guilty blush. Suddenly an awkward silence reigned between them. 'I suppose you heard I married Grant?'

Grant had been her boyfriend before Gibson; they'd broken up only a few months before Gibson and Serena got together. 'Yes, I heard. Didn't hear about that though.' He nodded towards her stomach and then quickly averted his gaze. 'Congratulations.'

'I'm sorry, Gibson.' She sounded genuine, but he guessed she might be sorrier for the small bit of guilt she harboured than anything else.

'Ancient history,' he said. 'Anyway, I'm supposed to be getting Charlie a pie. Better go.' He hoped he sounded cool and carefree, because in reality he felt like he'd been kicked in the nuts.

Somehow, he got a pie and a bottle of water for each of them; somehow he made it through the game. The Dockers creamed the Eagles in the second half but Gibson couldn't summon the energy to care. Charlie had a ball and Gibson told himself that's what mattered. That was why they'd come. It didn't matter that he'd seen Serena. He was more than over her.

But Charlie noticed his quietness as they began their journey. 'What's up with you? Told you my boys were going to kick the Eagles' butts, didn't I?'

Gibson managed a half chuckle and shook his head. 'I'm fine, Granddad. Things on my mind is all.'

He felt Charlie's eyes boring into the side of his head. 'Something happen at the game I missed? You were fine until you went for the food.'

Charlie's sharp observation made Gibson wonder if they were silly to be worried about him. He also knew his granddad wouldn't let up. He'd either have to buck up his mood or confess. 'I ran into Serena,' he said finally. 'She's pregnant.'

'Oh.' An awkward pause. 'Well, I suppose it has been a while since she left. How do you feel about it?'

'Fine. I'm happy for her. Just a shock, seeing her after all this time. I don't really want to talk about it.'

'Suit yourself.' Charlie opened the magazine from *The Weekend West* and settled in to read.

But not talking about Serena and her pregnancy didn't mean Gibson stopped thinking about her. When he and Charlie finally arrived back in Gibson's Find, the last thing he felt like doing was facing the pub, facing Imogen. But he'd promised to tell her how Charlie had been, and if nothing else, he was a man of his word.

★★★

'Imogen!'

She startled at Cal's call and almost dropped the glass she'd been polishing. She'd like to say she'd been going over her to do list – an extensive inventory of preparations for Man Drought – but that would have been a lie. She'd been daydreaming. Again.

'Do you mind serving Wazza?' Cal nodded towards the other side of the bar.

The pub was getting busy – unheard of for a Sunday night a couple of months ago, but now not unusual at all. It seemed the locals liked what she'd done to the place. There were even a few couples: women who never ventured into the bar before she arrived but whom she'd discovered did exist, sipping bottles of beer or glasses of wine with their smug husbands. They started to come out of the woodwork when she'd first raised the idea of the Man Drought weekend, and all voiced their enthusiasm for Imogen's plan to bring more oestrogen back to the region. Many of these couples had volunteered their spare rooms when the accommodation at The Majestic had filled.

'Imogen? Hello?' At Cal's voice, she realised she'd drifted off again. What the hell was wrong with her?

'Sorry Warren,' she turned to her patron. 'What can I get for you?'

'Just the usual, please. Got an early start tomorrow, so I'd better make it my last.' He leaned in close. 'What's the dress code for this … uh … Man Drought thing?'

Imogen tried not to smile at the first sign of uncertainty she'd ever seen in Warren. He was usually Mr Cocky. 'Smart casual on Friday and Saturday nights, and casual during the day. That help?' she asked, pouring him a glass of Carlton Dry.

'Yeah, great.' He passed her his money. 'My sister's sending me a couple of new shirts from Perth, but I didn't want to go overboard.'

'You'll be perfect.' And she meant it. Some smart woman would look past Warren's class-clown charms and see the genuine and sweet man inside.

'Thanks.' He held up his glass to show his approval, then swaggered off to join his mates around the pool table. Not Gibson, though. He was still at the football with Charlie. She glanced at her watch – almost eight o'clock. The game would be long over and they'd be on their way home. He'd promised to pop in after dropping Charlie home, but he could be tired after the round trip to Perth. He could change his mind.

She felt a hand on her arm and jumped.

'Jeez, you're on edge tonight,' Cal said. 'Are you okay?'

Imogen smiled at her employee, who'd become a good friend in a short space of time. 'Just tired.' It wasn't a total lie. She was tired – tired of not being able to think about anything or anyone else but Gibson. Tired of trying to work out what she should do about these feelings, *if* she should do anything at all.

'Go have a quick break upstairs.' Cal gestured to the rest of the pub. 'The rush is over now, I think. Quite a few people are starting to head out and I can always grab Pauli for a few minutes, if necessary.'

Cal was right. She really could do with a few minutes to try and pull herself together. 'Okay, that'd be great. Thanks.'

Imogen ran up the stairs to her apartment, drank a long glass of ice-cold water, and had just decided on five minutes with her feet up on the couch when her mobile rang. Jiggling the phone from her pocket, she glanced at the screen and smiled.

'Hey Jenna,' she said, leaning back into the couch again.

'Have I caught you at a bad moment?'

'Nope. I can talk. I'm on a break. How are you?'

'Pregnant,' Jenna said, in a tone she may have used to say 'fine' or 'great'.

For a second Imogen wondered if she'd heard correctly. 'Did you say "pregnant"?' Her heart began a heavy beat at the thought.

'Uh-huh. Surprised?'

Speechless, more like. Imogen took a moment to gather her thoughts and locate an appropriate response. 'Wow,' she said eventually. 'Is it Guy's?'

'You betcha.'

Imogen knew she should summon some enthusiasm, but a volcano of emotions had erupted inside her. Thankfully, Jenna started rambling. 'We only just found out. I had my suspicions this morning when I realised I was a couple of days late – you know how like clockwork my cycles are. I called Guy and he came to Perth immediately, armed with three pregnancy-testing kits. We did the lot and they all showed positive.'

Imogen struggled to get her head around everything Jenna told her, not the least her friend's excited response. Jenna had *never* been enthusiastic about motherhood.

*It's not fair*, Imogen thought, as a lone tear slipped from her left eye. She needed to pretend for Jenna, to hold off the avalanche of tears until she was off the phone. It felt like a slap in the face that her terminally single best friend was suddenly achieving everything Imogen had always dreamed of. Jenna had Guy. And soon, like Amy, she'd have a baby.

Meanwhile, Imogen had nothing. *Damn you, Jamie!*

'I know you're not supposed to say anything until three months or anything, but you know how terrible I am at keeping secrets.' Imogen tried to focus on Jenna's words, knowing she'd missed a bit in the middle there. 'But you're the reason we're together. If you hadn't bought the pub, I'd never have met Guy and … and … oh, look at me, I'm bawling.' There was noise at the other end of the phone and then Jenna blew her nose. Imogen heard Guy speak in a gentle, supportive tone, although she couldn't decipher his actual words.

'I'm really happy for you.' Imogen forced the words. She *was* happy for her friend – at least, she wanted to be happy. Jenna had been ecstatic for Imogen when Jamie had proposed, and now it was her turn to repay the favour. She would do it if it killed her.

'Thank you.' Jenna sighed happily. 'Anyway, how are you? I'm so excited about next weekend. Do you think—'

Imogen didn't hear the rest of Jenna's question because a knock sounded at her front door. She snatched the chance to get off the phone, but once she'd disconnected, the last thing she wanted to do was answer the door. Right now she needed that five-minute break more than anything.

The knock sounded again, followed by 'Imogen?'

*Gibson.*

Her heart jolted at the sound of his voice, and she wiped her palms over her eyes, thankful she'd held off the tears while on the phone to Jenna. 'Coming,' she called.

*His* visit was a welcome diversion.

She peeled the door back a fraction and Gibson's tantalising aroma hit her nostrils even before he stepped into the light. A warmth flooded her body as if she were starving and had just opened the door to a delicious delivery of her favourite takeaway meal. The happiness at seeing him tonight, when she hadn't been sure if she would, almost floored her. She couldn't fight the need any longer. Didn't want to.

'Hi,' she managed.

'Can I come in a moment?' A warm but tentative smile hung on his lips.

'Yes.' She pulled back the door the whole way and he slipped inside. 'How was the football?'

'Um … yeah … enlightening.' He stood awkwardly in the space just inside the door.

'Come sit.' His unsure tone and distracted words worried her. 'How'd Charlie go?'

Gibson followed her to the lounge room and sank down onto the couch. 'Actually, he wasn't as…' He didn't finish his sentence, lifting his butt slightly instead, as a confused expression flitted across his face. He slipped his hand beneath him and looked to be digging under the cushions. As he pulled out a thin pink box, her heart leapt into her throat.

*Oh! No!* No good was ever going to come from Jenna bringing that thing into her life, but this was worst-case-scenario embarrassing.

'Give that to me,' she shouted as she all but threw herself across the lounge room, stopping just short of landing on top of him.

He visibly relaxed before her eyes, grinning wickedly as he held the horrid pink box high out of her reach. 'Why? What is it?'

*Do. Not. Hyperventilate.*

She tried for calm and unaffected – bit late for that – as she spoke. 'It's a present.'

'A present for me?' His grin stretched even further, as if he liked this notion.

'God no.' Just the thought had her insides twisting into painful knots. Could this day possibly get any worse?

He shrugged. 'Then I don't see why I can't peek.'

'Because…because…' She lunged at him, unable to think of any reason that would both satisfy him and save her.

His reflexes quick, he caught her wrist with his free hand as her body collided with his and her own fingers closed around the box. Victory! Now she just had to keep her grip, extract herself and then distract him from pursuing the issue. Yeah, right, easy – about as easy taming a crocodile, that is. Right now, the only possible way she could think to distract him – and thus give herself the opportunity to escape – was by leaning closer and pressing her lips against his.

Once this thought entered her head it spiralled out of control. She felt everything she'd decided today – that she wanted more than just sex – slipping away along with her grip on the box. It thumped against the carpet, making a much bigger noise than she'd have expected. Gibson twisted, manoeuvring and lifting her off him so she landed on the couch, stunned and feeling more than a little hard done by.

The thought of kissing him evaporated as he took his turn to lunge. She watched as he dived in what seemed like slow motion onto the carpet and captured the box like it was a football in the AFL grand final. Smiling, he lifted his booty, and Imogen watched her victory slip away as the contents fell onto the floor.

*Kill me now*, she thought as her cheeks flashed what had to be tomato red to match her hair.

'Is that what I think it is?' Gibson sounded amused as he leaned to pick it up.

'I don't know,' she shrugged, trying to appear coy while her eyes focused on the object in his hand. 'What do you think it is?'

He raised one eyebrow, twisting the vibrator and gawking from every which way. She wanted to snatch it out of his grip and hurl it out of the open window. And she would have, if she weren't scared it might land on one of her patrons heading for their car.

'You're not going to make me say it, are you?'

'Hell, yeah.' She folded her arms and nodded. Why should she be the only one feeling a little awkward?

He straightened up. 'It's a vibrator.'

She held her chin high and nodded. 'Yes. It is.' What must he think of her? That she was so randy she kept the blasted thing tucked down the back of the couch for easy access? *Oh Lord*, there went that flush speeding up her neck and colouring her cheeks again. She clamped her teeth hard over her tongue at the urge to tell him she hadn't used it, and that she didn't need it, but that it was the safer – and less complicated – option than pushing him down onto the couch and crawling on top of him as every cell in her body was currently screaming for her to do. She squeezed her knees together and glued her feet to the floor at that menacing thought.

Even with him smirking and silently mocking her, she wanted him. Even knowing he didn't want commitment, she wanted him so bad it was maddening.

She sat there, frozen, waiting for him to say something, do something. Time seemed to stand still. He gazed at her, his eyes hot as molten lava, her body burning up wherever he looked. The room grew small and it felt like they were the only people in a world no larger than an elevator.

And when there were only two options left – to scream or to kiss him – when she couldn't stand the need a second longer, she leaned forward and grabbed hold of option two.

# Chapter Twenty-five

*Fuck. Fuck. And more fuck.*

Gibson's whole body tensed as Imogen's lips, tongue, her whole damn mouth teased his for interaction. For two long seconds his libido warred with his conscience – maybe she'd changed her mind, maybe she just wanted a fuck buddy. He could do that. He could *more* than do that!

But alarm bells rang in his head … alarm bells telling him this kiss wasn't fuck-buddy territory.

Summoning every inch of willpower in his body, he grabbed her upper arms and pushed her away. The cocktail of hurt, confusion and embarrassment in her eyes felt like barbed wire tightening round his heart. As he stepped back out of her personal space, his instinct was to apologise.

'I'm sorry.'

Fiddling with the collar on her work shirt, she blushed. 'Why are you apologising? I'm the one that kissed you when it so obviously repulsed you.'

He tore a hand through his hair, only just falling short of ripping out a huge great chunk. 'As if! You know you don't repulse me, but you confuse the hell out of me. What happened to just being friends?'

She sighed. 'How's that working for you, Gibson?'

*Terribly.* 'Fine.'

She raised an eyebrow and he shifted on the spot. Swallowed. Might have screwed his face up a little.

'Gibson, why don't you want to get married again?'

*Whoa!* His instinct was to kiss her just to get her to drop the topic, but one thing he'd learnt about Imogen was that she was persistent. If she wanted to know, she wouldn't give up. 'Why do you care so much? Why do you want to know?'

She looked right into his eyes, so that despite the distance he'd put between them, he felt as if she were pressed against him and he could see right into her soul.

'Oh Gibson, isn't it obvious?' Her voice trembled and tears glistened in her eyes. 'I think I'm falling for you. Big time.'

*No!* His heart sank as if injected with a deadly weight. She hadn't said *love*, but that's what she meant. In another lifetime, another world, her confession would be music to his ears, but he couldn't harbour such a fantasy.

'What about Jamie?' he asked, glancing across the room to the photos.

She didn't follow his gaze. 'I'll always love Jamie. And I used to think that meant to the exclusion of anybody else. But it doesn't, Gibson.' She sighed wistfully. 'I can't stop thinking about you, the things you say, the way you look at me, the way you make me feel. And the bottom line is, I don't want to. I think you feel the same way.'

He closed his eyes, thinking of the words his mum often parroted to him and Paris when they were kids. *Life isn't fair.* Well, that just sucked. He didn't want to break her heart, but it was kinder not to lead her on. She'd get over it – get over him – if she really were falling for him. He was the only one who had to live with this fate forever.

'It doesn't matter what I feel,' he told her flatly. 'You can't love me because you don't know everything about me. And when I tell you, you won't be able to love me.'

'Tell me then, Gibson, because right now, I can't think of anything you could have done that would change my feelings.' She spoke with such conviction, such love, that he hated what he had to do.

'It's not something I've done; it's something I'll never do.'

She frowned, her beautiful eyes crinkling at the edges.

He took a breath and tried to swallow the lump in his throat. Eventually, he spoke, exposing himself in a way he'd never planned on doing. 'I'm infertile, Imogen.'

'What?' She blinked, shaking her head slightly. He saw that she didn't want to believe him. 'How?'

'Mumps, actually.' He chuckled slightly, as if it didn't matter to him. 'My mum was a little bit of a hippy – she never believed in immunising us – so Paris and I didn't have any of your standard childhood vaccinations. When I was fourteen I got mumps pretty bad.'

'Oh.' Her hand was pressed against her mouth.

He couldn't stand the silence. 'I was unlucky enough to be in the minority of people who have lasting effects. Of course, we didn't know this when I married Serena – she wouldn't have gone through with it if we had. Like most women, having children was a major part of her life plan.'

'So that's why she left.' Imogen's realisation came out on one breath. She stepped back and sank onto the couch. He could see her mind ticking over. For the first time, she stood on Serena's side of the fence and looked at Gibson differently. As someone who lacked.

'Yes, that's why.' He stood straight, puffed his chest a little, pretending it didn't matter to him anymore. Before she'd landed in Gibson's Find, he'd almost fooled himself into believing it didn't. 'And let's face it, you don't blame her, do you?'

She went pale, her lips squeezed tightly together as if she didn't trust herself to give an answer.

It wasn't her fault, but the look on her face repulsed him. He just wanted out of there.

'Gibson, I…' As he turned to go, she launched off the couch and rushed to his side, but he shrugged her hand off his arm.

'Don't, Imogen. Unless you can look me in the eye right now and tell me you don't feel like she did, then please don't prolong the agony. It already hurts too damn much.'

She looked him in the eye, but she hesitated, and in that moment he knew she couldn't lie any more than she could change her feelings. 'Please, can we just talk about this?'

Talking was overrated. Talking couldn't change a thing.

'Goodbye Imogen,' he said, already headed for the door.

She hesitated only a moment, and then she let him go. 'Goodbye Gibson.'

***

As the door shut behind Gibson, Imogen wrestled with the urge to run after him and tell him she didn't care – that babies weren't the be-all and end-all, that she just wanted him – but deep down, she couldn't be certain.

Hadn't she been wallowing in self-pity only seconds before he knocked? And she hadn't been upset about Jenna's new relationship with Guy. No, the ache in her heart had come from Jenna's pregnancy announcement, which followed painfully close to the arrival of Amy's beautiful baby.

She always believed she'd be a good mother. She wanted to be fun – not afraid to squeal down the slide, paint her hands and feet, jump in puddles and dance in the rain.

That dream had died alongside Jamie, but for a tiny while there … for a tiny while, hope had returned in the form of Gibson Black, and she'd thought that maybe she wasn't destined to be a spinster publican with a bunch of cats after all. Not that she minded the publican bit – she was quite enjoying that, actually – but she wanted more. Didn't she?

Desperate for a painkiller but unable to summon the enthusiasm to search for one, Imogen flopped back onto the couch instead. Her eyes sought Jamie's photos on the wall, on the mantle.

'What do you think, hon?'

She waited, because usually when she talked to Jamie, things became clearer in her mind. But tonight he was silent. For the first time, she felt truly alone.

Gibson was a good man. He was a gorgeous man.

And she hated that that wasn't enough.

# Chapter Twenty-six

The day had finally arrived. It was almost 6:00 p.m. and there were only a few minutes to go until the Man Drought weekend officially kicked off. While Imogen couldn't summon the enthusiasm she'd initially had about matching like-minded couples, she tried to maintain some of her passion for the event. The whole community of Gibson's Find had thrown its support behind her and she owed it to them to make it a success.

Jenna, back from Perth for yet another weekend, had already taken her place at a table they'd set up for registration. She looked very professional – in a tailored grey suit that wouldn't fit her in a couple of months, her hair neatly tied back and a glow in her face. The band, a duo of brothers who were hoping to make it big on the country music circuit, had just finished setting up on a temporary stage that Gibson and Guy had erected, and the first few blokes who'd signed up for the event were straggling in. Cal and Charlie stood behind the bar, amped and ready, along with Gibson and Guy, who'd volunteered their services for the evening.

While Cal took cool drinks to the band, Imogen grabbed her camera from its hidey-hole under the bar and rushed forward to greet Warren and a couple of his mates, the first of her male participants. She moved in front of them and snapped before any of them could get camera shy, but it was quickly apparent that none of these blokes would ever suffer from any such thing. They leaned together and posed for her, big goofy grins stretching across their faces.

'Where's the chicks?' Warren asked, just as the first lady walked through the door. One of his mates dug him in the side and nodded in her direction, and the three men swung round, their mouths all dropping open at the sight.

'Hi.' A short brunette with a pale complexion and a shapely body smiled tentatively at Imogen and the guys. 'Am I in the right place for Man Drought?'

'No Man Drought here ,honey.' Warren stepped forward and offered his arm. 'Let me buy you a drink.'

The girl blushed slightly and fiddled with an owl pendant that hung around her neck. 'Okay,' she replied quietly.

'Warren, you can buy drinks in a moment.' Imogen introduced herself and ushered the woman away from the boisterous boys to Jenna at the registration table. As the band cranked up, launching into their first tune, Jenna gave their first female participant a badge with the name Michelle scrawled across it and also the key to the room she'd be sharing with another participant.

A few more blokes arrived after that, and then a couple of groups of girls who obviously thought this was a fun way to get away from the city and have a bit of a laugh. Imogen tried not to be disheartened, reasoning that there'd be at least some genuine women in the pool – Michelle didn't seem like the type to come all this way for nothing. Charlie and Cal offered around complimentary glasses of champagne, while Gibson and Guy (looking adorable in matching Majestic t-shirts) wandered through the mob with plates of Pauli's mouth-watering hors d'oeuvres. As Imogen welcomed a pair of identical twins, she caught Gibson's eye, but he looked away quickly, making her heart cramp.

She was glad he was here and very grateful for his support – he'd promised to keep an eye on Charlie so she could focus on the actual event – but she hated the wall he'd put up between them. She didn't blame him, but she hated it. And considering he'd never officially been a part of her life, she missed him so damn much.

'Excuse me?' One of the sisters cleared her throat. 'You were saying we need to register?'

'Oh, yes, sorry. Come this way.' Imogen swallowed and led the newcomers over to Jenna.

By seven o'clock, all the participants were registered. The mingling in full swing, Imogen found herself with a few moments to take in the scene before the first round of speed dating began. She joined Jenna again.

'I think it's going well.'

'Understatement of the century.' Jenna grinned back. 'There's sparks going off left, right and centre.' She scribbled something down on one of the sticky label badges and then held it up: HANDS OFF, I'M TAKEN. 'I'm going to put this on Guy, just in case. Back in a moment.'

Imogen glanced down at the last few empty labels. Her fingers itched to pick up a pen and scrawl the same words on a badge for Gibson, but she forced the urge aside and glanced around the pub at the diverse crowd. The men wore variations of smart jeans and dress shirts, but the women could have opened their own fashion shop. Some wore cocktail dresses and others opted for more casual, but casual that had taken hours to perfect. She only hoped they'd packed appropriate clothes for their trip to Roseglen. She could just imagine Gibson rolling his eyes if they rocked up in skirts and heels.

Pushing that thought aside, she crossed to the bar and grabbed herself a glass of water in readiness for the official part of the night. Gibson and Guy arrived back with empty platters. She nabbed Guy – hoping he didn't notice the tension between her and Gibson – and asked him to put the next lot of nibbles on the tables in the dining room. These tables were already set up in rows to cater for the quick movement from partner to partner during the speed dating session. Gibson and Guy on their way, she went over to the band and signalled for them to stop after the current song. Then she took a deep breath, sent up a silent prayer for a successful weekend, and climbed up onto the podium.

As she stood in front of the microphone, the music faded, causing all chattering heads to look up. She smiled at the faces looking back at her and took the mic.

'Good evening, folks. Welcome everyone. Especially to our fabulous ladies who made the long hike from Perth. And I believe we even have a couple of girls from Sydney, who have come all the way for Man Drought. Well, don't worry, ladies, there's no shortage of men in in Gibson's Find.'

The room exploded into whoops, cheers and wolf-whistles. She waited a moment for the excitement to die down.

'When I moved here a couple of months ago, I'd heard there were more men than women, but I didn't really believe it until I started getting to know the locals. Men are in the majority in Gibson's Find and it didn't take long for me to realise they are all fabulous men. My friend Jenna,' Imogen paused to indicate Jenna to the side of her, 'thought it would be wrong of us not to share all this testosterone with our fellow females. So, we came up with the idea for this weekend, and we hope you all have a lot of fun, and maybe start some amazing friendships.

'Tonight, we'll begin with some speed dating. Each of your name badges has a number, which corresponds to a seat on the tables. Ladies, you'll get three minutes talking to each man and then we'll ring the closing bell and you'll be asked to move on to the next guy. Easy, right?'

Imogen smiled at the audience. 'But before we get started, I'd like to explain the schedule for the rest of the weekend and introduce a few key people. Tomorrow morning, we'll be heading out to Roseglen, a local farm, owned and operated by Gibson Black.' She looked to the bar, her eyes meeting briefly with Gibson's before he lifted his hand and saluted the crowd.

'And…' For a second she was lost for words, still lost in Gibson's gaze. *Dammit.* She took a much-needed breath. 'There we'll be trying our hands at all sorts of farming experiences and enjoying a delicious lunch, packed by my staff: Pauli, Cal and Karen.' The girls waved from their position alongside Gibson at the bar.

'If you have any questions at any time, come and see me or Jenna. And have a fantastic weekend! Okay. I think that's about it for now. Grab a drink and let the speed dating begin!'

Participants rushed off eagerly to find their numbers at the tables.

As the night went on, speed dating continued between the meals. Imogen forgot about her own problems and got caught up in the romance buzzing around her. It hadn't escaped her that Warren and Michelle had bypassed the last round, instead choosing a private table in the corner of the pub to continue their conversation. And the local policeman had the twins hanging off his every word, although he couldn't seem to decide which sister he liked best. She laughed to herself. Even if only one long-term association came from this weekend, her project would have been a success.

★★★

At the sound of cars heading up his drive, Gibson took a deep breath and headed down the steps of the shearing shed where he'd been checking everything was set up and ready to go. Hell was on its way!

Outside, Jack and Jill patrolled the pens, confused that they only had a few sheep to keep track of, but excited nonetheless. He glanced up at the partially cloudy sky and then at the long line of utes making their way towards him – most he recognised, a couple he didn't – and made out the dusty outline of the local community bus following behind.

Within a few minutes, blokes leapt out of the utes, and the bus – driven by Tom – pulled up in the clearing between the sheds and the homestead. Gibson watched along with the male participants as the women spilled out of the bus. Some were sensibly dressed in shorts, t-shirts and boots. Others favoured the highly inappropriate farm attire – stiletto heels, short skirts, tight tops and dangly earrings – preferred by his ex-wife. He'd have bet money on which girls were serious about this weekend and which ones just wanted to have fun, but that wasn't his concern. His job was to help make Imogen's project a success. He may not have been able to offer what she needed, what she wanted, but he could at least do this.

The only thing he couldn't control was the weather. He looked up at the rapidly darkening clouds and hoped the wind would blow them away.

When he looked back, Imogen was stepping out from behind the crowd of excited ladies. The breath left his lungs before he could hold it back. Surely the sight of her shouldn't have had quite such a visceral affect on him after all this time, but if anything, it was getting stronger. He was a goner and he couldn't do any damn thing about it.

Inwardly, cursing the futility of his feelings, he stepped forward to greet her. 'Morning.'

She smiled, blowing her fringe off her face in that way only she did. 'Everything ready?'

'Yes.' He nodded as Guy and Tom came to stand beside them.

Tom, an ex-shearer who now drove the community bus and did other odd jobs around town, would teach the women who were game how to rid a sheep of its coat. Guy would be giving riding lessons on the quad bike, and Gibson would be on hand to show anyone who was interested how to fix and erect fences. He didn't expect to be swamped with volunteers but that didn't bother him.

'Okay, good.' Imogen looked up at the clouds, worry evident in her face. 'Do you think the weather's going to be a problem?'

The men followed her gaze to the sky. If anything, the clouds had grown more sinister. 'Relax,' Gibson said, before either of the other two could voice their thoughts. 'We'll do the farming activities first. Worst-case scenario, we can eat lunch in the safety of the shed until this passes over, and then hike to the old homestead this afternoon. It'll be fine, promise.'

'Okay.' She didn't sound convinced. 'Let's do this, then.'

Stepping forward, Imogen stuck two fingers into her mouth and whistled in a way that both impressed and surprised him. All heads swivelled in her direction, eyes wide as they waited for instruction. 'First, I want to thank Gibson Black for welcoming us all to his beautiful property, Roseglen.' She gestured to him and Gibson nodded to the crowd, trying not to think about how great his name sounded when she said it.

'Today,' Imogen continued, 'Gibson, with the help of Tom and Guy, will be running three farming stations. Each of you will select an activity from a hat. We'll stop for a break in about half an hour and rotate stations until lunchtime, when we've got a real treat in store. Gibson has kindly offered to give us a tour of the original Roseglen homestead, built by his great-grandparents in the late 1800s. It's a short walk from here, but I promise you, it's worth the exertion. If you think life on the land is hard in the twenty-first century, you'll be amazed at what the early settlers had to cope with.'

Even as Imogen spoke, the wind picked up and the air grew cooler around them. Several of the women, already on a first-name basis with the men, leaned in close to make the most of body heat. Gibson noticed Imogen's gaze flicking to the sky while she relayed the activity options. He too started to fret. The forecast this morning had been mostly fine with possible showers, but it wouldn't be the first time they'd been wrong.

Pushing the thought aside, he welcomed his group of participants. He rolled his eyes as Wazza approached. 'Don't tell me I have to teach you how to fix a fence. That'll be like trying to teach one of the dogs to knit socks.'

'Humph.' Wazza gave Gibson the finger. 'Don't listen to the Gibster, ladies, I'll be teaching him a few things.'

'This I'd like to see.' Gibson waved his hand at the tools lying on the ground in front of them. 'Don't let me hold you back.'

Wazza's chest puffed up and his shoulders snapped back as he swaggered forward and picked up a fence strainer. 'Watch and learn, ladies. Who's up first?'

Gibson folded his arms, leaned back against the fence and watched as Wazza took over, obviously trying to impress the short brunette. She seemed to be the only woman interested, and frankly, he couldn't blame them.

'It's bloody freezing out here,' whined a blonde after a couple of minutes. She had so much product in her hair the wind hadn't moved it an inch.

'Tell me about it,' added another, rubbing perfectly manicured fingers up and down bare arms. Troy, a guy Gibson played footy with, stepped forward and offered his shirt. Another bloke Gibson recognised from the neighbouring shire quickly did the same.

*Brownie points.* The shirt-receivers batted their eyelashes in thanks at the now-bare-chested blokes. As he glanced towards the shed, hoping Tom was having better luck entertaining the ladies with his shearing talents, a large drop of rain plopped onto Gibson's nose. The blonde with the fortified hair must have felt one too because she squealed, yanked Troy's shirt up over her head like a hoodie and started running towards the shed. Within seconds, rain began falling from the sky as if God had emptied his swimming pool. Big drops soaked into dusty red ground that hadn't seen a downpour in months.

Squeals of excitement mingled with cries of disgust as the others abandoned all pretences of fencing, chasing the blonde towards the sheering shed. Gibson took one look at the tools, wiped water from his forehead and launched into a run himself. It wasn't that the rain bothered him so much as that he wanted to be there for Imogen when these wussy women barrelled into the shed. They pushed and shoved ahead of him through the open doorway and then shook their heads, trying to rid their hair of the rain like a pack of wild dogs.

Gibson located Imogen across the other side of the shed, where Tom was in the middle of a shearing demo. As her gaze landed on the chaos spilling in the door, she started towards him.

'What's going on?' she asked.

'Rain.' He gestured behind him and she peered past. 'Lots of it.'

'Dammit.' She scowled and ran both hands through her hair. 'This wasn't forecast.'

'Relax,' he instructed, fighting the urge to squeeze her hand in a show of support. 'We'll have lunch early in here and hope it passes quickly. I'll heat up the urn and we'll give everyone a warm Milo to settle them. This weekend's about romance, right?'

She nodded and he swore he saw a lump travel up the column of her throat. He felt one in his too.

'Trust me, there's nothing more romantic than keeping warm and sheltered out of the rain. Where's the lunch?'

'Still in eskies on the back of Guy's ute.'

'I'll take care of it.' He was already scanning the crowd for Guy as she thanked him.

\*\*\*

Imogen bit into one of Pauli's gourmet chicken, avocado and sun-dried tomato wraps and sent a silent prayer of thanks skywards for Gibson. He'd not only kept her calm when the storm threatened to rain on her parade, but he'd made everything perfect for the complaining city girls as well. She only hoped that when this weekend was over, they could get back to some kind of friendship.

With the help of Guy and Tom, he'd trudged back and forth through the rain and puddles, fetching food, blankets to huddle under and, best of all, a massive stereo to really set the mood.

You could barely hear the wind howling and the rain teeming on the tin roof of the shearing shed over the country tunes blasting from the stereo and the tap of dancing feet against the floorboards. Spunky farmers spun the female participants round the shed in some sort of country disco ritual. Imogen couldn't help but smile. When the girls had run screaming into the shed only half an hour ago, she'd sworn any chance of a successful weekend was over, but now...

'Care to dance?'

One of the male participants – a guy who frequented the pub – jolted her from her reverie. She'd made the decision not to interact in anything but a professional manner with anyone, but he'd caught her off-guard. Before she knew it, his hand clasped hers and he pulled her off the ground, oblivious to the wrap in her other hand. As the man waltzed her onto the makeshift dance floor, she dumped her food on a trestle table and tried to smile, not wanting to embarrass him by turning him down in front of his peers.

She rocked uncomfortably to the music, glad that the current song was upbeat and she didn't have to get up close and personal. Counting down the minutes till she could politely escape, she glanced sideways and saw Gibson standing by the door – his eyes trained on her, his lips decidedly scowling. Her stomach dropped. She hoped he'd seen the man approach *her* and that he didn't think she could so easily switch her affections.

How far from the truth that was.

All around her, everyone looked to be having the time of their lives. Jenna, twirling underneath Guy's arm, swung past and winked at Imogen. She tried to smile back. Gibson's dogs, Jack and Jill, weaved in and out between the dancers, desperate to get in on the action too. But Imogen just couldn't feel it.

Then, as if solely to torture her, the music that had been loud and boppy seconds before turned soft and undeniably romantic. As each man snatched for his favoured woman, Imogen looked into her partner's eyes and cringed. Oblivious, he offered a cheesy grin, slipped his arms around her waist and crushed her against him.

The feel of his tall, hard body pressed up against hers sickened her. Her insides revolted and she racked her brain for a way to extract herself. She wriggled a little, then just as she was about to make her escape, thunder boomed overhead and the lights and music died.

'Aww!' Groans and moans echoed throughout the shed. Her partner dropped his hands to his side, blinking as if to decipher what had happened. She didn't stick around long enough for him to find out.

Gibson was already outside, surveying the scene. She jumped down the steps from the shed, joining him on the ground. Despite the rain they'd already had, the menacing black clouds hadn't lifted at all. All around them, heavy drops pelted down, turning the thick, muddy puddles on the normally dusty ground into lakes. Imogen thought briefly of Gibson's offer that they could use his swimming pool – this had not been what either of them had had in mind.

'Shit,' Gibson said as a bolt of lightning illuminated the sky over Lookout hill. Thunder cracked seconds later. He turned to her. 'You've got to get everyone back into town. I can't remember the last time we had a storm like this. Leave the shed as is. I'll clean up later, but right now, you've gotta move people and I have to move sheep.'

Imogen watched as Gibson started running towards his house. She wanted to call him back – to tell him she hadn't wanted to dance with that man – but now wasn't the time. She rubbed her arms – freezing – but knowing from the anxiousness in his voice that this was serious and she didn't have time to waste.

'Tom,' she shouted, as she turned back into the shed, 'we've gotta go.'

\*\*\*

His faithful dogs at his heels, Gibson reached his ute, yanked open the door and ushered Jack and Jill in ahead of him. He slammed the door, tugged the gears into reverse and took off towards a low paddock that had been known to flood in times of heavy rain – and where half his sheep just happened to be grazing.

Despite not wanting Imogen's weekend to be a flop, in a way he couldn't help being happy for the opportunity to escape.

Most of his mates had now no doubt abandoned the Man Drought project and were probably heading towards their farms, anxious to save their own stock.

A little bit of rain would have been okay, but this was something else. Where this storm had come from, he had no idea. All he knew was that he had to move the sheep to higher ground. If Charlie were here, he'd help, but he'd chosen to bypass the farm visit, saying he had things to do before his shift this evening. That had surprised Gibson, but now he was glad of it. As knowledgeable and useful as Charlie used to be, Gibson didn't want his recent confusion slowing the process.

As he drove, he tried to focus on the terrain. The rain pelted so hard he could barely see centimetres ahead. In a matter of minutes, the lightning had multiplied and the thunder sounded like a heavy metal band in the sky, only a few seconds' reprieve between each impressive episode.

Although he knew the track like the back of his hand, he had to ease back on the accelerator as he navigated the swampy paddocks. He may have slowed the vehicle but thoughts raced through his mind like high-speed helicopter blades. The image of Imogen and that bloke dancing together would be a nightmare for life. She'd told him she was ready to move on, to find love again, and it was only a matter of time before some smart guy locked on to that fact.

Sliding wildly in the mud, the ute careened over a bump and almost crashed into a fence. 'Dammit!' He took a deep breath, needing to concentrate on the task at hand. He'd finally reached the paddock where hundreds of sheep were scrambling about, sloshing through puddles in their quest for higher ground.

For the next half an hour, Gibson and the dogs worked hard moving the sheep to a higher paddock near the lookout. Normally, the view was breathtaking, but he couldn't see anything from up there today – wind threw grit and sticks hurling through the air, the low clouds made the sky look like night, and the rain was still heavy. At one point, a tree crashed to the ground to his right, just a little down from Lookout hill, and Gibson knew he had to get to shelter fast. Hoping he'd done enough to save the sheep, he ushered Jack and Jill back into the ute.

As he headed back towards the homestead – driving slower than snail's pace, frustration clawing at him every metre of the way – he thought about the old shack, how it had no doubt seen hundreds of storms and somehow weathered them all. He hoped it'd survive this one.

Only a hundred metres or so from his house, hailstones began catapulting out of the sky. As they slammed into the windscreen and belted on the ute roof, he realised these weren't your run-of-the-mill hailstones – these were golf ball-sized, capable of doing serious damage. The dogs barked in the seat beside him, taking turns diving towards the dash as if trying to catch the hail.

Even before he'd switched off the engine, he opened the door and yelled, 'Inside, now!' His dogs may have been excitable at times, but they knew when to obey their master. They bounded ahead of him, down the cobbled path and flew up the few steps onto the verandah. He must have left a window open, for the wind had almost blown the front door off its hinges. The moment he stepped inside, he slammed the door behind him, shivered and took a second to calm himself.

Having battened down the hatches, he went into the lounge room. Jack and Jill had already adopted prime position on the rug in front of the wood fire that hadn't been lit since last winter. Whoever said dogs were stupid obviously hadn't met these two, he thought as he set the fire. Luckily, he'd collected a bit of wood a week or so ago, anticipating that the cold would land suddenly.

Not like this though. He hadn't seen rain like this in years.

The fire roaring and the dogs settled, Gibson headed for the bathroom to peel off his soggy clothes and take a hot shower before hypothermia settled in his bones. He spent longer than he should underneath the hot shards – like every other farmer, he'd been trained in water preservation and usually kept to a three-minute limit. But not today. Today, he needed the warmth and the comfort and the time to just be.

When he emerged, the phone was ringing in the kitchen. Knowing that any sort of emergency could have occurred in this foul weather, he made a mad dash for it, wrapping a towel around his waist as he ran, and anticipating having to head out again with the ambulance or the SES.

'Yes,' he answered, his towel slipping as he grabbed the phone.

'Hi Gibson.'

'Imogen.' He breathed out the tension he'd been feeling since he'd left her at the shed. 'Are you okay?'

'Yes, thanks. It was a bit of a hairy ride but we all got back into town safely.'

Thank God she was out of harm's way. He wished he didn't care so damn much, but it was too damn late. Despite his best intentions, he was unable to control his heart. He'd fallen in love with Imogen in a way he'd never thought possible again.

'Most of the girls have retreated for showers and I'm not sure the guys will make it back from their farms, but anyway … have you heard from Charlie?'

Lost in his thoughts, he barely heard the first part of her sentence, but her mention of his granddad grabbed his attention. 'No. Why?'

'I tried to call him to tell him not to bother coming out in the rain for his shift – the girls and I can manage with Jenna's help – but he didn't answer his phone. I tried a couple more times and then gave up, thinking he'd likely venture out anyway and show up for work. It's probably nothing, but it's past his rostered time now and he's still not here. I was wondering if he mentioned going anywhere to you.'

'He did say he had something to do this morning, but he was definitely planning to work tonight.' Gibson racked his brain for a logical reason why Charlie wouldn't be answering the call. The phones were obviously still working.

'Okay, then, I'll go round to his place and check.'

Gibson peeled back the kitchen curtain and looked outside. As if on cue, lightning streaked across the sky and more thunder sounded. 'No way, you stay where you are. I'll head there now. He's probably just fallen asleep.'

'Yeah, probably.' But he could tell her chirpy optimistic voice was a front.

They were both thinking the same thing: Charlie hadn't been himself for weeks, and going missing in this weather could be lethal.

# Chapter Twenty-seven

After making sure the fire was safe, Gibson left the dogs lounging on the rug, and then dressed in his wet-weather gear, ready to face the storm. As he descended the steps towards his ute, he registered that the rain had finally eased a little. At least he'd be able to see through the windscreen as he drove into town. Halfway down the gravel driveway, a thought struck him, and he swung the ute left down the dirt track to the old homestead.

It was just a hunch, but the hail had stopped him taking a good look when he'd passed by earlier, so he wanted to be sure. From about a hundred metres away he registered Charlie's old beast. For a second, his heart relaxed, but the smile died on his face as he noted the disaster behind the car.

*Fuck!*

One of the old trees had been struck by lightning and now lay right across the old shack, dividing the building into two piles of devastation. The old brick stones were scattered left and right and the jagged sheets of corrugated iron that had once formed the roof were jabbed up in the air like an abstract sculpture. He'd never imagined lightning could do so much damage. Slamming his foot against the brake, Gibson leapt from the ute, not bothering to shut the door as he ran towards the debris.

'Charlie!' he yelled, his voice barely audible above the screaming wind. 'Charlie!'

Nothing. Although, if Charlie were injured, he might not be able to answer. Treading carefully so as not to lose his footing, Gibson arrived at what was once the entrance of the building and peered inside. He called again but still got no reply.

Taking a deep breath, he began trying to shift some of the rubble – careful not to make any sudden movements that could send the remains of the walls crashing down. He pushed and heaved and yanked, but barely anything budged. The huge sheets of iron were almost impossible to shift by himself. He couldn't see Charlie lying injured anywhere, but if he wasn't here, where the hell was he? The car was fine. Surely he'd have taken shelter there if he could.

Gibson ran one hand through his hair, his other hand already in his pocket, grabbing his phone. He dialled Guy. Maybe he was overreacting, but where Charlie was concerned, he'd do everything he could.

'Hey mate, how's your place?' Guy sounded carefree, so Gibson guessed he'd managed to get his stock to safety.

'Fine,' he replied. 'Are you back in town?'

'Heading there now. Why?'

'It's Charlie.' Gibson told Guy everything he knew.

'Oh shit,' was Guy's initial response, but he quickly switched to action mode, promising to make his way to Roseglen and alert the other SES volunteers to be ready if a search were needed.

Disconnecting the call, Gibson turned back to the shack and set to removing one tedious stone at a time until Guy arrived and they could really make inroads.

***

Imogen took a long slurp on the mug of Milo Pauli had insisted she drink and sighed. So much for a successful matchmaking weekend. The rain had finally eased and girls were only now straggling back into the pub, having showered after the storm. Only a couple of men had returned, but Jenna had spoken to Guy, who'd assured her the others would be back as soon as they could. Thanks to Karen, the wood fire was now roaring in the corner, creating a pretty scene, not to mention much-needed warmth. Just a Bunch of Cowgirls were doing their bit to try to brighten the mood, belting out tunes from the stage.

Despite the efforts, the long faces of her female participants told Imogen they were going to be a hard crowd to please, but right now, all her thoughts centred on Charlie. The Milo felt heavy in her belly and she didn't think she could stomach any more. Hopefully, the sixth sense that told her something had happened to him was wide of the mark. If only she'd braved the elements and checked his house before alerting Gibson. What if she'd worried him for nothing? Like he needed any more woe in his life.

Imogen felt an encouraging squeeze on her shoulder and turned to see Jenna taking the stool beside her. Jenna cradled an identical mug of Milo and smiled sympathetically. 'How are you?'

Before Imogen could reply, Jenna's iPhone rang. She glanced at the screen, grinned and answered. 'Hey sweet, what's up?'

The expression on Jenna's face changed from joyful to anxious in a matter of seconds. Imogen's pulse started a manic tap dance as she waited for the conversation to be over.

'What is it?' she asked the moment Jenna disconnected.

'It's Charlie,' Jenna said, confirming the worst as she reached out to take Imogen's hand. 'Gibson found his car near an old shack on his property. The shack was totally destroyed in the storm. Guy and Gibson have torn it apart, but there's no sign of him.'

'Oh Lord.' Imogen's hand rushed to her chest – she thought of Charlie's old homestead and all the cherished memories it held. Then, of course, she thought of Charlie. If he wasn't there, where could he be?

Jenna held Imogen's shaking hands and looked at her. 'He's going to be fine. The SES is preparing to start a search. They'll find him. Try not to worry.'

*Try not to worry?* She couldn't bear the thought of Charlie lost somewhere, alone and confused in this god-awful weather. Even worse was how Gibson would feel if they didn't find him alive. She closed her eyes, wishing she could imagine this nightmare away.

'What we can do?' She yanked her hands out of Jenna's and slipped off the stool, ready for action.

Jenna shook her head. 'We've got to concentrate on here; Guy said most of the men won't be returning now because they'll want to join the search.'

Imogen nodded, totally understanding. She wanted to join the search herself – nothing seemed as important as that right now – but Jenna was right. She couldn't just up and leave the women who'd paid for this weekend. 'Okay,' she said eventually, trying to swallow her fear and worry. 'I suppose I'd better tell the girls.'

'Do you want me to?' Jenna asked.

'No, it's fine. They're my responsibility.'

'Okay, then.' Jenna smiled then yawned, reminding Imogen her friend was in the early stages of pregnancy.

'Hey, since we're quiet here, do you want to go have a rest upstairs?'

'No, I'm fine. Honestly. I'm not ill, just pregnant, and right now I want to be here for you.'

Feeling as if she could burst with love, Imogen leaned forward and wrapped her arms around Jenna, hugging her tightly. 'I'm so happy for you,' she said, her own eyes finally welling with truly happy tears. She hadn't allowed herself to share her friend's joy until now, but everyone deserved what Jenna had found: someone to love and start a family with.

Yet when she closed her eyes and tried to imagine that for herself, all she could see was Gibson. Just Gibson and her. And they were blissfully happy.

As if her world had just tilted, Imogen pulled back slightly. 'It's because of Guy, isn't it?'

Jenna frowned. 'What's because of Guy?'

'You never wanted a baby until him. His love changed you: it opened up a whole new world.'

Jenna tilted her head to one side, thinking. 'Yes, I guess it did. But the truth is, as much as I'm looking forward to the baby, I would have been quite happy to wait a bit, enjoy some time with Guy. Hell, I'd have been happy to have him all to myself forever. Lucky he's got lots of love to go around.'

'That he does,' Imogen agreed, but her mind was elsewhere. When Jamie died, she'd thought all was lost – her chance of love, her chance of motherhood. Slowly, she'd begun to heal, to come to terms with a different life. She'd never imagined finding someone she loved enough to be able to move on, to be able to have children with. But coming here, she'd been given more than a new direction in her life. Her heart had opened itself up, healed so completely that there'd been room for Gibson to take over.

He may not have been able to have children, but she believed – oh, how she believed – he was capable of love. She could see it in his total devotion to Charlie – and in the hurt in his eyes when she told him she wanted more.

She could no longer deny her heart.

It didn't matter if Gibson couldn't have children. It was he she'd fallen in love with, him and only him. He was more than enough. But it would to take some kind of miracle to convince him.

'Earth to Imogen. Please, if you say any more, you're going to make me cry.'

Imogen wondered if she'd spoken her epiphany aloud, then realised Jenna meant her words about Guy and the baby. 'That I'd like to see,' she said, knowing warm fuzzy moments weren't Jenna's cup of tea. With a kiss on her friend's cheek, Imogen headed for the stage and turned to face the crowd. When the band finished their song, Imogen took the mic.

Even before she said anything, the yelling started.

'Where's all the men?' cried one of the twins, holding up a glass and sloshing wine all over her short red dress. Clearly, she'd already had way too much to drink.

Cries of support echoed around the room. 'Hear, hear!'

'Yeah, you promised us testosterone!'

'Please, ladies.' Imogen's used her loudest voice to be heard over the riot. 'If you'll just listen for a moment, I can explain. I know you're disappointed, but one of our locals has gone missing in the storm. He's over eighty and his memory's not the best at the moment.' She paused a second, trying to stop her voice from wobbling. 'Unfortunately, most of the guys have had to join the search.'

Silence ruled for a momen,t and then more boos and harsher derogatory words were thrown her way.

The other twin stood up. 'We paid for men. We want our money back.'

'Yeah, damn straight we do.' Another participant stood and started through the crowds.

Two other women followed. 'Yeah, us too. We're outta here.'

Imogen stood there, frozen with shock and disgust at their responses. Why had she ever thought this was a good idea? Gibson was right – this was never going to work. She'd painted the weekend as some sort of party, whereas in reality, life in the bush wasn't a party. It was about mucking in, becoming part of the community, caring about those around you in a way that just didn't happen in the city. She'd wanted so badly to help her gorgeous patrons to find the love and intimacy they deserved, but you couldn't manufacture love. Real love had a mind of its own – sparking where and when you least expected.

She could have screamed and yelled and told these women exactly what she thought of them, but that might have made them stay longer and she just wanted them gone. She wanted to concentrate on worrying about Charlie. She we wanted to be there when – if – Gibson needed her. So the decision was an easy one.

'Fine, come over to the bar,' she told them. 'I'm happy to give you a refund.'

'And so you should,' snapped one of the twins.

Imogen didn't dignify her with a response.

As the women lined up for their money and stormed from the pub, muttering angrily about collecting their things and heading back to the city, she couldn't summon the anxiety to care that the roads would still be slippery and most of them over the legal limit. If they wanted to be stupid, so be it. She had bigger things to focus on.

★★★

The rain picked up again, mixing with the tears streaming down Gibson's face. Stopping the quad bike for a moment (he'd taken it instead of the ute for better access on the rough terrain), he wiped his eyes with the backs of both hands. His mates weren't far, searching every metre of Roseglen for Charlie, but he was beyond caring if any of them saw his tears. He couldn't recall the last time he'd cried.

Even when Serena had delivered the final blow, he'd been more angry – at her, at himself, at the injustice of the world – than sad.

'God!' he screamed, realising it was a plea, not a curse. A self-confessed agnostic – he could never see the point in wasting time arguing for or against a superior being you couldn't see – he now found himself bargaining.

*Bring Charlie back, make him okay, and I promise I'll take him to the doctors. I'll talk to my parents. I'll side with Mum about putting him in a home.*

But it was no use. They'd searched every inch of Roseglen and not found even a trace of his grandfather. Looking up at the sky – darkening again now, because of the time as well as the return of inclement weather – he guessed Guy would have to call off the search until first light.

If anything happened to Charlie, his dad would skin him alive, but he'd have to wait in line, because Gibson's life wouldn't be worth living with that kind of guilt. He should have confronted him, should have made him see a doctor – and now the appointment he'd booked for two weeks away, giving him time to talk Charlie round, might have been too late.

The UHF radio clipped to his belt crackled and he could only just make out Guy's voice over the wind. 'Are you okay? Any sign of Charlie?'

'No. I'm heading back now.'

★★★

'Sorry,' Guy said the moment Gibson disembarked the bike. 'It's late and dark and I've got to send the troops home.' The searchers had congregated back in the shearing shed, their glum faces only a tiny echo of what he felt inside.

'Okay.'

'You're not going to stop looking, though, are you?'

'Hell no.' Gibson ran a hand through his hair, itching to get back out there.

'That's what I thought. And I'll be with you ever step of the way,' Guy said.

'Me too.' Wazza's firm hand landed on Gibson's back in a show of support.

'Thanks.' Gibson resisted the urge to hug his friends. He'd barely given them the time of day these last couple of years, but like true mates, they didn't hold that against him.

Then he turned to face the rest of the group. He swallowed the lump that had taken permanent residence in his throat to step forward and thank everyone.

***

Imogen's hand ached as she signed her name on the last cheque. She'd lost count of how many refunds she'd written, but it felt like a lot, so she was surprised to look up and find a few ladies still nursing cocktails at a couple of the tables. As if sensing her staring, a couple looked up and smiled warmly.

Michelle, the quiet brunette who'd taken a shine to Warren, spoke first. 'So sorry to hear about your barman. Is there anything we can do to help?'

The others nodded in agreement, and one said, 'Yeah, do the searchers need sandwiches or something?'

Imogen pressed her hand against her chest, trying to still the emotion that welled there at the show of support from these genuine ladies. Finally, she found the wherewithal to speak. 'Good idea.' She'd been too consumed with worry to think of such things. 'Jenna, do you think you could ring Guy and see if that would help?'

Jenna nodded and reached for her phone. Imogen looked to Pauli, who'd deserted the kitchen because up till now no one had felt much like eating. 'I'm on to it,' Pauli said.

The four remaining participants marched into the kitchen behind Pauli. A smile broke out on Imogen's face and she followed. It felt good – right – to finally be doing something proactive.

Jenna arrived in the kitchen a few minutes later. 'Guy said they've had to scale the search back till tomorrow.'

'What? How can they give up until they find him?'

'Gibson, Guy and Warren aren't giving up. And Guy said food would be much appreciated. He only hopes he can get Gibson to pause long enough to eat.'

Imogen bit her lower lip. She'd take the food out to Roseglen and force Gibson to eat. Then she'd force him to listen. She understood his anguish, but couldn't bear the thought of him collapsing from weakness and exhaustion. It would do Charlie no good if Gibson made himself ill, but it was herself she was thinking of now.

She'd already lost one love, and she'd be damned if she was going to lose another.

# Chapter Twenty-eight

As Imogen headed out to Roseglen, driving slower than she normally would on the wet, potholed roads, she squinted to try to see through the rain. It had worsened again. She'd switched off the radio in order not to get distracted, but the wind howling outside made quite a majestic tune on its own.

She shuddered to think of Charlie still out there – more than five hours after she'd alerted Gibson that he was missing. Where the hell could he be? Yes, persistence could be Charlie's middle name, but he couldn't have walked far in this weather. Could he?

Lost in thought, she almost didn't see the branch that had fallen across her side of the gravel road. She swerved, hit the brakes and struggled to keep control of the car as she moved across the other side of the road to safety.

She swore loudly, all the while praying, *Please Lord, don't let anything be coming in the other direction.*

Her heart pounded so hard and fast that once she'd crossed back to the left side of the road, she had to pull over to calm herself. She glanced behind her, but of course any chance of assessing the size of the branch was hindered by the unrelenting rain.

Dammit, she'd have to get out and look. She'd never live with herself if someone came after her and crashed. Sighing, she did a three-point turn so the car was off the road but its headlights shone on the fallen log. Then she hauled her heavy-duty rain jacket off the back seat and tried to wriggle into it before getting out of the car.

Rain that felt more like hail pelted down on her. It was dark and eerily creepy on the road, but Imogen tried not to dwell on the fact that she was alone – surely not even psychopaths would be out on a night like this. Not wanting to spend longer than necessary in the elements, she jogged the few metres to the log and then stopped at the edge of the road to assess it. But even before she stooped down and tried to wrap her hands around one end, she knew it'd be too heavy for her to lift on her own.

She dug into her pocket for her mobile and then realised she'd left it on the bar. *Dammit.*

'Do you want a hand with that, love?'

She startled, almost stumbling on the wet dirt, the shock of company triggering her reflexes even before she recognised the voice. At the realisation, her heart slammed into her chest and she spun on her gumboots, thinking she must have been hallucinating.

But no, Charlie stood only a few metres away, illuminated by the headlights and looking dishevelled but otherwise well, and determined with his offer to help.

'Where've you been?' she breathed, although she didn't think he heard her. She wanted to rush forward and hug him, to check him over and take him to her car, but she didn't want to make a sudden move in case it confused him.

He stepped closer and she saw that he was shivering, his clothes muddy and dripping wet. 'You're lucky you didn't hit that,' he said, nodding to the branch and seemingly oblivious to his state.

She blinked, having almost forgotten about the log-across-the-road problem. 'Charlie. It's Imogen,' she said. 'Do you remember me?'

His brow creased and he stared. She could almost see his brain ticking over as he tried to place her, and then a light went on inside. 'Yes, yes, of course I do. What are you doing out here at night all by yourself?'

She lifted one brow, still unsure whether he recognised her. 'I could ask you the same thing, Charlie.'

'Oh … well … I—' He scratched his head, seemingly unable to answer this question and so she interrupted, not wanting him to work himself up into a state.

'Doesn't matter.' She stepped slowly forward and gently slipped her arm through his, joyful to finally have him within reach. 'I'm on my way to Gibson's for a bite to eat. I'm sure he'd love you to join us.'

Charlie patted her hand. 'Now that you mention it, I am a little hungry.'

Slowly, she led him into the car and settled him in the passenger seat. She grabbed a picnic rug from the boot and draped it over his legs before closing the door. The heater in the car was already on full bore but she automatically tried to turn it higher, and then, unable to control her happiness, she leaned over and kissed Charlie on the cheek.

Feeling lighter than she had in days, she turned the car back onto the road towards Roseglen and sent another silent prayer skywards – first, of thanks, and then for her run of luck to continue with Charlie's grandson.

★★★

The lights looked to be on in every room of Gibson's house when Imogen stopped her car. Two utes – one red and one white, both dirty – were parked out the front but she couldn't see Gibson's. She got out and was almost at the passenger door when a figure started running down the path towards them.

'I've got him,' she called. 'I've found Charlie.'

Within seconds, Guy was at her side, hauling the passenger door open. 'Thank fuck,' he said, briefly slumping before springing into action again. 'How is he?'

'I'm fine, thank you very much,' Charlie grumbled, trying to climb out of the car, 'and I'll have you know I'm right here, so there's no need to talk about me like I'm not.'

Guy looked taken aback, but Imogen smirked. She understood why Gibson had been reluctant to broach the subject of seeing a doctor with his grandfather – in Charlie's times of clarity, he was a force not to be trifled with.

'So you are,' Guy said, kneeling down in the dirt. 'How are *you* feeling?'

'Bloody cold.' Charlie's lips formed a determined pout as if he were trying to work out how the hell he got this way.

Imogen guessed it was going to be a long and emotionally draining night.

'Well, let's get you inside to the fire, then.' Guy tentatively offered his hand and Imogen sighed with relief when Charlie took it. She didn't want him stubbornly insisting on walking to the house without assistance. He appeared unscathed, but his lips had turned even bluer since she'd found him and those wet clothes must have been heavy, not to mention unhelpful to his body temp.

Charlie let Guy help him out of the car. Imogen shut the door behind them and Charlie plodded, sandwiched between her and Guy, up the garden path. She'd come back for the food once she'd settled him, once she'd seen Gibson.

Warren was coming out of the bathroom and doing up his fly when the three of them entered the house. 'Holy hell, where'd you find him?'

'On the side of the road. Where's Gibson?' Imogen asked.

'He's still out searching,' Guy replied. 'Waz, can you get him on the two-way?'

'Sure.' Warren headed for the kitchen.

They had to get Charlie out of his wet clothes quick smart, but Imogen didn't want to embarrass him. She suggested he sit in the armchair in front of the fire. She wasn't sure you could technically call the seat an 'armchair' – it looked like something to look at rather than sit on – but it was the best thing available.

Guy trekked off to find blankets, and Charlie all but collapsed into the chair. Imogen knelt beside him, instinctively picking up his papery hand. *Ice.* She shivered, but didn't let go. She didn't quite know what to say to him, scared that in his agitated state he might take it the wrong way. 'Crazy weather we're having,' she decided on eventually. When all else failed, talk about the weather.

'Hmm.' Charlie nodded, his chin still stuck out as if he were deep in thought. Then, 'It's Elsie's birthday today.'

'Oh.' Imogen's heart contracted at his use of the present tense. She swallowed and found her voice. 'Did you get her anything?'

He looked at her as if she were the one with memory issues. 'She's dead.' His words weren't harsh, but resigned.

*Phew!* 'I know,' she nodded and gave his hand a gentle squeeze, 'but my husband's dead too, and I still like to acknowledge the special dates.'

He beamed. 'Me too. I make a special picnic every year, on her birthday and also on our wedding anniversary. I take it out to the shack and I eat and sit and talk to her. I feel close to her there. Not many people understand.'

'I do,' Imogen whispered. 'I still talk to Jamie's photos. I run things by him when I'm not sure. It eases the pain.'

Except she'd barely talked to Jamie in weeks. The thought didn't make her ache with guilt like it once would have. Deep down, she believed Jamie would be pleased she wanted to move on.

Guy came back into the room armed with thick blankets and followed by Warren, who carried a steaming mug.

'Would you like to take your shirt off?' she asked Charlie. 'You'll warm up once we get the wet clothes off.'

Charlie nodded and let her help him undo the buttons on his faded blue shirt – the farmer's uniform he still wore, years after moving into town. The moment it was off, Guy wrapped the first blanket around Charlie, draped another blanket over his legs and offered the drink. It smelled suspiciously like Milo with a shot of something more sinister in it. Whatever the drink, Charlie wrapped his hands around the mug and drank, his lips returning to near-normal colour with every sip.

Imogen stayed kneeling next to Charlie while he drank. Her knees were numb and she sweltered by the fire, but she didn't care. Guy and Warren hung back a bit, and when Charlie finished the Milo, he spoke again.

'The shack's damaged.' His voice cracked on the admission and she saw water in his eyes.

'I know, Charlie.' She struggled to keep her own voice level. 'I heard. But I'm sure it can be rebuilt. Gibson's pretty good with his hands. And we can help him.'

For the next few minutes, she tried to coax more information from Charlie about when the storm hit the shack, and about where he'd been between then and now. Soon, his lucid facts grew fewer and his eyelids began to droop.

'Should we let him sleep or keep him awake?' she asked the others. 'Hell, should we call an ambulance?'

Guy shook his head. 'Gibson will be here in a moment. He'll check him over and decide what to do.'

Imogen nodded, her ears pricking as the front door slammed.

Moments later, Gibson appeared. His tall, rugged physique filled the doorway and sent her heart racing, despite the anxiety on his face and the hellish day she'd had. She wanted to rush over and wrap her arms around him – so pleased was she to see *him* okay.

Instead, she offered him a smile and took comfort in Charlie's still-cold hand.

***

Gibson had never been more thankful to see anyone in his life, but he couldn't seem to move from the doorway. Sheer relief had frozen him to the spot. He took a deep breath, feeling as if he hadn't done so for hours.

Charlie was alive. And looked surprisingly well for his ordeal. The sight of Imogen at his side, holding his hand like she wouldn't let go until he begged her, almost broke his heart. How crazy that she'd been the one to find him. He caught her gaze, registered her warm smile, and snapped into action.

'Thank you,' he whispered, rushing forward to kneel on the other side of Charlie. He flung his arms around his grandfather's neck and rested his head in the nook between shoulder and neck. Fighting the tears pushing past his pupils was futile.

Charlie, who'd almost been asleep, stirred in Gibson's fierce embrace, lifted a hand and gently patted him on the back. 'There, there, boy. You can't get rid of me that easily.'

Smiling at Charlie's tone, but not moving his head, he stared at the wall behind them and thanked the Lord for answering his pleas.

'We thought we'd let you make the decision about an ambulance,' Guy said, reminding Gibson that he needed to check Charlie over before getting all sentimental.

He leaned back, ready to stand, and got Charlie's sharp response loud and clear in his ear. 'No ambulance, I'm fine.'

Gibson glanced at the time on the clock behind them – almost ten o'clock. Getting Charlie to a hospital could be a blessing in disguise. He'd be able to talk to the doctors and have them assess Charlie properly without him realising what was happening. But the plea in Charlie's eyes halted such a hasty decision. *Just one night*, he told himself.

'All right Charlie,' he said, straightening. 'Let me look you over, and if I think you're okay, you can stay here tonight. But you have to promise tomorrow we'll go to the hospital for a proper check-up.' He saw Charlie hesitating, so he added, 'Humour me, Granddad.'

Charlie huffed and rolled his eyes, but eventually agreed.

'I'll get my first aid kit.' Since joining St John as a volunteer, Gibson always made sure he had certain supplies available – one kit in his ute and another in the kitchen.

Guy caught him on his way out. 'If you're okay, Warren and I will head back now. I want to go check Jenna is okay and…' He seemed lost for words.

Gibson understood. Jenna was Guy's world; there *was* no other reason. Inappropriate or not, he felt the same about Imogen.

The innocent capturer of his heart piped up from her position on the floor. 'Oh Guy, I totally forgot. There's a branch across the road where I found Charlie.' She told them about the danger, and the boys promised to check it out on their way back into town.

It was only when he headed back into the lounge room with the first aid kit that Gibson realised that with Charlie almost asleep and his mates gone, he and Imogen were alone.

She stood as he approached and he thought maybe she'd voice her intention to leave as well, but her words told him the opposite. 'I'll give you and Charlie some privacy.' She lowered her voice and leaned near to him, an alluring aroma of vanilla perfume and wet clothes teasing him as she spoke. 'We managed to get his wet shirt off, but—'

'I'll get the rest off, give him a warm bath and put him to bed,' he interrupted, needing to put some distance between them before he did something they'd both regret. 'You can go now, if you like.'

She smiled and shook her head. 'I'm not going anywhere.'

# Chapter Twenty-nine

When Gibson returned to the kitchen almost an hour later, a veritable smorgasbord of food lay on the table before him. He thought he eyed some of Pauli's already-famous stuffed potatoes, and his stomach rolled in delighted anticipation.

'Take a seat,' Imogen said, stepping forward from where she'd been wiping his bench tops. Gesturing to the table, which she had laid with two place settings, she said, 'I figured Charlie would be sleeping.'

'Yep,' he replied, wondering if he imagined the wobble in her voice or it was his own nerves he felt. He'd been alone with Imogen before – hell, he'd been horizontal with the woman – but all that happened before he'd fallen in love with her. Or at least, before he'd recognised the feeling.

He didn't want this intimacy now – not when she was only here because of Charlie.

Part of him wanted her to leave. He couldn't stand her buzzing around his kitchen like everything was fine between them, like there actually was a 'them'. Still, she'd been the one to find Charlie and she cared about the old guy too. She had information he'd need to tell the doctor. Bracing himself for the conversation, he walked to the sink to wash his hands.

'How is he?' she asked when they were both sitting at opposite ends of the table.

'Sleeping now, but he seems physically fine.' Massacring a potato with his fork, he shoved a mouthful between his lips. After chewing, he looked to Imogen again. 'Can you tell me exactly how you found him?'

She nodded, launching into an account of how she'd almost driven into the log, and then how Charlie had offered to help. 'He scared me half to death.' Then she told him about their conversation when they returned to the house. He dropped his cutlery and almost slammed his fist into the table.

'Dammit, I should have remembered.' Charlie made a big deal of Elsie's birthday ever year. Gibson had never thought it strange, because it had always been that way. Most years, he also remembered the date, but he'd been too busy thinking of other things lately. Too busy thinking of Imogen.

'You didn't,' Imogen said logically, 'so don't waste your time dwelling on that. We need to move forward.'

He flinched at her use of the word 'we', as if they were a team. As if they were a couple. How could she be so cruel? She might be able forget his confession, to abandon thoughts of a relationship and jump on the friendship wagon he'd once marketed so well, but he couldn't do it anymore. It hurt too damn much.

'*I*,' he emphasised that word, 'will take him to the doctor tomorrow. It's obvious he can't go on the way he is, but whatever the outcome, *I'll* be there for him. He's all I've got.'

She put down her knife and fork, let out a long, slow breath and pushed her chair out from the table. Hallelujah. She'd gotten the message.

But Imogen didn't leave. No, she had to torture him by coming so close and kneeling right beside him so he could *smell* her again.

'What the hell are you doing?' He'd never be able to get that vanilla scent out of his house – it'd be infused here forever, like some ghost haunting him, reminding him of everything he wanted but couldn't have.

'That's not true,' she said, ignoring his question, gazing up at him and taking his hand off the table. He resisted, but she clamped her fingers down around his palm. 'You've got me too. If you'll have me.'

Yanking his hand from hers, he pushed back from the table, the chair clattering against the floor. He backed into a corner. 'Why are you doing this? I know you care about Charlie but this is going beyond the call of duty. We're not a charity.'

'I know.' Her voice wavered, her fingers lingering on the table where they'd dropped when he fled. 'I'd never think that. I love Charlie, but this has nothing to do with him. It's about you and me. Can you look me in the eye and tell me you want to be alone forever?'

'No.' He was far too human for that.

The tiniest smile graced her lips. 'Neither do I.'

Well, it was lovely that they'd established that sweet fact, but it didn't change one little – no, make that one *mammoth* – thing. He took a frustrated breath. 'The difference is, Imogen, you don't have to be. When you're ready to move on, you could have anyone you want – you're gorgeous, intelligent ... fertile.'

'Two things.' She held up two fingers, her voice suddenly strong and determined. 'I want you.' She stepped up close, jabbed her index finger painfully into his chest. 'I didn't think I was ready to be over Jamie, to move on romantically, but you made me. Without either of us intending to fall in love, I did. And I think you did too.'

When he neither denied nor confirmed this statement, she continued.

'Secondly, we have no idea if I'm fertile. For your information, Jamie and I were trying for a baby to no avail when he died. But none of that matters.'

Gibson rolled his eyes. This was where she'd try to convince him that there were other ways they could have a family – adoption, IVF through donor sperm, surrogacy – and that love would get them through any difficulties. He braced himself to argue, because while he wanted to believe in these possibilities, there were no guarantees. And if they all failed, then how could she possibly know she wouldn't feel like Serena did? But Imogen didn't mention children. Well, not in the way he'd been expecting.

'This isn't about babies. *This* is about us. After losing Jamie, I gave up on having a family. I came to terms with that, and I also never expected to find love again. But I did. You are my bonus, my second chance at love and life. You are enough for me. Am I not enough for you?'

He felt himself thawing. Her words overwhelmed him. And more than anything, he wanted them to be true. 'Enough? You're more than I ever dreamed of.'

'Hah!' A victorious smile lit her face. 'See? You do want me.'

'Dammit, Imogen, of course I want you. I never said I didn't.' And he was helpless not to drag her against him. His fists encircled her wrists and he brought her hands up against his chest. He didn't know whether he wanted to shake her or kiss her, but damn she felt good. So right. He summoned all the willpower he had – it wasn't much after such an exhausting day. 'But that's selfish,' he told her. 'Can't you see? I'm trying to put you first?'

She angled her chin up, looked daggers into his eyes. 'By taking away my freedom of choice? By not giving me the option of choosing you?'

'Honestly, woman!' No one had ever caused him so much frustration. No one had ever made his heart pound this much.

'Do you love me, Gibson?'

*Love!* That crazy, uncontrollable thing that had filled him, taking charge of his sensibilities the moment he first laid eyes on her. He had no doubt that was what he felt for Imogen, and he wanted to believe it truly was enough. He recalled Charlie's words – that growing old alone wasn't impossible, but it was lonely – and he knew he'd be crazy to turn her down. If she were enough for him, maybe he really was enough for her too.

'Yes, Imogen.' He swept a tear from his cheek as he spoke – she'd turned him into a right old sook. 'I love you more than I've ever loved anyone.'

While a bloke might have punched the air in victory, Imogen leaned forward on the tips of her toes and pressed her mouth against his in definite conquest.

\*\*\*

Gibson's kisses were nice – better than that, they were fan-bloody-tastic – but now he'd admitted he loved her, Imogen wanted the whole shebang. While his tongue explored her mouth, softer but equally as possessive as the first time they'd kissed, she roamed her hands down his chest, lingering at the buckle of his belt.

'Take me to bed, Gibson.'

His eyes were hot with need, but he sighed deeply. 'Are you sure this is what you want?'

'Oh yeah, I'm sure.' She placed a kiss in the hollow of his throat. 'And if I have to spend my lifetime proving it to you, the pleasure will be all mine.'

Claiming her lips in another desperate kiss, he scooped her up into his arms and carried her down the hallway. She'd never been into his bedroom before, and for a second she worried that it might have Serena's stamp on it as much as the rest of the house. But her worries were allayed the moment they stepped inside. This was a man's room – no pretty frills, no cushions, just a practical comforter and a lamp on one side of the bed. It smelled like him. She inhaled deeply, not that she needed any more of his personal brand of aphrodisiac.

He crossed to the bed in a couple of strides, pulled back the comforter and set her down in the middle of the mattress. 'Don't move.'

The only movements she had planned were ripping off her clothes. Smiling at that thought, she admired his butt as he turned to shut the door and turn off the light. She was glad when he returned and switched on the lamp – she wanted to see his face through every moment of their lovemaking.

'Last chance to back out,' he said. She could already see an erection straining in his trousers.

Getting to her knees, she grabbed him by his ears and yanked him down on top of her. 'Not going to happen, mister.'

He kissed her again, his mouth making sure hers felt purely adored. Tomorrow, she'd have stubble rash all over her face, but she didn't care one bit. Being cherished like this was worth it. After a moment, the damp from his clothes soaked into hers and she couldn't believe they were still fully dressed. It was a terrible over-sight on both their parts.

'We need to get you out of these wet clothes,' she whispered.

'I was thinking the same about yours.' His fingers trailed down her face, curved over her breasts and then down further, tugging her t-shirt and jumper up over her head and tossing them onto the floor.

'If I'm wet, it's for an entirely different reason,' she muttered, barely able to concoct a sentence with his hands moving lower.

His fingers slipped inside her jeans, he skilfully popped the button and then dragged them (knickers and all) down over her goosebump-covered legs. 'I won't marry you,' he said.

'Why not?' she asked, temporarily distracted from his hands, which were working their way back up the inside of her thighs.

'I want to give you time to be sure,' he replied seriously. 'I know you think I'm what you want, and I definitely want you, but I've been burnt before. I don't want to rush.'

What he didn't seem to understand was that she was already in so deep, there was no way she could turn back now. 'As I've said,' she murmured, her concentration slipping again as he dipped his head, 'I'm more than happy to prove my love.'

In reply, he pressed his lips between her legs and kissed her. Hard. Slow. Teasingly. She dragged her hands through his hair, caressed his earlobes, focused on the ceiling – anything to prolong this pure bliss. And then she felt it – her legs twitched, her body no longer her own. His hands cupped her buttocks, giving him greater access as he pressed his tongue deeper. In seconds, she was gone, hurtling over the edge, writhing beneath him, wondering if it had ever been this good before.

She was still panting when he rolled over and ripped off his jeans. *Oh my!* She was helpless not to stare. His shirt came next, exposing his tanned, muscular, slightly hairy chest – better than candy and every inch of it hers to explore. And, speaking of inches... She reached out and took his length in her hand. It was warm – make that hot – and pulsing. She moved her hand slightly and he moaned.

She stilled her hand. 'How long do I have to wait?'

'For what?' he choked.

'Marriage,' she said, smiling at him, squeezing tightly. 'I'm a traditional kind of girl, and when I'm in love I like the world to know. Officially.'

He pressed his hand into her wrist, looked into her eyes. 'Three years.'

She snorted in disbelief. 'Sounds like some arbitrary number to me.'

'Three years is longer than I was married. It's longer than you've been alone. It's my only offer.'

She sighed. 'I accept, but I guarantee you'll cave long before.'

'We'll see.' He tried to distract her with a kiss and the act of expertly removing her bra.

*Yes, we will,* she thought, loving the feel of her skin against his and vowing that after she'd finished what she was about to do, he'd want to marry her on the spot. Letting it go for now, she got busy with the inches, using both hands and tongue to take him to the heights he'd just taken her. He moaned her name, groaned beneath her touch.

Aroused beyond belief at her effect on him, she was more than ready, wetter than ever, when he stilled her hand and rolled her over so that he was on top.

He kissed her lips and then plunged deep inside. She clung to him, loving the feel of him inside her. The time in his ute had been off-the-radar terrific, but this was different. This was more. This was an act of love.

And when it was over, she lay back on his bed, let her head relax into his soft pillows, and grinned. Yes. Without a doubt, this was much better than a vibrator.

# Chapter Thirty

For a Sunday night, the pub buzzed with blokes. A few of them voiced their disappointment at not finding a willing woman over the Man Drought weekend, but most could drink their beer and laugh about it. All were happy that Charlie had been found and quite a few had already asked when he'd be returning to work.

Unable to provide an answer, Imogen checked her mobile for the umpteenth time to see if Gibson had called again. Although she knew he wouldn't mind her bothering him, she also knew he'd call when he had more news.

After giving her a memorable kiss goodbye early that morning, Gibson had roused Charlie from deep slumber and reminded him of his need to see a doctor. The way Gibson told it, words had been exchanged, but he'd remained firm and Charlie had eventually relented. Hearing Gibson's account and his fears about Charlie's memory, the doctor on call in Southern Cross had transferred him to Kalgoorlie Hospital for further testing.

Imogen wished she could have gone with them, but she was already one staff member down and Karen had been up early cleaning the hotel rooms after the participants had left, so she didn't want to ask her to do another shift.

'Evening, Imogen.' Warren's smile stretched from ear to ear. He leaned across the bar and whispered, 'I want to thank you for the weekend.' Then he held up a crumbled piece of paper. She could just make out a phone number.

'Well done, Warren.' Looked like she might not be the only one with a happy ending. 'Can I get you a drink?'

'Please. The usual.'

She fetched Warren's beer, and when she turned back to hand it to him, a tall, neatly dressed, middle-aged woman with a perfect platinum bob approached the bar. A man whom Imogen didn't recognise, but who looked like he could be one of the local farmers, walked right behind her.

'Thanks,' Warren said, taking the glass. He glanced sideways at the couple. 'Good evening, Mr and Mrs Black. Great to see you.'

'You too, Warren,' replied the woman.

'G'day, mate.' The man offered his hand, and Warren shook it quickly before slinking off in the direction of the pool table.

*Black?* Imogen's palms suddenly sweaty, she wanted to call Warren back. Were these Gibson's parents?

As she turned this thought over in her mind, the woman wiggled her nose, as if sniffing the air, and then swept one perfectly mani-cured finger along the bar. 'It's clean.' Her surprise was evident.

Imogen didn't know what to say. 'Can I get you a drink?'

'Just a Coke, thanks,' said the man. 'I've still got a bit of driving to do.'

'Just passing through?' she asked, wondering if she should intro-duce herself.

The man smiled wistfully. 'Yes. We used to live here, though.'

The woman just glanced warily around.

Imogen got the soft drink and placed it on the bar.

'Thanks.' He nodded as he lifted the drink to his mouth.

'Are you the new publican?' asked the woman.

Imogen smiled. 'I am.' She held out her hand and was almost surprised when she shook it. 'Imogen Bates, lovely to meet you.'

'My son said you'd done the old place up.' She snorted in a manner that didn't match her ladylike attire. 'He raved about your efforts, in fact. I suppose it's not bad if you like this sort of thing.'

'And we do,' Cal said defensively, arriving by Imogen's side.

Imogen shot her an appreciative look but shook her head to say she'd handle it. She returned her attention to the older woman. 'You must be Gibson's mum.'

The woman nodded. 'We're on our way to see him and Charlie in Kalgoorlie.' She sniffed and pulled a tissue out of her handbag. After blowing her nose, she continued. 'Dreadful business. I've been saying there's something wrong with him for months, but no one ever listens to me.' She looked to her husband, but he was studying the rim of his glass intently.

'We all love Charlie,' Imogen said. 'Please give him our best.'

Mrs Black opened her mouth to reply as Imogen's mobile began to ring. She yanked the phone out of her pocket, checked the caller ID and her heart did a happy high jump. 'Sorry, I've got to take this call. Cal, can you get Mrs Black anything she wants?'

Although Cal looked like she'd rather throw a glass of wine over the woman, she nodded. They'd all been waiting for this call.

Imogen retreated into the corridor that led to her office, hoping Gibson's news wasn't too terrible. Wondering if he knew his parents were in town. 'Hi there.'

'Hey sweet.' He didn't sound stressed, and she loved the sound of his voice, especially when he used a pet name.

'How's Charlie?'

'Actually, he's going to be fine.' She could hear the smile in his voice, but wanted answers before she let out a sigh of relief.

'Did he have tests?'

'Yes, but not for dementia. The doctor didn't think Charlie's symptoms added up to that, but they made sense relating to something else.'

'Oh?' Reaching her office, Imogen sank into her swivel chair to listen.

'Charlie has a heart condition – one he refused to let any of us know about. A minor one,' he rushed, before she could ask. 'I can't remember the medical term, but in layman's terms, he has heart flutters. It's really common and can be managed by medication. He takes a tablet daily, something called digoxin. Anyway, he's been on it for quite some time, and due to his kidney function, the digoxin has become toxic to his system. This is what they believe is responsible for his confusion and tiredness. He even admitted he's been having blurred vision, headaches and nausea.'

'But of course he didn't tell us any of this.'

'Of course not,' Gibson laughed. 'And Mum was partly right. At least she'll be able to own some smugness.'

'Um … speaking of your mother. I just met her.'

'You what?'

'She's here in the pub, running her fingernails along the bar and—'

'Checking for dust?'

It was Imogen's turn to laugh. 'Something like that.'

'Dammit, I was hoping to be there when you met her. To soften the blow. She's really not that terrible when you get to know her, at least not when she lives three hundred kilometres away.'

'Gibson,' Imogen spoke seriously, 'I keep trying to tell you, nothing is going to put me off. Your mother could be Cruella de Vil, for all I care.'

'Remind me to buy a lotto ticket tomorrow. I must be the luckiest man alive.' His words felt like a hot bath wrapping around her body, but there was more to ask about Charlie.

'This thing Charlie's got. Can it be fixed?' She picked up a pen from her desk and rolled it in her fingers, hoping the cure would take a long time for Gibson to explain. She liked the sound of his voice. She liked their banter and their serious discussions. She liked the normalness of speaking to him on the phone.

'Yep. He'll have to stay in hospital for a couple of days.'

Relief filled her heart. 'He's going to love that.'

Gibson snorted. 'He doesn't have a choice. He needs to be on a drip to get the toxin out of his system. But he wants you to know that he'll be back, so don't go getting any ideas about replacing him – his words.'

Laughing, Imogen said, 'I'll have a few words to say to him myself when I see him. Will you be home tonight?'

'No, I'm going to spend the night in Kal. It's late now and I want to be here for Charlie in the morning.'

'Okay.' Imogen hoped he couldn't detect the disappointment in her voice. She understood his desire to stay near Charlie. And his parents would want to spend time with the both of them. 'I told your Mum to give Charlie my best, but can you tell him I said hi as well? We're all—'

'Imogen,' his deep voice interrupted her. 'I can't stop thinking about last night.'

She grinned. 'Me neither,' she said, and then realised she'd been doodling love hearts on her notepad.

'So, no regrets then?'

She scribbled her initials at the top of one heart and then scrawled his underneath. 'None whatsoever, Gibson Black. And I promise you, there won't be.'

# Epilogue

Gibson did make Imogen wait three years, but every minute affirmed the fact that he was worth waiting for. He needed those years, and she was more than willing to give them. She'd walk to the ends of the earth for him, so three little years hadn't seemed so torturous in the end.

In that time, they grew closer than she'd ever believed possible.

She moved out of the pub and into Roseglen. She was still owner and publican of The Majestic, but was happy to hand over most of the daily running to Pauli and Cal, who surprised her, not long after the Man Drought weekend, by admitting they were crazy in love with each other. Looking back, perhaps there had been a few clues. They'd made Gibson's Find their home as much as she and Jenna had.

Yes, Jenna moved from Perth three months after conceiving Jasmine, and more recently opened a gallery on the main street of town. Showcasing local art and craft, as well as rural artists from right across the state, *Regal, Rustic and Rural* had become a must-see stop for tourists travelling along the highway – most of whom popped into The Majestic afterwards.

Once there, travellers were certain of a warm welcome, a cold or hot drink depending on the weather, and, if they were interested, a run-down of local history from Charlie. Three years after his stint in hospital, he was healthier than ever, and Imogen couldn't imagine the pub – not to mention their lives – without him.

And although she hadn't repeated the Man Drought weekend – too scared of another debacle – it hadn't been a complete flop. One romance had sparked, blossomed and thrived. Having beaten Imogen and Gibson to the altar, Michelle and Warren had just celebrated two blissful years of marriage. Thus, the female population of Gibson's Find was on the rise again.

Amy and Ryan still lived in Perth, but they were frequent visitors to the farm, wanting their two children – there were only fifteen months between Gibson and Mitchell – to appreciate the benefits of life on the land. And while Imogen and Gibson loved having the boys around, they were always happy to get back to it just being them.

After Amy and Ryan had driven away and the dust from their city car hurtling down the country track had settled, Imogen would step back inside the only place she could ever call home, into the welcoming arms of the man who made her smile every day. She'd come to Gibson's Find to build a new future, but nothing had prepared her for the joy of finding Gibson. Where she and Jamie had been waiting for children to fulfil them, with Gibson, she was now complete.

*****

# *Outback Dreams*

Turn over for a sneak peek of the new title
by Australia's home-grown

# RACHAEL JOHNS

OUT OCTOBER

# Prologue

'I *hate* you both and I'm not coming!'

Ten-year old Daniel Montgomery ran from the only house he'd ever called home, slamming the door behind him. He couldn't remember the last time he'd slammed a door—his little brother couldn't handle loud, sudden noises—but the rage inside him right now warranted it.

How could his parents do this to him? How could they even contemplate selling the farm and moving to the city? Of all the ridiculous places. What did the city have to offer except stupidly tall buildings and more shops than anyone would ever need in their life?

He tried to tell himself it wasn't his brother's fault—Will would be quite happy spending the rest of his life on the farm catching spiders and aligning furniture around the house—but of course it *was* Will's fault: his parents wanted more for him. Yet no one asked Monty. No one cared what he thought or what happened to him.

He ran to find the only person he knew would understand. He ran next door to Forrester's Rock where Faith lived. But next door in the country wasn't a mere leap over the fence like it would be in the city—he hated the thought of living so close to other people—it was a good few kilometres over paddocks and hills. He ran as the crow flies—that's what adults said, didn't they?—and he didn't see another soul until Faith's house appeared and he saw her swinging off the rope in the old gum tree. He'd miss that rope. On his few visits to Perth, he hadn't seen any ropes hanging from backyard trees. All the city kids had those bright-coloured plastic swing sets that you couldn't even make go high if you swung your legs as hard as ever.

Grimacing at that thought, Monty pushed his burning legs harder. He raced across the last bit of the paddock, leapt the wire fence and shouted, 'Faith!'

She glanced his way, smiled, let go of the rope and sailed through the air to meet him. When she got close, her face fell. 'What's the matter?' she asked.

He stopped, his breath ragged as he ran a hand over his sweaty face. He knew it would be as bright as a tomato. 'We're moving,' he panted, delivering the blow in two devastating words.

'What?' Faith screwed up her face as if she couldn't comprehend what he was saying.

He took another deep breath. 'Mum and Dad have sold the farm. We're moving to Perth. Next week.'

'What?' Faith said again. He wondered if it was suddenly the only word in her vocabulary. She sank down onto the lawn—about the only green grass in the region—and he sat down beside her. It was like a bad dream.

'They didn't tell me until now because they didn't want to worry me.' Monty scoffed and thumped his fist against the ground. 'That's what they said, anyway. Truth is, they didn't tell me because they don't give a damn what I think.' He'd never used such harsh language before and it made him feel grown-up, even while he was sulking.

'Why?' Faith asked, her voice quiet, as if she might be about to cry. Faith never cried—not like the girls at school who burst into tears at the tiniest thing, like if a mouse scuttled across the classroom floor. Her name and long brown hair in a messy ponytail were the only things girly about Faith. People called her a tomboy, but Monty didn't care. She was his best mate. Leaving her behind would be as horrid as leaving the farm.

'Because of Will. Mum's tired of driving back and forth to Perth for all his therapy. And the high school up here might not be equipped for him. They said they're thinking ahead.' But as far as Monty was concerned, they weren't thinking at all. How could selling the farm be a good thing? It had been in the family for generations.

'Oh. Well that royally sucks.'

'You can say that again. What am I gonna do in the city?'

'Maybe you could join a chess club or the Boy Scouts.' Faith tossed a grin his way, obviously trying to make him feel better.

He scowled and thumped her in the side. They both sighed and stared out across the garden to the paddocks of Forrester's Rock. Big cylinder hay bales littered the ground. There were identical ones back at his place. Hay baling was one of his favourite parts of farming. Only a week ago he'd been working alongside his dad, who hadn't mentioned even once that this would be his last chance to do it. Grown-ups were so unfair.

'I was always gonna be a farmer.' Monty felt tears welling up in the corners of his eyes. He fought them hard, trying to keep hold of his anger.

'You still will be,' Faith said with determination. 'The best.'

'But what good's a farmer without a farm?'

'Hmm…' Faith mused for a few moments and then said, 'Maybe you could marry me and live here.'

Monty snorted.

'You're right. It's ridiculous.'

Faith laughed. She didn't even know if she wanted to get married anyway. As far as she could see, the only reason to get married was to have babies, and she wasn't very sure about them either. She'd never liked playing with dolls, sitting around toying with tea sets drove her berserk, and you didn't want to get her started on make-up. Like Monty, she wanted to be a farmer— outside from dawn to dusk, ploughing the dirt, shearing, crutching, mustering stock. That's why she played with the boys at school and steered clear of the girls.

'Maybe your parents could adopt me,' Monty said, interrupting her thoughts.

'Now that would be fabulous.' He already stayed with them often enough when his mum and Will went to Perth. She grinned at the idea as she wiped her eyes, not wanting to cry in front of Monty. Not wanting to cry full stop. Only sissies cried. But how was she ever going to get through each day without him? Who would catch frogs with her by the dam? Who would climb trees and do silly dares with her?

Ryan never wanted to play the same games. He was only three years older, but thought himself a man already. She couldn't even interest him when mud pies and catapults were on the table.

'I'm gonna be bored out of my brains without you,' she said, staring glumly at the ground.

Monty grabbed her hand and squeezed hard. 'You won't forget me though, will ya?'

'Never. We'll be friends forever.' Although she squeezed back, Faith didn't look at Monty. If she did, she'd definitely cry.

# Chapter One

*What in God's name am I doing here?*

Faith Forrester didn't get her underarms or bikini line waxed, she didn't drink skim milk when there was perfectly good full cream stuff available from the cow, and she didn't run marathons, so why on earth had she agreed to come to a school reunion? She'd hated boarding school and hadn't stayed in touch with any of the girls in her year.

Taking a sip of expensive champagne, she glanced around the room—the one difference between here and Hell being that here they served good grog—and imagined Monty laughing as she described it. Overlooking the Swan River in all its sparkling night-time glory, the décor and atmosphere at the yacht club were about as far from The Palace in Bunyip Bay as you could get. But it wasn't just her surroundings that were top of the wazza; everything from the background music to the guests' outfits screamed glamour and class. She should have listened to him when he told her not to bother coming, that nothing and no one from school would have changed.

Trying not to look too awkward standing on her lonesome by the bar, she sipped another mouthful of the almost sickly-sweet bubbly and nearly didn't notice a tall, thin, peroxide blonde sidle up beside her.

'Oh my. If it isn't Faith Forrester.'

Faith tried not to flinch as the woman air-kissed her and scraped long, hugely impractical, bright red fingernails over her arms as she hugged her. She was surprised that Kat—Head Girl of Perth Ladies College a decade ago—even remembered her name. They'd not spoken more than two words in high school.

'What are you doing hiding all the way over here in the corner?'

Faith bit her tongue on a sarcastic reply. The better question was why she'd come in the first place. Lord knew she'd never had any inclination before—not since that first time, almost ten years ago, when she'd spent all evening alone.

Where many boarding schools were full of farmers' kids, hers had catered to the Perth elite, and she had never fit in with these posh ladies. Nothing had changed; she was still just a country girl, and now her school pals were married to lawyers and doctors, just like their mothers had been. Not that she'd ever called any of them pals. She'd got through private school hell with her head down, her nose in books (mostly novels about country kids) and her focus on the weekend when she could escape the prison and catch up with Monty.

But when the invitation to this year's old girls' function had landed in her post office box, something had twitched inside her. She'd forgotten the downside of these events and pounced on the opportunity to do something different for a change. Something to liven up her otherwise depressingly dull existence.

Mulling these thoughts over, Faith suddenly realised Katarina Lamberusco-whatever-her-married-name-was expected an answer. She was standing there smiling like plastic and looking Faith up and down like some sort of exhibit in the museum.

'Well? What's your excuse for hiding in the corner?"

'Just taking a breather,' Faith said eventually.

Kat giggled in a manner that grated on Faith's nerves. 'It is a bit overwhelming, isn't it? Catching up with all these old friends. So, what have you been up to lately?'

And there it was, a slight variation on the dreaded question, which was really just a polite way to ask if anyone had seen fit to marry Faith and let her breed.

The answer was no.

It didn't make an inch of difference that this was supposed to be a modern world. Things like husbands and babies still mattered, and if you fell short in that department, you'd better have a jolly good reason—such as becoming the youngest partner in a law firm or making it big-time on a catwalk in Paris. Unfortunately, Faith couldn't tick either of those boxes.

When she didn't reply, Kat leaned a little closer and wiggled her immaculate eyebrows. Her gaze glued on the unadorned finger wrapped around Faith's glass, she asked, 'Is there a lucky man?'

Faith swallowed and the words fell from her lips without her thinking them through.

'Yes. There is, actually.'

*Good Lord. Have I just invented a boyfriend?*

While she lamented this disturbing fact, Kat's eyes literally glistened with excitement as she beckoned to someone across the room. Faith downed half her glass of bubbly as a whole horde of women formed a circle around her. Just like something out of a horror movie.

'Faith's just about to tell us about her ma-an,' Kat sang, informing her little posse (the girls who'd hung on her every word at school apparently still did).

'Ooh,' came the replies. 'Do tell.'

Faith's throat went dry. She wanted another drink, but somehow her glass had emptied. 'Well…' she said, aware ten eyes were trained on her, 'His name's Monty.'

Eyebrows rose in unison.

'That's a nickname, obviously,' she rushed, wondering why she cared what any of them thought. She never used to. 'His full name is Daniel Montgomery.'

'Mont-gom-ery.' Kat tried the surname on for size. 'Sounds hot.'

Her posse laughed.

Faith thought about her best friend. 'Oh, he is,' she said, stifling a laugh because she'd never thought about Monty in that way at all. Ever. They'd grown up together, he was the brother she'd wished she could swap her own with. That said, half the women in Bunyip Bay had swooned after him at some stage or other.

'What's he look like then?' asked another former student as she raised her glass. 'Is he tall, dark and delicious?'

'He's tall,' Faith nodded, thinking about how she had to jog to keep up with Monty's big strides, 'but not dark. He's got golden blond hair.' She smiled. 'But he's very tanned from being outdoors lots.'

'I feel faint.' Kat placed a hand theatrically against her chest. The rest of them giggled. 'What does he do?'

Faith opened her mouth to say jack-of-all-trades but caught herself. This was supposed to be a fantasy. 'Monty's a farmer.'

'Ooh, so he's landed gentry.' One of the women actually clapped.

Faith summoned a smile, nodded and then pretended to take another sip from her now empty glass. This was why she'd hated boarding school. Even though her family were lucky enough to be fairly well-to-do—one of the farming families who could afford not to stress over the odd bad season—she'd never felt comfortable with the class system her prestigious boarding school classmates clung to. Quite frankly, she didn't give a damn how much money a person had, whether six generations had owned their property, what suburb they lived in, whether their father was a judge and their mother a charity queen, yadda yadda yadda.

She cared about what was inside—whether a person could make her laugh when she wanted to cry, was there for her in times of need and didn't judge her by her outfit.

Yes, she'd noticed the looks her fellow old girls had given her when she'd first entered the yacht club. So, she wasn't wearing a cocktail dress or heels that would give a ruler a run for its money, and maybe her mousy-brown mid-length hair wasn't shiny and straight, but she was comfy in her look.

While the women around her nattered on about her imaginary boyfriend, Faith giggled inwardly at the fact that this was her best going-out outfit. Knee-high boots, leggings and a chiffon tunic were far removed from her normal uniform of shorts or jeans (depending on the season), tee or flannelette shirt and her Blundstones. Tonight she was even wearing make-up.

'Good evening, ladies and gentlemen,' boomed a microphoned voice from a raised platform at the front of the room. 'Welcome to our annual alumnae cocktail party and the presentation of Ms Alumna of the Year.'

The women around Faith scattered to find their business-suited husbands and Faith stood alone at the edge of the room, nursing her empty champagne flute.

'As you know,' continued the principal, 'tonight we celebrate our former students' successes in fundraising for charities in need. Perth Ladies College is proud of our Ms Alumna award, and the continued support by our students and old girls is admirable. It's hard to believe the award is now in its twenty-fifth year. I'm going to hand over to Mrs Priscilla Morgan-Brookes, organiser of this outstanding initiative, to announce this year's finalists.'

Faith scanned the faces all around her. Amongst these women, being crowned Ms Alumna of the Year was akin to winning a Miss World title. To enter, you had to organise a fundraising event for a charity near to your heart, garner the support and attention of the media (thus giving the school good publicity) and raise the most money of all the entrants. Faith had never thought too highly of the award, which in the old girls' magazine always seemed like yet another way for some women to draw attention to themselves, but as she listened to the list of finalists and their achievements, she wondered if she'd been too quick to judge.

How could you be anything but positive about a woman who rode a tricycle all the way around Australia to raise money for sufferers of non-alcoholic fatty liver disease, and did the books of her family's business online at night?

And this wasn't an act in isolation. Most of the entrants had worked hard to achieve fulfilling careers, all the while starting families and giving back to the community. What the hell had *she* done?

She made a mental inventory of her achievements.

*Complete half a degree in agricultural sciences.*

*Coach Bunyip Bay's junior netball team.*

Um… This was a lot harder than she liked.

*Look after Dad and Ryan, help them on the farm when they let me.*

Nup, nothing else was jumping out at her.

*Sad, seriously sad.* Faith focused back on Priscilla Morgan-Brookes as she spoke about a woman who'd been a few years ahead of her at school.

'Lara Leeds has taken time off from the law firm where she met her husband Michael to home-school their three children. Somehow, whilst doing this and supporting Michael's demanding career, Lara managed to raise forty-five thousand dollars last year for research into childhood cancers.'

Faith joined in the applause while images flashed across a big screen—photos of Lara's fundraiser in which children with leukaemia had illustrated greeting cards, which had then been sold for big bucks across the country.

Another finalist had organised an art show for victims of post-traumatic stress. One woman raised almost thirty thousand dollars for homeless people by getting Western Australian actors to donate their time and put on a theatre production. Faith recalled reading something about it in *The West Australian*.

And the list went on.

Yes, Faith was guilty of serious judgement. If she'd been sitting, she'd have slunk low in her chair in shame. As it was, all she could do was smile and applaud along with the rest of the crowd as Lara Leeds took to the podium to be crowned Ms Alumna of the Year. While Priscilla Morgan-Brookes whisked Lara away to have photos taken with the other finalists, the principal took the microphone once again.

'It is with great pleasure,' he made elaborate hand gestures, 'that I declare our next Ms Alumna of the Year competition open.' He paused for a moment as more applause assaulted Faith's ears, then added, 'All old girls who'd like to participate are invited to come forward and pledge this evening.'

When Faith had arrived that evening, she'd never in her wildest imaginings have envisioned doing what she did next. As she handed her empty glass to a passing waiter, took a deep breath and went forward to join the other women lining up at the pledge table, she suddenly felt like this was a turning point in her life.

This was her year to make a difference.

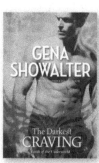

# Find out more about our latest releases, authors and competitions.

 Like us on facebook.com/harlequinaustralia

 Follow us on twitter.com/harlequinaus

 Find us at harlequinbooks.com.au